IN TOO DEEP

KIMBERLY KINCAID

Read hot,
Raw Reader!

COPYRIGHT PAGE

DEDICATION

This book is dedicated to Nicole Bailey, who is one
of the most patient people I know.

Thank you for juggling my crazy with such finesse.

ACKNOWLEDGMENTS

Writing a book is a serious tribe effort. I would be nowhere without mine. Specifically, my editor, Nicole Bailey, who achieved serious goddess status for this one. I am so grateful for your willingness to shift things around to make the magic happen. Rachel Hamilton, who gobbled up the pages and always encouraged me to tell Luke and Quinn's story the right way, *and* sent me Tumblr gifs when I needed "encouragement"—you are the best. Geoff Symon, who always leads me to the details that make the suspense aspects of these books shine, your brain is my favorite!

Huge thanks to nurse and fabulous friend, Dana Carroll, for schooling me on things like diabetic shock and how much blood is in the human body. You keep me in line, and I am so grateful! Michelle Forde and Danielle Barclay, thank you for always making me look so good. To my lovely friend, Beverly Early, who has such amazing insights into the deaf community and is always willing to have thoughtful conversations with me on the topic. I did take one small liberty with regard to ASL, in that there is no actual sign for "rutabaga". But I do respectfully hope the rest is on the mark.

Robin Covington and Avery Flynn, thank you for encouraging me/talking me off ledges/feeding me wine when I need to whine. Scarlett Cole, thank you for being my writing buddy in Orlando. A huge shout out to the incomparable Lori Foster for saying such lovely things about the Station Seventeen series (out loud and everything!) I am humbled to have such an amazing audience.

To my girls, who actually answer to Reader Girl, Smarty Pants, and Tiny Dancer now, you are the very best kids I know. Thanks for learning how to make grilled cheese so mommy could write. And Mr. K, thanks for putting up with all the security alerts from my Google searches. Also, for loving me like I love you. I do, however, love you more (heh.)

To all first responders, I'm humbly grateful for the risks you take on a daily basis. Thank you for running in when all others run out.

Lastly, I cannot thank you, my readers, enough. You make my job possible. Your emails, Facebook messages, appearances at book signings, reviews...all of it fuels me. I am so grateful to have you all on this journey with me. Thank you for loving Station Seventeen!

1

Luke Slater hung forty feet over the city of Remington by a hand, a harness, and a Hail Mary. Ironically, the situation didn't shove him into the brand of heart-slamming, utterly paralyzing panic it would incite in nearly anyone else; hell, it didn't even make him consider blowing his breakfast the way he almost had the first time he'd been up this high with no ceilings or floors or plate glass windows to comfort his brain's fear center. Then again, from all the practice drills he and his fellow fire-fighters ran during every shift to the "this-is-*not*-a-drill" risks they took every time a building started to burn, being Station Seventeen's rookie for the last seven months had given his adrenal gland one hell of an attitude adjustment.

Which was fine by Luke, really. If recalibrating his holy-shit barometer was the pre-requisite for helping people when they needed it most, that seemed like a fair trade.

After all, if there was one thing he'd grown gold-star good at in his twenty-four years, it was putting a tourniquet on his emotions when life handed over a big, bloody mess.

"Okay, rookie. Now what?"

His engine lieutenant, Ian Gamble, leaned his well-inked forearms on the neatly bricked edge of Station Seventeen's roof. The guy raised one dark brown eyebrow over a stare the exact same color as he leveled Luke with a look that read, *you got yourself into this, now get yourself out.* Luke had learned real fast not to take his lieutenant's sledgehammer-serious stare personally. When Gamble was rationing up shit, he was in a decent mood. When Gamble clapped his trap completely? Yeah, that was when Luke knew he'd fucked something up on a royal level. And seeing as how he was on the business end of the bricks and this was the first time he'd ever done this particular drill without Gamble right there at his hip talking him through every micro-movement, he really, really didn't want to fumble the job like a football on game day.

So he dug deep and said, "Now I assess the situation and execute the rescue protocol accordingly. Think, then act."

The corners of Gamble's mouth edged up by the slightest degree—barely a movement, let alone a smile—but from the six foot five former Marine, the gesture might as well have been a bear hug and a nice, hot cup of cocoa. "Good. But let's do both today, huh? I'm not getting any younger, and it's hot as balls up here."

Luke squashed his return smile before it could make the journey from his synapses to his lips. Yeah, Gamble was a good teacher, and beneath the rough, gruff badass thing he had going on, he seemed to be an even better guy. But as much as Luke respected everyone at Station Seventeen and even liked them on a professional level, he wasn't here to go the Kumbaya route with any of his fellow firefighters.

Arm's length was safer. Smarter.

Necessary.

So he gave up a clipped nod and applied an equally

clipped tone to his voice as he battened down his expression and said, "Copy that, Lieutenant."

Inhaling a large breath of courage and end-of-April sunshine, Luke eyeballed his current circumstances in an effort to formulate a rescue plan that wouldn't turn him into Elmer's paste. He was four stories above the fat ribbon of asphalt leading from the side door of the engine bay to the alcove where they kept their trash and recycling bins (surroundings, check). He'd just maneuvered himself over what any sane person would call the wrong side of the waist-high bricks mortared around the perimeter of the roof (situation, check). The thick, bright blue straps of his harness put equal, squeezing pressure where they were looped over his shoulders, hips, and thighs (gear, check). His "victim", a.k.a. his engine-mate, Shae McCullough, grinned up at him from her spot about fifteen feet below, where—for the purposes of this drill—her own safety gear had "failed" and Luke had to go rescue her (objective, check). He knew the protocol for a rope transfer like this backward, forward, and upside down, which meant he knew exactly what he needed to do next.

"Slater to Command, ready to lower," he called out, the words low but steady.

And then he let go of the building.

For a split second, Luke's heart declared mutiny on his brain, whacking out the Morse code equivalent of *have you lost your mind, you great big crazy jackass?* against his ribs. But the belay system he'd anchored around the steel-in-cement posts on the roof held him in place even though he'd let go of the ledge, and his engine-mate, Kellan Walker, was in charge of Luke's lift/lower from the far side of the roof. Everything was on the level—as much as it could be when you were dangling forty feet above terra firma, anyway. Just another day at the office, learning how to save lives.

The recognition firmed Luke's resolve. He ordered his shoulder muscles to loosen so he could balance out the physiological   find-solid-ground-right-now-right-now message radiating out of his survival instinct. Filling his lungs with a slow slide of oxygen just as he'd been trained to, Luke tightened his belly beneath the now-sweaty RFD T-shirt sticking to his skin under his safety harness. This might just be a drill today, but at some point, he'd be in a situation where he had to step up, to be calm and quick and save somebody's life. He'd need to turn this training into a solution. To fix the problem in front of him without emotions.

Whether that was tomorrow or in a thousand tomorrows, he was goddamn well going to be ready.

Luke looked up, shifting as much of his weight as possible into his pelvis as he sat back in the harness and pressed his boots against the sun-warmed bricks of the outer wall of the engine bay for steadier control. Lifting one gloved hand, he twirled his index finger in an exaggerated circle, making sure he had eye contact with Gamble before reinforcing the visual command with the matching verbal one.

"Slater to Command. Easy to lower."

"Command to Slater. Easy to lower," came the callback from Gamble. The first few seconds were a bumpy-ass ride, and hell if all the lurch and jerk didn't dare Luke's already questionable adrenaline levels into twitchy fucking territory. But then Kellan found a slow and steady groove. A handful of seconds later, Luke was face-to-Cheshire-cat-grin with McCullough.

"Aw. Of all the fire houses in all of Remington, you

scaled mine." Her gold-brown brows waggled toward the brim of her battle-tested helmet as she splayed both hands over her heart in an exaggerated gesture, and Slater couldn't help but let a snort escape from the side of his mouth.

"We're hanging nearly thirty feet above the ground, McCullough," Luke said, making a special point to look down so his brain might start getting hard-wired to the idea that he'd be scaling buildings from time to time. "Knowing you, you're probably disappointed to see me."

Of all the firefighters in the house on both engine and rescue squad, Shae was the most fearless. As evidenced by the fact that she looked more like she was relaxing in a hammock right now than locked into a safety harness high above the ground.

"Come on, Slater." She rocked side to side, as if all she was missing was a stiff drink in one hand and a good book in the other. "I'm always happy to see you."

"Careful," Luke warned, unable to keep a thread of teasing out of his voice. He might not be tight with anyone at Seventeen the way they were all tight with each other, but of everyone, he felt easiest around Shae. "Otherwise people are going to start thinking that moving in with Capelli has made you sappy."

Shae's grin shifted into something entirely deeper at the mention of her boyfriend, James Capelli, who ran all the tech and surveillance for the Remington Police Department's elite intelligence unit, and who she'd also moved in with last month. "Yeah, that's me," she said with a deep belly laugh. "I'm just a big ol' bag of sunshine and unicorns. Now do you want to help me out here? Apparently, I need to be fucking rescued."

"Copy that," Luke replied over a half-chuckle, looking up to lock eyes on Gamble again. "Slater to Command," he called out. "Victim is alert and responsive. Hold for line transfer."

"Command to Slater. Holding for transfer."

Calmly sliding his forearm over the bloom of sweat that had begun to escape from beneath the brim of his helmet, Luke nailed his focus on the hardware on Shae's harness. He'd pre-rigged the rescue equipment in the pack at his hip long before he'd thrown his leg over the side of the engine bay—funny how far the whole "be prepared" thing went when you had to rescue someone from a thorny situation on the fly—and he mentally catalogued his next steps before shifting to turn them into reality. But then Luke heard the shuffle and bang of someone moving through the station's side door below him, caught the flash of blond hair on the very edges of his peripheral vision as the person belonging to it walked over to the trash bin to toss a Hefty bag over the side, and his hands hitched without permission from the rest of him.

"You okay?" Shae asked. Her brows tucked in concern, and damn it, of course she'd noticed. She was helping train him, for Chrissake. She'd probably notice if he sneezed crooked.

"Yep." Luke knew better than to elaborate, especially since the answer was eighty percent untrue. It wasn't that he was *not* okay, necessarily. But if anything was going to crash his concentration, it'd be the sight of Station Seventeen's sweet-and-sexy paramedic, Quinn Copeland.

Great, now his pulse was hitching along with his stupid, traitorous hands.

Shae moved her gaze over their surroundings in a methodical sweep, the eyes she'd squinted against the glare of the late-morning sunlight going round and wide as they landed on Quinn. "So," she said, dropping her voice but not the ear-to-ear smile that told Luke nothing good was going to come from their now-private conversation. "About Quinn."

"What about her?" Luke stared holes in the pick-off strap he'd pre-rigged before the drill, willing his fingers to steadily fasten the stupid thing to the main attachment point on Shae's harness. *Rope rescue. Safe transfer. Focus.*

"You two have been spending some time together lately, huh?"

His stomach knotted before dropping toward his hips. "Quinn has been helping with my paramedic training," he said, selecting his words with care. After a really hairy call had led the house to a gruesome arson/murder scene three months ago, Luke had been surprised to discover he had a fear of blood. But since he also wanted to help people as a first responder, he couldn't let that fear—debilitating as it had been—stand in the way of him doing the job that would keep people safe.

So he'd done what he always did. He'd taken a step back to quietly attack the problem, devoting himself not only to the rest of his fire and rescue training, but to earning his certification as a paramedic at the same time. Yeah, the workload was intense, and no, balancing both didn't leave him much time for luxuries outside of sleep or hot meals. He wasn't exactly a stranger to balls-out hard work, though. In fact, he and hard work were more like what his seventeen-year-old sister Hayley would call "besties". Not that Luke had any freaking clue what that might actually entail, since he never got past the handshake and Heisman stage with anyone.

That whole arm's length thing? So not an overstatement.

At any rate, Luke had his sister and their grandmother, Momma Billie. He didn't need a bunch of Lifetime Original moments to distract him from his goal. He'd attained his full qualifications as an EMT six weeks ago. Official paramedic status would be in his reach before the year was out, provided he could continue to keep his seemingly sudden-onset fear of blood at bay. He was well on his way to becoming a full-fledged firefighter, like he'd always wanted. Just as long as he could keep both his focus and his distance, he'd be fucking stellar.

Quinn looked up with a grin and a wave before heading back into the fire house, and Christ, did she really *have* to have a set of cutely sexy dimples he could see all the way from here?

"Helping you with your paramedic training," Shae echoed, her quiet murmur tumbling him right back to the here and now of the side wall of the engine bay.

Luke concentrated on the equipment in his hands, the clink of the carabiners and the soft hiss of the nylon ropes as he continued with the rope transfer while he spoke. "Sure. She's been giving me tips and tricks to remember different procedures, telling me the fastest ways to safely do workups. Stuff like that."

"Ah." Shae waited a beat while he clipped the backup carabiner for the line transfer into place. "You know, it wouldn't be terrible if you liked her."

"I do like her." The words shoveled out of his mouth by default. He double-checked the carabiner. Adjusted the slack in his line. Mentally kicked himself square in the nuts. "She's nice."

Shae made a noise Momma Billie would have described as unladylike. "You know what I mean, Slater. Don't be a dumbass."

And that was the problem, right there. He *was* a dumb-ass. He didn't just like Quinn in a casual friends, good coworkers, she's-helping-me-with-my-training kind of way. Nope. He was *attracted* to her. From the minute he'd clapped eyes on Quinn on his very first day as a rookie, Luke had had this reckless desire to kiss her. To hook his fingers in that waterfall of blond waves spilling down her back, to part her lips with his tongue and taste her until he ran out of air.

And he didn't want to stop at her mouth.

Luke cleared his throat. Twice. "I'm not being a dumbass," he said. "She *is* nice."

His libido reached up and bitch-slapped him for the understatement. Big dark blue eyes framed by impossibly long lashes. Bow-shaped lips full enough to be both beautiful and distracting as hell. Long legs. Pretty, feminine curves that were evident even beneath her ho-hum paramedic's uniform, and who was he kidding?

Quinn wasn't just nice. She was totally fucking gorgeous.

As if Shae had zeroed in on Luke's deepest, darkest brainwaves, she said, "You should ask her out." And even though her delivery was purely matter-of-fact, his heart dumped into his gut. He needed to laugh, he knew. To make this into no big deal so he could change the subject. To *not* let Shae see that she was spot-on about his extra-curricular thoughts of Quinn.

"You don't strike me as the matchmaker type," he tried, putting a toe in the water with Diversion Tactic Number One: make it about the person you were talking to rather than yourself.

Not that Shae so much as nibbled on the line. "What can I say? Finding true love has made me squishy."

"You threw *actual* elbows with Kellan over which one of you would get to rappel down here to be saved," Luke pointed out, unable to help himself. "I'd hardly call that squishy."

"It's not my fault he didn't look. I'm sure that black eye won't last but a day or two.

Anyway"—Shae replaced the smile tugging at the edges of her mouth with a look of renewed determination—"if Quinn is so nice, why wouldn't you ask her out?"

Luke gave Diversion Tactic Number One the old college try. "Would *you* date someone you worked with?"

Annnnnd oh-for-fucking-two. "A for effort, trying to shift the spotlight there. But my answer's only 'no' because I've never been attracted to anyone I work with, and besides, we're not talking about me."

Shit. He shifted to Tactic Number Two: go vague to create distance. "Aren't there rules against that sort of thing? You know, department-wide?"

Shae watched him seamlessly remove the pick-off strap from her harness, nodding her approval at his handiwork before conceding. "Inter-house relationships probably don't make Captain Bridges want to do backflips of joy. But technically? They're only against the rules if the parties involved are both on engine or squad together, and they want to get married. Paramedics are totally fair game."

Luke bit back the pop of shocked laughter that wanted to emerge from his throat. This conversation had just gone from left field to bat-shit crazy in a few dozen syllables. It was time to tie it off, once and for all.

"Thanks for the primer on the RFD rule book, but getting on the captain's bad side isn't really on my wish list. Besides, Quinn and I are just friends." He gestured to Shae's safety harness, which was now tethered to his, prepped and ready for the next step in the drill. All that was left to do was release her original line and make the descent. "So should I keep going, here?" Luke asked, making sure he tied his manners into his tone. The last thing he needed was for

Shae to think he was throwing shade. Dodging the topic was hard enough, thanks.

After a pause he might not have noticed if he hadn't been funneling all of his attention into trying to boomerang the subject, Shae examined his work with a nod. "Affirmative. Nice job on that pick-off line. Now let's see if you can get me safely to the ground, huh?"

"Copy that," Luke said, his chest flooding with more than a little irony at the fact that focusing on being this high above the ground actually made him feel relieved. But since it was better than focusing on the topic he'd just managed to shake—not to mention necessary to successfully completing the drill—he dove in without hesitation.

Taking a minute to release the hardware attaching Shae to her own set of ropes, he did a lightning-fast double-check before barking out, "Slater to Command. Victim is secure on the primary line. Easy to lower."

Gamble stared over the edge of the roof, thankfully oblivious to the conversation Luke had just skirted with Shae. "Command to Slater. Copy that. Easy to lower."

He raised one hand overhead, looping his index finger in the signal to go. Slowly but steadily, Kellan lowered both Luke and Shae, who were now tethered to one another, all the way down until their boots made contact with the sunbaked asphalt below.

"Nice job not turning us into road pizza," Shae said, slapping the top of his helmet with one hand and using the other to lift a big thumbs-up at Gamble, high above.

"Thanks."

Luke's cheeks prickled with pride. Just when he thought he was in the clear for good, though, Shae hit him with a stare that made him feel like a biology-project butterfly pinned to a board.

"And by the way, I'm not suggesting you marry her, rookie. But you keep to yourself an awful lot around here."

Luke's pulse stuttered, but despite the warning bells clanging in his head, he replied, "It's nothing personal." This, at least, was the top layer of the truth. Not that he was about to dole out the rest—not even to Shae, who was the closest thing he had to a friend at the fire house.

Arm's length. Create distance. Right now.

"I like everyone at Seventeen, and I definitely like the job. I just don't...hang out," he finished quietly.

"Okay."

Luke didn't know what shocked him more—the no-bull-shit reply or the no-judgment manner in which Shae had delivered it. "Okay?"

She lifted one shoulder in a non-committal shrug. "I'm sure you have your reasons for playing it close to the vest. All I'm saying is if you're looking for someone to bridge that gap, Quinn's a really solid pick. That's all."

But before he could answer, let alone process what Shae said, the shrill sound of the station-wide all-call sounded off from the speakers just inside the engine bay.

Engine Seventeen, Ambulance Twenty-Two, person down of unknown causes, nineteen-twelve Maplewood Avenue. Requesting immediate response.

"Ah, look at that, Slater," Shae said, unclipping the cara-biners from her harness and his with brisk, sure motions. "They're playing our song."

And then they were hustling toward the engine, all thoughts of anything either of them had said—or hadn't said—summarily forgotten.

2

"Okay, Copeland. What's it going to be? Blood, sweat, or tears?"

Quinn looked from the GPS on the dashboard of the ambulance to her partner, Parker Drake, a wry smile slipping over her lips despite the fact that they were hauling ass through city traffic in a vehicle weighing approximately as much as a full-grown African bush elephant.

"First things first," she said loudly enough to compete with the siren. Adjusting her seat belt over the front of her navy blue RFD T-shirt, she settled in against the comfortably familiar backrest of the ambo's passenger seat. "What are the stakes?"

They'd come up with this game about three months into their now five-year work partnership, and she'd learned early on not to give him so much as a millimeter of leeway. Parker was like the slightly annoying, overly cocky older brother she'd always wanted but never had. At least, that's what Quinn imagined an older brother would be like. For as much good-natured crap as they gave each other, Parker seemed happy to fill the role. They'd been tight—and platonic, because even though Parker was objectively hand-some, *ew*—from the beginning. Not that Quinn wasn't close with everyone at Seventeen, because she really was. Heck, she could even get Gamble to crack a smile if she set her sights on it. But her and Parker? God, they'd probably still be riding around Remington, treating everything from hangnails to heart attacks when they were eighty.

Which was totally fine by Quinn, thank you very much.

"Stakes. Let's see. How about house chores for a week," he answered, prompting her to laugh.

"It's so cute how you think I'll fall for that when I know you're on kitchen duty this week. I've seen that science experiment B-shift has going on in the back of the fridge with that leftover Kung Pao chicken. It's a total biohazard. Try again."

"Okay, okay." Parker lifted his brows, since lifting his hands from the steering wheel was obviously not a spectac-ular plan. "How about loser takes the next cantankerous drunk who needs a banana bag?"

Cantankerous? Oh, that was just too good to pass up. Not that he didn't use four-syllable words on a very regular rota-tion, but hell if she wasn't going to give him a serving of shit to go with his high-pedigree vocabulary.

"Jesus, Drake. What are you, a Thesaurus with legs?"

Parker, of course, gave as good as he got. Which, come to think of it, was half the reason they worked so well together. "What can I say? I'm not just a pretty face over here. Now are you in, or not?"

"Yeah, yeah. I'm in."

Eyeballing the dashboard display to make sure no new updates had come through from dispatch on the call they were responding to, Quinn took a second to roll through her options and the odds that went with them. A person down of unknown causes could be anything from a sixty-year-old bank CEO who had choked on his caviar at the Plaza to an eighteen-year-old who had OD'd on heroin in a grimy alley, and there were a whooooole lot of in-betweens. She knew, because she and Parker had seen pretty much all of them. Hence the whole reason for blood, sweat, or tears.

To anyone who wasn't a first responder, Quinn supposed the game might seem uncaring; after all, she and Parker could have someone's life in their hands—literally—on any given call. But the gravity of those situations was heavy enough to sandbag even the most experienced paramedic. Compartmentalizing so you could stay sane and help people on their worst-ever days rather than letting the job scatter your marbles? Yeah, that was something Quinn had learned to do after her first shift.

She knew all too well how deeply no-holds-barred caring could hurt. And since she wasn't about to stop caring *or* taking care of people who needed it, she'd take compartmentalization for the win. Hell, she'd take anything that would keep her on the proper side of sane so she could do her job.

Shaking her head, Quinn re-routed her thoughts. *Person down of unknown causes, nineteen hundred block of Maplewood Avenue. Go.*

"Okay. The nine-one-one call came in nine minutes ago, so I'm going to rule out blood right off the bat," she said, thinking out loud. Dispatch stayed on the line with the caller whenever humanly possible, especially if they were right there with the victim. If the person down was bleeding badly, she and Parker would know by now.

"So no traumatic injury." Parker took a hard left onto Palmer Boulevard. "That leaves sweat or tears. What's your pick?"

"Hmm." Sweat was their own personal shorthand for any sort of stress ailment, like an MI or overdose or a seizure. Tears were anything that could be categorized as a mental health issue, because God, of all the calls they handled, those were often the most heartbreaking.

Quinn took a slow, deep breath. Looked out the window. Hedged her bets and said, "It's hot enough out today. My money's on sweat."

"Sweat it is. I'm taking tears," Parker said. "First hell-hot day of the year? Always stirs people up."

Ah, but he wasn't wrong. Mother Nature could kill a person in a dozen and a half ways if she put her back into it. This time last year, they'd had to treat a guy whose wife had stabbed him in the neck with a barbecue fork because he'd overcooked the steaks she'd blown her paycheck on.

Okay, so maybe "stirs people up" was the teensiest bit of an understatement. Still, Quinn felt pretty good about her odds, and either way, she'd get to help somebody who needed it. "Sweat versus tears. Deal."

A beat passed, then one more before Parker asked, "Hey, have you given any more thought to putting in for that lead spot opening up at Station Six next month?"

Her heart sucker punched her sternum at the swerve in subject, and damn it, she *so* didn't want to have this conversation right now. Or, okay. Ever. Which he totally knew, otherwise he wouldn't have blindsided her with the topic when they were on the way to a call and she was a captive freaking audience.

"Trying to get rid of me again?" Quinn finally managed, although the waver in her voice told her she hadn't quite stuck the no-big-deal landing she'd been going for. Parker had already asked her—twice, but who was counting—about the opening for a lead paramedic at Six. Looked like he thought the trifecta would be the charm. Poor misguided guy.

"Actually, I am. Not that I don't dig working with you," Parker quickly added, probably in a pre-emptive strike against the *seriously, what the hell?* that had just formed hotly on her tongue. "You're a kickass paramedic, Copeland."

"Thanks, I think."

Parker met her frown with one of his own. "That's exactly my point, though. You're good enough to be a lead, and spots like the one at Six don't open up every day. I'm not saying I don't want to work with you. But I *am* saying you deserve to run your own rig."

An odd sensation, somewhere between a jab and an ache, spread out in the pit of Quinn's stomach. She and Parker had had this conversation six months ago when a position for a lead paramedic had opened up over at Station Twenty-Nine. She was flattered that he thought so highly of her abilities—she busted her ass to be one of the best. But she'd spent her entire five-year tenure at the fire house they'd just rolled out of. She'd found her purpose there, not to mention the family she'd desperately needed when she'd walked in the door on day one. Her answer was still—and always would be—the same.

"I appreciate the atta-girl, Drake. But Seventeen is my home. I'm perfectly happy where I am, even if that means I'm not the lead paramedic."

"Okay," he said after a pause. "If you change your mind, I'm cool with writing you a letter of recommendation. I mean, hell"—he flashed her a sly grin while still managing to focus on the road in front of them—"you're even getting Slater to warm up a little, and *that* is really saying something."

Now Quinn's heart clattered for an entirely different

reason. "Slater's a good EMT," she said, and thank God Parker was as oblivious as an older brother when it came to things like sudden, out-of-control blushes.

"I'm sure he is. The city doesn't certify dumbasses, and judging by all the extra shifts he's taken since he started training, he's sure gaining enough experience. He's just a little, I don't know. Reserved, don't you think?"

Quinn hedged. It was true that Slater never hung out for after-hours beers at the Crooked Angel with the first responders and cops who frequented the place, just like he'd never gone to the Fork in the Road diner for the post-shift breakfast everyone at Seventeen usually indulged in once a week. Not that his no-show track record had ever stopped her from hoping he'd come around.

"Okay, so he might be a little quiet," she allowed, because there was no denying that Slater wasn't exactly the sharing-is-caring type. Still... "He's not *that* hard to talk to once you get to know him, though. I actually like helping him study."

"Do you, now?"

Parker's dark eyebrows traveled halfway up his forehead, his smile edging dangerously close to smirk territory, and ah, shit. For all his big-brother lack of awareness regarding the fact that she was both female and heterosexual, he wasn't dense.

And since Slater had neither made a move in the whole seven months they'd worked together, nor given her any overt sign that he'd be receptive if *she* made a move, it was time to save face by putting a cork in this conversation, stat.

"Don't." Quinn punctuated the word with her very best glare. "Or I'll be forced to tell Gamble you're the one who ate the last of the lasagna rolls Kylie brought in during last shift."

Parker's grin went on an instant sabbatical. "You wouldn't."

Okay, she probably wouldn't. But a girl had her pride. Mostly. Sort of. Okay, fine. She was completely prideless when it came to her one-sided girl crush on Luke Slater. "Do you really want to try me?" she bluffed.

"It's not my fault Kellan's sister is an amazing chef and Gamble's too slow on the uptake with the leftovers. Those lasagna rolls are ridiculous," Parker pointed out.

"Are they worth Gamble's wrath? Because slow or not, I'm pretty sure he'd—"

"I get it, I get it!" Parker said with a laugh that was half humor, half holy-shit fear he was trying to cover *up* with humor. "No questions about you and the rookie."

"Because there's nothing to question. I'm just helping him study," Quinn said with finality. Sitting back against the contours of the passenger seat, she checked the dashboard screen one more time before looking out the window at the downtown buildings flashing by.

Nothing to question, her ass. He might keep to himself more than the rest of them combined, but Luke Slater was sexy as strong-and-silent sin.

Heat crept over her skin as an unexpected pull of attraction settled low between her hips. Quinn had heard enough horror stories from first responders at other houses to know that crossing the streams between work and play probably had "bad idea" scrawled all over it in permanent marker. But between Slater's broad, muscular shoulders and the killer combination of his light brown skin and piercing blue eyes that were gorgeous enough to render a girl's panties useless, she really couldn't deny the truth.

The longer she and Slater worked together, the more she wanted to turn that bad idea into a very. Very. Good. Time.

The ambulance slowed, and the change in velocity kicked Quinn's pulse into a completely different sort of go-mode. Hunger, thirst, exhaustion, even pain—they all fell by the wayside when she was working a trauma, as if her physiology just seemed to know that it was more important for her to take care of a kid who had been hurt in a car crash than to distract her with something as lame as a stomach rumble or a yawn.

"Okay, here we go," Parker said, pulling to a full stop in front of a trendy-looking café with an overhead sign that read BREWED AWAKENING in big, bright red letters. "Nineteen-twelve Maplewood Avenue."

Per protocol, Quinn confirmed the address with a fast but careful glance at the dashboard screen. "Copy that," she said, her heartbeat accelerating in an ingrained physical response her body knew all too well as she reached for the two-way radio that linked them to dispatch. "Ambulance Twenty-Two to dispatch. We are on-scene at nineteen-twelve Maplewood Avenue. Over."

"Dispatch to Ambulance Twenty-Two, copy your location. Over."

Snuffing out the very last of the well-hello-there tingle that had accompanied her illicit thoughts of Slater, Quinn got out of the rig and locked all of her attention on the scene. Coffee shop, busy part of the city, a hundred and fuckteen degrees outside...God, this could be anything.

Engine Seventeen rumbled up behind them, the heavy thump of four sets of boots sounding off against the pavement just as she popped the handle on the ambo's side storage door.

"Hey, you guys," Quinn said over her shoulder, grabbing her first-in bag and tugging a pair of blue nitrile gloves from the side pocket, snapping them quickly into place. "Sorry for cutting your drills short."

Any time engine wasn't already on a call, dispatch tended to send them to accompany her and Parker on reports of a person down, just in case they needed help getting past a sticky obstacle in order to reach a victim. Falling out on this one must have given them a hell of a run for their money, considering they'd been harness-deep in rope drills when the all-call had gone off.

Funny, Shae—who just so happened to be not only Quinn's station-mate, but one of her closest friends—just grinned and shook her head as she stepped up next to Quinn on the pavement. "Ah, Slater's got to learn rescue skills on the fly, and it gave the rest of us some good practice at making fast work of things."

Quinn shut the compartment door just in time to see Slater and Kellan arrive behind Shae, the latter sporting a small, freshly formed bruise just below his right eye.

"Mmm. Some of us got more practice than others." Despite the sarcasm in his tone, Kellan smiled and fell into step with the rest of them as they hustled toward the back of the ambo for the gurney. "Speaking of which, if you need backup on this one, I've got dibs. McCullough owes me for the shiner."

Quinn couldn't help but go brows-up. "Do I even want to know?" she asked Gamble, who stood sentry at the ambulance's open rear doors while Parker unlocked the gurney with a loud clack.

"Do you even have to ask?" Gamble capped the question with a shake of his dark head, and even Shae lifted her hands in concession as they got the gurney to ground level and cut a brisk path over the city sidewalk leading up to the coffee shop.

"Probably not," she said.

Parker let out a short-lived laugh as he moved past one of the glass double doors leading inside, guiding the foot of the gurney while Quinn maneuvered over the threshold from the other end. "Okay, then. If we need an assist, Kellan it is."

Taking a few seconds to allow her eyes to make the adjustment from the bright sunlight outside to the much more dimly lit interior of the coffee shop, Quinn scanned the cozy L-shaped space. "Did someone call for an ambulance?"

"Yes! Over here!" called out a worried brunette wearing thickly rimmed glasses that matched her cherry-red apron. "Please, hurry."

Quinn's breath kicked slightly faster through her lungs, and yeah, the woman didn't have to tell them twice.

"Can you tell us what happened?" Parker asked the brunette while Quinn sighted in on the lifeless figure slumped over the floorboards alongside the bakery display case. *Female, late twenties-early thirties. Unconscious. No visible signs of trauma. Go. Go.*

She knelt down before she was even aware of the command from her neurons to move, pressing her index and middle fingers over the woman's neck with one hand while using the other to stabilize her spine. Relief splashed through Quinn's veins at the thump of the woman's heartbeat, strong and slow against her fingers.

"I've got a pulse." At least *that* was a win. The rest of this situation? Not so much.

"She was waiting in line." The woman in the apron, whose name tag read "Annie", stared down at them, her eyes as round as a pair of dinner plates behind her glasses. "She was standing right there when all of a sudden she...I don't know. Just kind of collapsed. One of the other customers caught her on the way down"—Annie pointed to a man kneeling on the floor by the woman's side, across from Quinn—"but she was out cold, and she's been really out of it since then. I called nine-one-one right away."

"So she didn't hit her head when she fell? You're sure?" Parker asked, and the man nodded, moving back to give them room to work.

"I'm sure. I was next to her in line when she passed out. She went down like a sack of potatoes. One minute, she was standing there, the next..." He trailed off, gesturing to the floor. "I did manage to get ahold of her and slide her to the floor, though."

Another win, although Quinn did a quick check for a head injury the guy might have missed, just in case. Good Samaritans might have kind intentions, but what they usually *didn't* have were medical degrees. "No sign of head or spinal trauma," she confirmed.

"Okay, let's get her on her back for an RTA," Parker said. "On my count. One, two, three."

Working in a rhythm she knew as well as her own signature, they rolled the woman to her back on the floor-boards. Later, Quinn would probably have bruises on her knees, she knew. But right now? She didn't even feel the slightest bite of the hardwood on her skin. Her brain caught clips and snippets from her peripheral vision as she prepped for the rapid trauma assessment. The dozen or so onlookers Shae and Gamble had corralled by the tables in the back of the shop. Kellan standing by the gurney, his sharp stare on both the situation and the scene. Slater, who was watching with enough quiet intensity to sink a battle-ship. Quinn had been trained to always be aware of her surroundings in case they became dangerous. But right now, in this moment, the only thing she really *saw* was her patient.

"Ma'am?" She curled her fingers into a loose fist, placing her knuckles over the center of the woman's now-loosened blouse for a nice firm sternal rub. The woman stirred, but barely. *Shit*. "Ma'am, can you hear me?"

"Heart rate is sixty-two, pulse ox is ninety-nine percent," Parker said, and damn, he'd been fast with those leads. The portable monitor beside him flashed as the numbers registered, the woman's vitals beginning to scroll over the screen.

"Okay, sweetheart. Let's figure you out." Quinn's brain spun through the most likely suspects. Airway was clear, heart rate was normal, albeit on the low side. The woman had gone lights out with no warning...

Of course. "Diabetic shock," Quinn said, just a nanosecond before Parker did. Reaching for her first-in bag, Quinn liberated the glucose test kit from the pocket where she always kept it, the sharp, familiar tang of alcohol pinching at her nose as she swiped a pad over the woman's middle finger and completed the test.

"Whoa. Blood sugar is thirty-four." No wonder this lady was so unresponsive. Anything under seventy was considered low. Thirty-four was in the freaking basement. But at least subterranean blood sugar levels were a relatively easy fix.

"Starting an IV," Parker said, although his hands were already halfway through the process. He'd always been a wizard with starting a line. He hadn't earned the nickname Ace for nothing. "Pushing half an amp of D50 and running normal saline, wide open."

Quinn eagle-eyed the woman's vitals for another minute before placing another sternal rub over the center of her chest, right between the leads. "Ma'am? Can you hear me?"

The woman's eyes fluttered, and Quinn exhaled a little easier. Right up until she swatted at Quinn's hands, anyway.

"Okay, it's okay." She dropped her voice to its most soothing setting, trying to reassure the woman. Judging by her dazed/panicked expression, Quinn was doing a piss-poor job.

She tried again. "Ma'am, my name is Quinn and I'm a paramedic. Can you tell me—"

The woman lifted her lids again in a series of heavy blinks. She took another swat—this one with a little more oomph—at Quinn's hands, the sloppy movements tangling her IV tube.

Quinn's pulse jerked in a reminder that her adrenal gland was fully functional. Coming around from diabetic shock was a slow road, and waking up to a gaggle of first responders all up in your personal bubble had to be a little frightening. But keeping this woman calm was key if they wanted to keep helping her, so Quinn mentally crossed her fingers and hoped the third time would be the proverbial charm.

"Ma'am, please. I need you to—"

The woman's hand shot out, connecting with Quinn's upper arm in a solid, ow-worthy thump. Her heart slapped faster in her chest, and even though the response was pure physiology, it threatened to upend the composure she needed in order to do her job.

Nope. Not today.

"Okay. Take it easy." Quinn gripped the woman's forearm in an effort to steady her. If that IV blew, she wouldn't get the fluids she needed, and they'd have no way of getting more meds on board if her blood sugar took another belly flop. The woman struggled against Quinn's hold, her free hand flailing in a series of wild, broken motions that meant nothing good for where they were headed.

"Copeland."

Quinn locked eyes with Parker, a nonverbal conversation moving between them in less time than it took to sneeze. Parker passed the IV bag to Kellan, who had been standing behind him, ready to assist as promised, and circled his fingers carefully but firmly around either one of the patient's forearms.

"Ma'am, I know this is scary, but we want to help you. We're going to give you something to calm you down so we can treat you and make you feel better, okay? Quinn, draw up two milligrams of Ativan."

"Wait. She doesn't need Ativan. *Stop*."

Quinn was so stunned to hear Slater's words that she actually hesitated with one hand on the vial.

Parker shook his head, adamant. "No. I get that you're fresh out of EMT training, Slater, but this isn't my first rodeo. We need to skip the pleasantries before this woman yanks out her IV or becomes more upset. Or worse." He turned back to the woman, his tone unyielding but not unkind. "Ma'am, please. You need to stop fighting us, okay? We don't want to have to restrain you."

But rather than standing down, Slater stepped closer, until he was less than an inch away from Parker at the woman's side. "If you restrain her, she'll only fight harder. And she doesn't need the Ativan to calm down."

Parker's brows winged up in shock, and didn't that just make him and Quinn a pair of freaking bookends.

"Slater," she started, but his determined, ice-blue stare made the rest of her words crash to a halt in her throat.

"Your patient isn't trying to fight you, Quinn. She's trying to *talk* to you."

3

"Your patient is deaf. She's trying to sign," Luke said quietly, moving past a drop-jawed Quinn and—shit, yeah, Parker and Kellan, too. But since Parker putting restraints on his patient would be akin to slapping duct tape over her mouth and Luke had been the only person to recognize that little fact, he didn't have a choice. Ignoring the lead-lined weight of their stares, he knelt down beside the woman, positioning himself directly in her line of sight and began to sign.

"My name is Luke," he said, accompanying the ASL with actual out-loud words, partly because he didn't know if the woman could read lips (or might be too groggy to the job even if she could), and partly because he didn't want to have to waste time translating for Parker and Quinn any more than he'd already have to. This woman needed treatment, and fast. "I'm a firefighter and an EMT. I need you to be calm so my friends can help you. Okay?"

The woman stilled, her eyes widening with recognition and relief, and she gave up a loose nod.

"Can you tell me your name?" Luke asked. Parker

released his grasp on the woman's forearms, albeit a little hesitantly, and she signed in a weak reply.

Elena. I feel tired. And scared.

His chest tightened beneath his RFD T-shirt. "It's nice to meet you, Elena. I know you feel tired and scared, but we're here to help you. Can you tell me if anything hurts?"

Nothing hurts. But I'm diabetic. I missed breakfast. Elena lowered her arms to her sides as if the conversation had been a four-minute mile, and Christ, with a blood sugar of thirty-four and a history of diabetes, no wonder the poor woman was wiped out.

"No reported pain." Although the words were for Quinn and Parker's benefit, Luke made sure Elena could still see him as he spoke. She was the biggest part of the equation, and excluding her just because she was deaf wasn't on his great big plan of *let's do that.* "Patient is diabetic and didn't eat breakfast."

Quinn got over her shock first. "Okay," she said, glancing at the monitor. "Her vitals are strong, and that D50 is obviously starting to kick in. Why don't we get her on the gurney so she'll be more comfortable? We can continue to monitor her blood sugar levels out at the ambo to make sure they're coming up."

After a heartbeat's worth of a hitch, Parker nodded. "Copy that. Sounds good."

Kellan grabbed the gurney from the spot where Parker and Quinn had parked the thing a few feet away, and Luke relayed the plan of action to Elena. He helped Parker get her situated on the white-sheeted mattress, staying close by in case he needed to translate further, and also a little selfishly to watch the treatment protocol as they relo'd from the coffee shop to the back of the ambulance.

"I'll call this in and get the paperwork started since she's stable. You two good to continue treatment back here?" Parker split his gaze between Luke and Quinn, and whoa, cue up the surprise.

"Sure," Luke said, the words tagging along with Quinn's nod. "I'm happy to stick around and help if you need a translator."

"Good deal. And by the way?" Parker paused, brows up. "Nice catch, rookie."

Oh, the fucking irony. But of course Luke had recognized Elena's efforts to sign, just as he'd been able to fluently communicate with her.

After all, his sister had been deaf for a decade, and he'd been raising her for just as long. Shame on him if he hadn't recognized it, or intervened on Elena's behalf. Even if he *had* just tipped his personal-life hand to Parker and Quinn and everyone on engine.

No, check that. He might as well have flung every last one of his cards face-up on the fucking table.

Luke's smile was about as comfortable as a sandpaper strait jacket, but he forked it over just the same as Parker swiveled on his boots to head for the front of the rig. "Thanks."

Dodging Quinn's unnervingly pretty, unnervingly laser-like dark blue gaze, Luke settled against the bench seat running the length of the left side of the ambulance. Between the dextrose and the fluids free-flowing through her IV, Elena perked up exponentially after only a few short minutes, her dark brown stare growing more focused and her sign language more fluid than it had been back in the coffee shop.

Now that she was stable, Luke asked and signed, "Would you prefer signing or lip-reading?"

She smiled, albeit weakly. *I can read lips, but don't mind you signing. Your ASL is quite good.*

Sure. To this day, Hayley wasn't shy about correcting even the subtle nuances when he got sloppy.

Luke's gut gave up a hard slap shot. "Thank you. How are you feeling?"

Silly, Elena signed. *I know better than to skip breakfast. I won't have to go to the hospital or anything, will I?*

"Don't feel silly," Luke replied, continuing to both speak and sign. "It's our job to help, and believe me, we've seen far sillier. As for whether or not you need to go to Remington Memorial..."

He let the statement dangle, turning toward the spot where Quinn sat across from him. Her stare flicked from the exchange—which she'd been watching with far too much curiosity for him *not* to have to do damage control on the whole why-yes-I-am-fluent-in-ASL topic later—to the portable monitor now tucked safely beside Elena on the gurney.

"Her vitals are normal, and she's pretty alert. We'll have to check her blood sugar again in about five minutes." Quinn left zero wiggle room in either her tone or her expression. "But if she's up to the nineties, I think she can opt out of a trip to Remington Mem. As long as she eats. *And* Parker agrees," she added.

"Seems fair."

Luke relayed the message. He shifted over the bench with the intention of going to scrounge up some orange juice and maybe a granola bar from the coffee shop to get Elena's levels closer to normal, but she reached out, grabbing his hand for a second before launching into some rapid-fire sign language.

"What?" Quinn's spine snapped to attention. "What's she saying? Is she in pain?"

"You can ask her yourself if you'd like," Luke said, taking care to keep his tone free of judgment. He spent so much time around Hayley that he sometimes forgot most of the world wasn't well-versed in deaf culture. "I don't mind translating her answers, but Elena can understand you just as long as you're face-to-face with her when you speak. And no. She's not in pain. She actually wanted me to tell you she's sorry."

"Sorry?" Quinn's brows furrowed before flying sky-high in obvious surprise. "What on earth for?"

But before Luke could answer, Quinn gave up a tiny head shake and turned toward Elena to repeat the question. She didn't crank up her volume or slow her words to toddler speed like most people who spoke to someone who was deaf, and hell if that didn't send a feeling Luke didn't want to contemplate directly through his chest.

Elena looked at him for only a second, then turned her gaze on Quinn as she signed her reply.

"She says, 'I didn't mean to hit you earlier. I was frightened and really dizzy.'" He paused to process the rest of what Elena was saying, to make sure he was getting the translation just right. "'I wanted to get your attention, but I didn't realize you were so close. I'm sorry.'"

"That's okay," Quinn said directly to Elena, who met the words with an apologetic smile. "I know you didn't hit me on purpose. I'm just glad I could help."

Again, Elena signed, and Luke translated directly, the way he'd learned to ages ago. "'Thank you very much for taking care of me.'"

Quinn's cheeks pinked in a blush that made him thank his lucky goddamn stars *he* wasn't the one having his vitals monitored. "Oh. Of course. You're welcome," she said to Elena. "Now go ahead and rest, okay? Your body has been through a lot. I'll re-check your blood sugar in a few minutes."

The second finger stick showed some greatly improved numbers, and after a snack, a once-over from Parker, and a sapling's worth of paperwork, Quinn removed Elena's IV.

"Okay. Your blood sugar is ninety-six, and you're obviously feeling better," she said.

Elena nodded, sitting up taller against the back of the gurney as if to prove it. "'Yes,'" Luke relayed. "'I feel much better.'"

"Good. Take it easy for the rest of the day, and be sure to monitor your blood sugar again in an hour. Do you have a test kit with you?"

"'Right here in my purse.'" Luke bit his tongue. Direct translation might be the accepted norm with deaf people, but that didn't mean it didn't get awkward from time to time.

The smile Quinn had folded between her lips told Luke —and probably Elena, too—that she'd heard the humor, loud and frickin' clear. "Then you're all set. If you feel light-headed or if your re-test levels dip below seventy, you need to call nine-one-one right away, though. Okay?"

"'I promise,'" Luke translated. Elena turned toward him, but rather than accepting the hand he'd offered to help her off the gurney, she squeezed his forearm and began to sign again.

You saved me today.

His breath stuck in his windpipe, and he cleared his throat even though he wasn't going to use the damned thing. *Quinn and Parker did all the work.*

Elena's brows traveled up, likely in a bit of surprise that he wasn't also speaking the words. Excluding Quinn from the conversation when she was right there across from him was borderline rude, Luke knew. But she *was* right across from him, and he was already going to have a hell of a time playing dodge ball with the topic as soon as Elena was safely on her way.

He couldn't air out anything else. Especially not anything personal.

Not that Elena was about to let him off the proverbial hook. Damn, she was fierce. *Quinn and Parker took good care of me, yes, but so did you. You were on my side. You* heard *me. Thank you, Luke.*

The words might not have been spoken, but God, they nailed him to that ambo bench just the same. *You're welcome,* he signed, although steadying his hands to get the reply out smoothly took effort. *I'm glad you feel better, Elena.*

Parker reappeared around the back of the ambulance then, reaching up to help her to the pavement. With one last wave, Elena turned toward the friend who had offered to come get her and take her safely home for some rest.

Luke braced for impact in three, two, one...

"I had no idea you knew sign language." Quinn's tone was far from accusatory, but her stare held enough interest to tangle his gut like a ninety-foot string of Christmas lights.

Tactic Number One. Right fucking now. "I'm sure there are lots of things I don't know about you."

"Well, yeah, but..."

Followed by a healthy dose of Tactic Number Two. "Do you need me to help with anything else? Paperwork or cleanup or anything?"

Luke tacked a polite smile over his face to knock the diversion all the way home. His gut tightened slightly when Quinn seemed to buy it—which was weird as shit, considering that it meant his duck and cover was actually working.

But after a blink, she sent her gaze on a tour of the back of the ambo, and he let out a great, big lungful of *mission accomplished*.

"I need to do a little bit of housekeeping before we head back to Seventeen. Just some quick sterilization in case we catch another call right away," she said, gesturing to the gurney between them. "But sure. I'd love a hand."

"You got it."

Reaching for the box in the storage compartment mounted to the wall beside him, Luke snapped a pair of blue nitrile gloves into place per health and safety regs for medical cleanup. He and Quinn put some easy teamwork to gathering the discarded materials she'd used while caring for Elena—blood sugar test strips, gauze pads, and the like —placing everything into biohazard bags. Having done no less than two dozen ride-alongs and training runs with other houses in the last couple of months, Luke was already familiar with the protocol. Still, just like rope drills, even the stuff that seemed like a no-brainer needed to be practiced if he wanted to help people when they really needed it. Plus, he couldn't deny that while this part of the job was pretty standard-issue, the view certainly didn't suck.

Even if he *was* singing an internal hallelujah for the bunker pants currently hiding his hard-on for the very set of sexy-sweet dimples that were probably going to be the end of him.

He could think of a hell of a lot worse ways to go.

"Hey." The sound of footsteps on the pavement U-turned him back to the rear of the ambulance in about two seconds flat. "You two nearly done back here?" Parker asked, leaning in through the open space of the back door.

"Yep." Luke nodded, dishing up a double dose of his most neutral smile as he tugged the end of a fresh white sheet over the corner of the gurney mattress. God, his sanity was on a serious leave of absence. He and Quinn *worked* together. Just because there weren't rules against them getting involved, even casually, that didn't mean anything about it was a good idea. Especially since he was a rookie, and—oh, by the way—as serious as a triple bypass about not just doing his job, but doing it well.

He'd come too far for anything less. No matter how pretty (and sexy. And smart. And sexy, had he mentioned sexy?) Luke found her.

"Ugh." Leaning down from her side of the bench seat, Quinn aimed a high-octane frown at the mechanism anchoring the gurney to the floor of the ambulance. "This thing is loose again. I think there's something wrong with the lock. See? It's not holding properly."

She placed a hand on the bright yellow frame and pushed, and sure enough, the gurney gave up far more movement than safety probably dictated.

Parker pulled himself inside the back of the rig, leaning down with a frown that rivaled Quinn's. "Again?" He reached beneath the gurney, his arm disappearing beneath the expanse of vinyl mattress pad and steel framing. "This thing has been giving us fits for—"

All at once, the gurney lurched on its moorings, causing Parker to yank his arm back with a yell and Luke's pulse to sit up and take notice.

"Parker?" Quinn shifted forward, concern covering her face. "What's the matter? Are you hurt?"

The guy grimaced, whipping his left hand over his right. "My hand got stuck in the goddamn mechanism trying to get it to lock."

"Oh *hell*." Quinn blanched, and Luke was pretty sure he must have, too, because fucking *ow*. "Let me see it," she said.

Parker shook his head. "It's fine."

Her look was pure *are you kidding me*. Judging by the blood streaming through Parker's fingers and starting to run down his forearm, Luke was inclined to agree.

"Don't mess with me, Drake. Let me see your hand."

She'd already gloved up—damn, Luke would have to figure out how she managed to do that so fast all the time—and had one hand out in expectation. Parker must have realized arguing would get him exactly nowhere, because he forked over the limb in question even though his expression said he was less than wild about the share.

"Whoa." Luke clamped down on his bottom lip two seconds too late. Showing emotion at an injury was a strict no-no around patients. The freak-out factor tended to make them panic. But since he was pretty sure Parker had just torn through half the musculature in his palm and maybe even a tendon or two for good measure, the reaction was sadly warranted.

"Sorry," Luke murmured, snapping up a pair of gloves and moving to the other side of the gurney, next to Quinn. "What can I do?"

"You can grab a couple of four-by-four QuikClot pads, please. From the cabinet over my shoulder," she added. To anyone else, she probably looked cucumber-cool, examining Parker's injury with efficient movements. But Luke watched and listened way more than he spoke, which meant that after working with Quinn for seven months, he had the luxury of knowing exactly what that hard press of her mouth meant.

Clearly, Parker had also gotten the memo. "Come on, Copeland. It's just a scratch."

"Nice try. Now pardon me while I call bullshit." Taking the pads from Luke's outstretched fingers, she pressed one to the top of Parker's hand and the other to his palm. "The lac is deep, Parker, not to mention jagged as hell, and it's right between the thumb and forefinger on your dominant hand. You know the drill," she said, this time more softly.

Parker huffed past a highly frustrated frown, but even that couldn't cover up the wince of pain underneath or the sheen of sweat on his forehead as he looked down at the gauze pads he was already starting to bleed through. "I'm telling you, this isn't a big deal."

"And I'm telling you, if the situation were reversed, you'd be hauling me into Remington Mem without question. So would you please do me a favor and let me take care of you? Otherwise Bridges is going to fire my ass for letting you go back to the house with a hand that looks like a Frankenstein field day."

A beat passed, then another, punctuated only by the street noise filtering in past the still-open rear door to the ambulance and Parker's resigned exhale.

"Fine," he said. "Let's get this over with, since I know better than to think you'll back down."

Smart man, Luke thought, and not just because Parker's hand really did look all sorts of Humpty Dumpty.

When it came to caring for people, Quinn was a barracuda. When it came to caring for the people she worked with? She was a great white that would make Jaws run crying for his mommy.

"Thank you." Quinn's shoulders loosened beneath her paramedic's uniform, just slightly, but it was enough. She swung toward Luke and asked, "You know the protocol for this, right?"

He nodded. "Place firm pressure on the wound, dress and immobilize the injured limb, transport to the ED for treatment."

"Perfect." Shucking her gloves, she sent an apologetic look at her partner before jumping down to the pavement from the back of the ambo.

"Slater, you take care of one and two while I tackle number three. I'll radio Remington Memorial and let them know we're on our way."

Quinn sat in one of the two chairs across from Captain Bridges's desk and tried with all her might not to scream. But seeing as how Bridges was a) the boss she highly respected, and b) on the phone with Dr. Keith Langston, who just so happened to be the head of the very same emergency department to which she'd rushed her partner ninety minutes ago, she bit her tongue in the name of propriety.

And what do you know, it mostly worked.

"Mmm hmm. I see. Of course. Well, thank you for the update." Bridges replaced the receiver in its cradle on his desk, looking at her over the thin black frames of his reading glasses. "First things first, since I know where your head is. Parker is fine. No broken bones, his tendons look intact, and Dr. Langston expects him to make a full recovery."

Her sigh of relief lasted all of a nanosecond. "How many stitches?"

"Quinn..."

"I saw the injury, Cap." Quinn's gut gave up a hard twist

at the freshly minted memory of Parker's hand, sliced wide and bleeding. "For God's sake, I treated him two seconds after it happened. I know the number isn't one or two."

Bridges steepled his fingers over his desk. "Twenty-nine."

Right. Looked like that twist in her gut had its sights set on becoming a full-blown cyclone. "How long will he be out of work?"

"A couple weeks, minimum, but realistically, probably three. It depends on how quickly he heals and regains his mobility. He'll work closely with the docs, and they'll evaluate his progress next week to give us a more specific timetable."

Quinn swallowed hard, but managed a small nod. God, Parker must be going crazy. Or at the very least, driving the medical staff at Remington Mem crazy.

Cue up another corkscrew in her gut. "He's my partner. I should be there with him. Helping him fill out the paperwork or...something," she said lamely, but Bridges met the sentiment with a shake of his head.

"I sent squad over to the hospital. If Parker needs anything, Hawkins will make it happen. In the meantime, we've got some shifts to cover here on ambo."

Well, hello, rock and hard place. But Station Seventeen was the closest thing Quinn had to a family—hell, it was the only thing she had, period—and she wasn't about to let Bridges down. Especially if the guys on squad had Parker's back right now. Hawk might talk a good game with his laid-back grin and that deep Southern drawl of his, but when things went mission critical? He was as steadfast as they came.

"Okay," Quinn said. "I'm happy to do whatever I can to fill in the gaps until Parker recovers."

"I'm glad to hear that," Bridges said, not skipping so much as a breath or a beat as he added, "because I'd like to put you in the lead paramedic spot."

"Excuse me?" Her spine did its very best rigor mortis impression against the back of her chair, but somehow, her captain remained totally unfazed. Holy shit, he was serious.

"Temporarily, of course. Just until Parker heals up."

"Okaaaay." The word stretched out with far more uncertainty than Bridges had surely been aiming for, but come on. There were so many whammies in the plan he'd just tossed out, Quinn couldn't even process them all. "Then who would be my partner? Someone from the float pool?"

Ugh, the thought of it sent a less than polite look over her face. Sure, it was only three weeks, but with the wrong partner? Those three weeks could turn into the third circle of hell super quick.

Bridges surprised her by shaking his head. "Actually, I'd prefer to stay in-house to make this as easy as possible. You've already been mentoring Slater, and he's expressed an interest in extending his first responder training to full paramedic status. I thought the two of you would make a good team."

"You want me to take lead and partner with Slater," she said slowly, a flush spreading out over her skin, and good *Lord* it was hot in this office.

Thankfully, Bridges didn't seem to notice she was having her own personal summer. "The city is short on paramedics right now, especially lead paramedics. You're more than qualified to take Parker's role for the time being, and you and Slater already know each other. Plus, he's already earned his EMT credentials, so he's qualified to ride on ambo under your command. This would be a good learning opportunity for him, and less of a disruption for you."

The man had a point. Several of them, in fact. Quinn thought of how smartly Slater had realized Elena was deaf when the fact had gone so thoroughly over everyone else's heads this morning—including her own. "Slater *is* a really quick study," she agreed.

"Moving Dempsey back to his old spot on engine and pulling a floater from the pool to cover squad would be far easier than trying to drum up another paramedic for three weeks straight," Bridges said. "Just as long as you're okay with the arrangement."

"Of course." The answer catapulted past her lips before it had fully taken shape in her brain. But she'd do anything for this fire house, just like she'd do whatever it took to care for the people who needed medical help when she was on-shift.

Including squelching her libido's dark and dirty thoughts of Luke Slater in order to work shoulder to shoulder with him for the next three weeks.

"Good." Bridges nodded, reaching for a sheaf of paperwork on his desk. "I've already run everything by Gamble, and he's on board with the shuffle just as long as Slater keeps up with his firefighter training on the side. I'd like to start the new assignments effective immediately so we don't have to take the ambulance off rotation for the rest of this shift. As long as you think Slater will be okay with that."

Quinn scooped in a deep breath and looked over her shoulder at the door leading back to the common room. "Guess there's only one way to find out."

∾

LUKE SAT in the back of Ambulance Twenty-Two, staring at the engine bay through the open rear doors and trying like hell to figure out what had just happened. One minute, he'd been on the couch in Station Seventeen's common room reading *The Practice and Principles of Paramedics, Volume Four*, and the next, he'd been in Captain Bridges's office, agreeing to temporarily swap his bunker gear for a T-shirt with the department's EMT logo emblazoned across the back.

So much for keeping Quinn at arm's length. Now he was about to work with her, up close and personal, for three whole weeks.

And oh, by the way, not only did he still find her as sexy as ever, but as of this moment, she was his immediate superior.

Fucking spectacular.

Quinn cleared her throat, pulling herself into the back of the ambulance from the floor of the engine bay. "Sorry to keep you waiting. I just wanted to check in with Parker now that he's been released from the hospital."

"That's okay. How is he?"

"More pissed than anything else. Although I'm sure he'll change his tune once the hi-test pain meds start wearing off. Anyway"—her chest lifted slightly beneath her uniform shirt as she paused to inhale, and Christ the next ten shifts were going to last an ice age. *Each*—"since you and I are going to be working together for the next few weeks, there are probably a couple of things we should talk about from the jump."

"Okay." Yes. Business. Medical things. Nothing personal, and for the love of all things sacred and holy, no more looking at her chest. Even accidentally.

Damn, she had a really nice chest. Curves just where he liked them. Pert, pretty breasts that would fit perfectly in his palms, with nipples that he'd guess were just one shade darker than petal pink...

Luke cleared his throat to mask the strangled sound rising from it. *Boss! Boss! This woman is in charge of your training. Stop fantasizing about her nipples, you fucking horn dog.* "Shoot."

Quinn sat on the bench across from him, her expression wide open and bullshit-free. "I know I'm supposed to be the lead, or whatever, and since you haven't completed all of your paramedic training, I'll obviously take point on decision-making and higher-level treatments and procedures. But for the most part, I'd really like for us to treat patients as a team."

"You take this partner thing pretty seriously, huh?"

Not that Luke should be surprised, he guessed. Quinn was close with everyone in the house. Well, everyone other than him, anyway. She was also stone-cold serious about taking care of people, from the tiniest scratches to the grisliest amputations. Of course she'd want to go all-in on them being partners.

"Well, yeah," she said, all case-in-point. "I mean, I know it's a little different than how things work on engine because there are only two of us. But we can't treat patients properly if we don't rely on each other. And I definitely take caring for people seriously."

Although a tiny kernel of him squalled at the potential risk involved in working that closely with Quinn, he shook it off. The last seven months of training on engine had taught him all too well that teamwork was an absolute job requirement. He'd been able to balance the job with keeping his personal life personal. This wouldn't be any different.

It couldn't be.

"I do too," he said, capping off the words with a nod. "Teamwork sounds good."

Quinn smiled, and yeah, he'd need to start building an

immunity to those dimples if he had a prayer of surviving the next three weeks without balls the color of the Pacific Ocean. "Great. Why don't I show you where we keep everything back here, and we can review some basics as we go?"

"Sure."

She gave him a quick but thorough tutorial on the lay of the land in the back of the ambulance, and he did his level best to mentally catalogue everything as much as possible. They were halfway through the third compartment above the driver's side bench when the all-call burst out its harsh, high-pitched tone.

Engine Seventeen, brush fire. Route Four Ten, mile marker thirty-two. Requesting immediate response.

Luke's boots had hit the buffed concrete of the engine bay floor for three steps of solid hustle before he realized his auto-pilot needed a reroute.

"Sorry," he half-shouted over the thumping footfalls of his engine-mates and the churn and clack of the automatic garage door doing its thing. "Habit."

Quinn waited out the throaty, diesel-fueled rumble of the engine as Shae guided it out past the flashing yellow caution lights in front of the house, smiling as she said, "Not a bad one. I'm sure missing all the action on engine is a little disappointing."

"Not sure I'll be missing *all* the action. Being a paramedic is hardly like watching paint dry," he pointed out, hoisting himself back up to the interior of the ambulance. He'd seen her and Drake remove a guy's arm from a wood chipper last month, for God's sake.

"Okay, that's definitely true." The curiosity that had bubbled over her pretty face earlier went on a giant comeback tour, her blue eyes narrowing over his face. "So how come you want to do it?"

Luke's heartbeat sped up. "I'm sorry?" he asked, hoping maybe she'd reconsider the question. Couldn't they just talk about non-personal stuff, like the best way to splint a shattered femur, or the weather, or something?

Quinn's expression refused to let go, and yeah, that was a great, big negative. "How come you want to be a paramedic *and* a firefighter? It's a hell of an undertaking, especially as a rookie. And by that, I mean it's practically unheard of."

"I guess I just really want to help people."

It was a pat answer, and in honesty, one that knotted Luke's gut. There was so much more to the truth than that. But ever since his mother had died and his father had walked out the door on the night before her funeral never to return, taking care of people had been his MO. He knew how to find solutions and fix things. It wasn't just what he did. It was what he'd been hard-wired for. What he excelled at. What he needed.

And if by splitting time between both meant he wouldn't get too emotionally attached to one versus the other? Yeah. All the fucking better.

"Ah," Quinn said, and funny, the lift of her light blond brows said she actually understood his deep desire to help other people. "Well, if this morning is any indication, you've got a hell of a knack for it. You made a great catch with Elena. Patients in diabetic shock are usually really gorked out, so I didn't think anything of her not answering us verbally, but..."

The guilt covering Quinn's pretty features finished her sentence as loudly as if she'd shouted "I should have" through a ten-foot long megaphone, and a pang spread out from his belly to his chest.

"I got lucky," Luke said, duking it out with his conscience over the lie. "Anyway, you shouldn't beat yourself up." Okay, at least *that* was all truth. "You diagnosed Elena's diabetic shock way faster than I would have, and you and Parker took great care of her."

Quinn nodded, although she still seemed unconvinced. "I'm just glad she's going to be okay."

Luke replayed the call in his head. "How did you know to skip right to a sternal rub to try and wake her?"

"How did you know she was deaf?" Quinn asked back, and shit, how had he not seen that one coming?

Deflect. "You first."

"Okay." Quinn shrugged, propping her first-in bag over the gurney and re-stocking the thing with fresh packages of QuikClot pads. "Elena's LOC was pretty spontaneous and she'd been out for at least ten minutes. When someone's lost consciousness for that long, it's a solid bet the shake and wake isn't going to work. A sternal rub isn't fun for the patient," she admitted, a tiny wince stealing over her face as if she hated the fact that she'd given the woman a bruise while simultaneously saving her life. "And I know your text-book says to start out with the shoulder shake to gauge responsiveness for that very reason. But given how quickly she'd lost consciousness and how long she'd been out, I knew I'd end up needing to do the sternal rub anyway. So I did."

"That makes sense," Luke said, processing the knowl-edge with care. "So how do you know the difference between cutting to the chase and cutting corners?"

Quinn closed her bag, the zipper sending a soft *thhhrp* through the interior of the ambo. "The same way I'd guess you do on engine. Lots of training, and even more practice."

"Now that, I can get on board with."

A chuckle crossed his lips, but it met an abrupt end a second later when she looked at him and asked, "Is that how you learned sign language? As part of some training program?"

"No." His heart took a whack at his rib cage. "I, ah. I know someone who's deaf. My sister, actually."

The words were out before Luke could alter them, leaving a mental path of *are you out of your ever-loving mind?* in their wake. But he had to hand it to her—Quinn's only sign of surprise was the slight parting of her lips before she replied.

"Oh. Well, sign language is a pretty cool thing to know. Maybe in our down time, you can teach me some basics. If you'd be willing to."

"You want to learn how to sign?" His brows shot up, his jaw dropping in the opposite direction, but Quinn just jumped down from the back of the ambulance like no great shakes.

"What, you think you're the only one who needs to learn new things?" she asked, sending a laugh over one shoulder.

Huh. When she put it that way... "No. I guess not."

Her laughter softened, a more wistful expression taking its place as she turned toward him. "Knowing sign language, at least enough to be able to recognize it, would have made me a better paramedic this morning. Practice isn't always about the medical stuff, proper. It's about taking care of people the best way I can. Which"—she paused for a self-deprecating eye-roll—"I'm sure sounds all touchy-feely. But it's also the truth."

"It does sound a little touchy-feely," Luke agreed, partly because Quinn wasn't wrong, but more selfishly because he wanted her laughter to make an encore. *Bingo.* "I get it, though."

"Yeah?" she asked, her smile growing even bigger as he nodded. "I'm glad."

Luke moved from the ambo to the engine bay, squinting against the bright sunlight filtering in past the row of windows set into the garage door in front of them. Maybe teaching Quinn how to sign wouldn't be *that* big a deal. Maybe they could even grab a cup of coffee, or go on a date or something, once they were done working together. His attraction to her sure as shit wasn't going to take a hike anytime soon, and in truth, Shae hadn't really been wrong earlier. Asking Quinn out was a far cry from marrying her, and just because he didn't want to let his feelings flag fly didn't mean he had to be a monk. Maybe—

The all-call blared from the overhead speakers, screeching his thoughts to an abrupt halt.

Ambulance Twenty-Two. Person down of unknown causes. Eleven-forty Beaumont Place. Requesting immediate assistance.

"Looks like I'll need a rain check on that lesson," Quinn said, her curl-filled ponytail swishing over the shoulder of her navy blue T-shirt as she turned to give the rear doors on the ambulance a firm slam. "You ready for your first med call, partner?"

Luke's nod was firm despite the adrenaline sparking through his veins.

"Absolutely."

5

Okay, so driving the ambulance was just weird. Not that Quinn was pioneering new territory by sliding behind the wheel, because she'd talked Parker into letting her drive way more than once over the last half-decade. But the passenger seat was broken in just the way she liked it, with the perfect ratio of support to cushion, and ugh, how did Parker last for even one shift on this slab of concrete?

Quinn let out an exhale and tamped down her inner voice with a steady shot of *suck it up, buttercup*. Yes, she hated that Parker was hurt, and yes, she *really* hated that there was nothing she could do to help him. She had to focus on what was in front of her, though, which meant taking care of whoever was on the other end of this call with Slater as her partner.

The thought made her belly tighten with twin feelings of excitement and curiosity. She'd known he'd probably take the assignment to ambo as seriously as he took everything else—which was to say that on a scale of one to ten, he was going to clock in at about a forty-two. What Quinn hadn't been expecting was the reveal on his sister, which—while it wasn't some huge go-viral-on-the-Internet-style bombshell —still had to make her wonder.

What other surprises was he hiding beneath that wickedly sexy turnout gear and serious ice-blue stare?

"Isn't engine supposed to go with us on person-down calls?" Slater asked from the passenger seat beside her, and okay, she needed a super-sized reality check. For God's sake, she'd been around turnout gear on a regular basis for the last five years straight. Never once had the word 'sexy' entered the equation.

"Not always," Quinn said, and at least her voice was normal even though the rest of her had clearly filed for temporary insanity. "They've almost certainly got their hands full with that brush fire, and we're not headed to a rough part of the city." If the call had come in from North Point, dispatch would've either sent them with a police escort or pulled the guys from Station Twenty-Nine to back them up, just in case. Granted, this one looked like it was a bit close to the fringe, but she'd been on a bazillion medical calls with no backup, and had never had so much as a hiccup.

"Most person-down calls are no big deal anyway, especially in heat like this," she continued. "Someone probably just got a little dizzy mowing their lawn or taking a jog. Fifty bucks says we get back to the house before engine does."

Slater gave up a half-smile that did nothing to un-sexy the whole turnout gear fantasy in her head. "I'm going to hold you to that, just so you know. But in the meantime, what should I be doing here?" He gestured to the dashboard unit, which was currently giving them an ETA of seven minutes.

"Just keep your eye on any updates from dispatch.

They'll come through on the screen. Anything urgent will come in over the radio, just like on engine. But other than that, just be ready to grab your first-in bag when we get there."

"Copy that."

Quinn navigated their route according to the GPS, her brain adjusting to the new punch list of being the lead para-medic even though the rest of her wanted to give the idea the finger. Guiding the ambulance down a long stretch of road lined with boarded-up warehouses and storefronts that looked like they'd been long-abandoned, she finally pulled to a stop in front of a plain, two-story building flanked by an alley on one side and a pair of industrial garage bays on the other. A weather-faded sign marked the place as HENDERSON SHIPPING AND SUPPLIES, a much newer-looking one warning that trespassers would be prosecuted to the fullest extent of the law. Quinn scanned the scene, her pulse doing its usual get-up-and-go despite the deep breath she took to set her focus.

"Okay. Looks like this is it. Eleven-forty Beaumont," she said, triple-checking the crooked black numbers nailed beside the front door, then grabbing up the radio to call in their arrival. "Ambulance Twenty-Two to dispatch. We are on-scene at eleven-forty Beaumont Place. Over."

"*Dispatch to Ambulance Twenty-Two, copy your location. Over.*"

Slater sent a wary look through the windshield. "Are you sure? This place looks totally abandoned," he said, and funny, Quinn couldn't disagree.

Still. "Could be kids who were messing around in one of these old buildings and got hurt. Or a squatter who OD'd, maybe. But someone called for help. We just need to figure out who, and why."

She got out of the ambo, heading to the side storage compartment for the first-in bag she'd thankfully stocked just before they'd hauled out of the fire house. Slater was on the ball enough to have mimicked her movements on his side of the ambulance—nice—and they met up behind the vehicle.

"You want to take the gurney in?" Slater asked, but Quinn eyeballed their surroundings in a brisk assessment and shook her head.

"Getting it over this gravel will slow us down too much. Let's see what we're dealing with first."

He swiveled a stare over the building, his blue eyes narrowing in the over-bright sunlight beating down from overhead. "Copy that."

They fell into step together, their boots crunching and popping over the rough gravel path serving as a walkway through the weed-choked grass. A sheen of sweat formed on Quinn's brow before they'd even reached the battered steel door to the building, and she pulled a pair of nitrile gloves from the stash in her pocket before pushing her way inside.

"Hello?" Her eyes struggled to adjust to the shadows of the space. "Did someone call for an ambulance?"

Annnnd nothing. The building, which appeared to be some sort of warehouse, opened to a large front room littered with old wooden shipping crates and enough trash and empty beer cans to make Quinn's radar ping.

"Keep your eyes open for squatters," she murmured, and Slater nodded from beside her.

"Paramedics" he tried, his deeper voice echoing eerily off the walls and the dust-encrusted windows set high above ground level. "We're here to help. Call out."

"Stop right there and let me see those hands. Right fucking now."

The words were so incongruous with anything Quinn had ever heard that for a second, her brain straight-up refused to process them. Then she turned and saw the snub-nosed gun in the man's hand, the blood covering his once-white shirt, the wild flash of menace in his pitch-black eyes, and fear turned her blood to pure ice.

"I...I..."

The man took a swift step toward her from his spot behind a shipping crate, reducing her stammer to a stran-gled cry. "I didn't say you could talk, bitch. Now shut up and let me see your fucking *hands*!"

Quinn's arms complied, raising out of sheer survival instinct. *Oh God. Oh God, oh God.*

"Radios," the man bit out, the thick black ink of the snake tattoo on his forearm flexing over his dark brown skin as he jerked the gun between her and Slater. "Both of you. Nice and easy, or I'll blow your goddamn heads off."

She chanced a fast, shaky glance at Slater, who had angled himself slightly in front of her on the dirty concrete floor.

"Quinn."

His voice was quiet, barely a breath in the tight space between them. Yet somehow it managed to penetrate the fear keeping her rooted into place. With trembling fingers, she lifted the radio strapped to her shoulder, ducking out of the thing and tossing it to the ground.

Think, think. She had to stop panicking and *think*. "Are... are you hurt?"

A muscle in the man's jaw ticked, and he thrust the gun toward her with enough intention to make her pulse go ballistic in her veins. "What did I tell you about not talking?"

"She's just trying to help you," Slater said softly. "If

you're bleeding, we can take care of that. No questions asked."

The man dropped his chin, the mention of the blood making him even more agitated even though Quinn couldn't detect any visible injury to attribute it to.

"You're gonna take care of it, alright. See, this blood ain't mine. It's my brother's. He got shot, and you're gonna fix him up."

"Okay." Slater's voice was low and steady, right there next to her, and the sound of it allowed Quinn to exhale, just the tiniest bit. "We can do that. You don't need the gun."

The snake tattoo jerked again, harder this time. So much for being able to breathe.

"Yeah, I do. Because my brother is at a safe house, and this here is a kidnapping. You're both comin' with me, and you're either gonna save his life, or I'm gonna end yours."

Fear climbed the back of Quinn's throat, hot, involuntary tears burning behind her eyelids. But Tattoo Guy either didn't notice, or—more likely, since he was, you know, pointing a freaking *gun* at her—didn't care.

"Listen real careful, 'cause I'm only saying this once. The three of us are gonna get in that ambulance of yours and put it in the alley beside this building, all nice and out of sight. Then we're gonna take a ride in my car, and you're gonna patch Jayden up real good. You even think of bein' a hero"—he paused to nail Slater with a glare that made Quinn's hair stand on end—"and I will shoot her in the face so many times, her dental records won't even have a prayer of holding up. And if *you* run"—she felt Tattoo Guy's stare on her like a living, slithering thing—"I'll do the same thing to him. You hear me?"

Quinn nodded. Slater must have, too, because the next thing she knew, Tattoo Guy was ordering them to turn around. Stepping up behind them, he pushed the gun between Quinn's shoulder blades. The cold, unforgiving press of steel made her flinch as her heart slammed even faster, but she forced the thought of the gun and the images that went with it all the way out of her brain.

Okay. Okay. This is still a call, with a patient who needs help. You know how to do this. You can do this. You're going to be fine.

She repeated the words in her head with every step toward the ambo even though she knew deep down they were a lie. She'd been around patients who were combative. People who had tried to hit her, bite her, and threatened to kill her if she so much as laid a pinky finger on their pulse point. But this was different. This man had a gun jammed directly over her spine, just behind her heart.

Quinn knew the sort of damage the weapon would inflict. She knew it would rip through flesh. Bones. Organs. She knew it could take long, terrifying minutes to bleed out from even the deadliest of wounds. She knew, because she'd seen it happen.

And now it was going to happen to her.

Luke lay on the floor of the black Cadillac Escalade he'd been forced into at gunpoint and wondered if he was going to die today. It was a fucked-up thought, but the abstract weirdness was the only thing between him and pure panic.

And wasn't that just even *more* fucked up? But when life went on a bender of bad and nasty, Luke buckled down. He put things at arm's length. He took care of business and fixed things. He didn't feel. Just did.

He couldn't die today. He couldn't leave Momma Billie

and Hayley. Not when they depended on him so much. He couldn't die, and he sure as shit couldn't let Quinn die.

Not. Goddamn. Happening.

Luke pulled in a deep breath and took in his surroundings as best he could, which—considering current circumstances—amounted to jack with a side order of shit. After they'd successfully hidden the ambo, their kidnapper had forced both him and Quinn into the back seat of the Escalade, then instructed them both to lie on the vehicle's floor. The wedge of space was barely big enough for Luke's six foot one frame alone, so he'd sardined himself into it as best he could and let Quinn lie curled in at his side. Her heart was beating against her chest, and therefore also his, like a fleet of hummingbirds, her breath moving against his neck in shaky, frightened bursts, and the feel of it would rip his guts out if it wasn't so busy making him angry.

Yeah, he needed to lose all this emotion before it got him into trouble. Or worse.

Releasing the air from his lungs, he flattened his palm against Quinn's back. He couldn't risk actually saying anything to her with their kidnapper only a handful of feet away in the driver's seat. The guy might have nine kinds of psycho in his dark, don't-give-a-shit stare, but he wasn't entirely stupid. He was covering his tracks to get them where he needed them to be.

Which didn't really bode well for what might happen after they were done.

He shoved the thought aside, concentrating on the feel of Quinn's back against his hand. Luke knew she was terrified—Christ, at this point, he was pretty fucking scared, too. But they'd both need every last one of their wits if they were going to live through this, so he channeled his energy into slowing his breathing so she might feel it and slow hers, pressing his palm over the damp cotton of her T-shirt to hold her close.

He should've asked her out. No, screw that. He should've kissed her, deeply, relentlessly, the way he'd wanted to since the minute he'd seen her that very first time in Station Seventeen's common room.

The Escalade slowed marginally, taking a series of turns that told Luke they had to be getting close to their destination. Quinn's body—which had gone a bit more lax against his—snapped right back to bowstring status against his rib cage.

It's okay. It will all be okay. Hoping the message came through in his touch was a last-ditch effort, and a crazy one at that. But since he was fresh out of options, Luke would scrape for anything he could to get them through this.

"Don't move," their kidnapper said, pulling to a stop. He hadn't let go of the gun during the drive, keeping it out of sight in one hand while steering the vehicle with the other. Now he trained the thing back on them with just as much menace as before, so Luke lay still and waited for instructions. The reality was, if the man's brother was injured badly enough to kidnap two paramedics, then he needed them. At least for a little while.

"I'm gonna open the door, and you're both getting out, nice and slow. We'll get your fancy bags from the back, and then you'll go inside and fix my brother. You got me?"

"Yes," Luke said, and Quinn echoed with her own affirmative. The guy scrambled out of the driver's side, tugging the door behind it open a second later. He swung a wild gaze over the surroundings Luke couldn't yet see before motioning with the gun for Quinn to get out. A few awkward movements later, the two of them were standing in the driveway of a small, run-down house clearly in the heart of Remington's North Point.

"Go." Grabbing Quinn by the back of the shirt—*shit*, Luke wanted to throat-punch this guy into next week just for putting that look on her face—he shoved the gun against the back of her ribs, forcing her toward the back of the Escalade while effectively keeping the gun from plain view.

"We'll do what you're asking," Luke said, trying like hell to keep his voice venom-free. "You don't have to do that."

As if he'd sensed Luke's desire to put the focus on himself rather than Quinn, the guy pressed the gun into her back even harder. "Shut up and get the bags, hero. You're wasting time, and that makes me antsy."

Luke didn't wait. Reaching into the back of the Escalade, he grabbed his first-in bag and the portable monitor they'd liberated from the back of the ambulance. Quinn shouldered her own bag, reaching into the pocket of her navy blue uniform pants likely out of sheer habit, and no, no, she needed to stop before—

Their kidnapper snapped the gun from her shoulder blades to the back of her neck in less than a second. "What the fuck do you think you're doing?"

"Gloves!" she cried out, holding them up as proof. "If I'm going to treat your brother I need gloves!"

He bit out a nasty curse. "Don't be makin' no sudden moves like that."

"How else am I going to do my job?" Quinn snapped. Her defiant tone shocked Luke firmly into place, but not before making his gut bottom out somewhere in the area of his shins. "Judging by the amount of blood on your shirt, I don't think you want me to take my time, so yeah. I need to glove up now."

Their kidnapper's eyes went wide, but only for a split

second before his gaze turned feral. "You're gonna want to keep this bitch in check," he said to Luke. "Before I decide I don't need both of you."

Luke didn't pause. Didn't think. Just stepped into the man's line of sight and stayed there. "I can promise that you do. Now do you want to scare her so badly she can't work, or do you want to show us where your brother is so we can start helping him out?"

The cadence of his words was steady even though his hands were shaking too hard to control, but the shift in focus did the trick. The guy strong-armed them over the cracked concrete driveway, past a row of anemic shrubbery to a front door that looked better suited for a bank vault than the dilapidated rancher it was connected to.

"It's chill," he barked out a second later, when a man in a backwards baseball hat welcome wagoned them by raising the gun in his grasp. Christ, these guys had a lot of hardware. "It's me. Damien. I brought help for Jayden."

Baseball Hat gave Luke and Quinn a once-over and frowned. "Boss Man tell you to?"

For the first time since he'd jumped out from behind that shipping crate, Damien paused. "I had to do *somethin'*, man. Jay's my brother." Poking his gun back into Quinn's spine, he ordered, "Walk. Both of you. That way, down the hall. Stop when you get to the first bedroom."

The directions, it turned out, were totally unnecessary. A steady trail of blood led the way, some in tiny drips, some in bigger, oily-looking puddles, and Luke's shoulders took an involuntary trip around his spine. His heart slammed despite the deep breath he'd just sent down the hatch, but he forced himself to focus. He'd worked in life and death situations before. Run into burning buildings. Scaled rooftops. Pulled mangled bodies from car wrecks. He could do this. If it would save his life—Quinn's life—then he would buckle the fuck down and face whatever danger was in front of him in order to help this guy.

Luke stopped just outside the bedroom door. His boots squeaked and slid over the blood spattered on the floorboards, but he didn't have time to let the grisly details sink far enough into his brain to scare him. Damien called out, pushing both Quinn and Luke forward at the same time. Since Luke's only options were to open the door or be crushed up against it, he went for Plan A and twisted the knob, stumbling his way inside the room.

"Damien." A huge hulk of a man dressed in head-to-toe black pushed up from the chair beside the bed taking up most of the space in the room. His body coiled in an immediate and utterly menacing defensive stance, his shoulders snapping into place around what would be the guy's neck, if he had one. Instead, they simply went from those linebacker-esque muscles right up to the back of his shaved head, his nearly black eyes glinting in the daylight fighting to get past the window blinds. Luke's boots slapped to a halt at the sight of the guy, who—of course—had rested his hand on the gun prominently visible at his hip.

"You have guests," the man said, his voice sending frost over Luke's spine. His tone of voice suggested that a) he was as surprised to see Luke and Quinn as they were to be there, and b) said surprise was taking a backseat to his extreme irritation.

Damien, however? Didn't seem to get the memo. "Jayden needs help," he said, his agitation visibly growing at the sight of the young man lying on the bed, bleeding freely from a wound in his chest. The kid's chest rose and fell in rapid, wheezing breaths, and if he was conscious, it was only just. The dirty-copper smell of too much blood hung heavily in the air, punching Luke in both his throat and his fear center simultaneously, and shit. *Shit*, this was bad.

Damien rambled on. "You said no hospitals, so I got the next best thing. I ain't letting my brother die. Especially not by the hand of no fuckin' Scarlet Reapers."

The big guy's stare turned cold and flat as he moved it first over Luke and Quinn, then back to Damien with a frown. "Let them get to it, then. In the meantime, get someone in here to watch them work. You and I need to have a word."

Forget bad, Luke thought as Baseball Hat stepped into the room and Damien and his boss stepped out. This was going to end horribly.

Luke just didn't know for who.

6

The man in front of her was going to die. Not that a little thing like inevitability would keep Quinn from doing all that she could to save him. But if her life, and Slater's, depended on this guy waking up tomorrow, she was well and truly fucked.

Quinn thrust the thought aside before it submarined what little calm she'd been able to regain. She had a patient. A purpose. Something to focus on other than the gun being pointed at her chest.

"Okay, we need to get him on the monitor, and I'm going to need to get a look at what we're dealing with here." She shifted toward the bed, reaching into her first-in bag for a pair of shears to do away with Jayden's shirt.

Up came the gun of their guard, a skinny guy with the same snake tattoo on his forearm that Damien had, and Quinn jumped reflexively.

"They're trauma shears," she said, holding them up in a solid mix of terror and exasperation. "I need to cut his shirt off so I can see the wound." For Cripes' sake, they weren't even pointy! What could she possibly do with them—snip her way out of danger?

After a minute, the guard said, "Fine. Just don't make no sudden movements."

Right. No sudden movements in a trauma. He might as well have asked her to conjure a Bentley out of thin air.

Shaking off her ragged nerves, Quinn covered the three steps between her and her patient while Slater moved to stand across from her on the other side of the bloodstained double bed. She propped her first-in bag next to Jayden on the mattress, taking a lightning-fast visual inventory of her patient.

Breathing—barely. Bleeding—profusely. One visible chest wound. No good options.

Quinn leaned down, making fast work of turning his shirt into scraps. "Hey, Jayden. My name is Quinn, and this is Luke. We're here to help you, okay?"

Her stomach clenched at the sight of the gaping bullet wound shredding the real estate between his right shoulder and his sternum, and the feeling didn't improve at the sound of his low, raspy moan.

"It...hurts..." he coughed out. His skin was beaded with a heavy sheen of sweat, his lips chalky against his pale brown skin, and oh God, they had to control this bleeding and get him to a hospital. Like ten minutes ago.

"I know it hurts, but I need you to stay with me, okay?" Without waiting for an answer, Quinn reached into her first-in bag for some QuikClot pads. But her efforts were cut short by the cold, hard press of a gun in her ribs.

"Jesus!" Quinn blurted, fear and adrenaline spurting through her chest. Luke snapped to attention, his ice-blue eyes flashing fiercely, but she gave up the slightest head shake. She couldn't let Slater get shot. Especially not over something as stupid as a knee-jerk reaction she should have been able to control.

"I said no sudden movements," their guard said, and screw this. If Quinn had any freaking prayer of saving Jayden, or at the very least keeping him from flatlining before she could convince someone to take him to the hospital, she was going to have to be able to *move*.

But before she could get that little nugget down the chain of command from her brain to her mouth, Slater shocked the hell out of her by interrupting. "Look, man. If we're going to do this, we're going to have to reach into our bags to get supplies, and we're going to need room to move. Taking care of your buddy here will be a whole lot more effective and a whole lot less nerve wracking if you don't shove that thing around every time we do."

The guy pulled the gun from Quinn's rib cage, his stare sliding into a sneer as he shoved it toward Luke instead. "You think this is about you bein' comfortable, bitch?"

"Do you think I'm going to be able to help him if you blow a fucking hole in me by accident?" Slater shot back.

Quinn's heart thundered, each beat pulsing the word *no* against her eardrums, and finally, she scraped in a breath. "You're not going to need to shoot anyone," she said, her throat threatening mutiny at the thought. *Breathe.* "All we want to do is help Jayden, okay? That's all. But my partner is right. We're going to need room to make that happen, and we're wasting time by arguing about it."

"Fine. Whatever," the guard said after a pause and one last dark look at Slater. "But either of y'all tries anything funny, and I'mma kill you both."

"That won't be necessary." *Please baby Jesus, let it not be necessary.*

Not wanting to lose any more time or dwell on the terrifying thought of either her or Luke getting shot, Quinn grabbed a fat stack of QuikClot pads from inside her bag. Luke got the monitor leads in place as she pressed the pads over the wound. Blood squished through her gloved fingers, and damn it, that bullet had to have hit something really major. The freaking problem was, there were too many possibilities for her to know exactly what had been damaged while she and Slater were flying blind in a crappy flophouse bedroom with nothing but a pair of first-in bags and a portable monitor.

She grabbed more pads and slapped them into place, but not before registering the tightness on Slater's face as he stared at the blood flowing thickly over her hands. Oh no. No, no, no, no, no. They were a team. Partners. She couldn't do this alone.

"Hey." Quinn tilted her head, moving into his line of sight until she caught his glacier-blue stare. He'd been managing his fear of blood ridiculously well over the last couple of months, but God, this bullet wound was one hell of a trial by fire. "I need you to stay with me here, too. Okay?"

Slater blinked exactly once, then nodded firmly. "Copy that. I'm with you. Pulse is tachy at one-eighteen. BP is sixty over eighty."

Not good. Not even close. Placing one more QuikClot pad over the wound, she pressed down, the give of Jayden's chest sending a ripple of dread all the way through her.

"Okay. We've got a single gunshot wound to the upper right chest. Let's roll him and see if we've got an exit wound," she said, locking eyes with Slater. The damage was on the right side of Jayden's chest, which meant Slater would have to be the one to look for an exit wound by default of where he stood. They didn't have time to switch places, and anyway, a shuffle would probably make their guard apoplectic. "You ready?"

"Yeah. Yes." Slater's face was a shade paler than usual, but set in determination.

Good enough for Quinn. "On my count. One. Two. Three."

Jayden screamed as they rolled him, his wound pumping out a steady stream of fresh blood from both the motion and the yell. *Shit.* "Hang in there, Jayden," she said, swinging her gaze to Slater's. "Anything?"

"Negative," he said. "No exit wound."

Of course not. It'd been wishful freaking thinking to start with. "Okay. Let's get him back. Here we go, Jayden. Nice and easy."

"Unnnh." Another low moan loosened from his throat at the repositioning, his eyes glassy as he turned them on her. Christ, he couldn't be more than eighteen. "Hurts...it hurts so much..."

"I know, and I'm sorry." Quinn's heart folded in half. She firmed her hands back over the dressing even though it was nearly soaked through. "But I have to put pressure on the wound to get this bleeding under control, okay?"

"Don't you got any of the good shit in that bag?" their guard interrupted from his spot on the far side of the room, but she shook her head.

"His blood pressure is too low for pain medication. What he needs is a hospital."

"No hospitals."

Quinn bit back the urge to loosen her frustration in a yell. "Look, I can try to control the bleeding and give him fluids and monitor his vitals, but those are all short-term solutions. Without trauma doctors and a surgeon to remove that bullet, there isn't going to be any way to help him."

The guy lifted a shoulder, then let it drop as he settled back into his chair. "You're just gonna have to figure out a way around that. 'Specially if you want to live."

She wanted to argue. Hell, she wanted to scream her fool head off. But she and Slater were being held at fucking *gunpoint*, and in truth, she didn't have either the time or breath to waste.

"Okay." She looked at Slater. Willed her hands not to shake. Failed spectacularly. "Let's start a large bore IV and run saline wide open. Keep an eye on those vitals, and we'll have to pack the wound with more dressing to manage this bleeding."

"What do you want to do after that?" Slater asked, his voice low enough that their guard likely mistook it for more medical exchange.

Dread and fear settled into Quinn's bones as she looked at Jayden, whose eyes had drifted shut, his breath coming in fast, shallow pants.

Please, Daddy, she prayed, her eyes pricking with hot, unbidden tears. *Please watch over me.*

"Damage control," she whispered. "Unless they let us take him to the hospital, he'll be dead in the next ten minutes."

Isaiah "Ice" Howard walked down the hallway in his safe house, his breathing carefully metered despite the anger writhing through him like a living, twisting thing. Not that either the composure or the stone-cold nastiness it covered were out of the ordinary. He'd built his livelihood around living up to the nickname he'd earned before his sixteenth birthday. Thirteen years later, he wasn't about to blow his business or his reputation on Damien fucking Washington.

No matter how badly he wanted to bury a bullet in the son of a bitch's face right now.

"Damien." Ice brought his black limited edition Timberland boots to an abrupt stop/about-face combo on the dirty kitchen linoleum. Goddamn flophouses. Disgusting as they were, they served so many purposes, not the least of which was that one didn't tend to care how much blood got on the floors. "Walk me through what you just did. All of it."

Damien had never been the brightest bulb on the Christmas tree, but at least he was smart enough to follow orders. Well, most of the time, anyway. Ice listened to the moron's story, and for fuck's sake. As if he didn't have enough on his plate with the impending weapons shipment from Sorenson and the very public drive-by those asshole Scarlet Reapers had just pulled to try and take that very deal right out from under him.

Ice inhaled, stockpiling the patience he was going to need to address this situation without getting brain matter on the walls. This gun deal was his. He'd earned it, just as he'd earned his reputation for being the most ruthless gang leader in Remington. He wasn't just on top of his game; he *was* the fucking game, and every last one of the rules besides. Nothing was going to stand in his goddamn way.

"So let me see if I've got this clearly," he said, crossing his arms over the front of his black T-shirt. "You lured these two paramedics to an abandoned warehouse where we've done business in the past, kidnapped them at gunpoint, and brought them here, to one of my flophouses, to treat your brother."

"You said no hospitals," Damien insisted. "Not no paramedics."

"And why do you think I said no hospitals?"

Damien, the little shit, actually had the balls to get indignant. "Because they'd report a gunshot wound to the cops. Everybody knows that. But this is different."

"A paper trail is a paper trail," Ice bit out. "They all lead somewhere, and now, because you called nine-one-one to get those paramedics to go out to that warehouse, I have one leading to me."

Damien shook his head. "I called from a throwaway, and I took their radios as soon as they got there. Come on, man. I ain't stupid."

Ice raised a brow. The display was as much emotion as he'd allow himself to outwardly show, but he wielded it like a machete, nailing Damien with a stare across the dingy kitchen. "You just kidnapped two paramedics who can ID you, me, Adam, and Jayden in a photo array, Damien. You sure as shit aren't smart."

Only a handful of people had ever seen Ice face-to-face *and* known who he was. Bumping that list up by two? Definitely not putting him in his happy place right now.

"Who gives a fuck about those paramedics?" Damien snapped, and oh, the cocksucker was lucky he could lean on the excuse of being distraught over his little brother having been caught in the crossfire of this morning's drive-by, because Ice had double-tapped people for far, far less. "When they're done fixin' Jay up, we can take 'em down to the pier and solve that problem with a couple of thirty-seven cent solutions. No big deal."

Under normal circumstances, Ice would actually have no problem popping two paramedics and dumping their bodies in the drink if it would suit his purpose. Hell, he'd done much nastier in the last couple of days. But circumstances weren't normal. Not that a hole-digger like Damien would understand that.

Ice shifted his weight on the blood-smudged linoleum, making a mental note to get someone in here to clean that shit up before it became evidence. Goddamn forensics. "What do you think is going to happen when two of RFD's paramedics go missing and eventually turn up murdered?" he asked Damien, waiting for the 40-watt to go off in the idiot's lizard brain.

Ding. "Nobody saw me kidnap them."

"You did it in broad fucking daylight. Am I wrong?"

"Well, no," Damien said, but it was the hesitation that preceded the words that made Ice slither in for the kill.

"Then somebody *could* have seen you. In fact, the Remington Police Department could be combing every inch of that ambulance right this very minute. Tell me, Damien. Would they find your fingerprints on the door handle? Or maybe the side panel? Or a little DNA from that blood-soaked shirt you're wearing?"

"I...don't know." The guy actually had the wherewithal to look sheepish. "Maybe, I guess."

"And how long do you think it would take RPD's gang unit to run that shit through the DB and figure out that it belongs to you or Jayden, hmm? Or for them to link you to the Vipers, then come after all of us with a vengeance?"

Ice knew he'd be safe from most of that fallout on a personal level. He rarely showed his face during business transactions, and thanks to a soulless sonofabitch hacker-slash-security expert, he had an ironclad alias on the few occasions that he did. Unfortunate that Conrad Vaughn had been taken down a couple months ago by Remington's elite intelligence unit. But the guy was one of the few bastards who matched Ice in the ruthless department. Ice knew his identity was safe with Vaughn. He'd certainly paid the guy enough to make it that way, in both money and respect.

And weren't they both just equal currency.

Ice shook off the thought, refocusing on the issue at hand. "If we kill those two paramedics, the cops are going to be so far up our asses we won't be able to sneeze without them saying 'God bless you' and passing over a box of tissues along with our arrest warrants. We've got two weeks before this job goes down with Sorenson. Do you honestly think Sergeant Sinclair over at the Thirty-Third won't turn over every fucking rock in North Point to find out who killed two of the city's first responders in cold blood?"

"Screw that asshole cop," Damien spat, but Ice didn't hesitate before lunging into the moron's personal space.

"You really are as dumb as you look. Brady Sorenson supplies weapons to more than half the gangs on the east coast." The guy was elite, the best of the baddest. It had taken Ice the better part of two goddamn years to get on Sorenson's radar. Not to mention all sorts of favors and payoffs. But he'd busted his ass, he had the juice for the job, and he was *going* to get his due. "This weapons deal he's got on the table will go to whichever crew in Remington proves themselves worthy. That job belongs to me. I'm not letting anything fuck that up."

Damien's bloodshot eyes flew wide. "So, what? You're gonna just let those paramedics walk?"

"I'll take care of those paramedics," Ice said, low and dangerous. "But you disobey my orders again, and I can guarantee I'll take care of you, too."

"What was I supposed to do? The Scarlet Reapers shot

Jayden, man." Damien's tone tightened with agitation. "They shot my little brother."

"This deal with Sorenson goes the way it should, and they'll be the first ones to pay. Nobody fucks with the Vipers, Damien, and nobody betrays *me*. At least nobody who lives to tell about it."

7

The monitor at the foot of the bed shrieked out a sound that, in all likelihood, had just signed Luke's death warrant.

"BP is forty over sixty and falling," he said briskly, focusing on what was in front of him because he couldn't focus on the alternative without wanting to puke.

He could *not* die today.

Quinn's stare snapped to the monitor. "He's crashing." The monitor confirmed it a second later, the shriek becoming a telltale beep that signaled a flatline. "Shit! We lost his pulse. Start compressions while I grab the paddles."

Luke flattened his hands over Jayden's chest, forcing himself not to react to the give of the poor kid's ribs, blanking out the thick-liquid ooze of the blood soaking through the QuikClot pads and the sound of bones popping and cracking even though his gag reflex had a stranglehold on his throat. *Don't think. Don't think*, came the words to the rhythm of the compressions. "Come on, Jayden. Come on!"

"You better save him. You gotta save him," said Baseball

Hat from his station at the foot of the bed, although his voice sounded less forceful than full of fear.

"We're *trying*." Quinn lifted the paddles. "Clear!"

"Clear."

Luke's hands shot up just as Quinn's fell into place, determination locked over her face as the portable AED buzzed, then thumped. Jayden's body jerked beneath the paddles, his back arching off the bloodstained comforter. But before Luke could throw so much as a glance at the monitor for a vitals check, the door flew in hard enough to bang loudly against the wall.

"What the fuck is going on?" Damien's stare whipped around the room, jumping wildly from Luke to Jayden to Quinn. His dark eyes were wild with about a thousand emotions, but it was the presence of the man behind him in the doorframe wearing no emotions at all that sent a bolt of icy fear through Luke's chest.

"Your brother is going into hypovolemic shock," Quinn said, and Damien released a noise of frustration.

"In English, bitch."

Luke had to move this guy's attention away from Quinn. Right now. "Jayden has lost more than a fifth of his blood volume," he said. The only mercy here was that the kid had also lost consciousness. "His heart is working too hard to get what's left in his body to his organs. His body can't keep up with the blood loss."

"Why ain't you fixin' him up like you're supposed to?" Damien paced a few strides to one side of the room before turning abruptly to complete the circuit. "I told you to fix him! Stitch him up!"

The steady beep of the monitor broke past the haze in Luke's mind, and thank Christ. Jayden had a sinus rhythm. At least the AED had bought them a few minutes to try and control this situation. He and Quinn would not—*would not* —die today.

"We're working on your brother," Luke said, proceeding with a truckload of care. Jayden wasn't going to live. Far too many minutes had fallen off of his golden hour for him to survive. Hell, with the wound he'd sustained, even if he'd been shot front and center in the ambulance bay at Remington Mem, his odds would've been fifty-fifty at best. But Luke could live—no, he fucking *would* live, and so would Quinn. All he had to do was get Damien and that huge guy back in the other room, and he could figure out a way to disarm their guard and get to the window on the wall behind him. "Look, we just need some more time—"

"What we need is a hospital."

Quinn's words sent Luke's gut into a free fall. "Quinn," he started, but she shook her head, adamant.

"Look, Damien. Your brother's wound is significant. He's lost a lot of blood, and the bullet may have damaged his lung."

The guy took a step back on the floorboards, his stare full of hair-triggered menace. "You don't *know*?"

"No," she said, before Luke could come up with any sort of buffer or distraction to soften the news. Her voice was low and steady, steeped in the same tone Luke had heard her use a thousand times on the job. The tone that said she meant exactly what was coming out of her mouth.

"I don't know," Quinn continued quietly. "I don't have the equipment to be able to see what's going on inside his body. Paramedics are trained to stabilize and transfer, not treat long-term. Your brother needs a blood transfusion and trauma surgeon to remove the bullet from his chest, and he needs them both right now. Otherwise he *is* going to die."

Damien's gun was out of his waistband before anyone

could move. Luke's heart ricocheted around his rib cage, a sharp-edged "no" barging out of his mouth. But then the barrel of the gun was against Quinn's forehead, and even though his mind and body both screamed for him to make a move, Luke knew he couldn't take the risk.

"You telling me you killed my brother?" Damien bit out, and Quinn released a shaky breath.

"N-no. Right now, he's alive. See? Look at the monitor."

Damien jerked his chin toward the machine at the top of the bed, and Luke sent up a wild prayer of gratitude that the fucking thug couldn't interpret the vitals scrolling across the backlit screen.

"I want to help him, Damien. I want to save his life." Quinn's voice wavered, her raised, blood-soaked hands trembling in a way that made Luke want to dismantle every single gang member in the room just for scaring her. "Please. Let us take him to the hospital. We don't have to say—"

The cold click of the gun's safety turned her words into a cry and Luke's pulse into a warzone. "No. You're gonna fix him like I told you to. I meant what I said before. He dies, you die."

Luke burned to find a way to knock Damien's gun from the spot where it was trained hard over Quinn's forehead. But Baseball Hat was still at the foot of the bed, the double mattress and Jayden's body between Luke and Damien. God damn it, even reaching the guy was a long shot. Disarming him and getting Quinn out of harm's way? The odds were probably four trillion to one.

Come on, come on. There has to be a solution. Think!

"I'll do it," Luke said, loudly enough to—*yes*—grab Damien's attention. "I'll save your brother's life. But you have to stop pointing that gun at my partner. I need her to help me work on Jayden."

Damien hesitated, but didn't budge. "She said he needs a hospital."

"And you said no hospitals," Luke countered. "So we'll do it your way, okay?"

"She said Jayden's gonna die anyway." Damien shifted on his thickly-soled boots, growing more agitated by the nanosecond, and no. No, no, no. "If he does—"

"Damien." The man standing in the doorway commanded attention with just the one simple word. "Put your piece away."

A heartbeat passed in tension-drenched silence, during which Luke prayed for the first time in a decade.

But then, miraculously, Damien lowered his gun. Quinn sagged in relief, her breath escaping in a near-soundless gasp, and relief coursed through Luke with so much force that he was sure his knees would forfeit his body weight right then and there.

His relief turned to pure shock when the man crossed his arms over his retaining wall of a chest and said, "Go on and take a walk. Score some H and find a girl on Delmar Street. Get yourself right while these two work on your brother."

Damien's brows popped up while his mouth popped open, and he turned toward the bed, where his brother's breaths were growing more and more labored. "But Jayden..."

"I'll take care of Jayden. You're too keyed up." The man stepped all the way into the room, sparing only the briefest glance at Baseball Hat, who had watched the entire exchange, dumbfounded, from the foot of the bed. "You get D here solid, you hear? Now both of you, go."

"Ice," Damien started, and in an instant, every muscle in the man's gigantic body coiled beneath his black T-shirt and pants.

"I said I'll take care of it, Damien. Now *go*."

Luke's gut bottomed out at the implication. Damien must've made the logic leap right along with him, because after one last lingering look at Jayden, he left the room with Baseball Hat. Ice—whose name was a flawless fit for his cold stare and unyielding demeanor—stepped back to shut the door, closing them in to the confines of the bedroom as he rested his hand on the gun at his hip.

Luke glanced at Quinn, but her eyes were on the portable monitor, her hands working swiftly to apply the last of their QuikClot pads over the small mountain of them already taped to Jayden's bare and bleeding chest.

"Which one of you is in charge?" Ice asked, measuring them both with an indecipherable look as he stood next to Quinn beside the bed.

Luke recalibrated from his surprise first. "What?"

"It's a very simple question. I want to know which one of you outranks the other."

"I do."

They both spoke the words at the same time. Quinn's lips parted in obvious surprise, but Luke forced his expression to remain quiet, calm. If Ice was looking for someone to take the blame for the fact that Jayden was dying, let it be him. Quinn had just had a gun shoved against her forehead. Enough was enough.

"I'm the senior paramedic," Luke said. A second that felt more like a century passed, and finally, Ice shook his head.

"No, you're not. I've seen enough people bleed out to know a dead man when I see one. Apparently, your boss here has, too. She clearly knows more than you. Jayden's not going to make it through the next five minutes."

"But—"

Lifting a hand that could probably span a dinner plate, Ice silenced Luke's argument, pivoting on his boot heels to address Quinn. "Do all you can for him until he dies. After that, we're taking a ride."

"You want us to do all we can for him even though you're going to kill us afterward?" Luke asked. Probably not too smart to get mouthy with a gun-wielding gang leader, but come on. It wasn't like he had much to lose at this point.

"I will."

Quinn took an audible breath. Squared her shoulders. Looked Ice right in his cold, dead stare and said, "I will do all that I can for him. No matter what you do to me afterward."

Ice's brows lifted almost imperceptibly. "Noble to the end. Interesting."

Anything Quinn or Luke might've said in response was cut off by the abrupt beeping of the monitor, and she cursed under her breath.

"We lost his pulse. Slater, start compressions," she said, but Luke was already there. For the second time today, he put himself a step outside of his actions—no blood, no ribs folding and cracking under the pressure of his ministrations, no slamming of his own heart as he tried desperately to jump-start his patient's.

It wasn't enough.

"Charging to one-fifty. Clear!" Quinn placed the paddles over Jayden's chest, shocking him once, pausing for a vitals check, then recharging the paddles to do the whole thing again.

Nothing. *Damn* it!

"Resuming CPR." She shoved the paddles back into the AED, flattening her hands on Jayden's sternum, the muscles in her forearms flexing under her exertion. Luke watched the monitor, willing the thing to fork over a blip, just one, that would buy them more time. Tears snuck from the corners of Quinn's eyes, disguising themselves as sweat. But Luke saw them because he was right here next to her, watching her try like hell to save the life of the man in front of her even though his gang leader was going to bury a bullet in her for her trouble, and Christ, she was the bravest, most beautiful thing Luke had ever seen.

"Charging again to two hundred. *Clear*."

They went for three more rounds before Ice stepped in, his eyes on Jayden's broken, bloodied body. "That's enough."

"Wait. Please wait," Quinn said, despair breaking over her face. "If you just—"

"No."

Quinn's chin dropped toward her chest, the tendrils of blond hair that had snapped free from her ponytail sticking to her damp temples. "Please," she whispered, the barely there sound ripping a hole in Luke's chest.

"Turn that thing off and pack up your gear," Ice replied, looking at Luke. "And you. Stay on that side of the bed until we're ready to go. Unless you want to watch me shoot your girl right here in this room."

"No." Luke's answer spring-boarded out, and he took a breath to try and stamp the emotions out of his voice. "I definitely don't want that."

"Good."

Luke removed the leads from Jayden's chest while Quinn shut down the portable AED. Her freshly gloved hands shook, and the obvious sign of her fear peppered holes in Luke's gut. He couldn't close the space between them to comfort her—not only had Ice been frighteningly clear about him staying on his side of the room, but Luke had spent the last ten years holding everyone at arm's length. Shutting everyone out. Refusing to let himself form any bonds or care for anyone other than his grandmother and sister. Chances were, he had no clue *how* to offer Quinn comfort. It was a nasty side effect of self-preservation.

One he would probably die regretting.

Quinn knew all the signs of a panic attack. Difficulty breathing. Rapid heart rate. Feeling weak, faint, or even dizzy. A sense of terror, impending doom. Death. She'd talked countless patients, or sometimes their family members, through the symptoms. Coached them to take slow, deep breaths. Helped them lie down, clear their minds, and in some cases, when it was medically appropriate, brought them juice or water to keep them hydrated.

Turned out she'd been full of shit for the last five years, because nothing—not one fucking thing—was going to make the feeling in her bones so much as budge.

She'd tried as hard as she could to save Jayden. He'd died under her supervision. And now she and Slater were going to die, too.

Quinn's heart fluttered so quickly in her chest, she was sure it would catapult right past her ribs and onto the floor of the Escalade where she was currently lying for the second time today. And since she was also wedged half beside, half on top of Slater again, surely that meant he could feel her racing heartbeat and shaky breaths by default.

Oh God. She didn't want to die. She didn't want Slater to die. Not like this. Not today.

Please, Daddy, Quinn prayed. *Please watch over me.*

Squeezing her eyes shut, she slid into her thoughts, settling on a memory as sharp and clear as if it had happened yesterday rather than seven years ago.

Quinn tucked the thin hospital blanket over her father's body, taking care not to tangle the half dozen tubes and wires and ports running under the sleeves of his green and white printed gown.

"There. All set," she said, although, like the blanket, the words were more for her own comfort than her father's. The potent cocktail of meds being used to manage his end-stage Parkinson's kept him so sedated, chances were high he wouldn't know she was here, let alone that she'd tucked him in. But Quinn had taken care of her father since he'd been diagnosed on her first day of eighth grade. Now that she was in her second year of pre-med at Remington University, she wasn't about to dial back.

Even if he did sleep through most of her visits now.

Settling in the rose-colored hospital recliner beside her father's bed, she reached for the anatomy textbook in her backpack. But the sound of his voice, thick and scratchy from non-use, snared every last bit of her attention.

"H-h-how's m-my girl?"

Quinn's heart tightened at the endearment he'd always used for her, even back before her mother had died. "Hey, Daddy. You feeling okay?"

He'd been having hallucinations lately, according to the nursing staff. Her research confirmed that they were, in fact, very common for Stage Five patients. Not that it made Quinn want to care for him any less.

"T-t-t-t-tired," he said, his head sinking back into the pillow. "It w-will be t-time. S-s-soon."

Tears sprang into Quinn's eyes. She didn't want to have this conversation with him. Not now. Not ever. But he was awake and lucid, and she knew the truth. She might not get another chance.

"Are you hurting?" she asked softly, relief spilling through her when he shook his head.

"N-no."

Biting her lip, she scooped up his hand, letting her tears fall because she had no other choice. He was her father, her only family. He'd always cared for her, even when she'd needed to care for him. "Will you watch over me from heaven once you go?"

For a moment, he said nothing, just looking at her with those dark blue eyes she'd come by so honestly, and Quinn thought he'd slipped back into a medicine-induced haze. But then he smiled and slowly said, "M-my girl. It w-will be the f-first thing I do..."

The Escalade hit a pothole, jarring her back to reality. She was on the floor of an SUV with no idea what was around her or where she was headed, and in less than thirty minutes, she would be dead. Ice was going to shoot her. Quinn knew exactly what would happen, how her body would fight the blood loss, how her organs would shut down anyway. She knew it would hurt badly enough for her to pray for death. She knew someone would find her, that someone from Seventeen—probably Captain Bridges— would have to ID her body. Bury her next to her father.

Please, Daddy. Don't watch over me. I don't want you to see this.

Quinn's lungs constricted, her heart beating even faster in her chest, and oh God, oh God ohGodohGod, she couldn't breathe.

The feel of Slater's hand on her back broke through the panic. He didn't say anything—not that he really could with

Ice a few feet away in the driver's seat. But he also didn't do anything trite, like rub little circles or, even worse, pat her like a fragile flower. Instead, he just wrapped his arm around her waist, flattening his palm between her shoulder blades in the same spot where Damien had shoved his gun, and all of a sudden, there was air.

Slater splayed his fingers wider, each fingertip pressing in that firm, quiet way of his. His chest rose and fell against hers, his left side flush with her right. Somehow, Quinn inhaled again, matching the rhythm of his breaths.

They would be her last ones. Slater's too, and—

"Easy."

Like the touch, his whisper was calm, steady. Shifting just slightly, he wrapped his other arm around her rib cage, his mouth coming to rest just shy of her temple.

"There. Breathe."

For a minute—or maybe it was an hour or a month or just a tiny nanosecond—Quinn did. She placed her hand on Slater's shoulder and breathed in the smell of him, part antiseptic wipes and laundry detergent and things she could identify, part something heady and masculine that seemed to belong only to him. In that pocket of time, lying there next to Slater, she was able to breathe. To move oxygen to her lungs. To keep the panic on the outer edges, away from her body and brain.

And then the Escalade slowed to a stop.

"Get out," Ice said a few seconds later, the rear passenger door opening wide to let in the harsh glare of sunlight. He held his gun at hip level, concealed and yet pointed at her in a way that said he wouldn't hesitate or miss if she didn't do what he'd told her, and Quinn had no choice but to push herself up from the floor of the SUV.

Keeping her right by his side, Ice pressed the gun against

her belly, ordering Slater out next. Quinn blinked, a tendril of surprise uncurling in her chest as she looked around and registered her surroundings. The empty street. The boarded up convenience store. The dilapidated warehouse.

"We're back where we started?" she asked, and Ice frowned.

"Walk."

He gestured toward the back of the Escalade with his gun, and after a short trip to reclaim their equipment, he herded them to the ambulance, which was still tucked in the alley where they'd left it.

"Put everything away. Slowly."

"No one else has to die today," Slater said. He kept his hands raised and his eyes slightly lowered, continuing in a quiet voice as he returned the portable monitor to the ambo's storage compartment, then followed it with his first-in bag. "We won't tell anybody what happened here."

Ice didn't hesitate. "I know you won't. Give me your cell phones and driver's licenses. One at a time."

He turned the gun toward Quinn, stepping in close enough for her to feel the cold, calculated evil rolling off him in waves. Her hands obeyed out of sheer survival instinct, fumbling for the latch on the drawer in the storage compartment where she always stashed her wallet and her iPhone. Slater followed suit, handing over his license and cell phone, and Ice lifted his chin at the warehouse.

"Walk."

Out of the corner of her eye, Quinn caught sight of Slater's expression. Most of the time, he had a crazy-good poker face, except for those rare occasions when she'd caught him smiling. But right now, the fear in his ice-blue eyes was unmistakable, and oh God. Oh God, they really weren't going to live through this.

"Breathe."

Slater started to walk, his boots in motion over the parched gravel before she could be entirely certain he'd loosened the whisper. But her neurons auto-piloted all the requisite messages to her legs, and she fell into step next to Slater, with Ice directly behind.

"Over here," Ice said, jerking the gun to the center of the dusty and dingy space. Quinn's heart slammed with every footstep. Her pulse grew even more erratic when Ice yanked two bright red strips of cloth out of his pants pocket, holding one out to Slater and dropping it into the small space between them.

"Gag her." When Slater hesitated, he tacked on, "Unless you want me to shoot her in the leg while you think about it."

"No," Slater said, all plea. He bent to pick up the cloth, gently brushing her hair away from her face as he stepped closer. "I'm sorry."

"I know. It's okay," Quinn whispered. God, she hated the look on his face almost as much as the cloth going around her mouth. But then Ice made her use the other cloth to gag Slater in return, and yeah, it was official. She hated that most of all.

Of course, Ice kept the hits coming. "Zip ties next," he said, a set of thick, figure-eight-shaped restraints clattering to the floor at Quinn's feet. "Put those on your partner. Hands behind his back, not in front. And make them tight, or I'll make you sorry."

She knelt for the zip tie, unable to do anything else. Slipping the black plastic over Slater's wrists, she paused to brush a brief touch over his fingers before snapping the closure on the restraints snugly.

Ice motioned her over with a jerk of his chin. "Your turn.

Nice and slow, or I'll shoot your partner here in the kneecaps just to watch him bleed."

For a second, Quinn was certain she would choke on the double shot of anxiety/adrenaline building beneath the cloth in her mouth. But unlike Damien, Ice didn't carry himself with sloppy bravado; for him, the gun in his hand wasn't just something to shove around as a scare tactic or inflate his power. He meant every word.

With no choices left, she covered the half dozen steps of concrete flooring, stopping less than an arm's length from where Ice stood. He turned her easily with his palm on her shoulder. Somewhere, in the back passages of her brain, Quinn was surprised he didn't manhandle her, didn't yank her hands together or fasten the zip ties so tightly they'd cut into her skin. Then again, she supposed he didn't have to.

The gun in his hand was the only fear tactic he really needed.

"Both of you together. Kneeling," Ice said, and now, Quinn's panic did surge. Her heart thundered in her eardrums, her breath turning to wet cement in her lungs and tears spilling down her cheeks as she stumbled toward Slater, her knees not so much obeying as simply giving out.

Ice took a few steps forward, parking his imposing, muscle-bound frame right in their line of sight. "You know this feeling you have right now? This fear of dying?"

A frustrated sound welled up from her throat. Why couldn't he just get on with it, for Chrissake? Not that Quinn wanted to die, because *God*, she didn't. But kneeling here, next to Slater on this filthy warehouse floor, just contemplating it? That was worse than dying.

"I want you to remember this feeling. I know who you are, Quinn Copeland and Luke Slater." Ice held up their driver's licenses, rattled off their addresses. "I know where you live. I know who your friends are." He flipped to Quinn's screen saver, where her own smiling face was surrounded by Parker and Shae and everyone else at Seventeen.

Ice didn't stop there. "I know who your families are." A photo of a black woman who Quinn guessed was in her late sixties flashed over the screen of Slater's phone, followed by one of a much younger girl bearing a strong family resemblance, and Slater went bowstring tight at Quinn's side. "I know everything there is to know about you. If either one of you so much as tells one person *anything* that happened today, I will make every single person you care about feel what you're feeling right now, and then I'll make you watch while I blow their fucking brains all over the floor. Am I making myself clear?"

Fresh tears burned in Quinn's eyes, and she nodded even though confusion clouded her brain. Of course she'd understood Ice's words. For God's sake, they'd be scorched in her mind forever. But why would he threaten them like this if...

"Good," he said, pinning them each with a stare full of promise. "Because I don't ever bluff. You tell anyone what happened today, and dying slowly will be the least of what scares you."

Without another word, he turned on his boot heels and walked out of the warehouse.

9

L uke was totally poleaxed to realize that from start to finish, their kidnapping had lasted only sixty-four minutes. But even after he blinked a couple of times for good measure, the clock on the ambo's dashboard still read fifteen thirty-seven, and even though Luke had seen some spectacularly shitty days in his life, the last hour had definitely slid into the top spot as the worst.

He turned toward Quinn, squinting at her through the painfully bright sunlight. "Are you okay? You're sure you're okay?"

Luke had wasted no time running to the ambo as soon as Ice and his Escalade had hit the past tense five minutes ago, and Quinn had followed closely behind. The latch on the storage compartment had been tricky as shit with his hands zip tied behind his back, but desperate times, and all that crap. Luke had made a holy mess of things in the process, but he'd managed to upend Quinn's first-in bag and grab her trauma shears, flipping the things to sever her restraints before she'd returned the favor on his with unsteady hands.

She blinked at him from the spot where she stood just outside the open passenger door. Her normally fair skin had gone troublingly pale, her lips pressed in a long, thin line that clearly outlined her distress, and okay, right. That had been one hell of a dumbass question.

Nothing about this was okay.

Luke rephrased. "Quinn, are you sure you're not hurt?"

"N-no. I..." She dropped her stare to her wrists, which were a little red from where the zip tie had circled them, but otherwise, her appearance seemed to back up her claim. "I'm not hurt."

Relief kicked through his chest. For one wild second, Luke had an urge to reach out and wrap his arms around her, to go over every inch of her from her blond curls to her boot heels to make sure she was truly unharmed. But since she looked fragile enough to shatter in a stiff wind, he curled his fingers into fists until the impulse to touch her passed.

"Okay, good."

Luke climbed into the passenger seat of the ambulance. His muscles ached with the sort of fatigue that accompanied a textbook adrenaline letdown, his less than stable breathing seconding the motion as he reached for the handset to the two-way.

"Wait. What are you doing?" Quinn asked, her voice panicked enough to screech his movements to a halt.

His brows tightened in confusion. "I'm calling nine-one-one."

"Are you *crazy*?" she chirped, immediately swiveling a panicked gaze over their surroundings even though the entire block—hell, probably the entire freaking neighborhood—was as still as a cemetery. "Didn't you hear what Ice said?"

Even if Luke lived to be a hundred and nine, he'd never forget what that evil bastard had said. "Of course I did. That's why I'm calling the police." He scraped for a breath. *Put this shit at arm's length and tackle the problem. Fix things right now.*

He exhaled, blanking the emotion from his voice even though it was a task and a half. "Ice obviously runs a gang. He held us at gunpoint. Threatened us. He's dangerous as hell, and he needs to be taken off the streets."

"That's exactly my point. He *is* dangerous! And if we tell anyone, especially the police, he's going to come after us."

"He couldn't possibly get away with that," Luke said, goose bumps rippling over his skin despite the hell-hot weather. No. *No.* He refused to give the thought any air time in his brain. There was a huge problem in front of him, and he needed to take care of it. Of himself. Of Quinn. Right now.

"We can go to January's dad," he continued. Their fire house administrator's old man ran the intelligence unit over at the Thirty-Third district. Luke might not be tight with all of the cops over there like everyone else at Seventeen was, but Kellan's girlfriend Isabella had visited the fire house enough for him to know she was a good detective. "The police will protect us and our families, and anyway, we won't have to worry about it, because Ice will be in jail."

He stuck the end of the sentence with an unspoken *where he fucking belongs*, but, funny, it seemed to bounce right off of Quinn, unnoticed.

"Do you honestly think a guy like that isn't used to dodging the cops?" she asked, her blond brows flying up toward her disheveled hairline. "Or that he doesn't have other people who would come after us if he can't do it himself? Or that even if he *does* get arrested, he can't make bail? God, Slater! We can't tell anyone what happened today."

"How could we *not* tell anyone?" Luke shot back, incredulous. "Damien kidnapped us at gunpoint, and Ice threatened our lives. The guy runs a fucking *gang*. Who knows what other kinds of crimes Ice is probably responsible for?"

Quinn stepped back on the pavement. She lifted a finger, probably to jam her point home, and the way her hand still visibly shook took a potshot at Luke's gut.

"Which is exactly why we can't take the risk. What about the two women in the picture on your phone? One of them is your sister, right? What if"—she paused, her voice wobbling before turning into a whisper—"what if he makes good on his threats against her, or someone at Seventeen?"

Just like that, the potshot turned into a riot. "He wouldn't. We'd be safe," Luke said, but damn it, his voice said he was suddenly only seventy-thirty in the balls-out certainty department. After everything Momma Billie and Hayley had been through ten years ago, he couldn't even bear the thought of one of them having a paper cut, much less being tortured by a sick son of a bitch like Ice.

Still... "Quinn, this is crazy. We were assaulted, and a man is dead. We have to report what happened."

"No, we don't," she insisted. "We haven't even been gone for an hour and a half. We can radio dispatch and tell them the call was a false alarm, then say we went to grab something to eat. Or that we went to go work on your training. Or, God, almost anything. But we can't call the police, Slater. We can't tell *anyone* what happened. Please. We can't take the chance that Ice will make good on his threats."

Tears filled her dark blue eyes, and she swiped at them angrily, as if she were supremely pissed at their presence. But her vulnerability disappeared as quickly as it had arrived, replaced less than a second later by a look of sheer determination Luke knew all too well.

And the more her words—hell, the reality of what had just happened to them—sank in, the more he realized she wasn't wrong.

Ice knew where they lived. Knew where they worked. Knew who was close to them and who they cared about. He couldn't take the risk, however small, that something might happen to Momma Billie or Hayley. Not when the stakes were that high.

"I'm going to call the false alarm in to dispatch," Quinn said quietly, looking at the handset on the dashboard in front of him. "We get them on a fairly regular basis, so they won't think anything of it. If everyone else is back at Seventeen when we get there, we'll just say we went on the call, and after that, we went to get a late lunch at Pizza Joe's. We already sanitized the equipment, and Ice made us leave the biohazard bags at the safe house. We'll re-stock our first-in bags before we go back to the house with the supplies in the rig. No one will be the wiser."

Luke paused. Christ, this was completely surreal. Had he and Quinn seriously been sitting in the back of the ambo, stocking tape and gauze and syringes like nothing-doing only two freaking hours ago? And more importantly, were they really about to cover up a crime?

Luke took in the frightened seriousness on Quinn's face, then replayed Ice's words in his head, the vicious threat sending a frigid chill up his spine, and yeah. Yeah, they really were.

"Okay," he said, the single word like sawdust in his mouth as he gave up a slow nod. "From here on in, the last hour and a half never happened."

~

QUINN WALKED SLOWLY and carefully through the engine bay, returning the chorus of cheerful hellos that January, Kellan, and Dempsey lobbed in her direction from the common room. Keeping her boots on a slow, steady line, she made it all the way to the locker room in the back of the house before promptly emptying the contents of her stomach.

"Whoa!" came a familiar female voice from the other side of the stall, and a minute later, Shae appeared at the crack in the door. *Damn* it. "You okay, Copeland?"

"I'm fine," Quinn shoveled out by default. "I..." *Was kidnapped at gunpoint. Lost a patient to a brutal drive-by. Thought for sure I was going to have my brain splattered on a dirty warehouse floor.* "I must have eaten something funny."

"That doesn't sound too funny," Shae said, stepping back on the tile as Quinn forced her legs to standing and auto-piloted her way to the sink to rinse her mouth. Ugh, at least she had the pale and shaky bit down cold. "You sure you're alright? If you've got food poisoning—"

"Nope. I'm totally fine." Quinn made sure to send her smile all the way up to her eyes even though it took more energy than she could afford to spare. But she didn't have a choice. She had to act as if everything was all systems go, because if she didn't, Shae would notice in about two point two seconds. And since backing down was far enough outside of Shae's wheelhouse to be measured in light years...yeah, Quinn was going to have to sell the hell out of 'fine'.

She amped up her smile until her teeth hurt. "One ride on the vomit comet does not food poisoning make. I'm sure it'll pass. How was the brush fire?"

"Ah, Station Six beat us to the scene, so it was mostly contained when we got there. Riding with Dempsey on engine again was kind of fun, though. Even if he does think he's hot shit now that he's on squad." Her green stare sparkled with sudden mischief. "Speaking of the shuffle, how's it going with Slater?"

"Fine." Ugh, Quinn was going to need to expand her vocabulary if she had a prayer of getting through this conversation unscathed. "I mean, you know, he's good. He made a great catch with that deaf patient this morning. I think we'll work together just..." *Shit.* "Fine."

Shae laughed, leaning one hip against the sink beside her and thankfully not seeming to notice Quinn's lack of verbal grace. "The way you two dance around each other is so freaking cute, I swear."

The words snagged Quinn's attention, and okay... "What way we dance around each other?"

"Oh, come on. Don't tell me you don't see it." At Quinn's drop-jawed silence, Shae added, "The way he looks at you so intently, but *pretends* he's not looking at you at all. He's so into you. In that weird, quiet sort of way."

The image of Slater's stare, brimming with intensity as he tied that bright red cloth over her mouth, crashed into her mind's eye unbidden.

"He's a serious guy." Her heartbeat accelerated. *Get it together, girl. You're right here in the fire house, no bad guys in sight. Everything's fine.* "But he's not into me. He looks at everybody like that."

A sound emerged from Shae's throat, somewhere between a scoff and a full-on snort. "Try again, sweet cheeks. Because it takes two to eye guzzle, and you, my friend, are guilty as charged. Not that it's a bad thing. Like I said, the back and forth is actually pretty adorbs. I'm just waiting for one of you to make a move."

Quinn wanted to make some crack about how Shae's relationship with Capelli was giving her couple-vision, or maybe even throw her hands up and admit that, yep, she totally *had* been ogling Slater on the (apparently not so) down low for the last handful of months. But instead, she found herself rooted to the bathroom tile with her brain honed in on how Slater's hand had felt on her back, calm and strong when she'd been anything but, and oh God, she needed to get out of here. *Fast.*

"You know what, you might've been right about that food poisoning thing," Quinn said, and bingo. Nothing like the suggestion that you might toss your cookies to make even the best of friends take a step back. "I'm not really feeling so great."

"Do you want me to go get Bridges?" Shae asked, but Quinn shook her head. The last thing she needed now was an expanded audience.

"No. I mean, I don't think it's anything major. But I'm going to go lie down for a while just to be sure. Better safe than sorry, you know?"

"Okay," Shae said, her gaze a mixture of concern and sympathy. "Just text me if you want me to break into C-shift's pantry stash to rummage for Saltines or Gatorade."

At that, Quinn managed a weak smile. "You're just looking for an excuse to get them back for always leaving the engine with barely any gas in it."

"Maybe." Shae waggled her light brown brows as she pushed off the sink. "But seriously, if you need anything..."

"I'm sure I'll feel better once I lie down."

Waiting until her friend's footsteps had disappeared from the locker room, Quinn let out a wobbly exhale. She had to treat what had gone down today like a really bad call. Yes, it had happened, and yes, it had been fucking terrible. But if she wanted to get past these stupid shakes, she had to forget about it and move on.

She had to be fine so no one found out the truth that would put everyone she cared about in danger.

Quinn poked her head past the locker room door, relieved to see a clear path between her and the hallway leading to the bunk room. At this time in the afternoon, it was pretty rare that anyone was sneaking in a nap unless they'd worked a double, and relief spiked when she discovered that today was no different than usual. She slipped past the curtained entryway leading into her assigned bunk, which was really just a ten by ten cubicle sectioned off from the other dozen just like it by a few sections of eight-foot cinderblock half-walls. The dimly lit space housed a twin bed, a metal chair, a small nightstand, and—most importantly right now—the biggest batch of privacy she was going to get under the roof of this fire house.

Funny, in her entire five years as a paramedic here, Quinn had never once *wanted* to get away from everyone.

With her body suddenly weary, she toed out of her boots and lay down on her bed. The shadows and silence tag-teamed to press against her from every direction, but when she closed her eyes to ward them off, their teeth only grew sharper.

You're either gonna save his life, or I'm gonna end yours...

You know this feeling you have right now? This fear of dying? I want you to remember this feeling...remember it...remember...

Quinn's eyes flew open, her pulse racing, her breaths sharp and erratic. She tried to focus on her surroundings—she should feel safe in the bunk room, in this fire house full of the best friends that were her only family. But Ice was out there—listening, waiting, watching—and her stomach cramped, her skin crawling with dread she couldn't shake. Quinn scraped for an inhale, a scrap of calm thought, God, *anything* that could serve as a lifeline, however tenuous.

Nothing came but the echo of Ice's words in her head. The blood-chilling fear in Jayden's eyes as he'd told her how badly his wound hurt. The bruising thrust of Damien's gun lodged between her shoulder blades. Pressed hard against her forehead.

I will make every single person you care about feel what you're feeling right now, and then I'll make you watch while I blow their fucking brains all over the floor...

Quinn barely got her pillow over her mouth before she began to sob.

10

Three false alarms, two minor calls who declined medical care, and one utterly sleepless night later, Quinn felt like pulverized shit. Skipping the house breakfast she knew she wouldn't eat, she opted for a quick shower before shift change, hoping the scrub down would calm her frayed nerves just a little.

No joy.

She managed to fake her way through shift change well enough even though she knew she looked like she felt (thank you, fake food poisoning). Looking Slater in the eye had been pretty much a no-go, but he was in serious quiet mode anyway, signing off on the shift roster and murmuring a quiet "see you later" before ducking out the side door three seconds after the clock hit oh-seven-hundred. Although it sent her heart into a dull ache, Quinn declined both Kellan and Gamble's invitation to hit the Fork in the Road diner for some "real breakfast" and Shae's offer to stop by her apartment later for a ginger ale and Netflix powwow while Capelli finished his work day at the Thirty-Third.

If Ice was out there watching, the last thing Quinn wanted was to let him know how spot-on he'd been about the people she cared for most. Anyway, the more time she spent with her friends, the more obvious it was going to be that she was a steaming hot mess right now. She just needed a day or two to figure out how to shake this ridiculous dread and move on once and for all.

After giving the street in front of the fire house two very thorough corner to corner examinations, Quinn slid on her Ray-Bans and kicked her feet into motion. The already-warm air made her grateful for the shorts and tank top she'd been smart enough to pull from her closet when she'd packed her work bag yesterday morning at oh-dark-thirty.

She looked down at the light blue cotton and white denim, a pang jabbing at her belly. It felt like a century ago that she'd packed the bag on her shoulder. Thought about things like Remington's first heat wave of the year. Whether or not her Mazda CX-3 had enough gas. What kind of beer she'd grab before heading over to Kellan's sister Kylie's place tomorrow for their weekly Girls' Night In with all the ladies from Seventeen and the Thirty-Third.

And now all she could think of was that gun between her shoulders. Pressing harder and harder...

"Stop," Quinn whispered, biting down on her lip with as much pressure as she could tolerate to ground herself in the here and now. She counted her steps until she reached her Mazda a half a block away, parked exactly where she'd left it yesterday morning before shift. Measuring her breaths —*inhale, one, two, three, exhale, three, two, one*—Quinn made her way to her apartment, her gaze firmly divided between the road in front of her and the reflection in the rearview mirror of what was behind her.

She'd never had an issue with security in her building; in fact, between the closed-circuit feeds in both the parking garage and the main lobby, the keycard readers installed at all the external doors, and the reputation the place had for being in a nicer-than-average part of the city, she'd never even thought twice about her safety. But now, as she made her way from the brightly-lit garage to the far wall in the lobby where the mailboxes stood in perfect, rectangular rows, she couldn't help but wonder if she'd just been fooling herself.

After all, she'd treated countless people who had been mugged. Snuck up on. Beaten. Worse. How many of them had been under the illusion of safety?

Stuffing the thought down deep with all the rest of the ones that had kept her mind racing all night, Quinn took the elevator to the third floor. Repeating the words *I'm fine* over and over again like a mantra, she keyed her way inside her apartment, not wasting a single second as she flipped the dead bolt, then latched the chain on the door. She got about three steps over the hardwood before a giant, geriatric furball that was more fat than cat launched himself against her shins. The tenuous reminder of her normal life sent a tiny spiral of relief through Quinn's chest, and she bent down to scratch the old guy between the ears.

"Hey, Galileo. Did you miss me?"

His purr sounded off like an El Camino with a busted muffler, and guess that answered that.

Quinn managed a smile, her first one in...God, she didn't even know how long. "I missed you too. Come on. Let's get you and Max fed, since I'm sure you hogged all the dry food from her while I was at work."

The normalcy of her routine took a chip out of her

nerves, albeit a very small one. Putting her bag away, she fed the cats—Max was nowhere in sight, but that was kind of a given—and surveyed her fridge out of habit before abandoning the idea of breakfast altogether. She considered texting Parker to see how his hand was feeling, but he was probably—rightfully—still sleeping off his pain meds. Anyway, she'd overheard Hawkins and the guys from squad say they were heading over to his place later today to make sure he was still standing, so she knew he wouldn't want for anything. She'd text him in a bit, though, just to be sure. For now, she should really catch up on some sleep.

Quinn slipped off her sneakers and padded down the hallway to her bedroom. Pulling back the sunshine-colored duvet, she didn't even bother with changing into pajamas before she slid under the sheets.

Her heart started to pound after only ten seconds.

"Okay. Deep breaths," she murmured. She shuffled through all the relaxation techniques she knew by heart, trying to ease the chatter in her mind. The squeeze of the zip ties against her wrists. The thick, coppery smell of Jayden's blood, invading her nostrils and flowing over her hands to soak the quilt beneath him. The pressure of Damien's gun between her shoulder blades. Pushing. Threatening. Capable of blowing a hole in her chest from behind...

Quinn ripped the duvet from her body, sitting up sharply and gasping for breath. Maybe she just needed something low-key to get her brain to settle down, like one of those astronomy shows on the Science Channel, or better yet, a Lifetime movie marathon. With a hero who had lean, sexy shoulders. And strong hands. And a piercing, ice-blue gaze—

The buzzer on her intercom system sounded off, startling the ever-loving shit out of her. She tiptoed back to the open space between her kitchen and her living room, where the unit stood mounted on the wall. No, she wasn't expecting anybody, but Ice hadn't exactly struck her as the Miss Manners type. If he was going to stalk her, would he really call from the front entrance and ask her to buzz him up first?

"Hello?" Quinn said, pressing the button on the intercom system before she lost her nerve.

"Quinn, it's me. Slater," he added, and cue up a big ol' batch of *whaaaaa*? "Can I come up?"

After a couple rapid-fire blinks, she realized the fear making her pulse race had turned into relief. "Sure."

She released the button in favor of the one next to it that would unlock the front door and allow him access to the lobby. Running a hand over her curls (which had air-dried, so they were probably more like giant tendrils of frizz that aspired to be curls when they grew up), she waited out the two minutes it would take Slater to get from Point A to Point B. After a quadruple-take through the peep hole confirmed that, no, she wasn't hallucinating from a lack of sleep, and yes, the knock on the other side of her door did in fact belong to her temporary partner, Quinn slid the security chain free, following it quickly with a flip of the dead bolt and a turn of the knob.

"What are you doing here?" she asked, unable to keep her curiosity in check. He looked so normal (also, gorgeous) standing there on her threshold in a pair of low-slung tan cargo shorts and a dark gray T-shirt that outlined just enough of his pecs to make her belly do a little flip, and it occurred to her all at once that she'd very rarely seen him in anything that wasn't his RFD uniform.

Welcome back, reality. You little bastard.

"I was..." Slater sent a furtive gaze over the hallway. "Would it be okay if I came inside for a minute?"

"Sure. Yes. Of course. Sure." Annnd on top of her French-fried nerves, she was babbling. Fantastic.

"Thanks," he said once he was inside and the door was re-latched to the nines. "I'm sorry to just show up like this, but I just wanted to be sure...you know, that you're okay."

"I'm fine," she answered automatically. Before he could put the high levels of doubt on his wildly handsome face to words, she asked, "So how did you know where I live, anyway?"

Slater paused, and score one for distraction. "Oh. I kind of looked up your address on January's computer before she got to work this morning."

Several things popped into Quinn's head in reply, but since *holy shit, that was ballsy* and *thank you, sweet Jesus* were just a smidge less than graceful, she went with, "Kind of?"

"I know it's against the rules. But I was worried about you."

Her spine stiffened, but she pasted a smile over her face. "That's sweet, really. But I'm fine."

"Have you eaten breakfast?" he asked.

Not wanting to heighten his concern, but also not crazy about this idea of lying outright, Quinn went with the mostly-true, "I'm not really hungry."

"I didn't think so." He raised the brown paper bag she'd just noticed he was holding. "I stopped at the Holy Roller. In case that changes your mind."

Quinn's mouth watered so hard, Pavlov would have been proud. *Well played, rookie.* "Best doughnuts in Remington." Probably the universe, if you wanted to go all brass tacks about it.

"Yeah," he said. "I had to run an errand, and the Holy Roller was right there, so...anyway, I got raspberry jelly-filled since they're your favorite."

Surprise shot her brows upward. "How did you know that?"

Slater smiled, just a half-lift of one corner of his mouth, but as far as her oddly overactive lady bits were concerned, it *so* counted.

"I've been at Seventeen for seven months, Quinn. Just because I don't share a lot doesn't mean I'm not paying attention."

Huh. He had a point, there. He did seem like a speak-once-for-every-ten-observations kind of guy. "Oh. Well, you really didn't have to bring me doughnuts."

"Actually, I really did."

"You didn't," she said, her face prickling with heat as soon as the words were out. "Don't get me wrong. I appreciate you looking out for me. I do. But yesterday is over." Her voice canted lower, as if she'd somehow be overheard even though they were standing in her foyer, behind a very locked door. "Ice let us go, and we're going to stay quiet like he told us to. Everyone will be safe. So honestly, I'm fine."

Slater took a slow step toward her. His expression was tough to read—nothing unusual there. But his sudden proximity had her instincts fired up, not with wariness or unease, but with a sudden urge to feel his arms wrapped around her again. To lose herself in the safety of him for just a few minutes. God, just to *breathe*.

"I'm glad to hear you're fine," he said softly. "But I meant I really did have to bring breakfast because I haven't eaten yet either, and I'm hungry."

"Oh. *Oh.*" The warmth on Quinn's cheeks doubled up.

God, she was an idiot. "I'm sorry, I just thought...you know what, why don't I make some coffee?"

Slater smiled, and even though the gesture was all manners, her nipples still had a field day against the thin cotton of her bra. "Coffee would be great."

He followed her into the kitchen. She was happy to have tasks to keep her hands—and her apparently untrustworthy brain—busy, making full use of both as she grabbed two single-serve pods from the stainless steel carousel next to her Keurig and filled the reservoir with fresh water from the nearby sink.

"Your place is nice," Slater said, spinning a look around her kitchen before taking a seat at the farmhouse table along the far wall of the room, across from the stove.

"Thanks. Do you live nearby?"

She should know that, right? After working with him for seven months, it felt like something she should know. Especially since not even two minutes ago, she'd had to fight off the urge to climb him like Mount Everest.

"Not far. Look, are we really going to do this?" he asked, sending Quinn's pulse skyrocketing and her panties into the damp zone.

She dropped the pair of plates in her grasp to the table with a *thunk*. "Do what?"

Slater looked up at her, his gaze perfectly steady and the complete opposite of the ruckus currently going on behind her breastbone. "Not talk about what happened yesterday," he said.

"No. Yes. I mean"—Quinn paused, forcing herself to reset—"It's not a good idea to talk about it. If we get into the habit, we might slip at the fire house in front of the others."

"Would it really be such a bad thing if they knew?" he

asked with so much calm that she had to fight a humorless laugh from climbing the back of her throat.

"Uh, yeah. We've already talked about this, Slater. We agreed not to say anything."

"Luke."

"What?" The answer caught her totally by surprise, her head jerking back as she stared at him, trying to make sense of his answer.

He pushed up from the table. Reaching around her, he carefully pulled out the chair across from the one he'd just abandoned, waiting until she sat before walking to the Keurig and grabbing both cups of steaming hot coffee.

"I know the last-name thing is a fire house standard, but we've been through a lot together in the last twenty-four hours. So"—he placed one of the coffee mugs in front of her before reclaiming his seat across the table—"you can call me Luke. If you want."

"Luke," she said, testing the name out on her tongue. It felt oddly personal to call him by his first name. Almost intimate.

Jesus, what was *wrong* with her? "If it's okay with you, I'd just as soon put what happened yesterday behind us. And that includes talking about it."

"You don't think we made a mistake, not calling the police?"

The way his muscle flexed tight over the days' worth of stubble on his jawline told her in no uncertain terms that he did, but oh no. No freaking way. She could not—*would not*—put everyone she cared about in danger.

"Do you not remember the threats Ice made? Or the fact that he has our driver's licenses? Our cell phones? And that he can see which contacts we call most often, not to mention all of our texts. He knows *everything*."

The realization of exactly how much detailed personal data the maniac had access to seemed to sober Luke up, lickety split. "I remember. But—"

"No." Quinn's voice shook, but God, at this point, she didn't even care. "I mean it. Yesterday is over. Done. We can't change that. We did all we could to try and save Jayden, and that's all that matters. I just want to forget the whole thing and move on."

"Okay," Luke said after a heartbeat's worth of a pause. "We don't have to talk about it if you don't want to."

Ooookay. Not what she'd been expecting, but... "Thank you."

"You're welcome." Reaching into the bag, he unearthed two softball-sized doughnuts, placing the slightly bigger one on the plate in front of her before brushing the sugar off his fingers and folding them just briefly over the edge of the table in what looked like prayer.

"So who's this guy?" Luke asked, the small action over and done before she could be one hundred percent certain she'd seen it, much less ask about it.

"Huh?" Quinn followed his downward gaze, her confusion morphing quickly to a small smile as Galileo slothed his way between Luke's shins with a hefty purr.

"Oh, sorry. That's Galileo. He's kind of an attention whore. And by 'kind of', I really mean 'completely'."

Luke's half-smile reappeared. "That's okay," he said, reaching down to scratch between the cat's ears with one hand while reaching for his coffee with the other. "I don't mind."

"Really?" Quinn's curiosity sparked, but he just gave up an easygoing shrug.

"Yeah, really."

She fiddled with her doughnut, breaking off a small

piece as she took her fishing expedition a little farther from shore. "You just don't seem like the cat type."

"What about you?" Luke asked, pausing to take a draw from his coffee cup. "How long have you had Galileo?"

"Oh, he and I go way back to when he was eight months old and I was a whopping fourteen." She couldn't help but smile at the memory, faded as it was around the edges.

Luke's black brows lifted up toward his nearly shaved hairline. "That's quite the partnership."

"Thirteen years," she agreed. "My father got him for me from the animal shelter just after he was diagnosed with Parkinson's. My dad, I mean. Not the cat."

"Oh." Luke's spine snapped against the ladder back of his chair. "I'm sorry."

But Quinn shook her head. Back before he got too sick, her father had made her promise to always remember him happily, the way he'd lived. With the exception of the months directly after he'd died, she'd honored that request. Still did. It wasn't easy, but it was what he'd wanted.

"Don't worry," she said. "He passed away seven years ago, but I'm okay talking about him. And thank you. I'm sorry too."

Luke paused for a second, seeming to consider his words. "So you and your father were close?"

"That is one hell of an understatement." She broke off another small piece of doughnut, the sugar and jam combo melting like perfection on her tongue as she popped it into her mouth. "My father was all the family I had. He and my mom were both only children who had lost their parents before I was born, and she died when I was six. She had an aneurism while she was sleeping. The doctors said she never felt a thing."

A shadow crossed Luke's eyes, darkening them to a stormy blue-gray. "I'm sorry to hear that, too."

Quinn nodded her thanks. "I don't remember her much, although I remember that I loved her, obviously. It was always really just me and my dad. When he found out he was sick, that's when we got Galileo. That cat was the runt of the litter, if you can believe that. So skinny and small, nobody wanted him."

"No way," Luke said, and she laughed. She wouldn't have believed her if she were him, either. The cat was practically spherical.

"Scout's honor. But my dad was a great caregiver. He fattened Galileo right up."

Luke ate for a minute, giving her a chance to do the same. The silence wasn't strained or overwhelming the way it had been before he'd hit the buzzer and interrupted her mini-panic attack, and she managed to get about half of her doughnut—and most of her coffee—down the hatch before he spoke again.

"So that's where you get it from. Being a great caregiver, I mean."

Huh. She'd never thought of it that way, but... "Yeah. I suppose so. And for the record, you're not a bad caregiver yourself."

"Come on, Quinn," he said, letting go of a soft laugh. "You make sure everyone in the house eats breakfast before every single shift, including at least one fruit or vegetable."

"Breakfast is the most important meal of the day," she semi-argued, although her smile probably watered down the effect.

Luke continued. "Right. How about when you rounded us all up to go to that flu shot clinic last winter? Including Captain Bridges."

"Hey, germs know no rank. And anyway, that was an act of self-preservation. When Faurier got the flu the year before that, he whined like a preschooler, and guess who had to start an IV of fluids just to keep him from driving us all crazy?" Quinn pointed to the front of her tank top with both index fingers. God, she loved squad's second-in-command, but honestly. Sam Faurier was probably the worst patient she'd ever had. Toddlers included.

"Call it what you want," Luke said, finishing off his doughnut with a wry quirk of his lips. "But you're always looking out for everyone. Especially at Seventeen."

"Okay. I guess I do focus on taking care of other people a lot," she admitted, because really, he wasn't wrong. "When I graduated from high school, I wanted to be a doctor."

"Seriously?"

Luke looked as shocked as she felt that she'd unearthed that little nugget. Not that it was a secret, necessarily. The fact just felt like ancient history, mostly forgotten and fully covered in dust.

But it was also out of the bag, so Quinn said, "Yep. I did two years of pre-med at Remington University. I'm here to tell you, organic chemistry is *not* for the faint of heart."

"What made you change your mind?" Luke asked.

"My dad's health started to decline after my first semester freshman year." Her heart twisted. Just because she wanted to honor his request not to be sad didn't make it an easy task. "He'd gone through ups and downs before, but this was a lot worse. He was in and out of the hospital—mostly in—and to be honest, I was lonely."

Luke looked at her from across the table. "What about your friends?"

"They sympathized. Or at least, they tried to," Quinn said. "But none of them really understood what I was going through. I mean, they were out playing beer pong and hooking up at last call, I was learning about end-stage Parkinson's and picking out caskets. Those two worlds don't really touch, you know?"

"So, wait." A flash of understanding dawned in Luke's stare. "You nursed your father through his illness by yourself? While you went to college at the same time?"

"Not entirely by myself, no. After that first semester, I wasn't equipped to do everything on my own. He spent the last three months of his life in a long-term care facility. But I was there with him every day until he died."

Quinn dropped her gaze to the coffee cup in her hands even though it was empty. Studying and grieving hadn't been easy; hell, it had been the hardest thing she'd ever done. But she'd promised her father she wouldn't stop. That she wouldn't give up her dreams, even though they'd changed.

"I wanted to work with people who understood how short life can be, but pre-med was so cutthroat. There was no camaraderie at all, only competition. So that's when I decided to switch over to emergency medicine and advanced paramedic training. After my very first ride-along, I knew that being a paramedic wouldn't just give me the chance to help people. It gave me a place to belong."

"And that's why you're so protective of everyone at Seventeen," he murmured, and even though his nod weirdly said he understood the connection, Quinn's pulse still knocked faster against her throat.

"I might not have anyone left who I'm related to, but Parker and Shae and Hawk and all those guys on engine and squad? *They're* my family. I'd do anything to take care of them."

"What about you?"

"What?" Her forehead creased in confusion.

But Luke's expression was all matter-of-fact. "I get that you want to look out for everyone at Seventeen, and I get why. What I want to know is, who looks out for you, Quinn?"

She opened her mouth to answer. Stopped. Started again. "I'm a big girl. I don't need anyone to look out for me."

"Are you sure about that?" he asked. Quinn's traitorous mind flashed back to the feel of his arms around her, holding her close. Telling her without words that she'd be okay. That she could breathe.

Just like she had to breathe now.

"Absolutely," she said. He looked at her for a handful of seconds in that calm, unreadable way of his, but she stood her ground, looking back until he slid his chair from the table with a polite smile.

"Well, I'll let you get on with your day. Those false alarms had us up a lot last night. I'm sure you want to catch up on your sleep. Thanks for the coffee, though."

Quinn let go of the breath she just realized had been spackled to her lungs, standing up to walk him to the foyer. "Sure. Thanks for the doughnut." She paused, her bare feet coming to a stop a few steps from the front door. "And thanks for stopping in to make sure I'm okay. It made me feel..." *Less alone. Secure. Safe.* "Well, it was just really nice of you. So thanks."

"You said that." His smile eased into teasing territory, his brows kicking up along with the corners of his mouth to form an expression that sent unrelenting heat right to her core.

Good Lord, she was losing it. "Right. Clearly I need some sleep."

But she didn't move, so neither did Luke, and, oh, screw it. She pressed forward, slipping her arms around his shoulders. It started out like just a regular hug, the kind she would exchange with Kellan or Shae or anyone else at Seventeen (except for Gamble, because yeah, the big, prickly lieutenant was so *not* a hugger). Only, after a handful of seconds, neither one of them made a move to break contact and step away, and Quinn couldn't help herself from tightening her arms and shifting even closer.

Although now she and Luke were standing and unencumbered by the restraints of the floor of an SUV, their bodies fit together in all the places she remembered—her head beneath his chin, her shoulders on the warm plane of his chest, his arms around her rib cage. His heartbeat was steady and strong, although maybe a little fast against her cheek, and she breathed in the clean, subtly spicy smell of him as her body melted against his.

With his arms around her, she could breathe. And oh God, as crazy and counter-intuitive as it seemed, she wanted far more than for him to hold her. She wanted his hands in other places. Dirty places. Touching her and stroking her and thrusting between her thighs until she screamed.

Quinn's breath caught on a sigh. She had enough knowledge of physiology to know it had to be a residual burst of adrenaline making her feel so strongly. This odd lust was fueled by a literal chemical reaction, and nothing more. But she'd been attracted to Luke before yesterday—for months, really. And right now, sitting here in the cocoon of her apartment with his solid, muscular arms wrapped around her, she felt safe. Good. Right.

Right *now*.

Pulling back just slightly, Quinn tipped her chin and flickered her stare to meet his. His mouth was an inch away from hers, two at most. She dropped her gaze to take in his firm lips, the light peppering of black stubble on his smooth, light brown skin.

"Quinn." The word was a whisper, part permission, part affirmation.

She answered it by pressing her lips over his.

11

L uke should have been rational. Reasonable. Calm.

But Quinn's mouth was on his, hot and needy, and fuck rational, reasonable, and calm.

He wanted to give her everything she was asking for.

Lifting his hands, he tunneled his fingers through her hair to hold her close. She made a little sound, just a quick burst of surprise in the back of her throat before her breath coalesced into a moan that had his dick responding with a whole lot of *hell yes*. Luke parted her lips with his tongue, fighting back a moan of his own when she answered by deepening the kiss. Quinn darted her tongue over his, tasting, taking, then retreating so she could start the maddening cycle all over again.

Her mouth was heaven. Or maybe it was pure sin. Either way, he wanted to spend all goddamned day finding out.

Quinn kissed him boldly, clutching his shoulders and running her teeth over his bottom lip. The move sent a shard of surprise, then realization, through his lust-fogged brain. As hot as kissing her was, it was probably the adrenaline from their situation yesterday making her—hell, making *both* of them reckless. He didn't want to stop, but he hadn't been raised to be a top-drawer asshole, either. He knew he'd never forgive himself if *she* didn't forgive herself for this later.

"Quinn." Luke broke from her mouth. "Are you sure—"

She answered by sliding both hands under his shirt and pressing forward to reclaim the sliver of space he'd put between them, and shit, he officially couldn't think. "I've wanted to do this since I first laid eyes on you seven months ago," she murmured against his lips. "Trust me. I'm *very* sure."

Later, he'd take the time to unpack that statement. Right now?

He was going to keep kissing her. A *lot*.

Lowering his grip to her hips, Luke swung her around and walked her backward to the nearest flat surface, which just so happened to be her living room wall. Quinn's shoulder blades bumped against the butter-colored expanse. She used the leverage to arch into his touch, her breasts swelling up to the round neckline of her tank top.

His cock jerked against the zipper of his shorts. Christ, she was so sexy like this, caught somewhere between soft and beautiful and fierce. Want blazed through Luke's blood, both hot and unrepentant, urging his palms to travel up to cup her over the soft cotton.

"Oh God." Quinn sighed her approval, pressing up to allow him better access. He took it—he might be turned on like fucking floodlights, but he damn sure wasn't stupid—and his fingers tightened around her breasts.

"I've wanted this for a long time, too," he said, his low, gravelly tone backing the words up all the way. He dragged his thumbs over the thin material beneath them. Her nipples stood out in hard relief against the fabric, the tight peaks pointed up and begging for more of his touch.

But before he could fully take in how pretty, how fucking *perfect* she looked beneath his hands, Quinn slid the straps of both her tank top and her bra from her shoulders. Pinning him with a devastatingly sexy stare, she said, "Then take it."

Luke's heart slammed, his dick pulsing with every beat. Light blue cotton and sheer, white satin pooled over his fingers, which were still cupped beneath the curve of Quinn's breasts. His fantasies about her nipples had been spot-on, the dark pink edges bared just enough to make him want to discover if she tasted as sweet as she looked.

Reaching out, she lifted his shirt over his head, then wasted no time letting her hands fall to his waistband.

"Hey, wait." He wanted her too—badly enough for the pleasure to kiss the boundaries of pain—but... "Slow down."

Quinn gave a frustrated moue. "I don't want to slow down." Her fingers closed over the button on his shorts, sliding the thing free. "I want *you*. Right here, right now."

Shock chipped past the want in Luke's chest, his instincts beginning to ping. "Standing up in the middle of your apartment?"

He was all for hot, spontaneous sex, he really was, and no strings? Even better. But suddenly her impulsiveness bordered on insistence, and her provocative little smile devolved into a defiant frown.

"Is there anything wrong with that?" she asked, and his answer slipped out, all truth.

"No. Nothing's wrong with that. I just want to take my time with you."

She exhaled over a joyless laugh, her blue eyes blazing

as she looked up at him. "What's the point in taking our time? You never know. We could die tomorrow."

Luke stepped back on the floorboards. Damn it. *Damn* it. "Is that what this is about? You want me to fuck you against your living room wall so you can just live in the moment?"

"No. I don't know. Maybe." Quinn pressed her kiss-swollen lips into a hard line. Even pissed off, she was still gorgeous. "Come on. You can't really tell me there's no appeal to some down and dirty sex."

Ah, she's kind of got you there. Luke really *couldn't* argue. He might not be the king of one-night stands, but sex without emotional attachments was pretty much his MO.

Funny, it seemed to apply to Quinn less and less the longer he stood here. "Listen, I really think we should talk about what happened yesterday."

"I already told you, I don't want to talk about yesterday," she huffed. "In fact, I don't want to waste time talking at all."

Luke opened his mouth to argue with her—how could they *not* talk about this? But her stare brimmed with emotion, her shoulders tugged so tightly around her neck that she practically wore them like a shield. Quinn had righted her tank top and knotted her arms over her chest, probably as a defense mechanism—one he knew well, thank you very much—and for all her bravado and claims otherwise, she clearly wasn't fine.

Yet her expression told him in no uncertain terms that pushing would get him exactly nowhere, just as it had yesterday when he'd tried to persuade her to call the police. Fighting her would only make her push harder to stand her ground. And Quinn was obviously rattled enough to believe that Ice would make good on his threats no matter what Luke said to try and convince her they'd be safe. That the right thing to do, the *rational* thing, would be to go to the cops.

Which meant his only option right now was to put her at arm's length. Fast.

"We've been through a lot in the last twenty-four hours. It's probably best if I just go," he said, the words sharp and bitter in his mouth.

His unease multiplied at the chill on her face. "If that's what you want."

It wasn't, of course. Christ, his cock was righteously indignant with him for having any conversation right now that didn't involve the phrase "please let me take your panties off with my teeth". What he *wanted* was to strip her bare and sink into the warm, wet heat of her pussy over and over until she screamed. To hold her afterward, to make good on the promise that they'd be okay if they went to the Thirty-Third and told Sergeant Sinclair everything that had happened to them yesterday. To erase the fear lurking in her dark blue eyes, once and for all.

But nothing about what he wanted was smart, or safe in any fucking way, so Luke did what he always did.

He walled off his emotions and fixed the problem in front of him.

"It is. I'll see you at next shift."

With that, he scooped his shirt from the floor, then turned and walked out of Quinn's apartment.

ONE LONG-ASS DAY and stupidly fitful night later, Luke was still disgruntled as hell. He'd weighed all the options. Thought through all the particulars no less than four thousand times. Measured the pros. The cons. The risks and the moral obligations of telling the cops what had happened versus staying quiet.

How could the right thing be the *same* thing that would make Quinn hate his fucking guts for the rest of all time?

Wow. His sister Hayley appeared in the doorway to the kitchen in the house she shared with Momma Billie, a sassy smile tugging at her mouth as she signed. *That is an even more serious face than usual. Which is totally saying something for you, big brother.*

"Thanks," Luke said wryly, turning to be sure he was all the way in Hayley's field of vision when he spoke. She preferred to lip read whenever possible since the majority of people didn't know how to sign, and even though he obviously didn't fall into that camp, he still wanted to respect what worked best for her. "I'm just tired from that extra half-shift I picked up on the fly last night. Are you ready for school?"

I have five weeks left to go in my senior year, Hayley signed, although her expression alone would've been plenty to get her disdain across. *School is pretty much optional at this point. Most of my friends aren't even going to their classes anymore.*

Luke reached for the pot of coffee that Momma Billie always had on the burner, thanking the Almighty that she made the stuff strong enough to take the paint off his car. "Yeah, but your friends also don't have a full scholarship to Remington University this fall. Something tells me you came out on top, there. And for the record, senior year or not, school's not optional. You're going."

He stuck the words with enough of a brotherly smile that Hayley caved even as she rolled her eyes. *Yeah, yeah. Education is important. I get it. And yes, I'm ready for school.*

"Good. I can drop you off on my way home. Just let me know when you want to roll out."

Hayley grinned, running a hand over her bright red T-shirt that read "Life Happens. Tacos Help" and grabbing a package of Pop-Tarts from the box on the counter. *Door to door service*, she signed after putting her breakfast in her backpack. *I could get used to that. Let me grab my shoes and we can get moving.*

Unable to shake his protective instincts, Luke kept his eyes on her until she'd disappeared down the hallway leading to the front of the house. Momma Billie took Hayley's place in the entryway to the kitchen, her gracefully graying head tilted in a way that said she saw the weariness he'd been trying like hell to hide.

"You look tired," she said, not unkindly.

Duck and cover. Do it right now. "You, on the other hand, look beautiful." He gestured to her blue and white flowered dress and her stylish but sensible shoes. "You'll be the prettiest lady working at the power company today."

"Hmm." Momma Billie clucked her tongue, but she couldn't hide the smile poking at the edges of her mouth. "If you know what's right for you, you'll save that sweet talk for a young lady instead of wasting it on an old woman."

Yeah, there were so many land mines in that sentence, Luke didn't even know where to swerve. "It's not sweet talk if it's true. Anyway, I just look tired because I picked up an extra half-shift last night. But I wanted to stop by and check on you two before I go home for some sleep."

He'd moved out of the house last year in order to spare his sister and grandmother the odd hours of his fire house schedule. He'd done it reluctantly, but Momma Billie had all but shooed him out the door, going on about how he deserved to have a personal life. Luke didn't have the heart to tell her that since one had to actually *get* personal with someone else in order to have a personal life, he wouldn't be doing that anytime soon. Or, you know. Ever.

"Hmm," she hummed again, which meant nothing good for Luke. "You've been checking on us a lot over the last couple of days. Everything okay in that head of yours?"

"Of course."

He bit back a wince. His default wasn't usually a bald-faced whopper. But since it was better than confessing he'd been kidnapped at gunpoint and was now wrestling with the mother of all moral dilemmas as a result, bending the truth would have to serve.

"I worry about you," Momma Billie said in that matter-of-fact way of hers. "So serious, like an old soul. You've always had so much on your shoulders."

The unspoken *ever since your mother died and your father did the unthinkable* hung heavy in the air between them, and shit, maybe the kidnapping conversation would be less messy.

"You don't need to worry," he said, but it only made her expression grow more stern.

"Luke Matthew, you might as well tell the sun not to rise. Grown man or not, you walk around with a look like that on your face and I'm going to fuss at you."

Luke's stomach knotted. Her wielding his middle name meant they were at the Slater family's version of DEFCON three. If he didn't reassure her, her concern would only esca-late. "I promise, everything's okay." Well, it would be. Once he figured it the fuck out. "I've been assigned to work on the ambulance for a while, and my partner, Quinn, and I had kind of a tough shift the day before yesterday. That's all."

Is Quinn a girl? Hayley signed, having popped back into the kitchen just in time to lip-read what he'd said, and great, this conversation had just turned into quicksand. *She is, isn't she! I bet she's pretty.*

God, he had to stick with the truths he could tell and kill this conversation. Fast. "Quinn is a woman, yes. She's also my boss."

Your pretty *boss. You're blushing!*

"Hayley Marie, put your manners on," Momma Billie murmured, and Hayley ducked her head, although her grin didn't subside.

Yes, ma'am.

Momma Billie turned to look at him, her dark gaze soft. "I'm sorry you had a difficult shift. Go home and get some sleep, then come on back here for supper tonight. I'll make a pot roast and we'll fill you up right. No arguing," she added.

Ah, busted. "Just as long as you let me handle the cleanup," he countered. The meal alone would take her a solid hour of work.

"You've got yourself a deal. And Luke?" Momma Billie lifted her brows, the quiet seriousness of her tone hitting him from across the sunlit kitchen. "You make sure you and Quinn take care of each other out there, you hear?"

Luke's heart pounded with sudden clarity, and in that moment, he knew exactly what he had to do. No matter how mad Quinn got.

"Yes, ma'am. I sure will."

ICE SAT in the driver's seat of the utterly nondescript Toyota Corolla he'd stolen from the satellite commuter lot outside of the Park and Ride. From behind a copy of the *Remington Ledger*, he surveyed Washington Boulevard, his stare traveling first over the coffee shop that had opened less than an hour ago, then the small grouping of mostly dark and quiet brownstones beside it before finally landing on the neatly bricked fire house he was there to keep an eye on.

He wasn't worried he'd get caught casing the place. Shit, he'd had eyes on both of those paramedics from the Jayden/Damien mess ever since he'd let them walk three days ago. Granted, this was the first time Ice had done the honors himself, but he'd learned how to slip surveillance cameras and take care of business quietly before he'd even been old enough to drive the cars he'd boosted to pull the jobs he'd done with the stolen vehicles. Anyway, he was only borrowing the Toyota temporarily to take care of a different sort of business. The POS would be back in the commuter lot before its hardworking fool of an owner had so much as a clue that it had been lifted.

Better smart than caught. Ice didn't have to get all showy to prove he was the best at what he did.

He just had to be meticulous. Calculated. And completely fucking cold-blooded whenever anyone crossed him.

His pulse perked at the sight of the blonde paramedic parking her little blue Mazda on the street a half a block away. She swiveled a cautious gaze over the street that glided right over him without so much as a hitch, and ah, human nature was a beautiful and highly predictable thing. This bitch was looking for bad guys she could label. Street thugs. Menacing men who made their presence known, not average cars with average men dressed as utility workers, thumbing through the morning paper.

Ice's lips curled into a smile behind the sports section. If he'd been a banker's son, he'd have been a hell of a banker, or if his old man had been a mechanic, he'd have fixed cars with the best of them. But neither of those had been his legacy. Instead, he'd been born to one of the meanest gang lieutenants Remington had ever seen, and Ice would be goddamned if he didn't command every bit of the juice his father would've expected from him.

He was a gang leader. The head of the Vipers. It wasn't what he did. It was who he *was*.

Ice watched the blonde walk into the fire house, his thoughts moving with her. She'd been fairly easy to track over the last couple of days. No strange outings or meet-ups, no emails or phone calls that had kicked up his hackles. She'd replaced her cell phone yesterday, and while Ice wasn't crazy about not being able to tap it—fucking Vaughn just *had* to go and get bagged by the intelligence unit with no decent hackers in his wake—but if she hadn't squawked to the cops yet, chances were, she wasn't going to.

The dude had been more of a wild card. Less fear in his eyes, that one. But he'd been protective enough of the blonde, albeit nonverbally, that Ice knew he had him by the nut hairs with the threats. The fact that the guy had checked in with that family of his in person for the last two days had just hammered it home. Human nature.

Those two paramedics would keep their mouths sewn up like Ice had told them to. The woman was weak, scared out of her mind, and the man? He'd wanted to be a hero, but in the end, he wasn't lacking a brain. He'd known Ice had meant every breath of what he'd said.

Just because killing an old lady, a teenaged kid, and a bunch of first responders would be a pain in the ass Ice didn't want or need right now didn't mean he wouldn't do it if he absolutely had to. Especially if it would keep intel on the Vipers out of the hands of the RPD's gang unit while this deal with Sorenson was on the line.

Ice's cell phone chimed softly, signaling an incoming

text. Lowering his newspaper but not his guard, he checked the street in front of him before casually sliding the thing into his palm.

Mikey and Donnie B. r solid. Scouting locations. More L8R.

He tapped off a quick "got it" in reply, but that was all. Vaughn might have taught him some nice tricks to keep his business dealings secure, but Ice knew the number one rule of evidence. No trail, no conviction, and that included an electronic trail. He wasn't sloppy like Damien. Not even when shit went sideways, although Ice had to admit, the guy was now extremely motivated to take this gun deal from the Scarlet Reapers and get his revenge. But risk went with the territory—after all, they weren't in the sort of profession where people grew old and retired at fifty-five with a nice pension and a gold watch as a parting gift. Jayden had known that. Paid the price like a lot of people who had come before him. Shit, like Ice's old man himself. It sucked, but it happened. You had to do business and move on.

As for Damien being pissed that Ice had let those two paramedics live? He could suck it the fuck up. Ice, and the Vipers along with him, needed to stay on the DL. Skirting the shadows and staying smart had been the key to his success for years. He wasn't about to upend what worked. Not when this deal—*his* deal—was right there for the taking.

Speaking of which... Ice tapped a phone number over the keypad on his cell phone from memory, waiting out the requisite two rings before the line clicked over on the third.

"Sorenson."

"Mr. Sorenson." The guy commanded enough respect to be addressed formally. Plus, business was business, and Ice wasn't sloppy. "I have an update for you."

A white-noise hum filled the pause for a beat, then two. "Mr. Howard. I take it this line is secure?"

A lesser man might have taken offense at the question and all the implications that went with it. But Ice wasn't about to fault Sorenson for taking strong security measures to protect his assets. Especially not when he wanted the other man's trust—and when he knew that Sorenson had already checked the damned line anyway.

"Of course," Ice said, sliding a pair of dark sunglasses from the Toyota's glove box now that the sun was breaking through the buildings on either side of the street. More cover was always best when you had to hide in plain sight. "I'm as interested in privacy as you are."

"My sources would tend to agree. Your reputation precedes you. As does your family name."

Ice smiled. Brady Sorenson looked, acted and sounded more like the CEO of a Fortune 500 company than a man who ran enough illegal hardware to fuel the uprising of a small nation. That he'd proved untouchable by both the Feds and the ATF as he acquired and distributed the weapons to every Tom, Dick, and Criminal on the Eastern seaboard? Even better.

"I take pride in both," Ice replied. "I believe in the value of a solid business plan."

"It shows, Mr. Howard." Sorenson's barely there pause was the only heads up Ice got for the blow that came next. "Heard you had a bit of trouble with Little Ray recently."

At both the mention of the Scarlet Reapers' gang leader and the perceived weakness that accompanied it, Ice's jaw clenched. "Little Ray thinks he can distract me, but he's wrong. He'll be dealt with in time."

Sorenson chuckled. "You have your priorities in the right

place, Mr. Howard. I like that. You have updates for me, you said?"

"I've got several parties interested in doing business with you." Anticipating Sorenson's next question, Ice added, "Enough of them to make working with me very worth your while. I have contacts Little Ray couldn't even dream up, much less secure."

"And a meeting place?" Sorenson asked.

Ice's pulse moved faster, his fingers twitching with the rush of the deal in front of him, but he couldn't get ahead of himself yet. He had to stay cool. Focused.

"I'm actively researching options as we speak." Finding the perfect spot to exchange a massive shipment of arms and ammo for a metric ton of unmarked cash took time. A fact that, thankfully, Sorenson seemed to understand.

"I look forward to hearing your findings. Until then, might I suggest that you continue to stay out of the spotlight. Your competitor hasn't impressed me with his carelessness. The job is yours to lose, Mr. Howard."

Ice stared at the fire house up the street, his mouth curling under the weight of his menacing smile. "Then the job is mine, period, Mr. Sorenson. I don't lose."

"Jesus Christ, Hawkins. You really need to get a food truck and sell this magic. These home fries are off the chain."

"Faurier, you ass. Stop hogging all the pancakes!"

"I'd listen to McCullough if I were you, dude. She's got sharp elbows, and she's not afraid to use them."

"Go big or go home, Walker!"

"Come on, y'all. No need to tussle. There's still plenty of grub to go 'round."

Quinn sat on the outskirts of Station Seventeen's common room, grateful as hell for the boisterous chatter going on around her. Not only did the conversations and the friendly jawing between her station-mates soothe her jagged nerves, but they served as proof positive that keeping her mouth shut had been worth the price of her shredded conscience.

Her family was safe. Even if she was still a hot freaking mess.

"Oh hey, Quinn. Glad to see you're feeling better."

The friendly, feminine voice at her side belonged to Station Seventeen's office administrator, January Sinclair, and Quinn gathered up a nothing-doing smile for her good friend in reply. She really had to get over this and move on.

"Yep! Good as new."

January smoothed the back of her light gray dress pants with one hand, tucking the stack of files she carried over her lap as she turned to sit next to Quinn on the end of the bench at the communal meal table. "We missed you at Girls' Night In. Although honestly, if you were still feeling queasy, skipping it was probably smart. Kennedy made a batch of mojitos that knocked everyone sideways. Addison and Kylie may or may not have done a karaoke version of "The Tide is High" by Blondie, and Kellan and Capelli *definitely* had to taxi everyone's drunk asses home."

Quinn's pulse tapped faster. "I was sad to miss it." *Truth.* "But that stomach bug was pretty nasty."

Liar, liar, pants on fire.

Although she had craved the normalcy and comfort of hanging out with her girlfriends, she'd known far better than to put herself on display in front of a firefighter, a police sergeant's daughter, two detectives, a professional bodyguard's girlfriend, and a shrewd-as-hell bar owner so soon after what had happened in North Point. She normally shared everything with them—she'd never had any reason not to. There was no way they wouldn't have seen right through her ugly-belly excuse, and since she couldn't fess up, she'd spent a fitful night at home, trying like hell to blank her memory of everything that had happened during her last shift.

The ultra-embarrassing kiss-and-dis with Luke that had followed the next day? Just the icing on the great big cake of things Quinn wanted to forget right now. Had she really asked him to strip her naked and fuck her against her living room wall?

And despite the short duration and the patently *un*happy ending, had it really been the hottest hookup she'd had in...God, who knew how long?

January squeezed Quinn's forearm, zinging her back to the common room with a smile. "Ah, no worries. We'll make up for it next time, girl. Anyway, I'm going to go grab some coffee and some of Hawk's home fries before these vultures swoop in and finish them off." January hooked a thumb over her shoulder, blond brows lifted in question. "Want anything?"

"Nah. I'm all good."

Quinn exhaled slowly as January beelined for the coffeepot at the front of the kitchen, although it did damned little to relax her. Despite all her efforts to make the words true, her gut still prickled with unease she couldn't explain, let alone loosen.

Which was honestly just plain stupid. She knew everyone here was fine. She'd seen every last firefighter at roll call thirty minutes ago—including Luke, who currently sat on the other side of the common room between Gamble and Dempsey, his expression as unreadable as ever. She'd spoken to Parker not once, but twice yesterday on the phone before he'd left for his brother's cabin in Virginia for some R&R, and even though she'd skipped the gathering at Kylie's, all of her girlfriends were clearly status quo. The last two days had been quiet. Calm. Completely normal.

So if she'd done the right thing, the smart thing, the *safe* thing, then why did she still feel so fucking rattled?

Pushing up from the table, Quinn grabbed her plate and headed for the sink. She'd forced herself to put bite after bite of Hawk's legendary belly-buster breakfast into her mouth, to chew and swallow and chew again even though she'd tasted nothing. She wouldn't be of any use if she keeled over from low blood sugar, she knew. But God, it had taken every ounce of her strength and sanity to clear even half the food on her plate. She needed to regroup, just long enough to get rid of this weird feeling still keeping her on edge.

Easy, came Luke's voice in her mind, making her heart flutter even as her shoulders unwound. *There. Breathe...*

She needed to get out of this room before she went bat-shit crazy.

Kicking her boots into motion, Quinn struck a path from the common room to the fire house's window-lined front lobby. Station Seventeen was made up of two main wings, one on either side of the lobby hallway and the common room, and she headed toward the side that housed the engine bay, the equipment room, and Captain Bridges's office. The pressure in her chest subsided with each step over the linoleum, her pulse beginning to slow at the thought of finally, *finally* getting back to normal.

She could do this. She could.

Her friends were okay, Luke's family was okay, and that was all that mattered.

"Hey." A very familiar, very masculine voice rumbled through the silence of the engine bay, and jeez, speak of the devil had never looked so ridiculously sexy. Then again, between those criminally long eyelashes and the curve of the lean, light brown biceps peeking out from the sleeves of his just-snug-enough RFD T-shirt, Luke might as well *be* the devil, because good Lord, he was hot as hell.

"Oh! Hey," Quinn said far too brightly. *Easy, girl.* "I was just coming out to, ah, do some inventory in the rig before we get too crazy with calls today."

Luke nodded, falling into step beside her as she put the rest of the distance between herself and the ambulance in the past tense. "Yeah, me too. How are you feeling?"

"Fine." Ugh, there she went again with the F-word. She re-set her smile even though it felt tighter than a Salvation Army drum. "I mean, better. Thanks."

Quinn reached for the heavy stainless steel latch on the back of the ambulance, but Luke reached out, his hand stopping just shy of hers but stopping her movements nonetheless.

"Before we get to work, I was hoping we could talk," he said, his eyes taking a lightning-fast tour of the quiet engine bay before he added, "about some of the things that happened at your apartment the other morning."

A flush heated the back of Quinn's neck. But better to face their impulsive kiss head-on so they could *move* on. "You don't have to say anything," she murmured. At least they were surrounded by the buffer of Engine Seventeen on one side and Squad Six's equally large rescue vehicle on the other. Even if someone did manage to tear themselves away from Hawk's breakfast of champions and stumble their way out here, chances were nil that she and Luke would be seen or overheard without ample warning.

Luke's eyes moved over her as he took a half-step forward. "I do," he argued, but Quinn cut him off with a shake of her head.

"You really don't. In fact, I should be the one talking. I owe you an apology. I was pretty hopped up on adrenaline, and I got"—she paused to swallow past her suddenly dry mouth—"a little carried away. I'm sorry I was out of line."

Surprise flashed through his stare before he cleared it with a slow, single blink. "We were both there for that kiss. And we both know how intense an adrenaline reaction can be. The whole thing was..." He trailed off, rubbing a palm over the back of his neck while Quinn's libido supplied words like *hot, so hot,* and *insanely fucking hot* to fill in the blanks. "Just a normal reaction to the endorphins," he finally finished. "But I was actually thinking we need to talk about the other thing that happened."

"Oh." Confusion sent her feet back a step on the buffed concrete floor. What the hell was he—"No," she said, snapping her arms over her chest as her brain played an ad hoc game of connect the dots. Was he out of his *mind*? "We don't."

"We do, and I think you know we do."

Quinn's breath grew shaky. How could his voice be so soft, so comforting, when the things he was saying terrified her so much?

"We need to tell the police about the call we went on, Quinn. All of it." Luke stepped in even closer, dropping his chin until she had no choice but to look right into those piercing, ice-blue eyes of his. Tears pricked the backs of her eyelids, and she channeled all of her energy into keeping them at bay.

"We've already been through this. We *can't* tell anybody," she said. But her words lacked conviction, wobbling upon exit. Luke might not be chatty about his family, but she'd seen his face when Ice had pulled up the photographs of his sister and the other, older woman on his cell phone. He was clearly close to them, just as she was close to everyone here at Seventeen. He wouldn't put them in danger unless he was sure they'd be safe from it. Would he?

Luke shook his head, adamant. "We can, and we should have right from the beginning. We aren't doing anyone we care about any favors by keeping what happened to ourselves. The longer Ice gets away with threatening us, the longer they're all in danger regardless. We're not taking care of them by ignoring what happened." He paused, an odd emotion flickering through his stare for less than a breath before it disappeared. "And we're not looking out for each other by pretending everything is fine."

Quinn's threadbare composure tilted further. *Easy. Breathe*, came Luke's voice from her memory, combining with the unwavering closeness of his body in front of hers to unstick the truth from her throat. "I...I'm scared."

"I know," Luke said, quiet and calm, and God, didn't *anything* rock him? "But we can't just move on like everything is normal, Quinn. It's not, and it won't be until we fix this."

"Fix this." She repeated the words on a whisper. As much as she hated it, he wasn't entirely wrong. Faking her way through this whole thing was only putting her nerves—not to mention her conscience—through a blender. She'd never last if she tried to keep it up, and the truth was, Ice could change his mind and come after everyone at any time if he felt like taking care of loose ends. He could be out there, hurting other people. Maybe even innocent people.

Still... "Ice is a cold-blooded killer," Quinn said. She might not have technically seen him commit the act, but she'd seen the look in his eyes when he'd threatened to kill her and Luke, and it had been enough to know he was neither bluffing nor inexperienced. "We can't just waltz right in to the Thirty-Third and spill our guts. He could be watching our every move."

Luke exhaled, scrubbing a hand over his clean-shaven face. "He could. Which means we'll have to come up with a plan to outsmart him."

"He's a gang leader, Luke. He's probably got tons of experience staying off the cops' radar, not to mention he's ruthless as hell and he knows everything about us. How on earth are we going to outsmart him?"

"I don't know."

For the first time since they'd come out here to the engine bay, Luke looked uncertain, and yeah, she felt his pain. They needed a plan—an *impossible* plan—and right now, they had no information, no advantage—God, all they had was each other.

Wait.

"I think I know what we need to do," Quinn said, her pulse threatening to outrun the air in her lungs.

Luke's brows popped, his stare widening in the harsh fluorescent light spilling down from overhead. "You do?"

She nodded. The idea forming in her brain scared the shit out of her, yes, but she couldn't deny the truth behind it.

She and Luke were in this together. They were partners. They needed to rely on the person they trusted most above all.

"I do. Now let's go before I lose my nerve."

13

For one of the good guys, Captain Tanner Bridges was still scary as shit under the right circumstances. Case in point, when you were about to tell him you'd withheld reporting a brutal drive-by shooting, and oh, by the way, a kidnapping/assault by a gang lord who could viciously kill your grandmother and sister with one simple phone call.

No. *No.* Luke hadn't watched his grandmother mourn her only child and nursed his sister through the debilitating illness that had destroyed her ability to hear only to lose them both to a cold-hearted bastard like Ice.

This wouldn't go pear-shaped. It couldn't.

He wouldn't let it.

Quinn sat next to him, her shoulders a rigid line beneath her dark gray RFD T-shirt and her spine straight against the chair across from Captain Bridges's desk. Luke had known bullying her wouldn't get her past her fear of coming forward, no matter how much they needed to tell the police about the kidnapping, just as he'd known she was both strong enough and smart enough to realize the truth for herself. What he *hadn't* been prepared for was how deeply that fear would tear at him, how the two simple words *I'm scared* would slice so cleanly through his carefully crafted composure.

How the hell was he supposed to keep her at arm's length when all he'd wanted to do in that engine bay was wrap his arms around her and hold her until she felt safe again?

"Copeland. Slater." Captain Bridges crossed the threshold into his office and shut the door. No turning back now. "You said this is urgent, so let's cut to the chase. What's going on?"

Quinn took an audible breath. "Well...there was an, um...incident at one of our calls last shift," she started, and Bridges pinned them both with a concern-filled stare as he took a seat at his desk.

"An incident."

"Yes, sir. We responded to a call for a person down of unknown causes, but the address turned out to be an abandoned warehouse with no victim present."

Although her voice was steady enough and her words sounded official, Luke could see her hands shaking where she'd folded them together in her lap, her fingers knotted in a white-knuckled grip. Her gaze said she wasn't having second thoughts—in fact, her expression was determined as hell. But that fear was right back in place in her eyes, and Luke's impulsive need to crush it roared back to life.

She'd had his back. When his fear of blood had broken free of its box and threatened to sink him as they'd started to treat Jayden. When Ice had asked which one of them was in charge. Shit, when she'd insisted on staying quiet about this whole fucking thing in the first place. Quinn had done those things because she'd had his back, without question.

And now he would have hers.

"We were kidnapped at gunpoint and taken to North Point to care for the victim of a drive-by shooting." Luke heard the words only after he'd let them launch, but now that they were out, there was no point in holding back. "We tried to save the guy, but he had a nasty GSW to the chest. He was barely alive when we got there, and obviously we couldn't transport him."

"Jesus," Bridges bit out, his frame having snapped to the sort of stern attention his crisp navy blue and white uniform usually commanded. "You two were kidnapped at *gunpoint* during last shift? Why didn't you report this?"

Luke's heart tripped. Still, he said, "Because our kidnapper belongs to a gang whose leader is pretty persuasive."

He outlined enough of the story to give Bridges the idea, but not so much that the fear in Quinn's eyes came rushing back with a vengeance. The tension in her shoulders actually seemed to ease (albeit only by the tiniest fraction) as he finished, and finally, Captain Bridges sat back to look at them both.

"First things first. Were either of you injured on the call?"

Of all the things the man could have led with, Luke had been expecting that the least. "No," he and Quinn both answered together, and Bridges nodded.

"Good. We're going to need to proceed with extreme care, obviously. But you did the right thing coming forward, and I can assure you both that we'll get this taken care of." Without another word, he reached for the phone on his desk, punching in a few numbers. "Yes, January? Will you do me a favor, please, and call dispatch? I need to have Ambulance Twenty-Two taken off rotation, effective immediately."

Quinn flinched, and for as big a fan as Luke was of the ol' poker face, he was right there with her. Taking them off rotation would be a huge red flag to anyone who might be tracking them. "Captain—"

Bridges held up a hand. "Yes, the vehicle is down for maintenance. It seems the repair on the gurney latch didn't hold. Copeland and Slater will stand by here for the time being until we can sort it out. Thank you."

Luke exhaled in relief. If Ice was watching, he'd think they were at the fire house, waiting for a new vehicle. A fact that Quinn had obviously realized, too, because she'd scaled back from panic mode.

"Okay," she said after Bridges had replaced the phone in its cradle. "So what do we do now?"

"Now we figure out how to get you two to the Thirty-Third without anyone seeing you."

Right. Luke frowned. "That's going to be easier said than done."

"Not necessarily," Quinn said, biting her lip as she fixed him with a stare. "I have an idea. But I don't think you're going to like it."

If Luke never had to lie down in the back seat of an SUV again, he'd die a seriously happy man. Granted, the much-roomier cargo space in Captain Bridges's department-issued Suburban was a far cry from the dirty floor in Damien's Escalade. But still. The flashback factor fucking sucked.

Nope. Not going there. They were fixing this. He needed to lock up his goddamn emotions while they did.

Calibrating his breathing, Luke turned on his side to look at Quinn. She'd curled up almost as soon as she'd stealthed into the back of the Suburban under the cover of the engine bay, closing her eyes and lying perfectly still beside him. Sunlight filtered in past the tinted windows, turning her blond hair into a sort of glowy halo and spot-lighting the tight crease between her eyebrows, and so much for locking up his emotions.

"Hey," he whispered. "You okay hiding like this?"

"Mmm hmm," Quinn hummed, although her eyes remained cranked shut. "It was my idea, remember?"

"That doesn't mean you love it."

That earned him a tiny smile. "Fair enough. I don't love it. But I'm okay. Anyway, the Thirty-Third isn't that far. We'll only be here for a few more minutes, tops."

Okay, so she was right. But Luke's fingers still itched to touch her, to erase the tension on her face even a little, and he nearly said fuck it to do just that. But God, he'd already blown past so many boundaries with her, so he settled for, "We're doing the right thing, Quinn."

"I know," she said.

"Okay." Captain Bridges's voice filtered in from the front seat of the Suburban. "We're nearly there. I've already called Sergeant Sinclair to let him know we've got a matter to discuss that requires discretion, so he'll be waiting for us at the rear entrance to the precinct."

"Copy that," Luke said. Unless Ice had X-ray vision, chances were pretty much nil that the guy knew he and Quinn had embarked on this little field trip to the Thirty-Third, Luke knew. But he was still grateful for the precautions. Just because he hadn't seen any hint of danger at Momma Billie's house in the last three mornings he'd dropped by didn't mean it wasn't there, and he sure as shit wasn't about to invite any by not being top-notch careful.

A minute later, the Suburban rolled to a stop. They all made quick work of getting out and walking over to the nondescript metal door where Sergeant Sam Sinclair waited as promised. Luke had only seen Sinclair a time or two when he'd come by to visit January at the fire house, but yeah, if anyone could protect him and Quinn, the lean, steely-eyed sergeant looked like a dead ringer for the job.

"Sam." Captain Bridges extended his hand. "Thanks for agreeing to see us so quickly. You know my paramedic, Quinn Copeland, and my engine rookie, Luke Slater."

"I do." Sinclair nodded, first at Quinn, then at Luke, before turning to use an electronic keycard and ID code to gain access to the building. "Gotta admit, you three have my curiosity piqued."

"I wish we were here under better circumstances," Bridges said. Sinclair seemed to take that for the bid for privacy that it was—thank fuck—because he didn't push. Instead, he led them deeper into the building, past a pair of uniformed officers at the metal detectors in the precinct's main hallway, then up one staircase that was open to the bustling lobby. Luke had never been to the intelligence unit's home base before, and after three days of trying to figure out a way to get here undetected, he couldn't deny the twinge of relief in his chest as he put the last of the stairs behind him and followed Sinclair past the glass double doors leading into the large office space.

Scanning a new environment for the basics was Firefighter 101, the habit so ingrained after only seven months that Luke now did it off-duty as much as he did on. The intelligence office was essentially a big, open rectangle, with four large windows on the wall to his left, and a narrow hallway shooting off from the back of the office that bore a backlit sign for another exit. Four desks—complete with detectives —filled the room at regular intervals, with one longer work-station along the right-hand wall. The crazy six-way monitor-type above the desk there told Luke it had to belong to Capelli, and hey, what do you know, there was the tech guru, sitting at the keyboard and looking as serious as ever.

"Whoa." Detective Addison Hale's head popped up from her laptop screen, followed quickly by her partner, Shawn Maxwell's, who had been reading over her shoulder. "Hey, Quinn," the female detective said. "Everything okay?"

Ah, right. Luke had forgotten Quinn was good friends with Hale. And Kellan's girlfriend, Isabella, who was now looking on with curiosity-slash-concern from her own desk a few feet away, too. Hell, there wasn't really *anybody* Quinn wasn't friends with.

"Oh, I uh…"

"Copeland and Slater are just coming in to make a report," Sinclair said. That probably would've been the end of the group disclosure—God knew the intelligence unit had to operate by the chain of command as much as they did at Seventeen, so if Sinclair wanted the full monty on discretion, Luke had a funny feeling the guy would get it.

But Quinn's boots didn't budge from the middle of the room. "Actually, Sergeant, this might be something the whole team will want to hear."

Sinclair's gray-blond brows winged up toward his crew cut. Quinn wasn't wrong, though—they were going to need the whole team in on taking down a guy like Ice—and Luke stepped toward her with a nod.

"Quinn is right. Sir," he tacked on, because a) his mother and grandmother hadn't raised him to be disrespectful, and

b) they also hadn't raised him to be a dumbass. "Having your detectives here for this is probably going to save time."

"By all means, then." Sinclair nodded to the pair of chairs that Isabella's partner, Detective Liam Hollister, had just pulled from beside their desks and placed at the front of the office. The detectives' faces were mostly business, and Capelli's was downright impassive, although Luke could see the covert glances being exchanged between the five of them like nonverbal shorthand. They knew something was up.

Hell if *that* wasn't a star nominee for the Understatement of the Year Award.

Sinclair leaned a hip against Isabella's file-covered desk, sending a quick gaze at Captain Bridges in the back of the room before focusing on Quinn and Luke. "So what's going on, you two?"

"We, ah..." Quinn stopped nearly as soon as she'd started. The expression she'd worn in Captain Bridges's office was back in all its tension-filled glory, and her whisper from the engine bay, so simple and yet so fucking complicated, flew through Luke's mind.

I'm scared.

"On our last shift, we were kidnapped at gunpoint while responding to a call," Luke said so Quinn wouldn't have to, and even though he'd fully expected the hiccup of pin-drop silence that ensued, it didn't make it any less deafening.

"I'm sorry," Hale said, her shoulders thumping against the back of her chair as she pulled back to stare at him. "You were...what?"

Luke inhaled on a three-count. *Give up the information. Fix the problem.* "We were kidnapped at gunpoint from a warehouse on Beaumont Place. The guy took us to a gang safe house in North Point—at least, I'm ninety percent sure it was North Point—to provide medical care for his brother, who had been shot."

The silence that followed combined with the balls-out seriousness on the faces of every last member in the unit, so Luke kept going. "Quinn and I administered as much medical care as we could. But the guys in the gang wouldn't let us take the patient to Remington Mem even though he had a GSW to the chest, so..." He dropped his chin slightly to get the message across, which seemed to work, because both Isabella and Hollister nodded slightly in return. "After he died, his gang leader took our cell phones and IDs and told us that if we said anything to anyone, he'd kill us and our families."

Sinclair didn't blink or budge. He simply looked at Maxwell and said, "Get Garza on the phone. Tell him to drop whatever he's doing and get his ass out here. Now."

"You got it, boss."

Luke didn't know who Garza was or why the guy was important, but he did feel a flash of relief at the seriousness in Sinclair's tone as he asked for the guy, then another when Maxwell reported that Garza was already in the building regarding a different case and was on his way up. Isabella excused herself to grab bottles of water for both him and Quinn, and Hollister and Hale used the wait-time to team up to clear the intelligence unit's schedule. Quinn sat quietly beside him, staring at the scuffed toes of her black work boots, and Christ, his gut panged with all sorts of shit he didn't want to contemplate but couldn't ignore.

"Hey. Are you okay?"

Her blond hair rustled over the shoulders of her uniform top, bringing with it a subtle, flowery scent that stirred something very primal under his skin. "I'm fine."

Damn, she used that word a lot. Too bad her eyes, her

shoulders—shit, everything else about her—told a very different story. But before Luke could say as much, the door to the intelligence unit's office swung open to reveal a tough-looking Hispanic guy in plainclothes with a gun on one hip and an RPD badge on the other.

"Hey, Sergeant. Heard you needed me?"

Sinclair nodded. "Garza, come on in. Quinn, Luke, Captain Bridges, this is Detective Matteo Garza. He works over in the department's gang unit." After a set of quick nods that translated to hey-how-ya-doing, Sinclair continued with, "Quinn and Luke have some information you're going to find of interest." He spared a lightning-fast glance at Capelli, who clacked out a few keystrokes on his computer, then looked at Luke and Quinn with all the seriousness of an acute MI with an open-fracture chaser. "We're going to need you to start at the beginning. And don't leave anything out."

Although Luke's pulse raced enough to make his hands unsteady, he didn't hesitate to do what Sinclair had asked. He recounted what had happened, the story punctuated by Quinn's nods and the tap-tap-tap of Capelli's keyboard as the guy recorded every detail on a big, digital board at the front of the office. The detectives listened without interrupting much, but Luke could sense the gravity of the situation from their still-stony expressions, and finally, he ended with, "Then Ice left us in the warehouse and took off. I'm sorry we didn't say anything before now, but..."

Sinclair quelled the guilt in Luke's gut with one shake of his head. "He has a lot of identifying information on you both, and he put you in a dangerous situation. But we're going to get to the bottom of this."

Isabella and Maxwell both nodded from their desks, and

Sinclair shifted back to look at the spot where Garza had been taking in the story with a shrewd, dark stare.

The detective asked, "This snake tattoo all of these guys had, was it exactly the same?"

Luke nodded, grateful that the whole attention-to-detail thing had been drilled into him from day one at the academy. "Yes. All four men had the same tattoo on their right forearms."

"Would you be able to identify it from a photo?"

"Absolutely." It was the first thing Quinn had said in a while, but her voice came out dead certain. "I remember it from when I started Jayden's IV. And from…" Her sentence skidded to an awkward halt. "Yes. I'd be able to identify it."

"Did it look like this?" Garza asked, flipping through his iPhone for a few seconds before handing it over to Quinn.

Her hand trembled, but only for a second before she and Luke said yes at the same time. Dark, coiled lines of ink, cold black spheres for eyes, mouth open to bare a set of menacing, pointed fangs—the tattoo in the photo was definitely a match.

"That's what I thought," Garza said, but funny, he looked none too thrilled at having made the ID on the ink. "The man who kidnapped you—Damien? Belongs to a gang called the Vipers."

"Shit." Hollister's apologetic expression was almost instantaneous with the slip. "Sorry. They're one of Remington's nastier gangs."

"Which means it's good that you came to us," Sinclair said, tipping his chin at the screen in the front of the room. "Garza, what can you tell me about this guy, Ice?"

"His legal name is Isaiah Howard, and he's a ruthless son of a bitch, not to mention a bit of a legend. He's been on our radar for at least a decade, but we barely even have verified photos of the guy, much less anything we can use to nail him."

Although he didn't say it, Sinclair's expression was the living embodiment of *fucking great*. "And the Vipers?"

"Ice inherited the top spot from his old man when the guy was shot to death in a DEA raid eight years ago. The Vipers are known for the usual list of bad and nasty— running drugs, illegal weapons, drive-by shootings over turf wars. There's been some chatter lately that they're looking to break out into some bigger gun running, but so far, we haven't been able to confirm that with anything concrete." Garza shook his head. "CIs are real reluctant to give up anything on this guy, and he's slippery. He covers his tracks better than most."

Quinn stiffened against her chair. "So you don't really know a whole lot about him, then."

"That doesn't mean we can't find proof of what he did to you two and arrest him for threatening your lives," Maxwell said, and Hale nodded reassuringly as she leaned closer to Quinn.

"Or keep you two safe while we work the case."

"But it's going to be really hard to do," Quinn said, and yeah, it sounded like she had one hell of a point.

"Yes." Both Isabella and Hale winced at Garza's reply, but the detective didn't scale back. "Building a case against Ice is going to be an uphill climb. He's as methodical as he is mean. If you two aren't dead, it's because he didn't want you that way. Sorry," he added, sending a sheepish shrug in Quinn's direction when she visibly paled. "But that's how he works. He was raised in that gang. Hell, he *is* that gang. Everything he does has a purpose."

Luke tamped down the very sudden, very unexpected urge to introduce his fist to Garza's face. He was all for the honesty, but for fuck's sake, Quinn was already scared. The reminder that they both could be dead? Not really helping.

A fact that Sinclair seemed to catch on to pretty quickly. "Right," he said quietly. "Now we just need to figure out what his purpose is here. Garza, I want you on this with the rest of my unit. I'll call Sergeant Mills to get him in the loop. As long as you're okay with working the case."

His tone made it sound like Garza would be crazy to decline, which was exactly how the detective answered.

"Yes, sir, I am. Although"—he paused for a breath—"respectfully, I have to say the gang unit may want jurisdiction. We've been dying to get decent intel on Ice for years."

The intelligence unit's detectives played a game of tag-team brow lifting, but Sinclair either didn't notice (unlikely) or didn't care (highly probable).

"And respectfully, my answer's no. We've got a dead body to go with our kidnapping, and who knows what else beneath the surface, which means the case falls to intelligence. Not to mention that as far as I'm concerned, an assault on the first responders at Seventeen is like an assault on our own." Sinclair's features hardened, his shoulders forming an unyielding line as he crossed his arms over the front of his dark blue button-down shirt. "This case is ours, and we *will* get to the bottom of it."

For the first time since they'd walked into the precinct, Quinn's shoulders seemed to unknot, which in turn sent a shot of relief through Luke's system. "Thank you," she said.

Isabella looked at Quinn, her smile soft but her words as tough as an MMA cage fighter. "This is what we do, sweetheart. Don't worry. We'll catch this guy."

Before his better judgment could remind him of the sharp edges Sinclair had just shown off, Luke asked, "And you plan to do that how, exactly?" It seemed like a monumental fucking job, even for an elite police unit.

"Very carefully," Sinclair said. "First, we're going to need any evidence we can get our hands on. Capelli, pull the transcripts of the nine-one-one call from dispatch. See if there's anything we can use there."

Capelli paused for a frown. "I doubt there will be. This kidnapping sounds like it was strategically planned, which means the odds are extremely high the call came from a burner phone," he said.

Hollister coughed into his fist, the noise sounding suspiciously like the word *dude*, and Capelli's eyes widened behind the thick black frames of his glasses as he caught sight of Sinclair's impressive death glare.

"You know what, why don't I just grab those transcripts anyway and see what turns up. I can also see if there are any street cams or security feeds from businesses near the warehouse. Just because it's a longshot doesn't mean it's statistically impossible."

"That's more like it," Sinclair said. "Hale, I want you and Maxwell on this body. Check all John Does with GSWs that have turned up in the last seventy-two hours. Check the department's database, the morgue, everywhere you can think of."

Maxwell gave up a dark and dangerous look that—whoa —actually rivaled Sinclair's. "On it."

The sergeant turned his attention back to him and Quinn and Captain Bridges. "Am I correct in assuming the ambulance taken on the call is at Seventeen right now?"

"Affirmative," Bridges said. "Ambulance Twenty-Two is at the fire house. The official status of the vehicle is that it's down for further repairs for some damage it sustained last week. Since that damage was already on the books, I thought it wouldn't raise any red flags to anyone watching."

"Smart thinking. Let's have the vehicle towed to central. I'll have a forensics team standing by to comb it for evidence. Slater, Copeland, what did you two do with the equipment when you were done at the flophouse?"

Quinn's expression went from realization to apology. "Ice made us sterilize everything before we left the house. We took the monitors and first-in bags back with us—obviously we'd never be able to explain losing such expensive equipment. But he made us leave everything disposable there with Jayden's body."

"Damn it," Hollister muttered. "So much for DNA."

"Not necessarily," Isabella interjected, but Luke shook his head.

"That ambulance has been on two and a half tours since we went on that call. It's been cleaned and sanitized by paramedics on all three shifts." Christ, Quinn alone was meticulous enough that the health department would probably green-light a four-course meal off any surface in the freaking thing when she was done with it.

The hard press of Sinclair's mouth said he likely agreed, but... "We'll check it anyway to see if we can find any DNA or fingerprints that match anyone in the system. The RFD can replace the vehicle with one you can use in the meantime."

"So we get to stay on-shift?" Quinn asked. Her voice was loaded with hope, and Luke had to admit, he shared every ounce of the sentiment.

Captain Bridges? Not so much. "With all due respect, Sam, is that wise? Shouldn't we be talking about protective custody, here?"

Luke's heart went full-on Whack-a-Mole with his rib

cage. "You think we need protective *custody*?" he asked, his question colliding with Quinn's emphatic "no".

"No. Not right now," Sinclair added as a caveat. "Look, we have to assume that Ice has eyes on you both. Right now, if we pull you from rotation at Seventeen, he'll know something's up and he'll either go below ground or he'll come after you two. Maybe both. We need to keep this investigation way under wraps if we want to keep you safe, *and* if we want to get any intel on the guy. Which means..."

"We go business as usual," Bridges said, although he seemed a mile and a half away from being convinced.

Sinclair shifted, angling his body toward Isabella, Hollister, and Garza to include them in the conversation. "It's not ideal. And we're going to have to take precautions. Talk to me about local family members. Boyfriends, girlfriends. Anyone you're close with."

Shit. *Shit.* Luke clammed up by default, letting Quinn take point on the question.

"I don't have anybody other than the crew at Seventeen. But Ice has my phone. He's got to know I'm really tight with everyone there, along with Isabella and Addison and Kennedy Matthews, from the Crooked Angel. Parker is at his brother's cabin in the mountains in Virginia, so he's probably far enough away to be safe. But everyone else..."

"Everyone else, we can keep an eye on. But you're right. Parker's far enough away to be out of Ice's reach." Sinclair swung his steely gaze at Luke, and fuck, suddenly it felt chock full of shrapnel. "How about you, Slater?"

"I, ah." *You don't have a choice. You need a solution. They need to stay safe.* "My grandmother is local. And so is my sister."

"I see. And exactly where do they live and work?"

Of course, Sinclair had to ask. Because—of course—Luke was all about penny-pinching the personal details.

He swallowed in an effort to buy time he knew he couldn't afford and wouldn't come anyway. "They live together in the house where I was raised in Mission Park. My grandmother works for Remington Gas and Electric, and my sister Hayley is a senior at Thomas Jefferson High School, over on Grammercy."

"Okay." Sinclair lifted his chin at Hollister, who turned toward the laptop on his desk and began to type. "We'll assign a detail to keep an eye on both of them, just to be on the safe side. Same goes for the fire house when you're all on-shift, and for you two all the time."

Luke took a breath, his first full one in at least ten minutes. Details were good. They meant there was a plan. A way to tackle the problem, step by step. "So everyone has cops looking out for them and we just go about everything like normal?"

"Essentially," Sinclair said after a pause. "You'll both have to be vigilant, and we'll require a voice check-in by phone every twelve hours. You also won't be able to discuss the case with anyone."

Quinn's chin lifted in surprise. "You're not going to tell anyone at Seventeen about this? Or Luke's family?"

"I know it sounds a little counter-intuitive and scary," Isabella said. "But our security details will keep them safe, and we'll keep you two safe."

"But—"

"Quinn, hey, look at me." Slipping from behind her desk, Isabella knelt down in front of Quinn, her lifted brows and soft expression proving in no uncertain terms that she not only understood the panic on Quinn's face, but she took it freaking seriously. "Kellan works in that fire house with you, doesn't he?"

Quinn blinked. "Yes."

The word was all question, and Isabella answered it as such. "Exactly. I would never put him at risk, just like I would never put the rest of you at risk. We need everyone to act normally so nothing tips Ice off while we work on our investigation, and the best way to ensure that is not to tell any of them what's going on. Captain Bridges is in the loop." Isabella nodded up at the captain, but never broke eye contact with Quinn. "Capelli runs the best security and surveillance around. This unit has your backs. I wouldn't bullshit you. I promise this is the best way to proceed. Okay?"

"Okay." Quinn nodded, and Luke echoed the movement when Isabella shifted her gaze to his. He might not like not telling his grandmother or sister what was going on—for Chrissake, he hated all of this, from the threat to the secrecy to the unease still locked in Quinn's dark blue stare. But he needed a solution, and involving the intelligence unit felt like the smartest, safest way to get one.

"What do we do in the meantime?"

"What you normally would," Isabella said. She stood back up and returned to her desk. "Work. Go to the grocery store. Have a couple of beers at the Crooked Angel. But be smart about it—stick to really public places and use the buddy system if you leave home after dark. That last one's not negotiable."

Not that it would be a problem for Luke. He didn't ever go anywhere to speak of other than work or Momma Billie's, although he'd have to skip post-sundown visits for now unless he stayed overnight because no fucking way was he taking anyone there. His personal life, scant as it was, was still personal. He wasn't about to share so much as an ounce of it if he didn't need to. "Copy that, detective."

"Got it," Quinn said. Although Luke's gut did a knot-and-drop at the thought of Ice watching Quinn—or worse yet, trying to hurt her if she was out in public—the buddy system certainly wouldn't be an issue for her. Her network of friends, *close* friends, had to be big enough to fill a base-ball stadium.

Sinclair reclaimed the conversation with one quick clearing of his throat. "Good. Moreno and Hollister will arrange a check-in schedule for you both. In the meantime, I'd like to get you set up with some photo arrays, see if we can't put a solid ID to Damien, Jayden, and anyone else we have in the system. Then we'll get you back to Seventeen in time to finish your shift."

"One more thing, if I could, Sergeant." Captain Bridges's tone carried enough non-request to send Luke's red flags flapping in the wind. "I'm going to have to insist that you two get cleared by Dr. Garrity over at HQ before you're put back in the active service rotation."

Quinn's ponytail snapped over the shoulder of her dark gray uniform top. "The head shrinker? Come on, Cap. No way."

"Dallas Garrity is one of the best psychologists in the city, and he just happens to be on the department's payroll," Bridges said, and yep, he wasn't backing down. "I'm sure I can arrange the appointments to look like routine mental health check-ins. But you were kidnapped at gunpoint and your lives have been threatened. I take your emotional well-being as seriously as your physical health, and as such..."

"Okay, okay," Quinn mumbled, but the frown tugging at the edges of her mouth broadcasted her disdain like a bill-board. In truth, Luke wasn't thrilled about the prospect of going, either. But resisting would only draw attention to the fact that he didn't want to do it, and anyway, pushing back was futile. If a session with the department shrink would get him a step closer to a solution, he'd suck it up for the greater good.

After all, he'd spent a damned decade keeping people at arm's length. Keeping his emotions on the down-low from yet one more person? Not gonna be that hard.

"Okay, then." Sinclair lifted his chin at Captain Bridges, then at Detective Garza. "Let's get everything in motion."

Nodding, Luke pushed up from his chair. Quinn stood up to follow Garza, who was clearly on the whole photo array thing, but then she turned back to look at Sinclair, her eyes brimming with something Luke couldn't quite identify even though he knew on sight that he hated it.

"Sergeant, I'm sorry we"—she broke off. Bit her lip. Tried again—"I'm sorry *I* didn't come forward sooner. Luke wanted to." Her emotion-filled gaze landed directly in his sternum. "But I didn't. So I apologize. We should have told you right after the, um...whole thing happened."

Sinclair regarded her carefully for a second while Luke fought twin urges to build a stronger defense against the look on Quinn's face and hold her until said look disappeared.

"I can't lie," Sinclair finally said. "We'd have made better headway if we'd had the jump on this. But it was a tough thing you did, coming forward. We're going to do everything we can to keep you and your families safe while we nail Damien for the kidnapping and Ice for threatening your lives."

"Thank you," she whispered.

Luke put one boot in front of the other as the group dispersed, his body following the commands from his neurons even though that deep-down visceral part of him that had wanted to hold Quinn was still screaming full-bore. As bat-shit as the idea was, though, he was her partner. He didn't have to let her in to have her back. He could still do the decent thing; hell, the *right* thing, and help the cops find Ice and his gang while still keeping Quinn at arm's length.

He didn't have a choice.

14

Quinn sat in the tastefully decorated office in the middle of downtown Remington and wished she could be anywhere else, including hell in the summertime and possibly even the mall on Black Friday. Sitting through a detailed re-hashing of the kidnapping with both Bridges and the intelligence unit had been bad enough, even though she'd known it would be necessary. But now she had to go round three with the department's brain peeper so she could get back to work like a normal person?

Fucking ugh.

The door beside her opened, and she fought the urge to try and make a jailbreak.

"Quinn, I'm Dallas Garrity." The guy extended a hand, and huh, can't say she'd been expecting the whole decently handsome, under-forty, polo shirt and chinos, doesn't-look-like-Freud-or-Satan thing.

Not that it made her want to be here for even another nanosecond. "Quinn Copeland." She shook his hand, eyeballing the door he'd just closed and angling her chair between it and his desk as she sat back down.

"How are you doing today?" he asked, and Quinn bit back the irony welling in her throat.

"Fine, thank you."

The doc took her answer in stride as he sat not behind his desk, but in the other chair on the "client" side of things, adjusting it to face her. "I've talked briefly with Captain Bridges and Sergeant Sinclair about the circumstances that have brought you here. Maybe we should start with you giving me your point of view."

Quinn's pulse tapped out a steady stream of *no, no, no, oh look, more no.* "If you've already gotten the story from them, then you're totally up to speed. My version isn't any different."

"Okay," he said, surprising her by not pushing. "If you don't want to talk about what happened, we can try talking about how you're feeling right now."

She stared at the carpet, focusing on the subtle, swirly pattern in the dark blue fibers. "I already told you. I'm feeling fine. Ready to get back to work."

Dr. Garrity nodded, but didn't look convinced. "You know, it wouldn't be unusual for it to take a little while to get your wheels spinning properly again."

"My wheels are fine. Great, actually. Just like the rest of me."

"You look like you want to leave."

"I'm sorry?" Her lips parted in genuine surprise, but the doc didn't bat so much as a single, sandy blond eyelash.

"The way you're sitting," he said, gesturing to the chair she'd repositioned the second she'd been ushered into his office. "Most people who come to see me sit facing the desk, but you're a bit of an exception. You're turned toward the door, like you want to leave."

Quinn lifted a shoulder halfway before letting it drop. "I'm a first responder. We like to know where all the exits are."

"I know." Dr. Garrity gave up a smile, and not the run-of-the-mill variety, either. "I was a firefighter myself."

Whoa. Talk about a plot twist. But come to think of it, that explained the whole broad-shoulders, alert-demeanor thing. "Oh. What made you decide to do this instead?"

"That's a long story for another day," he said, so easily that Quinn got the feeling he'd used the line more than once. "But we're here to talk about you."

Quinn trapped her sigh between her teeth. "Okay."

After a five-second pause for excruciating silence, Dr. Garrity said, "As your assigned psychologist, I'd like to tell you that if you'd prefer a female therapist, I can arrange for that."

"Why?" Her mental light bulb flashed a second later. "Because my kidnappers were all men?"

"Not to put too fine a point on it, but yes. That's exactly why."

Quinn had given enough people medical attention to know the whole gender preference/comfort zone thing was very real. Still... "I assure you, Dr. Garrity. I'm fine with you and your maleness. In fact, I'm fine with the whole situation."

"It's Mister, actually. Or Dallas, if you like. I don't quite have my PhD yet. And you're fine with having been kidnapped at gunpoint?"

"Dallas, then. And that's not what I meant."

"Okay. Why don't you tell me what you did mean?"

Oh, well played, Dr. Phil. Well played. "Look, no offense.

I'm sure you're great at your job, and I know there are lots of firefighters and paramedics who need therapy. I just don't happen to be one of them."

Dallas didn't even budge, and God, the guy had some serious staying power. "Your assault was pretty brutal, Quinn. Considering the circumstances, it would be perfectly understandable if you were experiencing anxiety. Trouble sleeping. A loss of appetite."

"I wasn't assaulted," she said, because it was so much better than admitting he'd hit the trifecta. But if she could just get back to work and take care of people and be *normal* again, all the other crap would go away.

"You weren't physically hurt," Dallas agreed. "But you were violently threatened. What happened to you falls under the umbrella of assault."

He said the words as gently as possible, his tone as soft and non-confrontational as a litter of kittens. But Quinn's stupid, treasonous heart slammed anyway.

"Let me guess. You talked to Luke about the whole...you know, thing."

Of course Luke had probably told Dallas all about how Damien had pressed his gun to her forehead and made her believe she was going to die horribly. How he'd also shoved that gun in the spot between her shoulder blades hard enough to brand her with a nasty bruise that still ached every time she freaking moved. How Ice had let it all happen, then threatened to turn every word of Damien's posturing into reality. How she'd believed him, and still did.

But Luke seemed to have mastered the normal that Quinn desperately wanted. Luke, who had been so smart and calm and rational when he'd told her what she'd already known this morning. Luke, who'd had the good fortune of having his appointment with Garrity first. Luke, whose arms she wanted to curl up in so she could forget the rest of the shit show that was her universe right now.

Jesus, maybe she did need therapy. Or at the very least, to get laid.

Dallas cleared his throat, reminding her not only where she was, but that she'd just had inappropriate and errant sex thoughts in front of a man who was trying his damnedest to hone in on her brain waves.

"Those are all very normal side effects a person can experience after a traumatic event," he said, dodging her question to maneuver back to the thing that made her look scared and weak, and before Quinn could check herself, she snapped.

"How would you know?"

Regret flooded through her almost instantly, heating her cheeks even though the office around her was nice and cool. "I'm sorry. That was really rude of me. What I meant was—"

"You want to know if I'm patronizing you with a bunch of pages from a textbook or if I actually know what the hell I'm talking about."

The wry smile lifting one corner of his mouth told Quinn he wasn't offended, and she exhaled in relief. "Yeah, maybe."

"I've talked to a lot of people who experience post-traumatic stress, and by a lot, I mean hundreds. Those three side effects seem to be the most common. If you're experiencing any of them, I can try to help you find the best way or ways to cope with that," Dallas said.

Annnnd welcome back to Square One. "I'm good, but thanks."

"So you feel like you're ready to get back on your rig and treat patients?"

Quinn nodded, making sure to look him right in the eye

as she answered, "Absolutely. I'd really like to get back to normal and take care of people who need it while the police do their thing."

"Ah. You like taking care of people, then." Dallas leaned forward to scribble something on the legal pad he'd propped on one khaki-clad knee. "No wonder you want to get back to work."

Her unease slipped. If he wanted to talk shop, she could do *that* for days. "Yep. I've been a paramedic for five years and only missed two shifts, so I guess you could say I like taking care of people."

"Only two, huh?" Dallas gave up a crooked grin that took another chunk out of Quinn's nerves. "Mind if I ask what for?"

"My partner, Parker, and I went on a call for a woman who was having trouble breathing. Turned out she, and the six other people living in her apartment with her, had a really nasty strain of tuberculosis. A handful of patients who had been diagnosed with the same strain had also been vaccinated, so we had to sit out the incubation period, just in case."

"You had to hole up for five days?" Dallas asked, his expression growing more curious at the face she'd made over the mandatory time off. "Some people would love a week-long excuse to catch up on *Game of Thrones*. Not you?"

Quinn laughed, her throat nearly forgetting how to let go of the sound. "I get enough gore on the job, thanks. Anyway, I'm a way happier camper when I'm at the fire house."

"So you've always wanted to be a paramedic, then."

"Ever since college," she said.

They spent the rest of the session talking about her dad and the job, two topics Quinn didn't usually mind going full-tilt on sharing. Dallas mostly listened, but she supposed that's what he'd signed on for. At the end of their time, he walked her back to the lobby, where Addison was waiting to take her back to the precinct so she could meet up with Luke and the captain and finally get back in service where she belonged.

"Hey, Quinn. You good to go?" her friend asked. But before she could answer with a great big hell yes, the woman behind the front desk cleared her throat in a bid for attention.

"Excuse me, Ms. Copeland? Before I can sign off on your temporary release, I'll need to schedule your next appointment."

Something twisted, deep beneath Quinn's ribs. "I'm sorry?"

"Your next appointment. It says here that your work release is contingent upon a follow-up visit next week," the woman said. "I apologize, did Mr. Garrity not explain that to you?"

Oh, that sneaky son of a... "No," Quinn replied through her teeth. "He must've forgotten to mention it." Or known Quinn would've pushed back on the decision with all of her might. *Damn* it!

"I see. I've got a nine thirty open next week on Monday, if that will work for you."

Knowing she had no choice, she tacked a too-tight smile to her face and said, "That would be great. Thanks."

Addison, being both a kickass detective and one of Quinn's closest friends, made the direct translation of her tone to *I'd rather have a root canal on my lady bits* in about two seconds flat. "Don't worry," Addison said as they left the office and headed down the hallway toward the elevator. "I'm sure Capelli can make it look like an official something-

or-other in the system. Even if this a-hole Ice is watching, the appointment will just pop up as your random drug screening, or whatever. Anyway, spending an hour with Dr. McHot Hot might not be *all* bad."

Relieved that Addison thought the safety factor was what had fueled her hesitation, Quinn nodded. She was going to have to get used to keeping this whole thing under wraps anyway. Might as well start now, no matter how weird it felt to hide her feelings from her friend.

After all, it was better than coming out with, "I keep trying to be fine, but I'm too busy being scared of my own freaking shadow".

"You think the psychologist is hot?" Quinn asked, shielding her eyes from the mid-afternoon sunlight with one hand as she followed Addison through the main door of RPD's headquarters.

"You don't?" Addison flipped back, but only after she'd given their surroundings a brief yet thorough three-sixty. "I mean, between that smile and the way he filled out those dress pants, I could eat those buns every night for dinner, if you know what I mean."

Quinn made a noise that meant to be a laugh, but it thudded way short of the mark. "I'll take your word for it until he's not my shrink."

She kept up with the conversation—notably about topics that didn't involve her case or her do-over trip to Dallas's office next week—as best she could, inserting enough mmm-hmms and oh-reallys and manufactured laughs to get by. They made it to the precinct, where Luke and Captain Bridges were standing by for the trip back to Seventeen.

Mashing down on the ball of dread that seemed to have made a permanent home in her stomach, Quinn climbed into the back of the Suburban and curled up on her side. Luke followed a second later, and really, how on earth did he smell so good?

"Hey," he said, his enviably steady voice making her heart pound even faster. "How did it go with Garrity?"

"Fine," she said by default, but God, she was really beginning to hate that fucking word. "How were the mug shots?"

Luke waited for Captain Bridges to slam the rear door and get the Suburban rolling before he answered. "I was able to ID Damien, Jayden, and the other guy, with the baseball hat."

"Me, too." *That's good news*, she told the dread ball, but funny, the stupid thing only seemed to dig in deeper. "Did you, um, get full clearance to go back to work?"

Quinn felt Luke's ice-blue stare on her even though she couldn't quite meet it, focusing instead on the spot where his cheekbone met his temple, up by the dark shadow of his hairline.

"I had to talk to Garrity for an hour so he could make sure I'm okay," he said. "But yeah. He signed off on the paperwork Cap asked for, no problem. Why? Didn't you?"

"Yep." The lie weighed a thousand pounds, but Quinn managed to scrape it past her vocal cords anyway. "I sure did. Like you said, no problem."

Then she closed her eyes and pretended she was anywhere but there.

15

L uke looked around the common room and tried like hell to process his thoughts. He and Quinn had been back from their "routine mental health screenings" for a couple of hours. She'd claimed a headache and headed to the bunk room not long after they'd arrived, and he hadn't seen her since. A not-small part of him had wanted to march a straight line down the hallway and not stop until he'd reached her, to talk to her or hold her or —*fuck*—whatever it took to erase the fear she was trying so hard to cover up.

But that was a terrible idea for several reasons, not the least of which was that Luke remembered in vivid detail how Quinn's body felt pressed against his. He knew how sweet she tasted, how sinful she sounded when he slid his thumbs over the tight peaks of her nipples with just enough friction to make her moan.

Christ, he was a jackass. No, scratch that. He was the high lord of jackasses.

Because despite how wrong, how *dangerous* it was, he still wanted Quinn.

Badly.

"Slater." Gamble stopped in front of the spot where Luke had camped out at one of the smaller side tables with a dog-eared study guide in one hand and a green highlighter in the other. Not that he'd used either since he'd parked himself in the chair. "Taking your assignment to ambo seriously, I see."

"Yes, sir," Luke said, grateful as shit that he'd mastered the art of the poker face before his eighteenth birthday. Had he seriously been thinking about Quinn's nipples right here in front of God and everybody?

"Come on, Gamble. Don't you know that geek is the new chic?" Shae called out from her perch on the arm of the couch.

"Says the woman whose boyfriend practically invented higher intelligence," Dempsey cracked, arching a dark brown brow at her. "You're maybe just a little biased on the whole geek thing, don't you think, McCullough?"

Shae, being Shae, just amped up her grin. "Uh-huh. Why don't you give me shit when you're *not* sleeping solo every night, okay? I might be biased, but at least I'm getting laid."

A chorus of "ohhhh"s rippled through the common room as Dempsey gave Shae a single-finger salute, both of them laughing too hard for any ill will to stick. Gamble rolled his eyes, although Luke caught the twitch of his lips that signaled as much of a smile as the guy ever gave up. The rest of the afternoon, then the evening, passed in a series of similar smartass remarks, along with more studying and fire house chores. Quinn kept her distance while Luke kept the loaner ambulance stocked and ready to go for calls that oddly never came, and when he finally turned in, he stared at the high, darkly shadowed ceiling in the bunk room, unable to shake one thought from his head.

Quinn might be a few dozen feet from him and everyone else at Seventeen, but right now, the space between them might as well measure a thousand miles.

TWELVE HOURS AFTER SHIFT CHANGE, Luke was pretty sure time had come to a rudely screeching halt. He'd agreed not to pick up any extra shifts at other fire houses for the sake of both ease and safety, but damn, the down time was driving him up the plain white walls of his apartment. How could he stick to normal when half of his routine had just been taken off the table and the other half had been shaken like a top-shelf martini?

Shit, he could use a drink.

Taking a deep breath, Luke sat down on the couch in his small but functional living room and palmed the new cell phone he'd picked up a few days ago instead. Although Hayley had already left for school when he'd driven by the house after his shift this morning, he'd texted her on the pretense of making sure she had his new number even though he knew damn well she did, dropping a subtle enough reminder for her to stay alert and safe. She might be a smart kid, and Momma Billie a tough lady, but Hayley's deafness added a layer of vulnerability he didn't like to contemplate.

Someone could sneak up on her and she wouldn't hear. Her vocal cords hadn't been used in a decade. Would her throat even remember how to scream?

Stop. You have a plan in place. You're fixing this.

Ah, hell. Maybe he should just go over there and check

on them, just to be sure. But if he did, he'd have to make sure he either left Momma Billie's before dark or got an escort home. Since the sun was already doing a little dance toward the horizon, and the option behind door number two was *definitely* not happening, he'd have to settle for another text.

Hey, H. You and Momma B okay over there?

The three dots that signaled an incoming message popped up almost immediately on his screen, followed by a photograph of her making a stern face.

We're fine, same as 12 hrs ago, big bro & yes, b4 u ask, I'm doing my HW.

Luke gave up a thin smile and thumb-typed, **Just checking. Goodnight.**

More dots, then, **You do know it's like 7:00, rt? But 'nite. ILU.**

Sitting back against the couch cushions, his fingers hovered over the icon just below Hayley's, the one labeled "QC". He and Quinn had said polite enough goodbyes this morning before parting ways, but the shadows beneath her eyes had said all the things the rest of her hadn't.

I'm scared.

Luke scrolled through his (admittedly short) list of contacts, tapping the icon a few below Quinn's.

Hey Isabella. It's Luke. I'm checking in from Omaha.

At seeing their special code word for the all-clear, she texted back, **Copy that. Sleep tight.**

He took a deep breath and exhaled on a fuck it. **Is Quinn okay?**

She's safe. Sitting here at the Crooked Angel surrounded by half the unit.

Luke's hands were steady even though his pulse wasn't. **I'm glad she's safe. But what I want to know is if she's okay.**

After a beat with no answer, he was certain he'd over-stepped. But then his phone rang in his hand, startling the shit out of him, and he lifted the thing to his ear.

"Hello?"

"You didn't hear this from me," Isabella said by way of greeting, the ambient noise from the bar filtering over the line as she paused to drop her voice. "But she looks like she could use a friend."

"Aren't Shae and January and everyone from Seventeen there?" Quinn had been thief-thick with them since far before he'd even signed up at the academy. Surely she was surrounded by a dozen people who would keep her from feeling alone. All of her friends were more like family than most blood relatives.

"Okay, let me rephrase," Isabella murmured. "She looks like she could use her partner."

A feeling tangled inside of him, one he couldn't readily identify. Luke knew, God, he *knew* he should step away, reclaim the arm's length he relied on to stay sane, to stay safe. This feeling was dangerous. Reckless. Wild. He needed to tamp it down. Snuff it out. Let Quinn's friends take care of her so he could keep her at arm's length and guard himself.

But instead, he heard himself say, "Copy that. I'll be there in fifteen minutes. Just don't let her leave."

One fresh T-shirt and fourteen-plus minutes later, Luke wasn't feeling any less bat-shit than he had when he'd hung up with Isabella. Still, he scanned the parking lot of the Crooked Angel, tucking the keys to his Nissan 370Z into the pocket of his jeans as he covered the space between himself and the door in just a few dozen strides.

This might be crazy, but it wasn't wrong.

Luke tugged open one of the heavy wooden double doors leading into the bar, letting his eyes adjust to the low light and loud music as he took the place in. The crowd was plenty healthy, especially for almost nineteen-thirty on a Thursday night, with more than half the tables in the dining room and most of the space at the bar in the back of the restaurant occupied by people in various stages of eat, drink, and be merry. A few couples dotted the dance floor on the far side of the dining room, including Sam Faurier and a very curvy, very *very* friendly looking brunette, and Detectives Maxwell and Garza sat with Addison Hale at a table by the front entrance. But since Luke had never actually met any of the detectives before this morning, he refrained from lifting his chin in greeting, although their brief gazes told him all three of them had registered his presence, loud and clear. A closer look at the bar in the back of the place revealed Gamble and Kellan on one end, both looking shocked as hell as they caught sight of him, and Isabella, who simply smiled into her beer.

Luke headed through the darkly paneled dining room, leaving the tables, the dance floor, and the jukebox in his wake. "Hey," he said, putting his hands in his pockets and girding up for the heavy ration of shit that was going to be inbound in three, two, one...

"Well, well, look what the cat dragged in!" Kellan said, reaching in to give Luke a brotherly clap on the shoulder despite the fact that Luke had never done anything more than work with the guy. Huh. "It's good to see you out, man, albeit a little weird. Everything alright?"

He stuffed down the events of the last few days in favor of a status-quo smile. "Yeah. Just felt like having a beer tonight, I guess."

"Definitely weird," Gamble said, but Isabella nudged him with her shoulder.

"Oh, don't be grouchy. I think it's great that Slater's out tonight."

Gamble frowned, but somehow Luke was certain she could hold her own against the guy. Gamble might be a big badass former Marine, but a) Isabella had clearly been served a double helping of badassery at the police academy, and b) she lived with Kellan, whose days as an Army sniper weren't *that* far in his rearview. Even if his days of being single sure were.

"I didn't say it wasn't cool," Gamble muttered, looking oddly chagrined. "Only weird. And for the record, I'm not grouchy."

"Oooookay," Kellan interrupted, pausing for a good-natured laugh. "So who needs a beer?"

Gamble crossed his arms over the retaining wall that was his chest, but funny, his frown held more confusion than irritation. "What? I'm *not* fucking grouchy."

"You got it, buddy. Let's go with that," Kellan said, waggling his brows at Isabella as he stepped up to the bar. "Another round? Slater, let's get you that beer, yeah?"

"Actually, I'm going to borrow Slater for a second to introduce him to Hollister. My partner," she added as she looked at Luke, and damn, she was good. "He's right over there talking to Quinn."

Luke took it back. Isabella wasn't just good. The woman deserved a fucking Emmy.

"Okay," Kellan said, dropping a kiss over her temple before unwinding his arm from around her waist. "I'll just hang here with Oscar 'til you get back."

Luke let Isabella usher him from his station-mates before Gamble let loose with a reply by way of his middle finger. The few seconds' worth of ease he'd felt at their back and forth disappeared in a quick strike as soon as he caught sight of Quinn sitting at the other end of the bar. She was still gorgeous—Christ, he'd think so even if she was wearing a clown suit. Her blond hair spilled over the shoulders of her gauzy white blouse, the neckline just low enough to reveal the edges of the lacy pink tank top she wore underneath. She smiled just enough to release those dimples that made him want to do unspeakable things. But the gesture looked cobbled together, too big and too forced for the sadness flickering in her hollow, dark blue stare, and that feeling behind his sternum came roaring back, full speed ahead.

"Hey, you two," Isabella said, smiling her way into the conversation as they arrived beside the two bar stools in the slightly out-of-the-way alcove where Quinn and Hollister had been talking. "Thought we'd come over and say hi."

Quinn made a small noise of shock, but Hollister covered for her, extending his hand to Luke for a firm shake-slash-shoulder bump.

"Hey, man. Good to see you."

Luke nodded, and for as awkward as he'd expected the whole out-and-about thing to be, he had to admit, being at the Crooked Angel could be worse. "Thanks. You, too."

The two detectives excused themselves a few seconds later on the premise of needing to talk shop, leaving him face-to-face with his suddenly wary-eyed partner.

"Why are you here?" Quinn asked.

Whether it was his need to scatter the tension between them or his deeply rooted desire to make her smile for real, even temporarily, Luke couldn't be sure. But he couldn't help it. He laughed.

"It's nice to see you, too."

Quinn's cheeks turned bright pink in the soft overhead

light, and shit, this was going to be an exercise in restraint. "I didn't mean it like that."

"Okay." Luke slid onto the bar stool Hollister had abandoned, his knee brushing against Quinn's in a slide of denim on denim that he felt fucking everywhere. "How did you mean it?"

"We're supposed to be doing what's normal, and for you this"—she paused to sketch an imaginary circle between them with one index finger, then extend the loop to the rest of the bustling bar behind him—"isn't really your normal."

"I was worried about you."

The truth was out before Luke could tidy it up or haul it back. He put the conversation on hold as a tall, edgy-looking brunette sidled up to their table wearing a dark red half-apron and a cat-that-ate-the-canary smile.

"Oooh, I was beginning to think you might be a myth. Slater, right?"

"Yeah," he replied, searching through his memory of all the stories he'd overheard at Seventeen to try and place her. *Ah.*

"Kennedy Matthews. I run the place," she said, just a heartbeat after he'd guessed her identity in his head. She extended a tattooed arm in his direction, her stare shrewd as hell beneath the heavy fringe of her jet-black bangs.

"Nice to meet you," Luke said, meeting her handshake halfway.

"You're keeping good company tonight, Slater. Can I get you anything from the bar?"

He dodged her good-company comment like the hand grenade it was. "Sure." Scanning the surprisingly impressive beer list on the chalkboard over Kennedy's shoulder, he ordered an IPA he'd been meaning to try.

She turned her attention to Quinn. "How about you, sweet pea? You good, or do you want another round?"

"Oh, by all means," Quinn said, her laugh holding very little joy. "Hit me."

The piercing in Kennedy's eyebrow glinted as she raised it, just slightly. "You got it."

Concern twanged in Luke's gut as Kennedy sidled away with their order and Quinn's empty beer bottle. Quinn didn't seem to have had more alcohol than was wise, but still... "How much have you had to drink?"

"Not enough," she muttered. But he didn't let up on his stare, so she added, "Two beers. I promise, I'm not wasted."

Luke exhaled. "Good to know."

"Look, I appreciate your concern, really. But you have nothing to be worried about."

Oh, look. His bullshit detector had just self-destructed. Again. "Right. You're fine, I know."

Her chin jerked up as her stare went from a simmer to a low boil. "Don't."

Luke's heart had risen halfway up his windpipe, but still, he didn't scale back. He *couldn't*. "Don't what, Quinn?" he asked quietly.

Her voice wobbled, although whether it was in anger or sadness, he couldn't be sure. "Don't patronize me."

His body leaned forward of its own volition, his fingers aching to touch her, his mouth ready to do anything to make her believe what he was about to say. "I would never do that to you. I meant what I said. You're clearly off the level here, and I'm worried about you."

For a heartbeat, she simply looked at him, those dark blue eyes churning with the sort of raw emotions he knew he should be guarding himself against. But right now, he could no sooner do that than he could move the goddamn moon to change the tides, so instead, he told her the truth.

"Look, I'm your partner. I told you we'd be in this together, and I want to keep that promise. So please, tell me how I can help you. Tell me what you need."

"Do you really want to know?" Quinn whispered, her stare making it seem like they were the only two people in the bar, or maybe even the world.

Luke swallowed, loosening a breath. "Yes."

Her expression grew steady, and her voice along with it as she said, "I need to get out of here. I need you to take me home."

16

Quinn sat in the passenger seat of Luke's sleek, dark gray sports car, finally able to breathe for the first time in hours. The unease that had clutched at her chest, tightening like a vise with each faked smile and passing minute she'd sat in the Crooked Angel, was finally loosening, allowing her the luxury of a steady inhale/exhale without having to hide the truth from the people who were closest to her. She was in Luke's car, sitting right beside him. His body was right there. Warm. Safe. Close enough for her to reach out and run her hand over his bare forearm, his fingers that were callused in some places, soft in others.

There. Easy. Breathe...

Luke pulled into the parking lot beside her apartment building, quieting the engine without pulling the keys from the ignition. His gaze moved covertly over their surroundings, mirroring the one Quinn had just sent over the adjacent parking spaces, the brightly illuminated walkway connecting the parking lot with the apartment building, the potential spots where someone might lurk or hide.

"Looks clear." It was the first thing he'd said since he'd quietly told Isabella and Hollister he was going to take her home, then paid Kennedy for the beers they didn't drink.

Quinn nodded in agreement. "Mmm hmm."

Heeding the detectives' advice not to dawdle, they both got out of the car, Luke locking the doors with a *click-CLICK* of a button on his key fob before walking her over the paved path leading to the front door of her building. The tension that had made a playground out of her shoulders faded with each step, and she and Luke made their way over the threshold, into the elevator, and down the tastefully carpeted hallway until finally, they were in her apartment.

"I should text Isabella," Luke said, briefly tapping out a message on his cell phone before sliding the thing back into the pocket of his jeans.

"Thank you for bringing me home." Heat climbed Quinn's cheeks as she grew aware of how very alone they were, standing there in her dusky foyer with nothing but the soft light filtering in from the one bulb she always left lit over the kitchen sink. But Luke was the only person she didn't have to hide anything from. The only person who could get her to breathe. The only person she could be truthful with.

And the truth was, she wanted him.

It seemed completely contradictory that her body should respond in such a primal, greedy way when her brain was a jumbled mess. That was just the thing, though. Her thoughts were a mess around her friends. They were a mess when she tried to work, and they were definitely a mess whenever she remembered the kidnapping. The only time her mind *wasn't* on overdrive was when she thought of Luke, with his hand on her rib cage and his breath in her ear, as steady as a heartbeat.

God, she wanted his touch so badly, she ached.

"Do you want to talk about what's going on with you?" he asked, his eyes steady on hers even through the shadows of her foyer.

"Honestly?" She stepped toward him and shook her head. "No."

"Quinn—"

"Please, just stop. I don't want to talk about the other day. I don't even want to think about it."

Luke opened his mouth, likely to argue, but she cut him off before he could say so much as a syllable. "Look, I'm not stupid, okay? I know I can't ignore things entirely. I'm not foolish or flighty enough to think I can magically make the truth into something it's not. But you asked me what I need, and right now I need to *not* remember what happened, just for a little while."

A pause opened between them. Quinn's heart raced so rapidly she was certain he had to be able to register the constant *thump-thump-thump* from where he stood.

Finally, he said, "What else do you need?"

For a question that had the potential to be so complicated, her answer was shockingly simple, and even though she knew it made her vulnerable, she didn't hesitate.

"Just for tonight, I need to feel something other than scared. I need to remember what it's like to feel good." She moved closer, until she could feel his exhale coast over her cheek. *Yes. This. I need this.* "So please, can you stay for a while and make me feel right again?"

"Quinn." He looked at her, his eyes flaring with emotions she couldn't read. "I don't want you to regret asking me that question."

"I don't want you to regret saying yes if it's what you want, too," Quinn whispered back. "But I wouldn't ask if I wasn't sure. I meant what I said the other day, just like I mean what I'm saying now. I want you. I've wanted you for a long time, Luke. I—"

He cut her off by closing the space between them in a single move. His mouth was on hers an instant later, hot and hungry and so unbelievably perfect that she nearly cried out. Letting her arms knot around his shoulders, Quinn pushed to her toes, lining up her soft, needy curves with the hard plane of Luke's chest and abs and hips.

Oh God, more. She wanted more.

She wanted *everything*.

Quinn deepened the kiss, darting her tongue over the threshold of her lips in search of his, and Luke tightened his hands around the back of her waist. His touch made a shiver rise up her spine, and it spread out over her skin as another shot of want built low in her belly. Swirling his tongue against hers, he tasted and took, retreating just long enough for her to return the favor before he pulled back on a ragged breath.

"Tell me."

"Tell you what?" Quinn blinked through the ambient light, thrown by the question.

But Luke remained perfectly steady. "Tell me what you want."

"I want you," she said, and—oh God, the soft chuff of laughter slipping past his ridiculously talented lips made her pussy grow hot and slick.

"I got that part. But I want to know *exactly* what you want."

Her breath caught in her chest, another tendril of wicked heat uncurling between her legs as she processed his words. "You want me to give you directions?"

One dark brow raised. His lips curled into a devastatingly sexy smile, and he lowered his mouth to her ear. Just shy of contact, he murmured, "You want me to make you feel good, right?"

"Yes." She arched up to give him better access, sliding one hand to the top edge of his jeans as encouragement.

But Luke caught her fingers in his. "You want me to kiss you?"

Quinn's sigh was her only answer as his lips coasted over her earlobe, more promise than action. He continued, "You want me to touch you?" His free hand ghosted over her bare collarbone, the contact so light she was sure she would explode from how badly she wanted more. Reaching lower, he gripped her hips, pulling her close enough to feel the unmistakable ridge of his rock-hard cock against her belly. "You want me to make you come?"

"Yes." Her answer collapsed into a moan. "Please, yes."

Luke stepped back to look at her, his eyes blazing with intensity that she felt in every last part of her body as he said, "Then yeah. Tell me what to do. I want to know everything that makes you hot. Because I promised to make you feel good, and I take both my promises and your pleasure *very* fucking seriously."

Oh. God. "Then kiss me," Quinn whispered, empowered by the soft demand. When he slanted his mouth over hers, she let him linger for only a second before doing exactly what he'd asked.

"Lower, Luke. I want you to take off my shirt and kiss me lower."

Time slowed down and rocketed forward all at once. Luke reached out, his fingers resting on the buttons on the front of her shirt. Funny that his large, strong hands—the same ones that had fought fires and worked tirelessly to save people from grave danger—moved so reverently over the

tiny little buttons on her shirt, gently freeing them from
their moorings as if he had all the time in the world. One by
one, he unfastened each button, revealing first her skin,
then the pink lace halter bra she'd carelessly thrown on
before she'd left her apartment, having no clue that anyone
would see it other than her. Finally, when Luke had loosened the last button, he shifted back to look at her, his eyes
finally settling on hers in the shadows.

"Jesus." His throat worked over a swallow. "You are so
goddamn beautiful."

It was the only thing he said before he did what Quinn
had asked. Tipping her head to the side with one hand, he
kissed a path down her neck, not rushing, but not taking his
time, either. His mouth felt so good, grounding her in the
moment with every slide of his lips and flick of his tongue,
and she was powerless against the moan rising up from
her chest.

"Like this, then?" he murmured against her skin.

She nodded, her hair spilling over them like a curtain.
"Yes, but..."

"But?"

Luke looked up at her, his stare loaded with intensity in
the dusky shadows. Quinn was in such foreign territory here
—all of her past bedroom experience had been give *and*
take. Having the focus solely on her was so unexpected that
she tested her words, and the want that accompanied them,
slowly.

"More," she said. "I want more."

His only answer was to move. Hooking his fingers in her
hair, he slid his mouth over her shoulder, the hammering
pulse point at the base of her neck, the top of her chest
where the lacy edges of her bra gave way to her cleavage.
Every touch sent sparks through Quinn's body, her nipples

tightening and her breath growing heavy with want as he lifted his chin to look at her.

"Tell me," Luke whispered, and understanding hit her all at once. This wasn't just some sexy brand of foreplay designed to turn her on.

He was asking permission to take things to each level, giving her the control to get *exactly* what she needed.

And that power was the hottest fucking thing she had ever felt.

"Kiss me here," Quinn whispered, pulling her bra aside just far enough to expose one aching, upturned nipple. Yes. *Yes.* "And do it until I come."

Luke didn't hesitate. Wrapping one arm around her back to hold her steady while he curled his opposite fingers around the thin lace, he tugged the fabric all the way from her breast, parting his lips over the peak of her nipple.

"*Ah.*" The sound broke from her throat, blending in with his pleasured groan in the shadows of her front hallway. But now that he'd started, Luke was far from shy. He swiped his tongue over her sensitive skin in long, sure strokes, alternating slow, open-mouthed kisses with harder, faster movements that turned the want in Quinn's belly into a screaming, lust-soaked demand. She arched higher, her fingers finding Luke's shoulders, her nails curving against the cotton of his T-shirt, the hard muscles underneath.

He didn't stop. Freeing her other breast from the soft triangle of lace over it, he repeated every kiss, cupping her with firm fingers and holding her fast while he licked and sucked and gave her everything she'd asked for.

"Luke."

Quinn meant to say more. To tell him how good his mouth felt, working her aching nipples in such perfect rhythm. To say how hotly he turned her on, how desperate she was to come, how she was more than halfway there. But somehow, he seemed to already know, as if he could read her simply by touch and taste.

Luke increased the intensity of his movements. There was no longer anything sweet about his ministrations, and God, that just ratcheted Quinn's need all the more. Her clit throbbed behind the seam of her jeans, the friction from his strong, wet mouth on her nipple making her desperate. Hands turning to fists on his shoulders, she clutched at his T-shirt as he took and gave all at once, until finally, she flew apart beneath his touch.

"Yes. Yes, *yes*." Her orgasm surged in from all sides, crashing through all of her pent-up tension. Luke carried her through every blissful wave, softening his touches by small degrees until Quinn released his shoulders, looking up at him in the hushed quiet of her front hallway.

"Are you okay?" he asked, and a laugh surprised her by surfacing from somewhere behind her breastbone.

"Are you serious? I'm *so* much better than okay."

He laughed, too, and God, he was so handsome with that rare smile reaching all the way up to his eyes. "You sounded pretty okay."

Not wanting to break the bubble of the moment, Quinn skimmed her palms over his T-shirt-clad chest, sending a look through her lashes as she pressed closer. "Is this still about what I want?"

Luke's pupils flared. "Yes."

"Then come with me."

Quinn paused for a lightning-fast readjustment of her bra before taking his hand and leading him to her bedroom. Thankfully for her recent untidy streak, the only light came by way of what little slanted past her blinds from the street-lamps below. She maneuvered them to the side of her bed, which was rumpled but, in her defense, mostly made. Pivoting on her heels, she slipped out of her shirt, then her sandals and jeans, putting the same treatment to Luke's T-shirt and jeans before shifting back to look at him.

She made a sound that was intended as an "oh", but it never quite formed an actual word. But honestly, who could blame her? Luke was sexy enough to flip all her switches when he was dressed. Standing here next to her bed in nothing more than a pair of boxers that did damned little to hide how mutual their arousal was? Yeah, he was absolutely *gorgeous*.

"Quinn." He lifted a hand to reach for her, his fingers curling against his palm at the last second.

Her heart pounded at just how much control Luke was offering her. "I want to look at you."

Some strange flash of emotion moved through his stare in response, and for a split second, Quinn nearly recanted. Then, so quickly she couldn't even swear she'd seen it, the emotion was gone, replaced by his usual brand of seriousness, and he nodded in the near-darkness.

"Okay."

Letting go of his gaze, she took in his shoulders and the flat expanse of his chest. His muscles were lean yet beautifully defined, dips and ridges she wanted to survey with her fingers, her lips, her tongue. His skin was dark and smooth, even in the delicious stretch of space between his navel and the waistband of his boxers, and desire punched through her at the outline of his cock pressed thick and proud against the cotton covering it.

Quinn had dropped to her knees before the realization that she would had even fully formed in her brain.

"This"—Luke paused to hiss out a sharp exhale that sent a shot of heat straight to her core as her fingers found the sinfully sexy muscles on either side of his hips—"is supposed to be about what *you* want."

"I know." Her breath grew shallow as his cock jerked in approval he was clearly trying to battle for the sake of propriety. "But I take your pleasure seriously, too. And right now, I want my mouth on you."

Wetness bloomed between her legs when he released a not-quite-steady exhale and lifted his hands in concession. Pushing fully to her knees, Quinn slid her fingers beneath the waistband of his boxers and lowered them with one purposeful tug. An appreciative sigh caught in her throat— sweet Jesus, Luke's cock was as gorgeous as the rest of him— but it lasted for only a breath before she'd parted her lips over him for a taste.

"Ah, *fuck*." His body went rigid, his teeth clamped over his bottom lip as if he were upset at having let the harsh swear fly.

But to Quinn, the word had been a testament to Luke's desire, and God, it just made the ache in her core even stronger. She swirled her tongue over the head of his dick, exploring softly for just a minute before releasing him from her mouth to say, "Tell me."

"What?" He looked at her through heavy lids, although that serious expression of his still showed through his stare.

"Tell me what you want," she murmured. "Please. Let me make *you* feel good, Luke."

She punctuated the request with another glide of her mouth, her breath tightening as he replied with a want-filled exhale.

"If you want me to feel good, all you have to do is not stop."

Taking him farther past her lips, Quinn experimented with everything from light brushes of her mouth to harder, faster draws, using his moans as a guide. She wrapped her fingers around the base of his cock, letting them follow the motions of her lips and tongue. Luke's hips moved in slow rhythm with her mouth, in, then out, rocking with intention over force. The provocative movement made her clit pulse with need so greedy, she dipped her fingers past the lacy edge of her panties, stroking herself with one hand while he filled her mouth with a slow thrust, then another.

"Jesus, Quinn. Are you..."

She fluttered her eyes open just in time to see his ice-blue gaze fixed on the spot where her fingers were buried in the slippery folds of her sex. The look on his face knocked her breath loose—so heated and wild, all she could do was pull back and nod.

An instant later, Luke had scooped her up and guided her over the bed. "You want me to tell you what I really want?" He parted her thighs with a strong press of his dark hands on her lighter skin, and oh God, her pussy felt so empty, she wasn't sure what she wanted more—to cry in frustration or beg him to bury his cock between her legs.

"Yes," Quinn whispered, not trusting her voice to do anything else.

"I want to be where your fingers were." As proof, Luke dragged one fingertip slowly over the seam of her sex, her whole body trembling with need in its wake. "I want to feel the heat of your pussy squeezing my cock." Another glide, and the friction of his finger on the want-soaked lace between her legs made her arch up for more contact, more pressure, more *anything*.

"I want to fuck you until you forget your name."

His words arrived at the same time she said "yes". Luke shifted back for only the briefest of seconds to—thank you, sweet Jesus—slip a condom from the wallet he'd left in the back pocket of his jeans. He returned to the bed, angling his body between her thighs as if he'd never left. But instead of doing any number of deliciously dirty things to her, he surprised her by placing his hands on either side of her face and brushing his mouth over hers. The kiss lasted for only a breath before Luke redistributed his body weight to his knees, his palms coasting over her waist, then her hips, taking her panties with them as they finished the journey down her legs. After rolling the condom into place, he slid the head of his cock over her swollen clit, rubbing deep circles against her overly sensitive skin.

"Ohhhh." Sparks flashed in Quinn's field of vision, begging to become explosions. She gave in to every sensation, each tremble and demand and stroke sending her closer to the release she craved. Luke's cock slipped easily through the wetness between her thighs, and he edged lower, pressing slowly past her entrance until he filled her completely.

For a second, her breath stopped, her pussy clenching at the sudden, stretching pressure. Luke was bowstring tight over her, his eyes squeezed shut and his lips parted with pleasure. The rare show of emotion arrowed right through Quinn, making her heart kick against her breastbone and her belly fill with brand-new want. She'd seen him look sexy, and she'd certainly seen him look serious, even to the point of wild intensity. But his expression right now surpassed anything she'd ever caught on his face, so wide open and pared down that it sent her pulse flying.

With his emotions front and center right here in front of her, Luke was beautiful.

Quinn lifted her hips off the comforter beneath them, just a tiny motion, up and back. It kick-started Luke's awareness, though, and his eyes opened, his gaze falling on hers.

"Christ, Quinn. You feel…"

Whatever he'd planned to say got lost on another press of her hips. Balancing his weight on his forearms, he shifted his position, the hard length of his cock sliding directly over her clit. A noise rumbled in the back of her throat, one part pleasure and the other part a lot more primal. Whatever it was, it seemed to cement his focus, and Luke splayed his hands wide over her shoulders while still keeping the bulk of his weight on his forearms, holding her in place as he began to rock harder.

Desire filled her belly, burning brighter and hotter with each thrust. "Ah, God. *Please*," Quinn moaned, digging her heels into the soft covers on either side of her for better purchase.

"Tell me, baby." Luke's exhale spread out over her shoulder, and he leaned in to place a hot, open-mouthed kiss just below her ear before sliding his dick all the way home.

Quinn's inner muscles contracted again, daring her closer to release, then closer still. *Yes. I want to feel this. Only this.* "Fuck me harder, Luke. Don't stop."

His movements changed, the thrust of his hips growing deeper and more intense as he levered into her, over and again. Keeping up with the same rhythmic tempo, he did just as she'd asked, fucking her hard and slow until the need at her very center reached critical mass. Luke found some sweet, hidden spot deep inside her core—*this. Feel this*—and she came undone with a ragged cry. Quinn knotted her legs around the corded muscles of his waist, leaving not even a sliver of space between their bodies. Luke's muscles flexed and released, the intensity on his face bordering on fierceness as he pistoned relentlessly against her hips, burying himself over and over until finally, he began to shake, her name on his lips as he climaxed.

Quinn kept her eyes wide even though her body felt boneless, spent and hyper-sensitive all at once. Luke lowered his chest over hers, connecting them from their shoulders to where they were still intimately joined, and she memorized every breath, each tiny movement. After some amount of time she had no prayer of measuring, he parted from her body, just long enough to move down the hallway to presumably deal with the condom. The reality they'd checked at the door lurked in the shadows of her bedroom, primed and ready to shatter the moment, but Quinn shook her head, her hair rustling over the bed sheets.

"Not yet," she whispered. Just until the sun came up, she needed to feel good. She needed this feeling of safety. Of being able to breathe. Of closeness to Luke.

Everything else would find her soon enough.

17

L uke sat back in the chair beside Quinn's bed with no less than a dozen feelings winging through his gut. Muted daylight had begun to color the shadows of her bedroom an hour ago, around the same time he'd slipped from her bed to the chair to keep from waking her up. He knew he should feel at least some level of unease at the intimacy he and Quinn had shared. After all, he'd hardly been holding her at arm's length when he'd been naked and buried deep between her legs, and she wasn't just some one-night stand. He needed to recreate the distance he'd sworn by for the last ten years. Arm's length was smarter. *Safer.* Luke knew this because he'd learned it the hardest way possible, from the person who had been closest to him. Letting people in was dangerous.

And yet he couldn't force himself from Quinn's bedroom, and wasn't that just the very definition of fucked straight up.

He frowned, tamping down the thoughts clogging his brain. Okay, so he was strangely low on caution when it came to Quinn. Fine. But being there for her wasn't the equivalent of an emotional exposé, and while he might not want to spill his guts, he also wasn't a dick. He was her partner. Her friend. Despite her insistence to the contrary, she was clearly still struggling with some level of post-traumatic stress from their kidnapping, and Luke had promised to help her. He *wanted* to help her.

Yeah, she'd asked him to make her feel good, and fuck yeah, they'd gone the mutual route to make that happen. But, while he didn't think she was experiencing enough PTSD to warrant an intervention, he did get the feeling she needed more than just a couple of orgasms to get right with her demons.

Luke didn't have to let her in to help her, though. For now, it could just be this.

Quinn shifted, a soft sigh moving past her lips as she rolled over in her sleep. They hadn't talked much after he'd returned to her bedroom post-sex, although oddly, they hadn't really needed to. He'd simply done what had felt right, gathering her up beneath the covers and holding her close. The whole skin-on-skin thing had led to another round of incendiary sex not long after, but again, Luke had wrapped his arms around her afterward, and Quinn had let him, both of them drifting off to sleep together. His eyes had popped open an hour ago in spite of the pre-eight AM hour —thank you, occupational hazard—so he'd just skinned into his jeans and grabbed a medical textbook from the shelf full of them over her dresser and gotten good and comfortable in the chair by her bed. Quinn's cat, Galileo, had moseyed on in to nestle in the covers beside her after Luke had gotten up, so the pair of bright green eyes currently snagging his attention from the bottom of the bedroom doorway? Yeah, can't say he'd been expecting those.

"Hey there." His whisper was barely a sound—a fact that seemed to be much appreciated by the lean, almost lanky black cat currently giving him a full perusal from his sentry spot. After a handful of minutes, Luke went back to reading about the guidelines for rapid sequence intubation. He was still keenly aware of the cat, especially when the little guy edged closer, finally settling directly between the spot where Luke sat and Quinn's bed, as if he wanted to keep an eye on both of them and couldn't decide between the two.

"See you met Max," came Quinn's sleep-heavy voice, and Luke's heart smacked him upside the rib cage.

He covered his surprise, although the whole heavy-lidded, mussed-hair thing she was rocking did nothing to lower his heart rate. "I think it's more like he let me stay."

"She," Quinn corrected gently, sitting up in her bed with a yawn. "And yeah, she had a rough life before I rescued her, so she's pretty skittish. I'm surprised she came out while you're here. She must like you."

"Actually, she seemed to be checking on *you*."

Quinn lifted a shoulder, her eyes dropping from his by a fraction, but it was enough. "I'm fine."

Nope. Not this time. Luke closed the textbook in his lap, placing it carefully on the nearby dresser before leaning forward to look at her. "Look, I'm not trying to pick a fight with you." He gave her a second to digest that truth before unloading the one that would sting more. "But we both know you're not fine."

Her blue eyes flashed in the early-morning sunlight slanting in past the blinds. "Yes, I am," she said. Still, her tone refused to back up the words, and as much as it made Luke feel like a limited-edition dickhead, he pushed back.

"I've watched you be fine for the last seven months. What's going on with you now"—he paused to gesture to the way she'd defensively yanked the covers over her tank top-clad shoulders even though the move had sent a sucker punch right to the middle of his chest—"isn't that, Quinn. You're not fine."

"I..." She trailed off. Pressing her lips into a tight line, she closed her eyes. "I *want* to be fine."

Emotion threatened, doubling up and growing teeth at the sight of the unshed tears brightening Quinn's stare when she reopened her eyes to look at him.

"But you're right. I'm not. I'm scared."

She aimed her whisper at the yellow and white covers in front of her. Luke fought the abrupt and very real urge to rip back the blankets and sheets, to hold her close and do damn near anything necessary to wipe the fear from her face.

Quinn needed room to let her emotions out. And even if it killed him, he needed to give it to her.

"I just...I keep waiting for this feeling, this terrible sense of dread to fade, you know?" she asked, her sights still locked on the blankets puddled around her. "I thought work would make things better. Maybe take my mind off being scared and help me focus. But this stupid fear keeps following me like a cloud. I can't get rid of it no matter what I do."

"Your fear isn't stupid," Luke said. Christ, she'd had a *gun* to her head. Ice had threatened to kill her and everyone she loved. If fear wasn't a legitimate response to the memory of that, he had no goddamn clue what was.

Quinn, however? Didn't look so convinced. "It is when it keeps me from doing my job. God, Luke, I can't even get through an entire shift without wanting to throw up. The only two things I've ever been able to rely on no matter what are the job and the people in that fire house, and now I don't have either."

Confusion washed over him. Not having her friends, he got—Sinclair had been wildly clear about not letting so much as a whisper drop about the kidnapping and the subsequent investigation the intelligence unit was currently up to their eye teeth in. But...

"What do you mean, you can't rely on the job?"

Quinn crossed her arms over the front of her tank top, Luke's confusion backsliding into something a lot more visceral at the sight of the uneasy flush climbing her cheekbones. "Garrity wouldn't clear me for work unless I agreed to go back and see him again."

Ah hell. No wonder she'd been so fully off-center when she'd returned from the guy's office two days ago. "Did he say why?"

"No. But be clearly feels like we have some unfinished business that needs to be talked out before I'm okay to do my job without a weekly check-in."

"Maybe," Luke allowed. But Quinn already seemed to know the score, and frankly, as much as he wanted to help her, he wasn't about to bullshit her in order to do it. "But he also clearly doesn't think you're totally unfit to be on the rig, otherwise he never would've let you go back to Seventeen at all, right?"

Her chin lifted as if the thought hadn't occurred to her. "Oh. Well, I guess not."

"And you feel like you'll be okay to be back on ambo tomorrow?"

"Of course," Quinn said, zero wiggle room in her tone. "I mean, yeah, this whole thing scares the shit out of me, but I wouldn't put anyone's health at risk just to make myself feel better. I want to get back to normal and take care of people again." Now her voice did soften, the waver traveling on a direct path from her words to Luke's gut. "I'm just so tired of feeling scared and alone."

"You're not alone."

Pushing to his feet, he covered the space between the chair and her bed in a pair of strides. Yes, this was dangerous, and yes, he knew he should be exercising a hell of a lot more caution—or at the very least, not cupping Quinn's beautiful face and brushing a kiss over her addictively soft lips.

But right now, in this moment, as he sat here in front of her and listened to her admit the fears that had been weighing so heavily on her shoulders for the past week straight, Luke didn't give one shit about caution.

"I'm your partner, remember?" he said, pulling back just far enough to look her in the eye. "I'll be with you at the fire house, and if you need me outside of Seventeen, I can be here, too."

Slowly, she nodded. "I would really like that."

Quinn lifted her mouth to his. The kiss quickly deepened, his cock growing hard at the feel of her eager tongue in his mouth and her hands on his body, and as he lay her back over the bed sheets to gain better access to the warm, wet heat between her thighs, Luke swore to himself it would only be this.

ICE LOOKED AT THE SKINNY, strung out blonde in front of him in the alley and contemplated murder. Not of the woman herself—to the contrary, she'd just proved pretty fucking useful, even if her loyalty was way more to the blow she got from Damien than to Ice personally. But if what she was telling him was in any way on the level, he was going to kill someone, and it wouldn't be merciful.

"Start at the beginning and tell me again."

The blonde—Cheryl? No, wait, Cherise—shifted her weight from one cheap stiletto to the other, picking at the already chipped polish on her stubby fingernails. Ice had exactly one more go-round with the intel before this chick went into full on tremors. Not that he wouldn't get her high as a motherfucking satellite to get the information he needed, but still. Pumping her for details he could actually use would be a hell of a lot easier if she was at least relatively sober.

"I was hanging out down on the pier last night, getting down with the usual Friday night crowd," she said, and Ice easily made the translation to her giving ten-dollar blowjobs and scoring whatever pharmaceuticals she could snort or shoot up. Not that he was offended by that—after all, business was business.

"Okay," he said, and Cherise continued.

"Around nine thirty, I got hungry, so I went to Three Brothers. You know, the pizza place? It's over by that bodega. They make, like, the best calzones."

Ice nodded, wanting her to get the hell on with the important shit, but not so much that she screwed up exactly what she'd seen and heard. "I know the place."

"Right. Well, I was sitting in the back, minding my own business and stuff, when these two people I'd never seen before came in and started talking to Carmen. She was working behind the counter. I know her from back when she used to be one of Bobby D.'s girls, like a year and a half ago, before he went up the river for killing that one chick. Anyway"—Cherise took a cigarette from the wrinkled pack in her purse, her Day-Glo pink lighter snicking softly as she lit the thing and blew a stream of smoke toward the brick wall over Ice's shoulder—"these two kinda caught my attention because they looked a little too clean to be on the pier on a Friday night. They seemed awful chatty, like maybe they knew Carmen or something. The woman was asking her how's business, and the guy ordered a couple of slices. Tipped her real good, too."

Cops. Nobody tipped the counter help at Three Brothers unless they were getting something in return.

"Did you hear any specifics from their conversation?" Ice asked, turning over the possible scenarios in his head. Just because he wanted to rip a path down to North Point's pier and beat the truth out of this ex-hooker directly didn't mean it was a smart move. With only a week to go before this deal with Sorenson shook out, he had to be more careful than fucking ever. Plus, if she was working an honest job, and a shit one at that, chances were high this Carmen bitch didn't know anything useful, anyway. He'd certainly never heard of her. She wasn't one of his boys' regulars, for sex or for drugs.

Cherise took another sharp drag from her cigarette. "Not a lot. They kept their voices low enough that I couldn't make out much. But I did hear Carmen say she didn't know anything about no guy named Damien." The words made Ice's exhale just a fraction easier as she continued. "The only guy I know by that name is right there."

She paused to point at Damien, who leaned against the graffiti-covered wall at the mouth of the alley, standing guard over Ice's conversation. It might be the middle of the day, but a man couldn't be too careful.

"When I told him these two randos might have been asking about him, he got all jumpy," Cherise said, shrugging her too-bony shoulders. "Didn't even want the blowjob he paid for. Just dumped me in his car and brought me here to you."

Ice tilted his head. At least Damien had had the mental capacity to realize this probably wasn't a coincidence. They'd been as careful as possible to cover up all signs of the drive-by and kidnapping, scrubbing both the flophouse and the abandoned warehouse of any potential physical evidence. Ice had been left with no choice but to dump Jayden's body—burying the guy in his backyard had hardly been a fucking option. But he'd chosen a remote location hours from Remington, one he knew would remain undisturbed for a good, long time.

So now all he had to do was figure out if those goddamn paramedics had gone squawking to the 5-0, or if Damien had stirred up some crap of his own that had gotten him noticed.

First things first. He had to put a proper ID to these asshole cops. "Can you tell me what these two looked like?"

"The woman was Hispanic. Long dark hair, leather jacket. I remember, because I liked it. The guy was a redhead. Sorta big. Nice ass. Oh!" Cherise's eyes brightened beneath the heavy layer of makeup weighing them down. "His name was weird, like one of those last names you use as a first name. Hollander, or something stupid like that. Carmen gave him a bunch of attitude and I heard her say it. But to be honest, I thought she was pretty stupid not to be nice to him. A guy like that, who's hot *and* giving her money?" Now her eyes glinted, her mouth curling into a mercenary smile. "If it were me, I'd be riding that shit all the way to the bank."

"I have no doubt you would," Ice said, all truth. "You were smart to come to Damien with this, Cherise."

"Yeah?" She cocked her hip, her thin black miniskirt riding higher over her thighs. "How smart?"

Ah, a negotiation. Ice's cock stirred at the prospect. "Smart enough for me to get you high right now. Or..."

"Or?"

"We could strike a deal. You know this woman who works at Three Brothers, right? Carmen?"

Cherise nodded. "We're not real close, but I know her good enough. Yeah."

"Get some information about how she knows these two and exactly who they are, and I'll give you a whole lot more than a one-time high."

Cherise took a step forward, crossing her arms over her skimpy top to push her tits front and center. "I'd be listening a whole lot better if you'd say a number."

Oh, yeah. Between the prospect of outsmarting these cops and the promise of punishing whoever was responsible for the sudden spotlight, he was *definitely* fucking hard now.

Ice rattled off a number that made Cherise smile. "That's for reliable information. Don't even think about giving me the runaround or double-crossing me."

"Wouldn't dream of it," she purred. "But I want half upfront *and* the high right now. Then you've got yourself a deal, sweetheart."

Of course she'd had to rely on an endearment, because he hadn't told her his name. Shit, between his sunglasses, his hoodie, and her post-high fog, she hadn't even gotten a halfway-decent look at his face.

"You drive a hard bargain. I like that," Ice said, reaching into his pocket for the roll of cash he always kept there and the small baggie of heroin he'd known he'd need the minute Damien had called him, and *bingo*. Cherise's pupils dilated, giving away her despair.

Peeling off a few bills, he held the money and the H just out of her reach. "But I drive an even harder one, so here it is. You'll get your high and your half upfront, but we're going to have to start on an even playing ground, and right now, you owe me."

"What?" Cherise blinked, and if Ice had been in possession of a soul, he might have actually felt bad for her. But she'd chosen to negotiate with the wrong businessman. He wasn't about to walk away from a deal without every single thing he'd damn well earned.

"It seems you still have an unsettled debt with Damien." He let his eyes drop to her mouth to get his meaning all the way home, his cock standing straight up as she parted her lips in realization.

"What, for the blowjob? He said he wasn't interested, remember?"

Ice laughed. "Oh, I remember. But it was bought and paid for, and Damien is my associate. You answer to him, he answers to me. Which means you owe *me* for your payday. So get on your knees and pay up like a good girl. Otherwise I'll make it so you can't score so much as a goddamn aspirin in this city ever again."

And as she undid his jeans and started sucking him off with that not-so-clever mouth, Ice grabbed her hair, fucking her face hard enough to make her gag as he thought of nothing but revenge.

18

Quinn blew out a breath and looked at Washington Boulevard for the ninetieth time before she declared herself totally insane. The street in front of Station Seventeen looked just as it always did at six thirty in the morning, with daylight beginning to illuminate the brownstones and storefronts on either side of the block and the yellow caution lights blinking out a steady sign that the fire house was business as usual.

"Just breathe. You've got this." Quinn repeated the words Luke had said to her in some form or another over the course of the last twenty-four hours. She hadn't meant to open her mouth and let her fear spill all over the place yesterday morning. But there he'd been, sitting next to her bed with that calm, quiet stare that made her feel so safe and yet strong at the same time, and her feelings had been out before she could press them back.

Luke had been there. He'd been threatened by Ice, just as she had. He understood.

And when he said they were going to be okay, she believed him.

Getting out of her Mazda, Quinn triple-checked that the locks were engaged and the sidewalk was clear before walking the half-block to Station Seventeen's front door. They kept the house locked up tight during non-business hours and the garage bays closed whenever they weren't in use, but the keypad mounted next to the doorframe gave her access to the front lobby, and she stepped all the way inside the warm, empty space.

Her heart tapped faster in her chest, but for the first time in a week, it was rooted in more comfort than fear. Laughter-tinged voices filtered in from the hallway leading to the bunks and the locker room, just like it always did pre-shift change. The buttery scent of Hawk's homemade biscuits wafted from the kitchen, making Quinn's mouth water and her stomach sound off in a snarl that probably would've made even the meanest of junkyard dogs quake and head for cover. The unease that had gripped her so tightly just a few days ago slipped, and she managed to get an inhale past the pressure in her lungs.

She was okay. She was back at work, ready to spend the next twenty-four hours taking care of people who needed help. The intelligence unit was going to find Ice and eliminate the threat to her and to everyone she cared about.

She would be safe. She *had* this.

"Hey. There you are," came a voice from behind her, and despite the fact that she was smack dab in the center of one of the most secure facilities in at least a five-mile radius, Quinn whirled around with a full-body flail.

"Oh *jeez!*" she yelped, her pulse rocketing fast enough that, truly, someone should probably alert NASA. "You two scared the crap out of me."

"Sorry," January said, and Shae matched the blonde's apologetic expression. "We didn't mean to startle you."

Quinn splayed a hand over the front of her green and white top, readjusting the duffle bag on her shoulder as she managed a soft laugh. "No, it's okay. I must've been distracted by the smell of Hawkins making breakfast." Eh. Not the best twist of the truth she'd ever brewed up, but for a pinch, it'd do.

Shae, bless her, fell for it hook, line, and biscuit. "Preach, sister. That man's culinary skills are amazeballs. I would do unspeakable things for his chicken cacciatore. Just saying."

The three of them fell into step together, headed toward the locker room. "At any rate, I'm glad you're finally feeling better," Shae continued. "You hightailed it out of the Crooked Angel pretty early the other night. Dempsey and Gates had a beer or six too many and talked Kennedy into busting out the karaoke machine. You missed out on some serious fun. Also, *major* blackmail material."

Quinn eked out a laugh. "That does sound fun."

"Mmm," January said, turning toward Shae, and—oh no, no no—Quinn registered the knowing glint in her eyes just a half-second too late. "I don't think she missed out on *all* the fun. Slater gave her a ride home."

Shae's boots clattered to an ungraceful halt on the linoleum at the same time Quinn's heart clattered, full-speed ahead. "Shut up! I didn't even know he was *there*, much less that he gave you a ride home!"

"He was, and he did." January's smile turned contrite when the heat tearing a path over Quinn's face had clearly translated to a blush. "Sorry," January said. "But I work at the Crooked Angel, too, you know. No way was Kennedy not sharing that dirt with me."

Quinn inwardly cursed her jumbled brain for blanking

on the fact that January filled in behind the bar a couple nights a week when Kennedy needed extra hands.

"It's not *dirt*," she argued, spectacularly failing at her effort not to fidget. For God's sake, she'd never needed a poker face with her friends in her life. Of course she sucked at this. "I wasn't feeling great, so Slater gave me a ride home." Truth.

Then he stayed and didn't leave until five o'clock this morning, and, oh hey, here's a fun fact: I actually lost count of how many mind-altering orgasms he gave me with his mouth alone.

Hashtag moretruth.

"How did you not tell me this, you tricky bitch?" Shae asked, although her monster-sized grin canceled out any heat the words might have possibly carried. "Seriously. Does the girl code mean nothing to you?"

Quinn couldn't help it. She let a soft puff of laughter escape. "There's...you know, not much to, um. Tell?"

At her friends' twin expressions of *are you kidding me*, Quinn caved. "Okay. Okay!" she admitted, shushing the immediate stream of near-giggles that followed even though —damn it—she was giggling a little, too. "There might be a teensy bit to tell."

"Oh my God. You besmirched the rookie!" Shae crowed, clapping her hands with glee. "You did, didn't you? Please tell me there was besmirching. I have been *dying* for you two to get it on!"

Quinn shot a glance up and down the hallway. She might be willing to confide in two of her closest friends, but telling the whole fire house she'd had thirty-six hours' worth of white-hot sexcapades with her co-worker so wasn't part of her game plan. "There was some...God, Shae, Capelli's giant brain is really rubbing off on you. Is besmirching honestly even a word?"

"Oh, I'm sorry, would you prefer the term wild monkey sex?" Shae asked.

January snorted. "Gotta admit, she has a point. The deed is the deed, girl. No matter what you want to call it."

The thought made Quinn pause. Yes, she and her friends were closer than most, and yes again, they usually did a fair amount of dishing on their sex lives. That didn't change the fact that a) Luke was a pretty private guy, who—oh, by the way—also worked with them; and b) Quinn couldn't really explain to January and Shae what had brought her closer to Luke without talking about the kidnapping. She had to keep things close to the vest, at least until the intelligence unit put Ice behind bars.

"Okay, yes. Luke and I slept together," Quinn said, because no way would either of them let her off the hook without at least that much. Speaking of which... "And before you badger me, Shae, yes. It was fantastic."

"I knew it," Shae sing-songed, but now it was time to nip the rest in the bud.

"It's also not that big of a deal," Quinn said, although ouch, the words felt as ill-fitting as a five-inch stiletto after a long day of work. "We're spending more time together now, and things just sort of...happened. But what's going on with us is casual." Annnnd more ouch.

January either seemed to get the hush-hush vibe or be content with the sparse details, because she said, "Well, I think it's great."

"I told you he was into you," Shae murmured, straightening a second later when Faurier came whistling down the hallway from the locker room.

"Oh, hey, Copeland." He stopped to give her a charming smile, per his MO with any woman over the age of twenty-one who also maintained a steady heartbeat. "You feeling better today? You kinda had us worried with that stomach thing."

"Oh, she's feeling better, all right," Shae said, letting out a soft *ooof* when Quinn directed a not-so-subtle elbow into her friend's rib cage. Both January's and Shae's expressions suggested they were T-minus one heartbeat away from devolving into a fit of laughter, and gah, Quinn bit her lip as hard as she could to keep herself from following suit.

"I feel great," Quinn managed. Barely. "Thanks for asking."

Faurier's light brown brows tucked in confusion. "Okaaay. Did I miss something major, or is this one of those feminine mystique things I'm not going to get because I'm from Mars, or whatever?"

"Mystique," Quinn barked out before Shae or January could say another word. "Mmm hmm. Yep! Definitely that."

"Right." He took a cautious step backward on the polished floor tiles, and God, Quinn really couldn't blame the poor guy. "Well, I'll see you ladies at roll call."

"See you, Sam."

As soon as he was out of earshot, Quinn turned toward January and Shae, stuffing back her smile and trying on her very best and-I-mean-it face. "Cone of silence, you two. Seriously."

They both sobered. "Okay. Of course," January said, and Shae lifted one finger to draw an imaginary *X* over the front of her uniform, right next to the RFD crest.

"We've got your back, girl. Even if Slater's got your front."

With one last round of laughter, Shae and January resumed their trip toward the common room, while Quinn aimed herself at the locker room. She knew she couldn't forget what had happened last week. Hell, she'd had to coach herself through walking the half a block from her car to the stupid building less than fifteen minutes ago. But these small pockets of goodness were better than nothing, and they were *definitely* better than the full-time dread she'd felt directly after the kidnapping.

They reminded her how to breathe.

Going through the motions of changing into her uniform and stowing her street clothes in her locker, Quinn got ready for the shift ahead of her. Her heart played epic-battle hopscotch with her rib cage when Luke ducked into the locker room, but other than to give her a quick, too-sexy-to-be-just-friendly smile, he treated her exactly as usual—nothing awkward or out of the ordinary. The pure comfort of her routine wrapped around her like a blanket, and by the time she got through both roll call and breakfast, the dread that had threatened to sideline her had been mostly relegated to a back shelf in her mind.

"So." Quinn pulled herself up into the back of the loaner ambulance, sliding a glance at the spot where Luke sat across from her as she unzipped her first-in bag to check her inventory. "We never did get to that sign language lesson last week."

His expression went blank, his unreadable blue stare traveling out over the engine bay. "No. I guess we didn't."

Although they'd talked quite a bit in between trips to her bedroom (and her living room couch...and once to her shower, which she'd never be able to look at the same way again, thank you very much), the conversations had mostly focused on her—what kind of movies she liked and what she did in her spare time and fire house stories from before he'd joined Seventeen. But whenever Quinn had tried to ask Luke about himself in return, he'd adopted the same impenetrable expression and either given the bare minimum of a reply or swung the focus back around to her.

She trapped her tongue between her teeth, and for a heartbeat, she nearly kept it there. Maybe she hadn't been off the mark when she'd told Shae and January what was happening with Luke was no big deal. They might be partners—okay, partners with benefits—but that didn't mean he owed her an all-access pass to his personal life.

But then Quinn caught a flash of emotion in his eyes, brief but definitely *there*, and the truth slapped into her all at once.

Luke wasn't blowing her off. He was trying to build trust.

And Quinn wanted him to trust her with his emotions, the same way she trusted him with hers.

"Look," she said, keeping her voice wholly matter-of-fact. "I know you don't like to go prime time with your personal stuff. We don't have to talk about your sister if you really don't want to. But I'd still like to learn some sign language. You know, if you're still willing to teach me a few things."

Luke sat back on the bench seat, his dark brows lifted up toward his closely cropped hairline. "Okay. Sure."

After a quick pause to make sure their first-in bags were properly stocked and their equipment was in good working order, Luke motioned for her to sit in the seat across from him in the back of the ambulance.

"It'll be easier to teach you if we're face-to-face," he explained, settling back on the gray vinyl of the bench. He sent another quick glance out to the engine bay, where the sounds of both engine and squad getting their house chores done echoed off the walls in muted tones.

A smile tugged at the corners of Quinn's mouth when he turned his attention back to her and kept talking. "Being fluent in ASL is more than just memorizing a bunch of signs. It's like any other language, with its own grammar, terminology—even slang."

"Wow," she said. "I had no idea it was so complex."

"Most people don't. A lot of signs are based on letters, and some things like names have to be finger-spelled, so the best thing for you to learn first is the alphabet."

Made sense. "Okay," Quinn said, but after twenty minutes of Luke's teaching and her subsequent fumbling, she couldn't help but frown.

"You're wondering how you got yourself into this mess, aren't you?" she asked, letting him adjust her finger placement for the letter P.

Funny, Luke shook his head. "Not really." He let go of a small smile, his fingers brushing over hers with just enough heat to be both encouraging and distracting as hell. "I mean, you've been patient with teaching me how to start IVs and run rapid trauma assessments. I have to imagine that's harder than this."

Quinn looked at her hands, which clunked along in such a poor imitation of his fluid motions, and ugh, she doubted it. "Nah. You're a really quick study." She laughed, because it was either that or throw her hands up in frustration. "Okay, seriously. You make it look far too easy. How are you so good at this?"

"I've had ten years of practice," Luke said, the words sending a prickle of surprise up Quinn's spine.

"Your sister wasn't born deaf?" The young woman in the photo on his phone had definitely looked older than ten. Luke had told Sinclair she was already in high school, so...

"I, ah. No." His shoulders snapped together beneath his navy blue RFD T-shirt. "She wasn't born deaf."

Shit. She hadn't meant to push. "You know what, we can just—"

"Hayley contracted bacterial meningitis just after her seventh birthday."

Luke's words arrived so quietly that at first, Quinn wasn't entirely certain she'd heard them. Her chest squeezed in response. But she wanted to give him room to share at his own pace, so she didn't say anything, and after a beat of silence and a few more small tweaks of her letter-signs, he continued.

"At first, my grandmother and I thought Hayley had the flu. She had a nasty fever and chills and aches."

"Those are all symptoms that point to the flu," Quinn agreed gently. God, they saw it all the time, especially in the colder months when people were cooped up inside.

"That's what her pediatrician said, too. Then, after a couple days of not getting any better, she began to get confused. Her fever spiked to a hundred and five, so we took her to the ED. But by then, her infection was already off the charts."

Luke braced his forearms over his thighs, her lesson temporarily forgotten as he dropped his chin toward the floor of the ambulance. His expression was loaded with remorse, and even though Quinn found it odd that he hadn't mentioned his parents, she also knew that pushing to find out why only had the potential to make him clam up.

So she voiced what was in her heart rather than in her head. "I'm so sorry, Luke. An illness like meningitis is just awful."

He nodded, although he'd blanked the emotion from his face as if it had never existed. "Once she was diagnosed, the doctors treated her aggressively. She recovered well, all things considered, but the damage was done. Hayley's been profoundly deaf since then."

"Wait." Quinn did some rudimentary math in her head, still coming up confused. "This was ten years ago, right? So you were, what..."

"Fourteen," Luke said.

Whoa. "That seems like a lot for a fourteen-year-old to have on his shoulders."

A shadow flickered through his eyes, turning his stare to steel. "It's been just the three of us for a long time. I didn't really have a choice."

"Of course you didn't," Quinn said, and oh, how she meant it. She knew all too well how much of a non-question it was to care for a loved one when they were sick and needed help. Even when you were too young for the role. "But kids aren't usually vaccinated for meningitis until they're eleven or twelve. Plus, there's no way you or your grandmother could have known Hayley would get so sick, so fast, or that she would have the complications she did. I'm not saying you shouldn't have taken on such a big responsibility." Her heart squeezed, pressing hard against her breastbone. "But I *am* saying you shouldn't blame yourself. It sounds like you're a pretty great older brother."

For a minute, then another, Luke simply looked at her, his face as unreadable as ever. But then his fingers flexed, his body shifting like he was about to reach out to her...

And the jarring sound of the all-call stopped him short.

Engine Seventeen, Squad Six, Ambulance Twenty-Two, Battalion Seventeen. Structure fire, ninety-two ten Bayside Avenue. Be advised. Police are en route to the scene. Requesting immediate response.

Quinn's heart rattled in her rib cage. The police were never called to a scene unless there were reports of an active crime. "That's down on the pier." Despite her best efforts, her voice shook. "Right in the middle of North Point."

"We've got this," Luke told her, his boots thumping on the concrete floor as he jumped down to the engine bay. Rather than hustling toward the ambo's passenger seat, though, he swiveled on his heels and reached up for her hand. "We're in it together, remember?"

There. Easy. Breathe.

Quinn inhaled. Set her resolve. And took his hand.

"Then let's go help someone who needs it."

19

L   ike many of the other establishments on North
     Point's pier, Three Brothers Pizzeria was a nonde-
     script little hole in the wall. Small space. Aging
storefront. Faded sign.

What set the place apart from everything else right now
was the dark gray smoke puffing from the pair of shattered
front windows and the handful of people either looking on
or filming the whole thing with their cell phones.

Quinn's heart pounded not only at the possibility of
someone posting a potential rescue—or worse, a fatality—
online, but of said post going viral when all she wanted to
do was keep every single person at Seventeen on the down
low for their safety.

God, sometimes the information age really fucking
sucked.

"Okay, everybody, listen up." Captain Bridges's voice
snapped over the two-way from the spot where he was
stationed in front of the pizzeria. "We've got reports of one
person still inside the kitchen on the Charlie side of the
building. A nine-one-one operator had the woman on the

line until a minute ago when the connection cut out, but the woman also reported a break-in and an assault, so we are waiting on RPD to respond."

"Damn," Luke murmured from beside her, and the dread in Quinn's belly knotted harder as she scanned the scene. The fire didn't look terribly bad, but now that Bridges mentioned it, the windows did appear to have been purposely smashed, one of them bearing several spider web-style points of impact around the actual hole in the plate glass. Still, if there was someone inside with bad intentions, protocol dictated they wait for the police to arrive on-scene.

"That fire's not getting any smaller," said Hawkins, not mincing any words. "If we have entrapment, we need to get in there, Cap. Bad guy be damned."

Especially if dispatch had lost contact with the woman inside, Quinn thought to herself. Between the fire and the reported assault, she could be hurt any number of ways. But the brass on both sides took active crime scenes very freaking seriously. No action without approval.

"Hold. I'm getting a police update from dispatch," Bridges said. Although the pause was literally only about seven seconds long, it felt like an eternity passed before he continued. "A suspect was seen fleeing the scene five minutes ago. RPD will be on-scene in two minutes, but they've given us the go-ahead to respond with caution. Hawkins, you and Gates take the primary entrance here on the Alpha side for search and rescue. Gamble, you and Walker take the point of entry on the Charlie side. McCullough and Dempsey, get those lines prepped. Go. And keep your eyes open, all of you."

A stern "copy that" came in over the radio from each responder. With her already-gloved hands wrapped around the bright yellow push bar on the gurney she and Luke had taken out of the ambo just in case, Quinn measured her breaths, in and out. Her stomach pitched at the idea that the guy who had done all this damage was still out there.

You know this feeling you have right now? This fear of dying? I want you to remember this feeling...remember it...remember...

Quinn's blood froze, taking her limbs along for the ride. Clammy fingers of dread ghosted up her spine, chilling her skin despite the already-warm late spring morning, and she swiveled a sharp three-sixty over her surroundings, unable to shake the feeling of being watched.

"Quinn?" Luke's voice, quiet with just a tinge of concern, broke past the sudden rush of adrenaline making her shaky. "Hey, are you okay?"

God, she was losing it. "Yeah. Yes." She drummed up a weak smile, feeling surprised when the gesture actually seemed to work on both her and Luke. "I'm a little jumpy," she admitted, giving the smoldering storefront and the growing crowd of onlookers one last careful perusal before turning to look at him fully. "But it sounds like this woman needs help. I'm good to take the call. Really."

"Okay," he said. His belief in her bolstered her confidence another notch, and she cemented her focus. Running through her mental checklists and listening closely to the exchanges on the two-way, she let the routine of the job she'd always relied on calm her as Kellan located the woman in the kitchen and Hawkins and Gates cleared a safe path for him to fall out.

Go. Go now. Do your job. Take care of this woman.

Quinn and Luke met Kellan halfway over the worn, silvery boards lining the pier's main drag. "Found her in the kitchen, away from most of the smoke. She's breathing and conscious, but out of it," he said.

"Let's get her on the gurney so we can see what we're dealing with," Quinn instructed. Her muscle memory won out in the throw-down against her jitters at being back in North Point, and she reached out to do her part in securing the woman, her brain immediately launching into a rapid trauma assessment.

"Strong pulse. Good breath sounds. Multiple facial contusions and lacerations." Quinn's pulse kicked, and she reached for the C-collar she'd thankfully grabbed out of the rig when they'd unloaded the gurney. Stabilizing the woman's spine was a precaution, but with the beating she'd obviously taken, it wasn't one Quinn was willing to overlook. "No obvious deformity to the extremities." At least they had *that* on their side.

"Copy that." Luke got the leads into place while she got the C-collar around the woman's neck and shifted into her line of sight. Kellan hadn't been wrong—she was definitely dazed, her blinks slow and sluggish as she clearly tried to track what was going on around her. Not unusual for a little smoke inhalation with a whole lot of shock on top.

"Ma'am? I'm here to help you. My name is Quinn, and I'm a paramedic with the Remington Fire Department. Can you tell me your name?"

"Her name is Carmen." The revelation—from Kellan, of all people—whoa-Nellied Quinn into place. But then he went for broke in the holy-shit department when he reached for the two-way on the shoulder of his turnout gear and said, "Walker to Command, requesting dispatch call Detective Moreno from the Thirty-Third to the scene immediately."

"Ugh," Carmen moaned, as if the words had broken through some sort of haze. "She's gonna...be a pain in my ass over this, pretty boy. It was just a stupid smash and grab."

"Yeah, yeah," Kellan said, the look on his face tough even though his voice was softer than Quinn had ever heard it. "She's coming anyway. Now behave while Quinn and Luke take care of you. I've got a fire to help knock down."

He was gone before Quinn could ask how the hell he knew a woman who worked at Three Brothers or why Isabella would need to haul herself to North Point for a robbery call on a Sunday morning, but it was just as well. Quinn had bigger fish to fry; namely making sure Carmen didn't have any bigger injuries lurking beneath her superficial cuts and bruises.

"Okay, Carmen," she said, checking the woman's vitals as they flashed over the monitor. BP and heart rate were a little elevated, but considering the circumstances, that was pretty damned understandable. "Can you tell me if anything hurts?"

"I got the crap kicked out of me, Blondie. Of course shit hurts."

"She's just trying to help you," Luke interjected with a frown, but Quinn had treated enough people to know that everyone reacted differently to pain.

And fear.

"It's okay, Carmen. I get it," Quinn said, because she really freaking did. "I'm just trying to figure out how to fix you up and get you out of here, alright?"

That bought her a pause. "Can you take this neck thing off?" Carmen reached blindly for the C-collar, her body tense and her frown on full display. "It's too fucking tight."

"Tell you what." Quinn eyeballed the group of onlookers, which had more than doubled since they'd arrived with lights and sirens blazing. "Let's get you to the ambulance so we can do an extended workup with a little more privacy. Then we'll talk about the C-collar. Good?"

Another pause, and man, she was tough. "Fine. Whatever will get me out of here, *chica*."

Because Three Brothers faced the pier directly, Quinn hadn't been able to park the ambulance as close to the place as she normally might. The crowd of looky-lous extended out to where all the emergency vehicles were parked nearly a block away, and God—even on a Sunday morning, a robbery/assault/arson trifecta would bring folks out of the woodwork.

Quinn shook off the prickle on the back of her neck and did her part in getting Carmen into the back of the rig with care. While they left one of the rear doors open, the mostly enclosed space offered them enough quiet to do a full workup.

"Okay. What do you see?" she asked Luke, who didn't hesitate to do an assessment.

"Patient is conscious and alert." He rattled off her vitals from the monitor. "Moderate contusion to the left orbit. Superficial lacerations to the mouth and chin. Deeper lac over the left eye."

Yeah, that one was going to need stitches. If Quinn was a betting woman, she'd say four. Maybe five. "Good. What else?"

"No signs of head or neck trauma," Luke said after double-checking for both. His penlight clicked on. "Pupils are equal and reactive."

"Even better."

Quinn went through a handful of questions with Carmen, ranging from where they were and what day it was ("I'm in the back of a damned ambulance and it's Sunday. I should have listened to *mi abeula* and gone to church.") to whether she'd lost consciousness or felt any numbness, tingling, or sensations of electrical activity anywhere in her body ("If I was, don't you think I'd lead with that? I watch *Grey's Anatomy*. I'm not stupid.") Finally, after they'd rolled her on her side to get an unimpeded view of her spine, Quinn set down the tablet where she'd been charting all of Carmen's info and looked at the woman.

"Good news. You passed with flying colors. The C-collar can come off."

"I *told* you I'm fine," Carmen said, her words loaded with sharp edges even though a whole lot of gratitude snuck into her dark brown stare as Quinn removed the C-collar and propped up the gurney so the woman could see what was going on.

"Mmm. You don't have a spinal injury, but I'm not sure about fine. You've got some pretty nasty bruises on your ribs that will require X-rays, and that cut over your eye is going to need to be stitched up."

Before Carmen could let loose with the argument her expression said she was working up, a familiar female voice sounded off from the rear door of the ambulance.

"Jesus, Carmen. Are you okay?" Isabella looked from Carmen to Quinn to Luke, likely gauging everyone's reaction to the question.

Carmen's eyes widened with uncharacteristic vulnerability for just a flash of a second. Then she released a heavy sigh. "*Dios mío*, here we go. The only thing that would be worse is if you'd brought—"

"Carmen, what the hell happened?" Hollister asked, nudging past Isabella to get a good look inside the back of the rig.

And just like that, Quinn's what-the-fuck-o-meter was pegged out.

"Okay, I've gotta ask. What is going *on* here? Are you two responding to the nine-one-one call for this robbery?"

Isabella and Hollister were both holstered up with their badges in plain view on their hips, so all signs pointed to yes. But this seemed like a pretty small-time call for the most elite police unit in the city. Quinn had seen enough big-time calls to know.

Isabella shifted her weight on the asphalt, exchanging a look with Hollister that Quinn couldn't read but she knew she didn't like. "It's complicated," the detective said. "But yes, Hollister and I would like to get a statement from Carmen. As long as she's okay to do that."

Now it was Quinn's turn to swap stares with Luke. "Medically, we can do the rest of her workup and monitor her while you talk, as long as she remains stable. But Luke and I have to stay in the rig with her, just in case her vitals change."

It didn't look like Isabella's first choice, but ultimately, she didn't refuse. She pulled herself into the back of the ambulance with Hollister on her boot heels, both of them sliding in next to Luke on the bench seat while Quinn held tight to her spot in the single chair across from them.

"Hey, girl," Isabella said. Before she could get any further, Carmen unleashed a string of angry rapid-fire Spanish in reply, and damn, Quinn had thought she was ballsy in English. She didn't need an interpreter to know Carmen was spitting nails over something.

"Okay, okay, okay." Isabella held up a hand. "I hear you, and I know you want to leave, but we've got to do this, *chica*. You know Liam and I need to know what happened."

"Oh, is that whole first-name thing supposed to make me all warm and fuzzy so I'll feel better about spilling my guts, here? *Liam*," she added, arching a brow at Hollister.

A flush drifted over his face beneath the auburn stubble peppering his jawline, and funny, Quinn had never seen the detective blush before. "We're trying to do you a solid, Carmen. So can you just give us a rundown so we can do our job and find the bastard who did this to you, please?"

She crossed her arms over the front of her body-hugging black and white top, wincing before she could achieve the full knot. "Fine. I closed last night, but Luis wasn't here. Not that he ever is. Make somebody a manager and they think they don't have to show up anymore. Anyway"—Carmen paused to let Luke tape a gauze pad over the cut on her brow—"I didn't want to take the cash to the bank's night-drop box by myself, so I left it in the safe and came back this morning to get it. This *cabrón*, I guess he was following me, or waiting, or whatever. But I didn't see him until he'd kicked in the back door and started trashing the place."

"Did you get a good look at him?" Hollister asked, and Carmen's laugh in reply held no joy.

"Dude didn't exactly make small talk, you know? I only saw him for a second before he went all MMA on me."

A muscle tightened at the hinge of Luke's jaw, and Hollister wore a matching expression. "Anything you can remember would be helpful," the detective tried again. "Was he black? White? Tall? Skinny?"

"Black," Carmen said, then followed it with, "I'm almost positive, but I guess he could've been Hispanic, too. Definitely not white. I think he was tall, but it was hard to tell, and everybody's taller than me. He was wearing a baseball hat with a hoodie over it. Both dark. Maybe gray? I don't know for sure."

"Okay, that's good." Isabella paused to ask Quinn to radio the details in to dispatch to help the uniformed officers with their search. "Someone saw a guy who might fit that description running out of here at the same time your nine-one-one call came in."

"That description fits half the guys in North Point," Carmen muttered, but Isabella shook her head.

"With any luck, the unis we have looking right now will find the *one* guy who did this. So what happened after he kicked in the door?"

Carmen shrugged, her shoulders shushing against the sheet covering the gurney behind them. "He didn't waste any time. He dragged me out of the office and started smacking me around, asking me weird questions. I fought back as much as I could."

The defensive scrapes and bruises on her knuckles certainly backed that up. "After, like, the ninth time I told him he was talking crazy, he finally stopped hitting me," Carmen continued. "Then he grabbed the money I'd taken from the safe, smashed up some stuff in the dining room, and lit something on fire, I guess. I didn't come out of the kitchen to see for sure. I was just glad he left."

Quinn's chest tightened at the thought of Carmen being assaulted by someone bigger than her, someone stronger, and Isabella looked equally unhappy about it.

"You said he asked you weird questions. Like what?" she asked, and Carmen frowned hard enough to stain her split lip a shade of fresh crimson.

"Questions about the guy you two were asking me about the other day," she said quietly. "Damien what's-his-face."

Luke's chin whipped up at the same time Quinn's heart ricocheted off her sternum. "Does this assault have something to do with our case?" he asked.

Hollister held up a hand. "The chances of that are extremely low."

"But not impossible," Quinn said. After all, Damien

wasn't exactly a garden variety name. Damiens who were linked to nasty crimes in North Point? Even less common.

Oh God. Oh *God*. If Ice knew she and Luke had gone to the Thirty-Third...

"Look, let's not get ahead of ourselves." Isabella's calm, cool voice broke through Quinn's rising panic, but just barely. "Carmen, I need you to think really hard, okay? Can you tell me exactly what this guy said?"

"He kept trying to intimidate me, you know? Yelling, asking how I really knew Damien, what I really told the cops and why I lied to that stupid *puta* Cherise last night. Every time I told him I didn't know what the fuck he was talking about, he'd hit me harder. Call me a liar. But it's like I already told you. I don't *know* nobody named Damien."

"Wait. Hold up." Hollister's hazel eyes narrowed, and he leaned in a little farther over the bench seat. "Who's Cherise?"

A noise of frustration crossed Carmen's lips, and although Quinn tried as hard as she could to process the conversation, she couldn't get much past the fear slinging its way through her system.

"Cherise is some junkie who turns tricks for Ricky Benton. Or she used to. I don't know about now," Carmen said. "I never used to hang with her much. Too skanky. But she came in to the pizzeria last night, all nice and shit, trying to talk about old times."

She clamped down on her lip even though it looked like the move hurt, and Isabella's normally titanium-reinforced gaze softened.

"Nobody here is judging you, Carmen."

"I get it," Carmen snapped, dragging the back of her hand over her bleeding lip. But not even the fear pooling in her belly was enough to keep Quinn from reaching for a

gauze pad and silently tucking it between the woman's
fingers.

"Thank you," Carmen whispered. The softness lasted for
less than a breath. "So Cherise comes by last night and
offers me some blow. I said no, by the way. Then she's all
going on about this guy Damien, and don't I know him from
back in the day, didn't she hear me talking to my new
friends about him when she was in here the other night.
Stupid shit. I told her to stop shooting up so much. I don't
know what the hell she was talking about."

Hollister's frame went rigid, his chin snapping up. "Oh,
shit. Cherise wouldn't happen to be the skinny blonde who
was sitting by the door in the pizzeria when Moreno and I
were here the other night, would she?"

"Yeah, now that you said it, I think she did come in for a
slice the other night," Carmen confirmed slowly. "But what
does that have to do with this asshole who broke in? Seriously, I don't know anybody named Damien."

"Be glad about that," Luke said, turning to pin Isabella
and Hollister with a stare as he voiced the question running
rampant in Quinn's brain. "This is related to what happened
to me and Quinn, isn't it?"

Isabella side-stepped his question neatly, but didn't cut
the conversation off at the quick, either. She looked at
Hollister. "We need to get a BOLO out on Cherise, and I
want the guy who did this in a holding cell with my
goddamn name on it. The sooner, the better."

Hollister nodded. "I'll have Capelli get Luis on the
phone. We're going to need all the pizzeria's surveillance
video from last night and this morning."

"You think those video cameras actually work?" Carmen
snorted. "Not since Christmas, honey. Three years ago."

Quinn's mind raced to outpace the rapid push of her

pulse as Hollister winced, then landed on his feet. "This is Capelli we're talking about. He might be able to pull something useful from one of the city cams out on the pier, proper. Carmen"—he turned back toward the gurney —"we'll have you go through some photo arrays, but is there anything else you can remember about the guy who did this? Anything at all."

She shook her head, but then gasped in contradiction. "He had a tattoo. Some kind of weird tattoo on his arm. I saw part of it sticking out from beneath the sleeve of his hoodie when he hit me. I don't know what it was, though. Maybe a rope or a chain or something?"

"Was it this?" Hollister pulled up an image on his cell phone, and Carmen turned the same color as the sheet on the gurney holding her up.

"Oh no. No fucking way. You think this is a Vipers thing? You can *forget* it. I'm not talking to you anymore."

"Carmen—"

She whipped a finger into the space between her and Hollister, her expression fierce as her dark eyes flashed. "Don't you 'Carmen' me, Charm School. I'm not messing around. If this has anything to do with the Vipers, I'm not saying a word."

But even though her bravado was pretty much bullet-proof, the heart rate monitor she was hooked up to didn't lie.

Carmen was scared, and hell if that didn't make at least two of them.

"We're not saying that," Isabella interrupted, her low, quiet tone making her the voice of reason. "We're just trying to figure things out. That's all."

"But you think this break-in *could* be a Vipers thing?"

Isabella hedged, but it was Hollister who nutted up with the truth. "Yes, Carmen. That's possible."

"Then no." She shook her head, adamant. "It's *possible* I'm keeping my mouth shut."

"Please," Quinn said. She knew she was probably overstepping her bounds by a nautical mile by intruding on the interview. But if Ice knew she and Luke had gone to the police, or God, if he even suspected something was off, then everything that mattered to her was on the line. "I know you don't know me, and maybe you don't care, but I know what you're feeling right now. I know these guys are dangerous."

"Trust me, Blondie. You don't."

Something deep in Quinn's belly snapped, making her bold. "Actually, I do. Just like I know that if Liam and Isabella don't catch whoever did this, a lot more people are going to be hurt than you. Do you really think they'll let you off with just a few bruises?" she asked, although the thought sent a shiver directly up her spine. "You know just as well as I do the Vipers don't mess around. If they're behind what happened here today, they have to be stopped. And you can help make that happen."

Please, God, let this work. Please, please...

Carmen huffed out a breath before frowning at Isabella. "You'd better know what the fuck you're doing."

"I do. I promise." She sent a scant nod of thanks in Quinn's direction before turning toward Hollister. "We need to call in the rest of the team and have Garza hit up every contact he has for chatter. We're also going to need a crime scene unit down here on the off-chance that this douche bag left behind any DNA that'll pop in the system."

"Before she does anything else, Carmen needs to go to Remington Memorial for stitches and X-rays," Luke said, his quiet yet unwavering tone doing something very funny to Quinn's chest.

"Of course," Isabella said. "Since time is obviously a factor here, can we make that happen as soon as possible?"

Quinn inhaled deeply to keep her pulse from knocking at her throat. The intelligence unit would figure this out. They'd keep her and Luke safe. They *would*. "Sure. I just need to radio Captain Bridges to let him know we're taking her in."

"I'll ride with her," Isabella said at the same time Hollister did, the female detective's brows winging up in obvious surprise at her partner's response.

"Right," he said, clearing his throat. "I'll just grab the squad car and meet you there, then."

"Copy that." Isabella waited until Hollister had gotten out of the back of the ambulance and disappeared from sight before splitting her stare between Quinn and Luke. "We'll keep you both posted."

"That's it?" Luke asked, but Isabella's nod was as firm as her answer.

"For now, yes. Look, as crazy as this might sound, waiting until we have something reliable to act on is the smartest play. If we went off half-cocked on every might-be and maybe, we'd burn ourselves out, not to mention probably lose our real leads. The best thing to do is continue to stay vigilant and let the team work the case. Trust me, I learned that the hard way."

The detective eked out a smile. "We're going to keep doing everything we've been doing to make sure you stay safe, okay? And if things change, we won't hesitate to change with them."

After a minute, Luke nodded. "Can you check on...you know, my grandmother and my sister? Just to be sure."

"Of course. I'll ask Maxwell and Hale to drive by your grandmother's house on their way in. Good?"

"Thank you."

Luke's expression looked calm on the surface, with the strong set of his jawline and his no-nonsense stare. But Quinn could see the worry lurking in his eyes, the tension strung across his shoulders, and suddenly, her heart thudded for an entirely different reason than it had only five seconds ago.

Oh, screw it.

She reached out to wrap her fingers around his, knowing but not caring that both Isabella and Carmen were within sneezing distance.

"Everything will be okay," Quinn said with a tiny squeeze. "We've got this, remember?"

He paused, then squeezed back. "Yeah. I remember." They stood there for a beat, then another, before Luke brushed his thumb over her forefinger. "I'll stay back here and finish Carmen's chart during transport. Okay?"

"Okay."

Quinn jumped down to the pavement on legs that qualified as Jell-O. Yeah, she was scared—fine, freaked out of her ever-loving mind was probably more accurate. But this could just be a coincidence. They'd taken every precaution possible. There was no way—

The hair on the back of her neck stood at sudden and complete attention. Quinn stopped abruptly, her boots rooted to the asphalt for just a split second before her throat slammed shut over her scream.

L uke liked to think that, barring anything wildly unnatural, he was prepared for anything. Quinn whipping open the back door to the ambulance and wearing a look of uncut terror when she was supposed to be getting them to Remington Memorial for a patient workup?

Not what he'd been expecting.

"Quinn? What the—"

"Ice. It's Ice. He's out there in the crowd."

Every part of Luke froze except for his heart. "What?"

"Are you sure?" Isabella asked at nearly the exact same time, and Quinn nodded in a broken movement.

"He held a gun to my head and threatened to kill everyone I care about. I'm never going to forget his face."

Carmen released a soft string of what Luke would bet were top-shelf curses in Spanish, and he fought the very irrational, *very* strong urge to elbow his way out the back of the ambulance, pluck that motherfucker out of the crowd, and rip him to shreds with his bare hands.

Thankfully, Isabella was a touch more level-headed. "Okay, Quinn. Where is he, exactly?"

"H-he's standing with the onlookers at about ten o'clock. Black T-shirt, sunglasses. Baseball hat pulled low over his face."

As carefully as they'd looked, he and Quinn hadn't been able to find a photo of Ice in any of the photo arrays or surveillance footage they'd looked at down at the Thirty-Third. They had, however, given up detailed descriptions of the guy—ones that Isabella seemed to have memorized, because she didn't ask for more details before she nodded. "And he's just standing in the crowd, watching the scene?"

A visible shiver moved over Quinn's body, turning Luke's fingers to fists. *Christ*, he wanted to dismantle this guy.

"He was, but when he saw me looking at him, he lifted his sunglasses up and stared back. Then..." She trailed off for a second, her voice pitching to a whisper as she said, "He looked at the pizzeria, then back at me, and he smiled this cold, dead smile and started to walk away."

"Damn it," Isabella bit out. She placed one hand on her gun, reaching for the door to the ambo with the other. "Stay in here with Carmen. Do *not* get out of the rig until I come back. You copy?"

Quinn nodded, but nope. Not today.

Luke followed Isabella out the back of the ambulance, his boots thumping against the ground next to hers before she could protest. "Your partner isn't here," he said from the side of his mouth, his eyes roving over the crowd as calmly and covertly as possible. "Plus, I can ID Ice if he's still out here. Let me help you."

"Fine," she said with a frown that said he'd get an earful from her later. "But only because arguing would waste time.

And if we put eyes on him, you stay here and call for help. Do you understand me?"

"Copy that," Luke said, because he knew that even though her sentence had technically ended with a question mark, she really wasn't asking.

"Good. You see him?"

Luke had to hand it to her. Isabella's laid back, nothing-to-see-here stance was flawless, even though he had zero doubt she had their surroundings under a microscope and would be able to put the weapon her hand still rested on to defensive use in about two seconds flat if she needed to.

"No." *Damn it.* He surveyed the crowd, which still looked as big as it had earlier even though the fire seemed nearly— if not all the way—dispatched. "I don't see him anywhere."

After another three minutes of surreptitious scrutiny from as many vantage points, they both came up empty.

"Still nothing." Luke shook his head. He'd seen a handful of men that had made him do a double-take, but no Ice. No Damien or Baseball Hat, a.k.a. Adam Simpson, either. "The only way he's still here is if he's invisible."

"Shit," Isabella said. "That's what I was afraid of."

Luke's pulse tapped in a steady rhythm of unease. "That he's in the wind?"

"That he suspects you and Quinn came to us. I'll radio dispatch to add Ice to the BOLO list, and they'll update Bridges. In the meantime, let's get Carmen to Remington Mem. I'm sure Sinclair will meet us there."

LUKE SAT BACK in his hard plastic chair and examined the small, sterile conference room in Remington Memorial for the nine thousandth time. Also for the nine thousandth time, he wished that the bottle of water in his hand was a triple shot of tequila. The only silver lining of the last two hours had been discovering that Momma Billie had left this morning to take Hayley on an overnight trip to Asheville to visit their Great-Aunt Margaret. Everything else—from the fire call to the assault on Carmen to the possibility that Ice knew he and Quinn had gone to the intelligence unit—had ranked somewhere between being audited by the IRS and having his nuts slammed in a drawer.

All painful as shit with the high possibility for permanent damage.

Quinn sat next to him with her own bottle of water in-hand, watching as Hale fiddled with the laptop on the conference room table and the other detectives from the intelligence unit filtered in from the hallway. The flicker of hope that had lit her dark blue stare when she'd grabbed his hand in the back of the ambo earlier was gone, replaced by that guarded fear Luke had thought was in the past tense. That Quinn was scared again was bad enough. That right now he'd do anything, however irrational, to erase the fear from her face?

On second thought, screw a triple shot of tequila. What he really needed was the whole damned bottle.

Sergeant Sinclair followed Captain Bridges into the conference room, shutting the door with a firm thump behind him. "Copeland. Slater. How are you two holding up?"

"Fine," Quinn said, the word stabbing into Luke with all the subtlety of a scalpel. "How's Carmen?"

"She's hanging in there," Isabella said, sitting down next to Quinn. "Her ribs are bruised and she's got four fresh stitches over her eye, but after a week of rest, she'll be as good as new."

"Probably as mouthy, too," Hollister added. "But you guys did a great job taking care of her."

There was no mistaking the gratitude beneath the detective's attitude. Luke wondered—not for the first time—exactly how Hollister and Isabella knew the woman. But considering the circumstances, it was a question for another day. "She's lucky that whoever assaulted her didn't do worse," Luke said. "Do you think it was Ice?"

Sergeant Sinclair took point on that one. "No. She put a positive ID on someone else for the break-in, a guy named Marcus Dixon."

He nodded to Maxwell, who pulled up a mug shot on a tablet and turned it toward Luke and Quinn.

"I've never seen him before," he said, confusion filling his brain as Quinn also shook her head to the negative. "So does that mean the assault *isn't* related to our case?"

"It means things are complicated."

Quinn stiffened beside him, her ponytail bouncing over the shoulder of her uniform top as she asked, "Okay. What's *that* supposed to mean?"

"Dixon's a bit of a wild card," Garza said from the spot where he leaned against the doorframe. "He's not a known member of the Vipers, but he's definitely not a choir boy, either. His rap sheet's as long as my arm, and he's got some nasty B&E's headlining the list. He just got out of county lockup a couple of weeks ago. It's possible he hooked up with Ice for this smash and grab."

"Or?" Captain Bridges put the unspoken question to voice, and Luke connected the dots a second later.

"Or you think this is some weird coincidence and the Vipers aren't involved at all."

"We've still got a BOLO out on Cherise, and we know she was at Three Brothers the other night when Moreno and Hollister were talking to Carmen. We also know that someone out there is fishing for intel on Damien," Hale said, looking across the table at him. "But without a connection between Cherise and Dixon, or either of them to Damien and Ice, we're left with a lot of maybes."

"I don't understand." Quinn spun a gaze from Hale to Sinclair. "We know Ice is involved. He was *there*."

A beat of silence filled the room, making Luke's gut pang. One of the bonuses to staying one step outside of any group was that he could read most people like the Sunday paper. Those loaded glances all five detectives had just swapped? Yeah, they might've lasted for only a split second, but he still hadn't missed them.

Finally, Sinclair said, "Eyewitness testimony isn't always ironclad, and you've been under some very understandable stress for the last week."

"Are you saying you think I was seeing things, Sergeant?" Quinn covered the words in a not-small amount of frost, which was the same way Sinclair answered them.

"That depends. How sure are you that you saw Ice in that crowd today?"

The legs of Luke's chair had scraped over the linoleum before he'd even realized he would move, but Quinn put out a hand, beating him to the figurative punch.

"You've been a cop for a long time, right?" she asked, and the question was so unexpected that it stunned Luke into place.

It must have shocked Sinclair, too, because his gray-blond brows had just taken a one-way trip toward his crew cut. "I have."

"So it's fair to say you've probably had someone point a gun at you. Threaten your life. Maybe even try to kill you."

Detective Maxwell and Captain Bridges both opened

their mouths simultaneously, but Sinclair shook his head, his eyes never leaving Quinn's. "That's an accurate assessment. Yes."

Quinn nodded, and although her chin trembled ever so slightly, the words she said next didn't. "Then you know you don't forget the faces of those people. *Ever*. I might not be able to prove it, but am one-hundred percent certain I saw Ice in that crowd. I'd stake my life on it. And the lives of my station-mates."

The silence that followed was punctuated only by the rapid thump-thump-thump of Luke's heartbeat pressing against his eardrums, until finally, Sinclair broke it.

"Okay, then. Let's figure out what the son of a bitch is up to." Turning toward Garza, he asked, "You know the guy's patterns. What are you thinking?"

Garza tugged a hand through his hair, and the way the stuff stuck up in about six different directions told Luke he'd made the move into a habit. "Ice isn't your average gang leader, and he's certainly not a run-of-the-mill street thug. To him, the Vipers are a family business—one he takes very seriously. He's ruthless and as mean as they come, but he's also methodical. Smart. Always under the radar."

"I'm not so sure about that." Capelli's voice sounded through the laptop positioned at the head of the room, the click of the keys in the background proving that the guy could Skype and run research from home at the same time. "Not entirely, anyway. He might not have taken a mid-day stroll down Main Street, but if he's behind this assault *and* he showed up at the scene, he's certainly above the surface."

"It does sound less cautious than his usual MO," Isabella said, and Maxwell lifted his chin in agreement.

"Which means he's got a good reason to risk being sighted."

"The question is," Sinclair said, "what is it?"

Luke's stomach dropped as the silence stretched out to fill every crevice of the room, but oh no. No fucking way. There had to be a plan. Some way to figure this out. Ice was completely diabolical. If he made good on his threats...

Of course. "He's trying to intimidate us."

Luke felt every stare in the room on his skin, but Quinn's most of all. "He's already done that pretty well, don't you think?" she asked.

"No, you might be onto something," Garza said. "Ice may be strategic, but he doesn't mess around. If he knew for sure that you and Quinn had come to us—"

"He'd have already made good on his threats to hurt us," Quinn whispered.

Luke shook his head, taking care to hold on to her stare with his. "But he didn't. Hell, he didn't even try."

"So he's got to be up to something," Sinclair said slowly. "He clearly wants to know what we know, if he got Cherise and Dixon to do his recon."

"And his dirty work," Hollister muttered, tacking on, "fucking asshat," for good measure.

Garza nodded, his boots echoing off the floor tiles as he paced in obvious thought. "It's not unusual for Ice to put other people into play. He runs one of Remington's most notorious gangs. To him, Cherise and Dixon are like employees. That they both seem to be freelancers with no clear connection to him doesn't hurt."

"He's definitely proving hard to track," Capelli said. Luke didn't have to look at the laptop screen to know the guy was frowning. His voice said it all as he continued. "Street cam footage in North Point is hit or miss, and most of the other businesses on the pier are like Three Brothers. No security cams to speak of. The crime scene unit couldn't find any DNA in the ambulance from the day of the kidnapping. Not that any defense lawyer worth his salt wouldn't scream reasonable doubt at the top of his lungs even if we did, or point out the pretty obvious fact that—at least as of right now—we don't even have a body to try and match it to. I'm willing to bet connecting him to Cherise and Dixon—even if you do find either of them—is going to be just as hard."

"Is he always this cheerful?" Garza asked. Whether it was the detective's deadpan delivery or the fact that simply no more unease could possibly fit in the damned room, Luke wasn't sure. But the question scattered the tension, and Isabella chuffed out a soft laugh.

"In a word? Yeah. But he's really awesome at *Jeopardy!* so we keep him around."

The strange sense of humor they also shared at the fire house took another chip out of Luke's stress, and more importantly, out of the stranglehold Quinn's shoulders had on her neck.

"Okay," she said, sitting back in her chair. "So what do we do now?"

Sinclair didn't hesitate. "We step things up a bit. This all started from a drive-by. Garza, let's find out more about the beef between the Scarlet Reapers and the Vipers, see if that'll give us an angle on what Ice is up to. We still have BOLOs out on Cherise and Dixon. Capelli, talk to me about where to find these two."

"The DMV has Cherise's last known address over on Delancey Street," Capelli said after a few seconds' worth of clacking, and Sinclair nodded.

"Good. Maxwell, you and Hale go for a knock and talk. Bring her in on whatever will stick."

"You got it, boss," Hale said, swiping a set of keys off the conference room table less than a breath before Maxwell could.

"Capelli, pull up Dixon's address along with his parole officer's contact information. Moreno, you and Hollister work all the leads you can get on him until you find his sorry ass. Let's see how cooperative he is when he realizes he's about to go back to the clink for a robbery/assault with a little arson on top," Sinclair ground out, and okay, yeah. Good. This was starting to sound like a plan.

The sergeant turned back to fix Luke, Quinn, and Captain Bridges with a steely, no-bullshit stare as the detectives filed out of the room.

"We're in some dicey territory in that we don't technically have any new or escalated threats to either of you or your families. That said"—Sinclair lifted both hands, probably in response to the way Captain Bridges had just shifted forward in his seat. Sinclair might be a badass police sergeant, but Luke's captain wasn't shy about standing up for his people, and hell if that didn't send a spiral of something sharp and unexpected all the way through his gut—"I think it's in our best interest to make some adjustments for the sake of everyone's safety."

"What did you have in mind?" Bridges asked.

"A few things," Sinclair said, his focus lasering in on Luke. "I understand your family is out of town for the day."

Instinct, the tough old bitch, had him nailing a cover over both his emotions and his expression, even as he made the disclosure. "Yes, sir. Until tomorrow afternoon, actually. They're in Asheville."

Hayley's spring exam schedule had offered up a rare Monday off, and Momma Billie had taken full advantage. She'd never liked driving in the dark.

"Good. That's far enough outside Ice's reach for us to

breathe easy until they get back. *If* he's going to act, he'll do it closer to home first."

That his grandmother and sister were safe reassured him. That Quinn and everyone else at Seventeen might not be...not so fucking much.

"So what do we do here, then?" Quinn asked, stealing the question directly from his brain.

"We stay sharp. Ice is smart, and we know he's watching. If we tighten up too much, he'll spook, so we've got to walk a pretty fine line to stay ahead of him." Sinclair turned toward Captain Bridges. "The RPD will put extra eyes on Station Seventeen and you'll get a police escort on any calls your people go out on for the rest of today's shift. We can pin it on heightened precautions from your response to this morning's crime scene."

The steady stream of keystrokes sounding off from the laptop on the table said Capelli was turning Sinclair's words into reality, and the sergeant's gaze hardened as he continued. "We'll keep to non-disclosure to the rest of your firefighters for now, but Copeland and Slater are off rotation until at least next shift."

"What?" Quinn chirped at the same time Luke's pulse sped way up.

"Come on," he said, trying to keep his voice level. "You're sending us home?"

Sinclair looked about as moveable as a skyscraper. "Ice might not have overtly threatened either of you today, but I'm not taking any chances. For now, we need you both to lay low and let us see what we can turn up. Garza will get you both secure at home, and of course, we'll complete regular sweeps and check-ins, just in case."

"I'm in perfect agreement," Bridges added. "With this guy still out there, taking you both off shift and having you hunker down at home is the safest way to handle this for now."

"Great," Luke said, but between the emotions in his gut and the *lack* of emotions currently on Quinn's face, the truth was, he felt anything but.

21

I t took exactly forty-nine minutes before Quinn wanted to scream just to break the silence in her apartment. Detective Garza had checked every inch of her living space to be absolutely certain it was safe, and she supposed she should be thankful the man had an obviously high tolerance for the free-range dust bunnies in the back of her closets and under her bed. Probably, she should also be thankful for the more-obvious fact that her apartment had been both unoccupied and undisturbed.

Too bad for her she was funneling all of her energy into trying to blot out the memory of Ice's cold, dead stare when he'd set his sights on her this morning and smiled.

"Come on, come on. Get it together," Quinn muttered past her ragged nerves and racing pulse. Yes, this morning had been terrifying, and God, yes, the very real possibility that he might come after her or Luke or someone they cared about was even more frightening than that. But Ice had meant what he said when he'd threatened her and Luke. She knew it in her bones and breath and blood. Something was holding him back, and it sure as hell wasn't a conscience.

She just prayed that the intelligence unit made good on their promise to stop him before Ice made good on *his* promise to torture her and all of her friends, then slowly end her life.

Snatching her cell phone from the kitchen counter, Quinn paced the hardwoods beneath her bare feet. She needed something to keep her overly active mind calm and occupied. She'd already showered and changed into a pair of yoga pants and her favorite big, off-the-shoulder T-shirt after Garza had left to take Luke home. She could call Parker to keep her brain busy, she supposed. Although they'd exchanged a handful of texts since his accident, she'd been a little remiss as far as actual phone calls. But Parker knew her as well as he knew his own reflection—one word, and he'd be able to hear her tension from the moon. Quinn had admittedly danced around calling him for that very reason. He hadn't exactly been blowing up her phone from his brother's cabin, either, but still. Even if her life was a shit storm right now, she owed the poor guy a check-in text, at the very least.

Except she knew that, while texting Parker would make her feel better in the sense of being a good friend, it wouldn't calm her. What she needed right now was to breathe. Not just to think everything would be okay, but to *believe* it.

What she really needed, above all else, was Luke.

Quinn's cell phone vibrated against her palm, making her jump, and the accompanying text message that flashed across the top of her screen didn't do anything to calm her pounding heartbeat.

Hey. It's me, checking in from Omaha. Are you okay?

Quinn took a breath. Considered going the I'm-fine route. Went the fuck-it route instead.

Truth? No.

Barely a beat passed before her phone vibrated again.

Okay, then buzz me up.

She blinked, but surely Luke didn't mean...

Are you serious? You're downstairs?

Yes and yes. I even come bearing gifts.

Quinn padded over to the intercom and pressed the button to allow him access to the lobby. She barely had time to pull her hair into a sloppy twist, let alone try to wrestle herself into a bra, before a soft knock echoed from her front door.

"It's me, Quinn," Luke said, as if he'd known her heart was tapping away in full force on the other side.

She checked the peephole, slid the chain from its mooring, flipped the dead bolt, and tugged the door an inch from the frame. God, she'd never been so happy to see someone in her entire twenty-seven years. "Um, hi?"

"Hey. It's just me. I promise."

Holding a loaded grocery bag in each hand and balancing a small duffel on his (hello, gorgeous) shoulder, Luke smiled at her.

Quinn let him in without thinking twice. He crossed her threshold, quickly letting her thump the door shut behind him and do up every last one of the locks before he said, "I know it's not much, but I had a six-pack of beer in my fridge and one of my grandmother's chicken pot pies in my freezer. I also grabbed some chips, some fruit, and some cans of cat food on my way over. I'm sure you're usually prepared, but I figured it wouldn't hurt to have extra. That way maybe poor Max will get a shot at the good stuff before Galileo hogs it all. No offense, buddy," he added, lowering the bags in favor of placing a quick scratch behind the cat's ears. "But you've gotta let that poor girl eat, too."

What...the...hell? "How are you here?" Quinn finally managed past the heavy haze of shock clouding her brain. "I thought Garza was bringing you home for lockdown."

"He did," Luke said, picking up the bags and heading into her kitchen like please and thank you all rolled into one. "Then he brought me back here."

"Seriously? Are we even allowed to do that?"

Luke shrugged. "I didn't ask permission. But Garza agreed it seemed dumb for the intelligence unit to keep tabs on both of us separately when they could keep track of us together with half the patrols. Plus, I saw the look on your face in that conference room, Quinn." His voice quieted. "I know you're scared. You shouldn't be alone."

Something she couldn't define jabbed at her chest. "I'm a big girl. I'm fine."

He put the beer and the pot pie in her fridge before turning to look at her with that ice-blue stare that saw everything. "I know you're a perfectly capable person. Just like I also know you're not okay."

A pop of frustration sizzled through her veins. Okay, so she wasn't made of Kevlar like Isabella or Addison, or even Shae. Still. "Look, maybe I'm not thrilled about...this..." She gestured to her apartment, and the fact that she was standing here in her kitchen, which should be terribly empty at this time of day when A-shift was at the fire house, frightened out of her goddamned mind. "But I don't need a babysitter."

"Is that why you think I'm here? To babysit you?" he asked, so honestly that Quinn's answer just shoveled on out.

"Why not? Everyone else thinks I need looking after. Garrity wants to keep tabs on all my feelings. The RPD literally won't let me out of their sight. I get the safety part, I really do." Anger and fear and frustration combined to form a great big emotional cocktail in her rib cage, and damn it, she wouldn't cry. She *wouldn't*. "I just hate feeling so fucking helpless. I'm not *helpless*."

Luke took a step toward her. Her stopped just shy of contact, though, as if he wanted to be close to her, but wanted to look her in the eye even more, and hell if that didn't make her chest ache harder.

"I know you're used to taking care of other people," he said. "You're very good at it. But a really bad thing happened to you, Quinn. Needing someone to take care of *you* a little while you figure out how to cope with that is okay. It doesn't make you helpless. It makes you human."

Her throat knotted. "I don't need..."

She stopped, the argument feeling too hollow for her to finish giving it voice. The truth was, she did. She did need help. Right now, in this moment, she needed Luke.

Quinn closed the slight space between them, her hands finding his shoulders, her belly brushing the spot between his hips. "How are you so calm all the time?" she asked, and his answer was immediate.

"I'm not always calm."

There was no helping the laugh that flew past her lips, which loosened her tension at least enough to strengthen her focus on the moment. "You are ridiculously calm. You're *always* ridiculously calm. I'm over here, losing my mind and vomiting my fear all over the goddamn place, and you're just standing there...perfect."

Luke's eyes blazed with sudden emotion Quinn didn't expect. Her heart twisted at the sight of it, her pulse tripping even harder as he slid his callused hands up to cradle her face.

"I'm not perfect. I'm a liar. You think just because you can't see my fear that it isn't there, but that's not true. I'm scared just like you. I stay awake at night, just like you. And fuck, I want this, just like you, so no. I'm not perfect. I'm not perfect, because I want you like I want my next breath. I shouldn't"—his hands moved to cup her neck, pulling her close enough to feel the heat of his words, of how much he meant them, on her skin—"but I do. And do you want to know the biggest sign of all that I'm not perfect? I'm not holding back anymore."

And then he kissed her.

LUKE HAD MADE MORE risky moves in the last week of his life than he had in the last ten years combined. But as foreign as it felt, as downright dangerous as he knew it should be, he didn't want to hold Quinn at arm's length anymore. He wanted to ease her fear. To hold her close. To strip her bare and take in every inch of her, every curve and every nuance, and he wanted to let her see him right back.

He wanted to let her in.

She sighed against his mouth, the soft vibration making him bite back a moan. Luke pressed his fingers against the hot skin where her neck met her hairline, holding her steady as he dragged his tongue over the line where her top lip met its counterpart. Quinn opened easily, her tongue meeting his for a provocative game of give and take that quickly had his cock growing hard behind the zipper of his jeans. Instinct combined with something even stronger, though, and Luke forced himself to slow down.

He might not be able to erase Quinn's fear entirely, but

he could give her other things to remember. He could take care of her.

Starting right now.

"Follow me."

Without waiting for an answer, he took a step back, grabbing her hand as gently as the need in his bloodstream would allow and leading her to the large, well-cushioned chair in her living room.

Luke looked at the windows along the wall a handful of feet away, taking in the sheer curtains covering them and the amount of afternoon sunlight and privacy they allowed into the room, and yeah, this would do. In fact, it was perfect.

"You want to have sex in my living room?" Quinn asked, and even though her voice didn't carry any reservations, he still answered with a nod meant to reassure her.

"I want you to be able to see."

She followed his gaze to the ample daylight spilling in from the windows. Her gold-blond brows tucked just enough to mark her confusion, but Luke didn't hesitate.

"There are things in your memory that scare you. I know I can't replace them." He paused to kiss her, to ground her in this moment, here, now. "But I can make you feel good, Quinn. I can give you new things to remember. Better things. All you have to do is let me."

Her blue eyes went wide. She nodded, a tendril of hair tumbling down from the knot at the crown of her head, and impulsively, Luke reached out to capture it between his fingers.

"You are so beautiful," he said, although Christ, the words were honestly tiny in the face of how he meant them.

Quinn coughed out a laugh, her cheeks coloring a shade

of pink that made Luke want to do the most wicked things he could think of, just to keep that blush in place.

"You don't believe me?" She hardly struck him as vain, but still. She had to know she was pretty.

The color on her face intensified. "I don't know. I guess I never gave it a ton of thought."

"Oh, we're fixing that right now." Turning her toward the mirror over the nearby side table, he stood behind her, catching her stare in the reflection. "Do you see yourself?"

"Of course."

"No," Luke said. "Do you *see* yourself? Do you see how pretty your skin is when you blush?"

He traced the apple of her cheek with two fingers, smiling when her body proved his point.

"I guess," she said, but oh, no, that wasn't going to be good enough.

Luke reached down for the hem of her shirt, lifting it slowly, first over her hips, then higher, until it was over her head. He wasn't prepared for her not to be wearing a bra, and fuck—*fuck*—this whole thing just might kill him. But Quinn needed to see everything he saw, exactly as he saw it, so he forced his resolve into place even though his cock was hard enough to be damn near painful right now.

"Look. Look how beautiful you are. How strong." His fingers coasted over the muscles on her shoulder, finding the hollow where they met her neck. He tasted the spot, his mouth curling into a smile when she shuddered. "How sweet."

Quinn did as he asked, her eyes unmoving from the reflection in front of them. Luke tugged his own shirt over his head, partly because he didn't want her to feel self-conscious and partly because he wanted selfish access to her, skin on skin. He pressed his chest against her back, his hands tilting her head gently to one side as he explored the warm stretch of her neck with his mouth. Her pulse hammered against his tongue, her breath moving in shallow sighs, but he refused to speed his movements.

"I could take all day to show you how pretty you are. Here." Luke traced her earlobe with the edge of his tongue before pulling the soft skin past his lips. "Here." His fingers found the indentation below her throat, right where her collarbones joined above her heart. Quinn dipped her head back, her eyes still on their reflection in the mirror as she arched up in search of his touch.

God, he couldn't deny her. "Here." Reaching up, he cupped her breasts, running his thumbs over the tight, rosy points of her nipples. Her moan twined around his, and the sound made Luke's cock jerk at the small of her back. The contrast of his darker skin against her cream-colored body, the flush of her nipples that grew deeper with every pass of his fingers, the way her eyes glittered in the mirror—all of it combined like an erotic slideshow.

And Quinn watched every move. She watched as he dropped his mouth to her ear and whispered all the filthy things he wanted to do to her. She watched as his hands moved downward from her breasts, skimming her waist, then the flare of her hips before reaching the waistband of her pants to lower them.

His heart hitched when he realized—sweet Jesus—she wasn't wearing panties beneath the black cotton. Something primal broke free in his chest, moving his fingers on a direct path to the spot between her thighs. But Quinn didn't seem to mind his impulsiveness. On the contrary, she parted her legs wider, tipping her hips up for more contact.

"Please," she whispered, and funny how one sound, one tiny syllable, could wreck him so fucking thoroughly. Wrapping one arm low over her belly, Luke parted her legs with his other hand, flattening his palm over the tidy strip of blond curls leading to the bare, sweet skin of her sex. He brushed his fingers over Quinn's slick folds only once before his hot, reckless desire to give her what she wanted won out. Luke curled his fingers to cup her pussy, pressing his middle finger inside her body with ease.

"Ah!" The cry that rushed out of her was more sound than actual word, and his balls pulled up tight at the greedy clench of her inner muscles around his finger.

"See?" he ground out, hearing the gravel in his voice as he began to work her in slow, sure strokes. "Look how pretty you are. How wet. How pink and perfect."

Quinn's eyes were nearly navy blue in the muted sunlight streaming in past the curtains. Sliding her arms over his, she anchored his hold on her belly and his fingers between her legs, urging him deeper with a push of her hips. Luke retreated only to add another finger to the first, letting his thumb slip up to graze her clit as he fucked her with his fingers. Her nails dug into his forearm, harder with each thrust of his hand, and before he could control anything about his movements, he withdrew from her body and swung her toward the chair.

"Keep watching."

Guiding her down over the cushions, he knelt between her legs, pulling her forward until her ass was on the very edge of the chair. The blush on her face was a complete juxtaposition with the provocative picture of the rest of her, naked and needy and open, and god*damn*, Luke had never wanted anything as much as he wanted this woman right now.

He fit his shoulders between Quinn's thighs, leaning in to run his tongue over the seam of her pussy in one long glide. He smiled against her body, making sure she saw it in his eyes as he lifted them to meet her stare.

Luke felt the way she was looking back at him in every part of his body.

With his pulse flying faster in his veins, he channeled all of his attention to Quinn. The sweet, musky taste of arousal that belonged only to her, the unchecked sounds she made when he explored her with his lips and tongue, all of it combined to form a deep-seated desire in his gut. Pressing her legs farther apart, he licked her in slow circles and faster, firmer flicks, finally closing his lips over the tiny bundle buried deep at the top of her sex.

"Oh *God*. Please. Please, please," Quinn cried, her hips arching off the cushion beneath them.

Luke pulled back, but only far enough to say, "Watch. Watch how pretty you are when you come."

He returned his mouth to her pussy, a spiral of dirty pleasure uncurling at the base of his spine at the way she moaned so openly. Her skin was so soft, so slick with want, that Luke let his fingers play at her clit as he buried his tongue deep inside her for a better taste.

Quinn made a sound, part pleasure, part need. Her hips shifted, her knees falling wider as the cradle of her body jerked higher against his mouth, her ass lifting up in invitation. A dark, half-forbidden yet highly sexy sensation sparked in Luke's mind as he realized what she was wordlessly asking for.

And there was no fucking way he wasn't going to give it to her.

Circling the pad of his forefinger over her clit, Luke dropped his mouth even further. Quinn sucked in an audible breath as his opposite hand cupped the curve of her ass, the breath becoming a moan as his pinky finger brushed over the ring of muscle centered low between her legs.

"Luke." Her exhale coasted over the bare skin of his shoulder, and damn, she was watching him as intently as ever. "Show me. Make me come."

His composure evaporated with those five little words. He stroked the slippery skin at the apex of her thighs while lowering his mouth to trace slow circles over her tight, sweet hole. Quinn's body tensed, just for a heartbeat, before she began to move with him in obvious pleasure. Luke tested and took, the movement of both his fingers and his tongue growing firm with intention as her cries grew more ragged. She clutched at his shoulders, her hands sliding up to hold him exactly where she wanted him, his tongue at the entrance to her ass and his fingers teasing the rigid knot of her clit. Finally, her thighs began to tremble, and—yes, fucking *yes*—she came undone with a screaming cry.

"There. There you are," Luke murmured, his dick as hard as iron at the sight and smell and taste of her orgasm. "See? So goddamn beautiful."

Quinn went lax a minute later, and he shifted back to look at her. With her disheveled hair and her flushed skin and her erratic breaths, she was pretty enough to be painful.

But then her eyes glinted, and within seconds, she'd pushed forward to tug him to his feet.

"Quinn. What are you—"

"Shh." The borderline sassy command sent an involuntary smile to the edges of his mouth, but the gesture turned into a want-soaked moan when she quickly removed his pants, then his boxers, pausing only long enough to grab a condom from the spot where they'd blessedly stashed a few in her side table drawer the other day. She treated him to a minute's worth of sheer heaven with her fingers, cleverly rolling the condom onto his cock as she did, and a pulse of surprise rippled over him as she turned to push him into the chair.

"Now it's my turn," Quinn said, straddling his lap and balancing her weight between her shins. The wet heat of her pussy brushed over Luke's insanely sensitive cock, and okay, yeah, he was going to last about four more nanoseconds if she kept that up.

"Your turn for what?" He dug his fingers into the armrests for focus. But then Quinn leaned forward, notching the crown of his cock just far enough inside her pussy to make him forget his fucking name.

"To let you watch." Her hips lowered another beautiful, excruciating inch. "Show me what *you* need, Luke."

He levered up to fill her in one swift push. "I need you." He gripped her ass, lifting her over his dick only so he could seat himself to the hilt again.

"Just you."

Quinn's eyes blazed, her lips parted in surprise and desire. But Luke's thoughts were hazy, the carnal part of his brain too wrapped up in the pressure of the sweet spot where his cock was buried to process anything else. Keeping his hands in place, he guided her into a steady, provocative rhythm. She answered easily, spreading her fingers wide over the arms of the chair, leaning back just enough to give Luke an unimpeded view of where they were joined. The sight of his cock sliding all the way home, the eager sighs that turned into moans, the pure pleasure on her face, all made his need intensify. He thrust into her over and over, speeding his movements to the beat of her cries, slipping one hand between them to stroke her clit as he watched her fuck him.

"You are the most beautiful thing I've ever seen. Come for me, baby. That's what I need."

Luke thrust deep, filling her pussy until no space at all remained between them. Holding Quinn in place, he let her roll her hips, grinding against him until his cock hit that hidden spot inside of her. Curling her arms around his shoulders, she pumped her hips against his in a hard, steady motion, taking what she wanted and giving him what he craved all at the same time. Luke's climax began as hers ended, the squeeze of her inner muscles triggering a chain reaction he had no hope of controlling. His orgasm rushed up from the base of his spine, stealing his breath and his ability to move as he held her close from shoulders to chest to hips. Vaguely, he was aware of calling Quinn's name, of her body tightening in another burst of release, but those things seemed small in comparison to the one feeling taking over his chest and his mind.

Even though it was neither safe nor smart in any way, Luke wanted to let her in and never let go.

22

Quinn lay tangled in her bed sheets, watching the sun give way to shadows on her bedroom floor. After their mind-blowing session in her living room chair, Luke had led her in here, letting her pause just long enough to throw on a tank top and a pair of boy shorts before pulling her beneath the covers and holding her close. She'd dozed for a little while —this morning's fear-laced adrenaline rush might have been strong, but it had also paled temporarily in the face of both the preternaturally amazing sex she and Luke had shared and the comfort of his closeness afterward.

Quinn's fear hadn't remained at bay for long, though. Reality crept back in with the early evening shadows, turning her nerves ragged and reminding her that not even great sex could distract her forever.

Are you sure great sex is all it was?

Her heartbeat sped beneath the light gray cotton of her tank top, so quickly that if Luke were awake, he'd surely have felt it. Okay, so what they'd shared this afternoon had felt like more than sex, like maybe they'd been connected on a different level than before. The emotion in Luke's eyes had been obvious, even though his words had been wicked and his actions even more so. There had been no mistaking the truth in his words.

I need you. Just you.

"You know, if your heart rate goes any higher, I might be forced to do an exam."

Even though Luke's voice was quiet, Quinn jumped all the same. "Maybe my heart is beating fast because you just scared the shit out of me," she said, but of course, he was too smart to let such a lame answer squeak by.

"Or maybe you've got something on your mind that you need to talk about." He shifted from beneath the covers, sitting up to look at her, and damn it. Damn it! How could he see so far into her with one little stare?

"I'm worried that Ice is going to hurt someone I care about," Quinn said, because Luke wasn't going to let her off the hook until she did. "But I don't need to talk about it. I don't even want to *think* about it. I'll feel a whole lot better once I can just get back to work like normal."

Unease built in her stomach, forming a hot, heavy ball. The longer they sat there in silence, the more tempted she was to fork over the truth, to admit that she wasn't just worried but terrified, and that she didn't know how to make the feeling go away.

Luke's eyes remained steady even though his voice was soft enough to take another chunk out of her resolve. "What you're feeling right now isn't your normal. You're trying to drown yourself in taking care of other people so you don't focus on the fact that who you really need to be taking care of is you."

Her heart slammed with how right he was, how much

she wanted to tell him so, yet her defenses sank in with teeth and hooks. "Oh, really? And how do you know that?"

"Because I do the exact same thing, Quinn. I do it every. Single. Day."

His undiluted honesty hit her like a wrecking ball, and Quinn had no choice. She pushed up from the bed, wrapping her arms around his shoulders.

"I'm just so scared," she said, her words as rickety as an old staircase. "I thought by now I'd be able to shake it. For a while, I *did*. But then I saw Ice today, and it was like nothing had changed at all, and...God, I just don't know how to make this fear stop. Every time I think I'm okay, it comes back like a boomerang. I don't know how to make it go away."

Luke's arms tightened around her, his hands flattening over her shoulder blades, reminding her how to breathe. "I don't either," he admitted.

"You don't?" she asked. His honesty took her by surprise, but rather than frustrating her—or worse, making her more frightened—the simple admission allowed her the chance to breathe.

"I don't." His fingers pressed into place. *There. Breathe.* "I can't pretend to have all the answers, no matter how badly I want to. But I can promise I'll be here to help you find them."

The truth of it grounded her more than any nicety or pat "there there"-style answer, and she pulled back to look at him. "You don't think I'm crazy?"

"Because the week-old memory of being threatened at gunpoint still scares you? God." His eyes widened. "Of course not."

When he said it that way, her fear seemed a lot more logical than it felt. Still... "It's just that you're handling all of this so much better than I am. To be honest, I'm a little jealous."

"You shouldn't be. Believe me." Luke blew out a breath. A flare of emotion moved over his face, a corresponding pang of shock moving through her when he didn't blank it or cover it up. "You know a minute ago, when I said I bury myself in taking care of other people so I won't have to look too hard at myself?"

Quinn turned toward him, her knees brushing over his bare legs beneath the bed sheets. "Yes," she said. This was the point at which Luke usually clammed up or re-channeled the conversation.

Only this time, he didn't.

"I wasn't exaggerating. My mother was…killed in an accident when I was fourteen." The words were rusty, as if they hadn't been spoken in ages, and they stunned Quinn into momentary silence. "A gas main explosion destroyed the real estate office where she worked. No one inside the building survived."

Quinn's heart wrenched, and even though she knew from her own personal experience that no words existed to erase the ache, she said, "Oh, Luke. I'm so sorry."

He nodded. "We were totally blindsided. Hayley was just shy of her seventh birthday, and I was in middle school. One minute, we were a normal family, going to work and school and having dinner together every night, and the next… everything was wrong."

Tears burned behind her eyes. As much as she'd hated it, she'd had time to adjust to the thought of losing her father, and she'd been too young when her mother had died to really understand the loss. But this? God, no wonder Luke didn't talk about it.

Except now, he was. "My grandmother, Momma Billie,

came up from Asheville. She was devastated, too—my mother was her only child, and my grandfather died before I was born. But after the accident, it was my father who was completely non-functional."

"Your father?" Quinn's cheeks blazed with the heat of her graceless blurt, and she bit her lip hard in penance. "I'm sorry," she said. "I assumed he wasn't in the picture since you didn't mention him, but I shouldn't have—"

"No, you're right," Luke said, his mouth set in a hard line and his body rigid beside hers in the bed. "He's not in the picture. He hasn't been since the day my mother died."

After a minute of silence, Quinn gave in to her confusion. "I'm sorry. I don't understand."

"My father spent two days locked in his room after the accident. He refused to see me or Hayley, or anyone. Then, the night before the funeral, he walked out of the house. He said..." Luke paused for a deep draw of breath, the look on his face making the hairs on the back of Quinn's neck prickle even though she couldn't pinpoint why. "He said he needed some air. So he walked to the park where he and my mother used to take me and Hayley all the time when we were little. Then he sat down under an old weeping willow tree and shot himself in the head."

For an odd clip of a second, the combination of words was so strange, their meaning so utterly foreign, that Quinn was certain she'd misunderstood.

And then she realized she hadn't.

Oh God. *Oh God.* "Luke," she whispered, her heart bottoming out in her belly. But it was as if, now that he'd kicked the conversation into motion, he couldn't stop it, and he kept going, the words pouring out.

"Some nearby neighbors heard the gunshot and called the police, but he'd planned it well. The wound was instantly fatal. We buried them together, then Momma Billie moved to Remington to raise me and Hayley. I found out later that he'd left a note asking her to look after us. But that was all it said."

"I don't..." Quinn's throat closed, so she swallowed hard and said the only true thing she could think of. "I don't know what to say. That must have been really awful for all of you."

Luke made a sound that would have been a laugh, except there was no happiness in it. "It was surreal. Hayley was too young to understand a lot of what had happened. She kept asking where our mom was, and when our dad would be coming home."

God, Quinn could relate. Every time her phone rang in that first year after her father died, she'd had an irrational pang of hope that it was him before remembering he couldn't possibly be calling.

"Anyway," Luke continued. "After two months, Momma Billie decided to sell the house. I think she knew it would be too hard for any of us to live there. So we moved to Mission Park."

"That doesn't sound like a bad decision," Quinn ventured, and he nodded.

"It helped Hayley, and even though she never said so, I think it helped Momma Billie, too."

Quinn whispered, "But not you?"

He lifted one shoulder halfway before letting it drop. "Not really. They were both sad, so the distance worked for them, but I wasn't just sad. I was angry. I thought my father was selfish to leave us. A coward who took the easy way out while the rest of us were left to figure out the hard parts. Sometimes, on the really hard days, I'm still angry," he said quietly. "But my mother was the love of his life, and we were such a happy family. I guess losing her just broke him. I don't really know. Then Hayley got sick and lost her hearing, and suddenly, there were bigger things to worry over than not having parents. So I did the only thing I could do."

Quinn recognized the look in his eyes like an old friend. *Of course.* "You took care of your family."

"I threw myself into doing everything I could for my grandmother and my sister," Luke agreed. "I took extra jobs after school to help pay Hayley's medical bills. I learned sign language right along with her once we realized she wasn't a candidate for hearing aids or surgery. I figured out how to make plans and fix things. Don't get me wrong—there were a lot of rough moments. But eventually, we had a bunch of good ones, too. I still take care of them both the best I can."

"That's why you pick up all those extra shifts, isn't it?" Quinn asked, realization sinking through her like a stone in still water. "And why you don't hang out with everyone at Seventeen in your spare time?"

He hesitated. "That's part of it."

"What's the other part?"

Another hesitation, this one longer. "I'm, ah. Not so good at letting people in."

His voice played back in her head from only a few minutes ago. *You drown yourself in taking care of other people so you don't focus on the fact that who you really need to be taking care of is you...I know because I do it every damn day...*

"Getting close to people means you might lose them, and that scares you," she said, the last piece to the puzzle falling into place with a startling snap. The way he'd always stayed one step outside of things at the fire house, how he subtly shifted the spotlight of each conversation off of himself, the calm, cool way he managed the emotions from the same situation that had threatened to upend her completely—God, all of it made so much sense.

Luke hadn't been building distance. He'd been building *armor*.

And now he was taking it off to show her what was underneath.

"Yeah. I just..." His voice caught, and Quinn's heart along with it. "I remember how much losing them hurt, you know? How scared I felt. How lost."

"Oh, Luke." Her chest ached, but she firmed up her words. She wasn't foolish enough to think she could take away the pain of him losing his parents. But she could be here for him now. "Of course you felt scared and lost. You lost your mom and dad too early, and you loved them very much."

"I did. I still do." He released an unstable exhale, and she didn't think. Just grabbed his hand and squeezed.

He squeezed back, holding her fingers tight as he continued. "I guess I just thought if I took care of other people but didn't let them get too close, I'd be able to keep myself from ever feeling like that again."

For a minute, Quinn sat there in the sunset shadows of her bedroom, trying to find the balance between her racing heart and her spinning thoughts. But Luke had trusted her with the truth. The least she could do was return the favor.

"I'm scared to lose the people I care about, too. But you're funny, and smart, and probably the kindest person I've ever met. You deserve to share that. You deserve to be cared for, too."

"We're kind of a matched set, huh?" he asked, and the irony of it made Quinn laugh.

"I'll tell you what. I promise to lean on you when I need help if you can promise me something in return."

Luke's dark brows went up. "And what's that?"

She moved forward to put her forehead on his, stealing a kiss from his lips before she said what was in her heart. "You'll let me help you, too. Ten years is a long time not to let anybody take care of you. I'm not saying you have to share everything, all the time," she added, because while she wanted to be there for Luke whenever he needed her, she wasn't about to force her way in. "But we're partners. We're supposed to hold each other up."

"We are partners," he said, brushing a return kiss over her mouth.

Quinn's breath hitched, and God, she would never get enough of this man. "So does that mean we have a deal?"

Luke pulled her close, his smile growing as he kissed her more deeply.

"Yeah. We have a deal."

23

Quinn sat in front of RFD's headquarters with her chest full of butterflies. More accurately, they might be giant moths, or even possibly an entire colony of full-grown bats.

Not that it mattered. Even if she was harboring every last species of Wild Kingdom under her shirt, neither Dallas Garrity nor Captain Bridges was going to let her bail on this damned appointment.

"You okay?" Detective Maxwell asked from the spot where he sat beside her in the driver's seat of his unmarked police car. He'd been at the helm of the cloak and dagger mission to get her from her apartment to her appointment with Garrity, slipping into her building disguised as a delivery man and sneaking her out through the complex's parking garage. The precautions were for Quinn's safety, she knew. But God, she'd be one happy-as-hell camper when she didn't have to stealth her way out of her own freaking house for fear of being watched, followed, or worse.

Breathe, girl. Breathe. "A little jittery, but I'll be alright," she said. "I don't suppose you'd be willing to humor me by giving me the case update again to help kill some of these nerves?"

The rough, gruff detective had never struck her as a particularly chatty guy. But thankfully, he took one for the team, nodding in the affirmative even though Hollister had given both her and Luke a thorough rundown less than two hours ago during their morning check-in.

"All of last night's patrols were quiet," Maxwell said. "No one fitting Ice's description has been spotted anywhere near your apartment, or Luke's. Seventeen finished A-shift without incident, and Luke's family's house is secure for when they return later today. There's no sign of increased or overt threat to any of you."

The good news bolstered Quinn's calm, but she also knew that was exactly why he'd led with it. The rest wasn't as promising. "Has Cherise turned up yet?"

The corners of Maxwell's mouth hinted at a frown. "No, but we're still looking as carefully as we can without tipping Ice off. It's not unusual for junkies to disappear for a day or two from time to time, though. It's possible she just went on a bender and she's crashed out somewhere."

A fact Quinn knew all too well from being called to resuscitate those who had crossed the limit of what their bodies could handle. God, she hoped the intelligence unit found the woman soon, and not just for the selfish reason that it might lead them closer to Ice. "And Dixon?"

"Still not talking," Maxwell said through his teeth. Isabella and Hollister had grabbed the guy off a street corner not long after they'd gone looking for him yesterday. But for as easy as he'd been to find, he was proving just as difficult to crack, having apparently spoken only the words "fuck" and "you" at various intervals before being thrown into city lockup for the night.

The detective continued. "We'll take another run at him today, though, after he's been formally charged for the robbery/assault. He's likely to change his tune once we tell him our crime scene unit found his prints in the kitchen at Three Brothers, the stolen bank bag in the bottom of his closet, *and* traces of Carmen's blood on the pair of jeans next to it. With her testimony, plus the surveillance video Capelli dug up that puts him a block from the place at the time of the incident? Even Dixon's attorney will be advising him to cooperate."

"So for now it's just sit and wait?" God, they were quickly becoming Quinn's least favorite words in the English language.

"For you," Maxwell said, giving up the closest thing he had to a smile. "But Garza and I are onto a couple of really solid leads with the Vipers' rival gang. We're getting closer to figuring out what Ice is up to, and once we do, there won't be anywhere that asshole can hide. Don't worry. We'll get him."

Quinn nodded and managed to smile back. They might not have Ice in custody, but they were closer than they had been. The intelligence unit had been smart and careful from Day One. She had to believe they'd break this case, because it was that or lose her marbles.

"Thanks, Shawn. I really appreciate it."

"Believe me, Copeland. Nailing this guy for kidnapping you two will be my freaking pleasure."

His dark eyes glinted with enough intensity to remind Quinn never to piss him off (*ever*), and she turned her energy toward tackling the next mountain in front of her. "Well, I guess we'd better go in before Garrity comes out to get me."

"Lead the way," Maxwell said. "I've got your back, and I'll be here to take you home when you're done."

Getting out of the unmarked Dodge Charger, Quinn scanned the busy city street in front of her. Maxwell did the same, of course, and he was the one with all the firepower, but staying alert never hurt a girl.

She blew out a sigh before making her way up to the building's double doors, then through the lobby and over the well-polished linoleum until she reached the glass and wood door marked *Dallas Garrity, Licensed Psychological Associate*. Her chest thumped its displeasure at the prospect of being back under the department microscope, but she managed a polite enough smile for the receptionist, then another for Dallas himself as he led her back to his office.

"I'm glad to see you again," he said, letting her choose her seat (same as last time) before choosing his own across from her (not shockingly, also the same as last time). "I heard you had a busy day on shift yesterday. Do you want to talk about it?"

Unease prowled through her rib cage. "It sounds like you already heard what happened."

"I saw the report from your captain," Dallas said, but the agreement was as much as Quinn was going to get. "What I'd really like is to hear your version of events. As long as you're willing to share it."

She sat back in her comfortably cushioned chair. If she wanted to get out of another session, she was going to have to throw him a bone, and the truth was, he really did seem nice enough. Now that Quinn looked at him closely, she supposed Addison wasn't *entirely* wrong. Dallas was kind of good-looking in an objective way, with that slightly tousled blond hair and that cleft in his chin that was just defined enough to make him handsome without throwing him over the top into *GQ*-ville. Plus, the look on his face right now was genuine, as if he really did want to hear what she had to say. She might not want to go skipping down memory lane all tra-la-la, but would it really be that bad to tell him about yesterday's call?

Quinn lifted one shoulder, although the move felt just a touch stiff. "Seventeen was called to the scene of a restaurant fire that turned out to be a robbery/assault."

"How did you feel about being back on ambo?"

"Pretty good," she answered honestly. "I mean, there's always a little adrenaline when that all-call goes off, you know? But otherwise, I was happy to be back at work, and definitely happy to be helping someone."

Dallas smiled, his pen pausing over the legal pad on his knee. "I remember the adrenaline."

Ah, right, he'd been a firefighter. Judging by the eight by ten photo of him and his squad-mates that hung on the wall below his diplomas, it hadn't been too terribly long ago, either.

His smile faded a bit. "So once you got to the scene of the restaurant fire, what happened then?"

"Oh. Ah, Luke and I took care of the woman who had been attacked."

Quinn's gut jabbed at the memory of Carmen's injuries and the fact that the man who had engineered that assault had been the same man who'd promised to murder everyone Quinn loved.

Easy. Breathe. "She was pretty banged up," Quinn said, clearing her throat. "But she'll be okay."

Dallas nodded slowly. "That's not what made the call tough for you, though," he led, and Quinn's breath grew suddenly heavy and thick.

"No." She tried to wait out the silence he gave her to

keep going, but God, he was *really* fucking patient. "Um, Ice was...there. In the crowd, watching. I saw him."

"Ice is the man who threatened you when you were kidnapped."

Dallas delivered the words as carefully as anyone could, yet still, they stuck into Quinn like a thousand razor-sharp needles. Talking with Luke about the kidnapping was one thing—he'd been there. He understood. But looking all vulnerable and weak in front of Dallas, when he potentially held her job in his hands? That fell square under the heading of *danger, Will Robinson!*

Quinn's heart—traitorous thing—beat even faster in her chest. "Why did you refuse to clear me unless I came back to talk to you again?"

Dallas's pause marked his surprise at her question even though his expression didn't. "I thought you might have some more things you needed to say about your kidnapping."

"I was there when it happened. Honestly, what's the point of rehashing all the details?" Quinn asked. It wasn't as if she could change any of them, from last week or from yesterday, and she damn sure couldn't make them less frightening whenever her memories snuck up on her.

You know this feeling you have right now? This fear of dying?

"That's a legitimate question," Dallas said, the words finding a path past the anxiety beginning to build behind her breastbone. "The short answer is that some assault victims find it cathartic to talk about their attacks. It allows them to move forward and begin to heal."

I want you to remember this feeling...remember it...remember...I know who you are, Quinn Copeland...

Her pulse rattled at her throat, defying her brain's

command to slow down. "Not me. Remembering won't help."

Dallas's sand-colored brows went up, and really, why did his smile have to be so kind? "To be fair, you haven't tried it."

"Sometimes, I feel like I'm crazy," Quinn blurted. Realizing just a beat too late that that was probably the last thing she wanted to say to the department-appointed psychologist in charge of keeping her cleared for work, she added, "I mean, not in the clinical sense. I'm functional, and I want to go to work and be with my friends. I just...it's like a boomerang. Most of the time I feel like I'm fine. Like, *really* fine."

"That's good."

Dallas seemed to mean it, and since Quinn couldn't stop talking now without him writing something potentially damning on that legal pad of his, she continued.

"But other times, like when I'm trying to fall asleep at night or if I'm by myself, the memories come back and I get so scared. I remember everything that happened and how I felt so helpless, and I can't control the fear. It gets so big, I can't move or breathe."

"Panic attacks can be a very normal side effect of post-traumatic stress, Quinn. They mean you're weak or helpless," Dallas said.

She frowned. "Well, they suck."

Dallas laughed, and at least that was a decent sign that he didn't think she'd lost it entirely. "That they do. But there are ways of pinpointing specific triggers so you can try to head them off at the pass, and there are also methods of dealing with them if your anxiety starts to become overwhelming on a regular basis."

"Right. I know how to breathe into a paper bag and stuff like that," she said. Not that it really worked when you were remembering in vivid detail the way a psycho gang leader had promised to murder you slowly.

Dallas surprised her by shaking his head. "While medical options are valuable in a lot of cases, the methods I'm talking about here are a bit different."

"Okay," Quinn said, turning the word into enough of a question that he answered it.

"Let's try this. Is there anything that calms you? A word or a place or a memory that makes you feel safe?"

"Yes. Luke—" She clamped down on her lip. But her relationship with Luke wasn't against the rules, and what's more, being around him really *did* calm her. "Sometimes, when I get shaky, Luke will put his hand on my back and remind me to breathe. That makes me feel safe."

If the personal reveal shocked him, Dallas didn't show it. "Good," he said. "Let's start with that."

They talked for a while about when she felt most scared, and Quinn was surprised at how well a few of the tricks Dallas suggested actually worked to at least ease her fear a little. Others didn't, but when he promised her that was okay, she believed him. Not having to hide how scared she was felt kind of comforting—not vulnerable like she'd thought it would—and by the time her session was almost up, she was glad (albeit grudgingly) he'd made her come back.

Well, right up until he said, "I've noticed you don't talk about your kidnapping in specific terms", anyway.

"Haven't we been talking about it in specific terms for like, the last forty-five minutes?" Quinn asked, although her hackles had kicked right back into a defensive position.

"Yes and no." Dallas smiled that funny little smile that made Quinn like him despite the fact that she'd had to sit in his office twice in the span of seven days. "What I mean is, you've made some really nice progress today in recognizing what triggers your anxiety. But you're very vague when you talk about what happened to you. You never use the words 'kidnapping' or 'assault'. I'm not faulting you for that," he added. "But it's something I've noticed. And at some point, you're going to have to address everything that happened to you if you really want to heal."

"I don't..." The words stuck in Quinn's throat, her inhale jamming right along with them, and damn it. *Damn it!* "I don't know if I can do that today." Or tomorrow. The day after that? Not looking so hot, either.

"I'd be surprised if you could," Dallas said, flipping his legal pad closed to look at her. "Coping with mental trauma takes time. But I want you to know that in here, you're not weak, and you're not helpless. In fact, I think today you were pretty damned strong."

Quinn paused. "So if I, ah, came back next week, maybe we could keep talking so I can start getting my head around my"—*Easy. Breathe*—"kidnapping? As long as that's okay."

He looked as shocked at her words as she'd been to say them. But Quinn couldn't deny feeling at least a little more grounded at having talked to him about being scared, and God, even though she knew it wouldn't happen overnight, she really did want to start getting back to normal, for real.

"I think that's a great idea," Dallas said. "In the meantime, do me a favor and stay safe out there, okay?"

Quinn nodded and promised, "I will."

~

ICE HAD JUST ABOUT HAD it with sloppy work from careless idiots who couldn't find their asses with both hands and an anatomy textbook.

Crossing his arms over his chest, he sat back in the private booth in the VIP room of The Tunnel. At least the nightclub was Viper territory through and through, out of the reach of both the police department and the Scarlet Reapers—a little fact that made it easier for him not just to show his face in public, but to have a business conversation without having to worry over locked doors and secure phone lines.

Ice took a deep breath and worked up the patience he was going to damn well need in order to handle this shit. "What do you mean, Dixon's agreed to a deal with the DA?"

Adam, who had been with the Vipers long enough to know Ice regarded loyalty above all, adjusted his baseball hat and kept his voice low even though the thumping bassline of the music coming through the club's speakers was more than adequate cover for their conversation. No one in here would dare betray Ice, but they didn't need to know his business, either.

"That's what my brother told me," Adam replied. "Said it happened a coupl'a hours ago. He knows someone with the same parole officer as Dixon. Dude asked the PO if he could get in on Dixon's work release placement since he heard he was going back to the clink for busting up that pizza place, but the guy said nope, Dixon cut a deal. No jail time."

Ice took a swallow of the Grey Goose in front of him, barely feeling the burn of the liquor as it went down. The fucking idiot must have sung like an opera soloist to sleaze his way out of any jail time at all, considering the charges he'd been looking at. Of course, Ice really shouldn't be surprised at this point. Dixon had been dumb enough to rob the place when Ice had specifically told him to go only for the intel and the beat down on that ex-hooker informant, just like he'd been dumb enough to get caught even though Ice had told him to lay low.

While the robbery had been unplanned—at least, by Ice —the fire had been part of the strategy. No way was he going to pass up the chance to rattle that weak-ass paramedic *and* send the intelligence unit a message that their informant wasn't safe from him. Showing up at the scene himself had been a risk, he'd known, but one worth taking. He'd been able to smell the sharp tang of the blonde's fear from fifty yards away, and by the time she'd been able to go squealing to her cop friends, he'd been long gone.

Unfortunately, time had been a factor after the break-in at Three Brothers. He'd had to choose between Cherise and Dixon. Ice had known she was the weaker link, far more likely to believe the cops' fairy tales about shit like immunity and being able to keep her safe than Dixon, so he'd made the strategically smarter move. The bad news was, Dixon—the disloyal son of a bitch—had turned out to be as loose-lipped as Cherise would've been had the cops gotten to her first.

The good news was, the only way the cops would get near her now was with a body bag. It'd been a shame he'd had to pump her full of heroin laced with enough fentanyl to drop a linebacker. Her mouth hadn't been half-bad, even if he hadn't been convinced she'd keep it shut when things really mattered. He might not be able to murder those two paramedics—yet—but no one would bat an eye at Cherise turning up as a poor, sad statistic. Shit, she'd even injected the first dose herself, and Ice had been certain to dump her in prime Scarlet Reapers territory once her body had been cold. No one could tie the Vipers to her death. No one could even prove Ice had ever had contact with her. The whole thing had been flawless.

Of course, Dixon had gone and shit on his carefully laid plans anyway, the fucking traitor. Ice had been willing to wait out killing those two paramedics until after the deal with Sorenson went down in five days—he'd had to be. But now there would be heat on him when he needed to be invisible, and that, he couldn't abide. It was time to give the RPD something else, something far bigger and nastier, to worry about other than digging into his business.

He'd have to be extremely careful. No more loose ends. No more maybes.

He needed an expert, one with a foolproof plan to keep the intelligence unit off his trail, the Vipers' assets safe, and his business alive and kicking.

"Get Rusty on the phone," Ice said, and Adam's eyes went appropriately wide in the flashing lights of the club.

"You want the firebug? Man, that guy is off his fucking rocker."

Ice smiled. There was such a fine line between dedication and insanity. Rusty was brilliant. The pyromania was just a nasty side effect. But since the man's *other* specialty was what Ice needed right now, he'd deal with whatever he needed to in order to reach his goal, and reach it fast.

"Tell him I need him here in an hour for a job that'll get his hands dirty and make a whole lot of noise."

24

L uke had never been so happy to see oh-six-thirty in his life. Never mind that Sinclair and Bridges had agreed to let him and Quinn go back to work today after having missed only that one half-shift three days ago, and that his family and friends had all remained completely safe since then, too. But the RPD had pulled together an impressive amount of intel in the last two days, from Dixon's confession that Ice was behind the break-in at Three Brothers to a bunch of details about some arms deal that was allegedly going down within the week.

They'd sadly lost any leads they'd have gotten from Cherise when her body had been discovered in the back alley of a nightclub frequented by the Vipers' rival gang early Monday morning, but even though it looked like a straight-up OD, the intelligence unit was still working whatever leads they could find to try and connect her to Ice. Quinn had even had what she'd called a "decent" session with Garrity.

Despite the fact that Ice seemed to suspect the RPD knew about the kidnapping, he wasn't acting on it. The case against him was coming together. There was a plan. He and Quinn were safe. About to head back to the jobs they loved.

Annnnnd cue the segue.

"You ready?" Luke asked, sending his gaze to the passenger seat of his Nissan.

Quinn flung off her seatbelt, grinning in reply. "Are you kidding? I've been up since four."

"I know." A bolt of heat moved through him as his short-term memory gave up a very wicked slide show in his mind's eye. "Or did you forget I'm also an early riser?"

"Luke, please," she murmured, closing the space between them to brush a sweet-and-sexy kiss over his mouth. "After what you did to me this morning, I won't even forget that when I'm ninety."

His lips parted into a smile as he kissed her back. "It *was* a pretty nice way to wake up." That's what she got for not wearing panties to bed. But no way had he planned to pass up saying good morning with his mouth between her thighs.

"Just nice?" Quinn asked, and his smile became full-blown laughter.

"Better than nice," Luke agreed, arching a brow. "Hot." He kissed her again. "Insanely sexy." Kissed her longer. "In fact, I might need to make a habit of waking up right here more often."

He slid his hand from her rib cage to the seam of her jeans. A sigh tumbled past her lips, threatening to wreck him, before she pulled back.

"We're going to be late," she cautioned, apparently thinking better of turning him down outright when she added, "Rain check for tomorrow morning after shift."

"Yes, ma'am."

Laughing, Luke got out of the car. Putting a solid visual

on their surroundings, he took in the vehicles parked along Washington Boulevard, the brick and neatly kept siding of the brownstones and shopfronts on the other side of the tidy sidewalk, the bakery that was already beginning to bustle with the pre-workday crowd. He and Quinn had heightened awareness down to a science, and she repeated his scan in reverse out of the corner of her eye as they walked toward the fire house. Changing out for their shift quickly became roll call, then morning house chores, and even though he wasn't headed back to the firefighter side of things for another week and a half, Luke walked into Station Seventeen's engine bay fully expecting a gigantic ration of shit from his engine mates.

Which worked out great, because that's exactly what he got.

"Well it's about freaking time!" came Shae's voice from the equipment room doorway, accompanied by a smile so genuine, he had no choice but to smile back. "I was beginning to think the department was going to keep yanking you two out of here for training indefinitely, you fucking slackers."

"Yeah, that's us," Quinn said from beside him, her laughter ruining any chance she had at nailing the sarcasm she'd almost certainly intended. "Luke and I are total delinquents. As a matter of fact, we had to drag ourselves away from Netflix and naptime just to be back here with you grunts."

"*Daaaamn.*" Kellan laughed, and Dempsey along with him. "Give a girl a rookie and she'll take a mile."

Quinn's cheeks flushed, but still, she said, "Mmm. Slater's mine for the next week and a half. And don't you forget it, Walker."

Not even the sly glances Kellan and Dempsey

exchanged at the subtle innuendo could crush the good vibes brewing in Luke's chest. The normalcy of fire house banter—and more importantly, the genuine, wide-open smile it put on Quinn's face—made any potential brow-raising worth it.

Damn, Luke really liked her. And the crazy thing was, it felt far too good to scare him.

Shae waggled her brows, popping off with one last comment about him and Quinn being back in the trenches before she turned to grab the inventory clipboard off the wall beside the storage cage where they kept the SCBA tanks. Luke aimed himself at the ambo—he and Quinn had a ton of work to catch up on after their morning inventory was under their belt. Who knew, if they got lucky enough to have a gap in their day, he might even be able to teach her a little more ASL, too.

But he barely got two steps past the back of Engine Seventeen before the look on Gamble's face stopped him dead in his tracks.

"Lieutenant? What's—"

"Slater. *Stop.*"

Quinn, who was right on Luke's boot heels, stuttered to a halt right next to him, her smile evaporating in an instant. "Gamble? What's going on?"

He looked up with an expression Luke had never, ever seen before, and God, what could possibly make Gamble, who was the saltiest SOB Luke knew, turn so pale?

"I need you to very carefully, very quietly get everyone out of the engine bay and tell Captain Bridges to put us on lockdown. *Immediately.*"

"What? Why?" Luke asked, the muscle in Gamble's jaw the only part of him that moved as he replied.

"Because I just did a security sweep of the engine, and

there's a bomb underneath it that's big enough to blow the entire engine bay halfway to the moon."

Quinn choked out a noise that Luke barely heard past the freight-train slam of his heart against his eardrums. "T-there's…"

"A bomb under the engine," Gamble said, his voice low and quiet. "It's not on a timer, which means the detonator's got to be on a remote. But I also found this."

He held up a cell phone, the kind convenience stores sold in those prepaid deals, and the message flashing across the screen turned Luke's blood to ice.

NO ONE IN, NO ONE OUT. EVACUATE THE FIRE HOUSE AND DIE LIKE ALL TEN OF YOU DESERVE, MOTHERFUCKERS.

Oh. Christ.

"Gamble—"

"Listen to me," he said, cutting Luke off with a tight nod. "I don't know how much time we've got here. This thing is sophisticated enough to put all the IEDs I've ever seen to fucking shame."

Jesus. Luke didn't even want to know how Gamble recognized what a complex explosive device looked like, let alone how many IEDs he'd ever come across.

The lieutenant continued. "It doesn't look like there are any pressure sensitive triggers on this thing that would set it off on contact, so I'm going to try to get a good look at it, since getting the bomb squad in here is obviously out of the question. But you need to go, both of you. Get everybody out of this room. Now."

"Quinn." Luke turned toward her, something odd turning over in his chest like a boulder that had been lodged in place for far too long. "Go tell Shae and Kellan and

Dempsey to get out of the engine bay and get Bridges. Go right now."

Miraculously, she nodded. "O-okay. I can do that." She pivoted and disappeared at a swift run.

"Slater," Gamble ground out, his dark eyes boring holes in Luke from ten feet away. "You need to go, too. Go with Copeland."

"No. Respectfully," he added, because not even life-and-death trumped manners as far as Momma Billie was concerned, and the least he could do if he was going to bite it was do so in a way that would make her proud. "But I'm not leaving you, so tell me how I can help."

Gamble bit out a vicious curse. "Jesus, rookie. You've got balls the size of Texas, you know that?"

"Hey, Lieu," came Kellan's voice from over Luke's shoulder before he could respond. "Uncle Sam gifted me with a little expertise in this field, same as you. Thought you might need a hand."

"Get your ass out of here," Gamble growled. But then Shae chimed in, too, and the big guy was totally outnumbered.

"Oh, quit bitching. Everyone here knows you secretly love to be cuddled."

"I'm serious," Gamble said, his dark stare darting from Luke to Kellan to Shae. "Get the fuck out of this room, all three of you. That's an order."

"No." Luke shook his head even though his heart (and yeah, maybe a few other parts of his anatomy) was lodged in his windpipe. "We're a team. Tell us how we can help."

Before Gamble could re-up his argument, Quinn's voice echoed through the engine bay.

"Captain Bridges is coming. Everyone else is in the common room. All accounted for."

A not-small part of Luke screamed for her to get as far away as possible, like maybe a cave in India or somewhere in the Australian outback, just for safety's sake. But the look on her face said that, like him, she wasn't budging, and since they had *way* bigger issues in front of them, Luke tamped down his wasted argument for the time being.

Captain Bridges arrived in the doorway of the engine bay directly behind Quinn, his face drawn tight with worry.

"Gamble, talk to me," he said, his voice calm even though he was clearly out of breath from having run down the hallway.

"We have an affirmative 10-89," Gamble replied, using the police department's code for a bomb threat. He relayed the basics to Captain Bridges, who let out a rare curse under his breath.

"Quinn, go tell Lieutenant Hawkins to initiate lockdown protocols immediately," he said, turning back to Gamble as she broke into a sprint down the hallway. "We're going to need a secure line to call this in."

"Cell phones are a no-go," Gamble said, and Kellan nodded in agreement from beside him. "The two-ways have private frequencies, so those will be our best bet. Dispatch can patch us through to the RPD and the bomb squad."

"Copy that. I'll get Sinclair on the line," Bridges said, heading quickly for the equipment room. Luke scraped for a breath—not an easy task, considering the circumstances—and settled on the first thing he could think of.

"Why no cell phones?"

"Not for the reason you'd think," Kellan said, moving next to Gamble, both of them kneeling down to look under the engine. "With a device this sophisticated, on a remote detonator to boot, only a very specific frequency is going to set it off. Cell phones are safe in that they won't interfere with the device..."

"But not if you don't want someone eavesdropping on your plans to defuse their bomb," Gamble finished.

Luke's brows shot up. "You think this guy can tap our cell phones?"

"I think this guy planted a highly complex explosive device under our fucking noses. I'm not willing to risk finding out how good he is at playing Big Brother. The RFD radio frequencies are encrypted to keep the media out of our shit. Whoever planted this thing would have to either be clairvoyant or in this room to hear the two-way coms."

Luke had a gut-sinking feeling he knew *exactly* who had planted this bomb. Or at least, who had commissioned the elaborate handiwork.

A thought slammed into him all at once. "Quinn." His gaze whipped toward the door to the engine bay, adrenaline free-flowing through his veins. No, no. *No.* "My sister and grandmother. I need—"

"Already done," she said, indicating the radio on her shoulder. "Bridges just got Sinclair on the line, but I had dispatch call Maxwell and Hale separately. There was a patrol car already at your grandmother's house, and they're taking her and Hayley to the precinct."

Luke's breath released in a whoosh of relief. It lasted for only a second, though, before he felt the weight of his engine-mates' stares.

"Long story," he said, and Kellan was the first to break the silence.

"How about you tell it over beers at the Crooked Angel when we get out of this mess, yeah?"

"Deal." Speaking of which... "And how are we going to do that, exactly?"

Captain Bridges moved over the concrete, stopping a few paces from where they stood. "I have Sergeant Sinclair on the line, and Detective Moreno is getting someone from the bomb squad patched in right now."

At the mention of Isabella's name, Kellan flinched. "Tell her I'm fine. Everything's fine."

"You'd better be," came Sinclair's voice over the line. "What's your head count, Captain?"

"Ten, just like the bomber's text said," replied Bridges. "Squad's riding light with Dempsey on engine, and January had a meeting down at RFD headquarters this morning. She's safe."

"Copy that." Although Sinclair's voice didn't betray him, Luke had to bet the guy was feeling a massive amount of relief that his daughter wasn't in the fire house right now. "We have to assume our bomber has eyes on the building," the sergeant continued. "He's got to be close by, and if he's smart—which I'm guessing he is—he's watching all the exit points of the fire house."

"We have security cameras at all the doors. If he's smart enough to potentially tap our cell phones, he might have hacked into the feed," Quinn ventured from the spot where she stood next to Bridges, and another thought made Luke's gut heavy with dread.

"Or he might have an accomplice who's out there watching." If Ice was behind this—and really, who the hell else would be—there could potentially be a whole gang's worth of eyes out there.

A conclusion Sinclair had obviously reached, too. "We can't risk cutting the feed and evacuating anyone in case he's got eyes on the ground. Moreno's still working on getting the bomb squad on the line, and the RPD has units on the way to block off the street and start evacuating all the adjacent buildings. In the meantime, can you tell me what you see?"

Gamble edged one hulking shoulder under the shiny bumper lining the back of the engine. "I can get a look at part of this thing, but I'm too big to fit far enough under the engine to see all of it clearly." For the sheer size of Engine Seventeen, the vehicle really was pretty low-slung.

"For God's sake. I swear you boys would be screwed without me," Shae said, although Luke didn't miss the shaky inhale that followed as she planted herself on the floor of the engine bay between Kellan and Gamble. "Move over and let me under there."

"Shae." Capelli's voice was quiet, yet serious enough to make the hair on the back of Luke's neck stand at complete attention. "You don't have any experience taking a visual inventory of an explosive device. Stop."

"No can do, Starsky," she murmured. "I hear you, but my team is my team."

"Shae," Gamble started, but she cut him off with one look.

"Don't, you big oaf. If you three are out here, I'm out here, too. Plus, it's not like being in the common room is going to save me if things go tango uniform. The least I can do is help."

"Nothing's going tango uniform," Luke said, a sudden burst of determination pumping through his chest. He hadn't come this far to die in a bomb blast, or to let anyone else he cared about die that way, either. *Focus.* "We've got a plan. Shae's going to take a look under the engine so the bomb squad guys can tell us how to defuse this thing, and we're all going to walk out of here once we do."

He looked at Quinn, holding on to her wide, dark blue

stare as he promised, "We're going to fix this. All of us, together."

A beat of silence passed, then another before Bridges said, "Slater's right. We need to know what we're dealing with here. But McCullough"—his expression brooked zero argument—"be careful. And don't touch *anything.*"

"Yeah, no worries there, Cap. I'm reckless, not brainless."

Palming the flashlight that Kellan had pulled from a nearby storage compartment, Shae slid back over the smooth concrete, edging her way beneath the engine until only her boots showed. She described what she saw in details that scared the hell out of Luke, but he marshaled every last ounce of his energy into keeping his adrenaline in check.

This was a call, just like all the others they went on. They were a team. They would find the solution.

He just prayed that happened before Ice blew up the fire house and everyone in it.

25

Quinn stood frozen in place among the concrete and cinderblocks, willing herself not to vomit as she listened to Shae describe the bomb strapped to the undercarriage of Engine Seventeen. Her brain twisted with an overload of terrifying questions—how could someone have snuck in here to plant a device that sophisticated and insidious while they'd been inside for roll call? How was that person watching, and could he see them all right now?

Was Ice watching? With that stare he'd given her the other day and the message on the bomber's cell phone—*die like all ten of you deserve*—there was no way he wasn't behind this.

Most importantly, how the hell were she and Luke and everyone else she loved going to get out of this without dying right where they stood?

Easy. Breathe. Luke is right. There's a plan. Breathe.

The message got past her fear center, albeit only by a hair. Quinn inhaled, watching closely as Shae slid out from beneath the engine.

"Okay," Sinclair said over the two-way. "I've got Captain Logan Pierce on the line from S.W.A.T.'s bomb squad. He's got jurisdiction until the immediate threat has been neutralized. He's en route to the scene with the rest of his team. The intelligence unit is also headed your way, ETA ten minutes."

Quinn's heart pounded hard enough to make her dizzy. "But you can't come in. If this guy sees you—"

"We're not coming in," Sinclair assured. "The last thing we want to do is give this guy a reason to detonate that bomb before we can defuse it. But the RPD has to evacuate the block, and S.W.A.T.'s presence is standard operating procedure for a bomb threat of this nature."

"Something your bomber likely knows." Quinn didn't recognize the masculine voice on the line, which meant it must belong to Pierce, who continued with, "With a device like that, there's no way this is his first trip to the big dance. We're not going to break any of his rules, but I'm sure as hell not going to let him blow up your fire house, either. So let's get down to business, shall we?"

"Affirmative," Bridges said, everyone else in the engine bay nodding in unison. "Just tell us what to do."

Pierce didn't pause. "From what you're describing, this device is pretty complex. It doesn't mean I can't defuse it, but walking you through the process is going to take time, and you're going to need at least a couple sets of very steady hands to make it happen."

"That, we've got," Luke said. He sounded so calm, so certain everything would be fine, that the pressure in Quinn's chest eased enough to allow her half a breath.

"Good. Two of you have military experience, is that correct?"

"Affirmative." Bridges nodded. "Both Gamble and Walker did multiple tours in the Middle East, one as a

SpecOps Marine, the other as a Ranger. But McCullough is the only one who can fit all the way under the engine."

"That's okay. I think we can still make this work."

Pierce talked Shae through a return trip back beneath Engine Seventeen. Luke lay down on the floor beside the engine's rear driver's side tires, holding the two-way as close to Shae as possible so she could communicate with Pierce hands-free. After a few minutes of slow back-and-forth, Pierce gave Quinn a list of tools to gather—all of which were thankfully standard issue for rescue squad and readily available in their vehicle's storage compartments—and began walking Shae, Kellan, and Gamble through defusing the bomb, step by excruciating step. Quinn's breath caught with each command, every tool Luke passed over making her pulse race faster and her stomach twist into softball-sized knots. Although it was rocky and definitely not swift, the team seemed to make some tentative progress, Pierce's tone lifting with each step in their exchange.

Right up until an odd buzzing sound caught Quinn's attention. "What the..." She looked around the engine bay, her heart launching into her windpipe as she realized where the sound had originated.

She scooped up the cell phone with a shaking hand. Oh...*God*. "Captain Pierce! A message just popped up on the cell phone that was left with the bomb."

"I need you to read it to me, Copeland. Word for word."

"It says, 'Tick tock. Time to die'." Quinn's throat threatened to close over the rest, but she managed to shove the words past her lips. "And there's a timer under the message. It just started counting down." Her voice trembled. "From five minutes."

Silence punched through the engine bay, swallowing all of the air around her until Pierce said, "We're all just going to keep doing our jobs here, okay? You guys have been great so far and my team is right up the block. I *will* get you out of this."

"Okay," Gamble grated. "What's next?"

Pierce gave them a few more directives each before he said, "Alright. McCullough and Walker, you're good to disengage. Gamble, I'm going to need you to cut that final wire on my command. But first, we need to clear that engine bay."

"Captain—" Bridges argued, but Pierce cut him off in less than a breath.

"Time is of the essence here, Captain Bridges. As soon as Gamble cuts that wire, I want everyone to fall out through the front door of the fire house. S.W.A.T. is standing by in an armored personnel carrier at your ten, and that's your rendezvous point. We have less than three minutes left. It needs to be now."

Bridges blew out a breath, turning his chin into the two-way on his shoulder. "Copy that. Hawkins, get squad to the primary exit and prepare to evacuate to the APC on Pierce's command." Lowering his hand from the radio, he spun his stare from Quinn to the rest of the crew on engine. "Everybody but Gamble out."

"Go," Gamble said, cutting off any would-be arguments from the rest of them at the quick. "No time for fucking around. Let's get this done."

Quinn looked at the lieutenant, tears pricking at the backs of her eyelids. Shae, Kellan, and Luke did what he said, though, moving from the engine bay floor to the doorway. But two steps shy of the threshold, Luke turned back.

"Gamble. I owe you that story and a beer at the Crooked Angel."

"Don't worry, rookie," he said, the brief flash of emotion

in his dark stare sending Quinn's heart into a full corkscrew. "I intend to collect."

The group hustled from the engine bay to the front lobby, where Lieutenant Hawkins met them all with turnout gear at the ready. The coats were a small precaution in the face of the big-ass bomb beneath the engine—*don't think about it, don't think about it*—but they were better than nothing against the heat of a potential blast.

"Breathe, baby." Luke's whisper found her ear, and he grazed a kiss over her temple even though they were in plain sight of every firefighter at Seventeen, save Gamble. "We're going to be just fine."

"Okay." Reaching down, Quinn grabbed his hand, gripping tight as they listened to Pierce give the command to cut the last remaining wire in three...*Oh God*...two...*watch over me, I know you'll watch over me*...one.

Gamble's voice sliced over the line. "The wire is cut and the timer is dark. I repeat, the timer is dark."

"Fall out, fall out, fall out!" Pierce yelled.

Everything that happened next was on fast-forward, a jumbled blur of images and sounds. Quinn surged through Station Seventeen's front door, pushed on a tide of firefighters and adrenaline, still clutching Luke's hand. She ran as fast as she could, her boots stabbing into the pavement and her muscles burning with exertion. Bright late-morning sunlight threatened to fry her vision, but she didn't stop running. With every slam of her feet, she expected the full-body impact of an explosion less and less, and she chanced a glance behind her just in time to see Gamble clear the front door of the fire house, the building still intact.

Holy shit. Holy *shit*.

Everyone was out. Everyone was safe.

They'd done it. They'd defused the bomb meant to kill them all.

Even though the fire house hadn't exploded and the normally busy block had been emptied of traffic and bystanders, chaos still rippled around her. Quinn had lost hold of Luke's hand in the frenzy, but a pair of well-armed S.W.A.T. officers were guiding the firefighters toward a large, armored vehicle sitting in the middle of Washington Boulevard. Sweat bloomed between her shoulder blades as she hustled alongside her station-mates, but a flash of a familiar face caught in her peripheral vision, a hard prickle of dread following in its wake.

There, standing among the smattering of people either brave or stupid enough to be standing behind the bright yellow RPD road block barriers, stood Ice, staring her down from beneath the brim of his baseball hat. Only this time, he wasn't smiling.

This time, his dark, soulless stare pierced right through her, and it promised nothing short of murder.

Everything in Quinn's brain screamed at her to freeze, and her feet clattered to a sloppy halt on Washington Boulevard. Her survival instinct shrieked at her to run, to find Sinclair, to give in to the cold, sharp fear daring her to break down and fall to pieces right there on the street.

But she didn't do any of those things.

Instead, she snatched her cell phone from her back pocket and started snapping pictures.

AN HOUR LATER, Quinn's adrenal gland was still firing on all cylinders. She was safe; hell, between the S.W.A.T. team and the intelligence unit, she was probably surrounded by enough grit and firepower to protect a small nation. Still, from the near miss of the bomb scare to the way Ice had tried yet again to intimidate her with his stealthy presence, her nerves had pretty much gone through a blender.

"Hey." A bottle of water appeared in front of her, and Luke along with it. "Drink this. You need to stay hydrated."

"You do know that if I was going to go into shock, I'd have done it by now, right? Plus, the paramedics from Station Twenty-Nine gave me the all-clear, just like everyone else." Quinn lifted enough of a brow to mark the words as not entirely serious. Too bad for her, Luke didn't bite.

"Yep. And *you* know I'm going to worry about you regardless of how many medical facts you throw at me right now, right?"

Fair enough. After all, she'd blatantly listened to Luke's exchange with the paramedics who had done his assessment to make sure they'd done a thorough job. "Okay, okay. I get it."

"Good. Then drink up."

Taking a healthy sip of water, Quinn looked around the interior of S.W.A.T.'s mobile command post, which had been situated two blocks south of the fire house for safety's sake. The last of A-shift had just earned a green light health-wise, and they'd all been shepherded into the S.W.A.T. team's tour bus-like vehicle along with all the members of the intelligence unit. Although the firefighters wore no less than a hundred questions apiece in their stares, they waited as Sergeant Sinclair finished privately talking to both Captain Bridges and Captain Pierce in the back of the vehicle.

"Okay." Sinclair walked to the center of the space, taking everyone's attention with him. "Let's get the most important information out of the way. Captain Pierce's team has confirmed that the bomb has been fully disarmed. They've obviously got a task in front of them in getting the device thoroughly dismantled and safely disposed of," he added. "So until then, Station Seventeen—and the entire block—will be shut down. RPD's crime scene unit will also be working in conjunction with S.W.A.T. to gather any evidence from the scene that will point us in the direction of the perpetrator."

"But you have a theory about who did this," Gamble said, and Quinn had to hand it to him. The lieutenant wasn't just tough and gruff. He was also sharp as hell.

"We do," Sinclair said slowly, looking first at Captain Bridges, then at her and Luke. "As most of you have probably guessed, it's our feeling that Station Seventeen was chosen as a specific target for today's bomb threat. While the investigation is ongoing and we can't disclose a lot of details as such, here's what we can tell you right now."

Quinn's heartbeat accelerated as he gave a bare-bones account of her and Luke's kidnapping, along with the intelligence unit's belief that Ice was 'a person of interest' in both the assault on Carmen as well as today's bombing. She felt her station-mates' shocked stares on her throughout the debriefing, but she did her best to keep her fear over what had happened today far from her face.

Ice might have tried to hurt everyone she cared about, but they'd been stronger. Smarter. And the intelligence unit *would* catch him.

They had to.

"So obviously, we're going to need to proceed with caution now that the threat level has increased," Sinclair finished.

Lieutenant Hawkins was the first person to break the two-ton silence that followed, leaning forward to brace his forearms over the tops of his navy blue uniform pants.

"Just tell us what to do, Sarge. Copeland and Slater are two of our own. We'll do whatever it takes to keep 'em safe."

Sinclair nodded, and Quinn's heart went for broke against her ribs. "I appreciate that, Hawk, but it's going to be a matter of keeping all of you safe. A-shift is obviously done for the day while the S.W.A.T. team and the crime scene unit work," the sergeant said. "We're actively pursuing several leads in this case, and we're not going to stop until Ice is behind bars. That said, until we get him, we have to ask that you all keep a low profile. Walker and McCullough"—he paused to pin each firefighter with a stare—"because of your living arrangements, you're obviously covered. But the rest of you will have to check in at twelve-hour intervals, and no unnecessary outings for anyone, especially not alone. If anything around you looks suspicious, don't wait. Call it in. Any questions?"

After everyone shook their heads, Sinclair continued. "We've got officers standing by who will escort you safely home. Copeland, Slater." He slid a steely glance at the two of them, his expression making her breath and her pulse play a full-contact game of *tag, you're it*. "If you could stay behind for a word."

"Of course," she said, her reply mingling with Luke's "copy that." The group began to disband, with Isabella talking in low tones to Kellan and Luke giving up a quick, "be right back," as he took a few steps toward Gamble. Shae appeared in front of Quinn, not hesitating a microsecond before grabbing her into a fierce hug.

"Jesus, girl! *That's* why you've been off rotation so much for the last week and a half? You were kidnapped and threatened at gunpoint by some psycho?"

"Yeah." Quinn disentangled herself from her friend's

grasp, torn between fear at the reminder and relief that finally, she didn't have to hide the truth anymore.

Shae shook her head, her disheveled ponytail bouncing off one shoulder. "I can't believe you didn't say anything."

"The case has been..." Right. There was no good way to finish that sentence, so Quinn went with, "Sinclair wanted to be really careful not to tip Ice off."

Shae waved a hand through the air. "Oh, the safety part, I get. After what happened with me and Capelli and that hacker-stalker-wingnut Vaughn a few months ago, I trust the intelligence unit a billion percent. But I had the support of everyone around me then. I just hate that you had to go through this alone."

"I wasn't alone." Quinn glanced at Luke, who was talking quietly to Gamble and Dempsey a handful of feet away. Her heart squeezed, but God, the feeling was frighteningly good. "I had Luke."

Shae followed her gaze, her smile surprisingly sweet. "I'm glad." She squeezed Quinn's shoulder, leaning in to whisper, "But when all of this is said and done and this jackass Ice is rotting in jail, I am *so* feeding you margaritas until you dish on the rookie."

Quinn should've known her friend's devious streak wouldn't stay at bay for more than a second or two. "Let's get there first, okay?"

"Mmm. 'Til then, call me if you need anything." Shae hugged her one more time for good measure.

"Please stay safe," Quinn said. They might've stopped Ice today, but if he tried again...

Shae surprised her by letting out a long laugh. "Something tells me Capelli isn't going to let me out of his sight anytime soon. I'll be fine. I promise."

She winked, turning on her boot heels to head for the

front of the vehicle. The rest of A-shift followed, giving Quinn various shoulder pats and we've-got-your-back chin lifts as they filed out. Everyone in the intelligence unit remained inside the command post with her and Luke and Captain Bridges, and Sinclair didn't waste any time diving in.

"We're going to need to put the two of you under around-the-clock surveillance for at least the next day or so. It's not the same thing as protective custody," he added quickly. "You can stay at your own apartments, and you're not on total lockdown. But you won't be able to go anywhere without a police escort and your check-ins will be frequent and mandatory. In light of the bomb threat, the constant eyes-on is a necessary precaution until we can zero in on Ice's location and make an arrest."

"Agreed," Bridges said with a nod, and Luke's brows went up, seconding Quinn's surprise.

"And no one else needs that kind of protection?" he asked.

"Everyone needs to be vigilant," Sinclair said, both Isabella and Maxwell's nods confirming the statement. "We're all on heightened alert, and Capelli will arrange for both check-ins and more frequent patrols for your family after they've been briefed. But we're about to launch a man hunt for Ice that he wasn't expecting, and he's not stupid. We want to make sure he doesn't try to retaliate before we can take him down. I know he threatened your loved ones"—Sinclair's voice dropped low enough to send goose bumps over Quinn's arms even though the interior of the command vehicle was plenty warm—"but at this point we have to consider the two of you his primary targets."

Slowly, Quinn nodded. She was far from in love with the idea of having a perma-shadow—God, she was on edge enough as it was. She *was* pretty fond of the whole living-and-breathing thing, though, and anyway, she trusted Sinclair. "Okay."

Luke nodded in agreement, then asked, "While we're busy laying low, what's next for the investigation?"

The detectives volleyballed a secret-code glance around the command post, and eventually, it landed on Sinclair. "Officially, I can't disclose any details pertaining to your case. Unofficially..."

He looked at Garza, who answered with a jerk of his darkly stubbled chin. "One of the guys from the gang unit just heard from an informant connected to the Scarlet Reapers that this arms deal is going down on Saturday night. I can't substantiate this yet, but he says the seller is Brady Sorenson."

"Whoa." Hollister's shoulder blades smacked against the back of his chair. "*The* Brady Sorenson? As in, the guy who supplies weapons to more than half the cartels in Miami?"

"Along with most of the gangs in Jacksonville and Atlanta," Garza agreed, the look on his face making Quinn wonder if this could possibly get any worse. "His reach is huge. Word is, he's looking to keep branching out, and Ice is his guy."

"Not anymore," grated Sinclair. "What've we got from the foot patrols and city cams?"

Isabella frowned. "Unfortunately not a lot, although we're still waiting on the footage from RPD headquarters and a couple of the private businesses on the block. There was a ton of chaos directly after the evac. We did a thorough sweep of the surrounding area as soon as we could, but there was no sign of anyone who could have been the bomber, or of Ice."

"I'm one hundred percent sure it was him." Quinn willed

her voice to steadiness even though the rest of her felt like dry leaves in a wind tunnel. "The photos don't lie."

Hale reached out to put a hand on her forearm. "We'd believe you even without them, Quinn. He's just really good at hiding, that's all."

"It was really quick thinking to grab pictures." Garza flipped through the images on Quinn's phone, which she'd immediately handed over the second Ice had whipped around and disappeared into the churning crowd. "He hasn't shown his face in ages. These will go a long way toward helping us find him."

"I'm sorry, I don't understand," Luke said, leaning in from beside Quinn to look carefully at Sinclair. "I mean, Ice *has* made a career out of hiding well, and like you said, he's not stupid. So why would he do something as brash as planting this bomb right before this huge gun deal goes down?"

"Because that bomb was meant to cause the sort of destruction that would have taken us weeks to recover from."

Shock rippled up Quinn's spine as the sergeant's bone-chilling words sank in. "You think the bomb was just meant to be a diversion?"

"Actually, we think his intent was twofold," Maxwell ventured. "If the bomb had gone off like Ice had meant it to, then yes, that would have been one hell of a distraction from the gun deal with Sorenson. But he's also a mean SOB, and he knows you told us about the kidnapping."

Luke's eyes went wide with sudden understanding. "So he *was* trying to make good on his threat to hurt us."

"It's why we're going to go after him with everything we possibly can." Sinclair looked at Capelli, who had set up not one, but two laptops at the desk built into the side wall of the command vehicle. "Let's get all the security patrols set up. And I want all that street cam footage run under a goddamn microscope. Find out who Ice is working with."

"You got it, boss."

"Garza, talk to your buddy's informant. Get everything you can on this gun deal. Maxwell, you and Hale take another run at Dixon. See if he knows anything we can use. Moreno." He turned toward Isabella, his expression as serious as Quinn had ever seen it. "You and Hollister wallpaper the goddamn city with the photos Quinn took. I want everyone with a pulse to know who Ice is and what he looks like. In the meantime, I'll reach out to my contacts at the ATF to see if they've got anything on Sorenson that can help us with this case."

Although Quinn hadn't thought it possible, Sinclair's stare grew sharper, his tone growing even more frost-filled as he said, "This asshole took a serious jab at some of our own today. I want him behind bars where he belongs. Let's go, people."

"So for now, Luke and I just lie low and wait?" Quinn asked, reaching for Luke's hand.

Sinclair nodded. "We're going to catch him. With those photos you took and the intel we've got on this gun deal, it's only a matter of time."

26

Luke stood on the sidewalk in front of five-sixty-three Balmour Avenue and waited for a feeling that didn't come. Not that he *wanted* the jagged nerves and the rapid heartbeat he'd been expecting when he'd arrived in front of his grandmother's house in an unmarked police car with two armed officers at the helm. Still, after ten years of his instincts warning against any sort of relationship that didn't have a sell-by date stamped on it in big, bold letters, he'd been expecting at least a few jitters over the familial meet-and-greet that was about to go down.

Still nope. Although from the way Quinn kept smoothing her hand over the front of her flowy white tank top and chewing on her bottom lip, he might be the only one.

"Are you sure about this?" she asked, swiveling her gaze from the neatly kept brick and clapboard cottage to the spot where Luke stood beside her. But they'd spent the last twenty-four hours holed up in her apartment, per Sinclair's request. While he couldn't complain too much—they'd been perfectly safe and perfectly naked the whole time—he was reaching his absolute limit of patience for only hearing about his sister and grandmother's safety secondhand. Plus, there was a bigger truth at play, one he could no longer deny.

Quinn was beautiful. Kind, yet fearless. Wide-open. Perfect. And Luke didn't just want to let her in.

He wanted to show her everything.

On second thought, it looked like his heart would go for that rapidly beating thing after all. "Yes, I'm sure about this," he said as he wrapped his fingers around hers and squeezed. "I already know your family. It only makes sense for you to meet mine."

Quinn laughed, and bingo. Her nerves seemed to fall away. "That's not fair," she said, her steps finding a rhythm with his as they began to cover the path leading up to the front walkway under the careful watch of the plainclothes officers standing guard just out of earshot. "You work with my family."

"Uh, your 'big brothers' are Hawkins and Gamble. The scary-factor on those two alone makes this more than fair," Luke pointed out.

Another laugh, and yeah, that was officially his favorite sound. "Mmm, you may have a point there. Although for the record, once you get past all that country-boy bravado, Hawk actually has a secret squishy side."

"I will take your word for that," he said over a laugh of his own. "I'm just glad they're all safe."

It hadn't taken long after they'd disbanded yesterday for Capelli to set up a secure section of the RPD network so everyone at Seventeen could check in with each other since their cell phones couldn't be guaranteed as safe. While Luke had the distinct impression the guy had done so at Shae's urging—and that Shae had pushed for the sake of Quinn's sanity—seeing the messages from all of their station-mates had gone a long way toward nailing his hope into place.

They'd overcome the impossible; Christ, they'd dismantled a fucking *bomb*. There hadn't been so much as a peep of disturbance anywhere near Quinn's apartment or Luke's, which the RPD had kept an eye on even though he hadn't set so much as a baby toe in the place since Garza had taken him there to grab some clothes yesterday. Likewise, Hayley and Momma Billie had been safe—albeit "totes bored" according to Hayley's messages over the secure network— ever since they'd returned home from the precinct via police escort.

Well. At least this visit of his would give them a whooooole lot of something to talk about while the intelligence unit closed in on Ice and put him in jail for the rest of his devious scumbag life.

Luke pulled a set of keys from his pocket, letting himself into the house to the tune of the alarm system's door chime. He'd made sure to have Isabella call over to let his sister and grandmother know he was on the way. Per security protocol, he hadn't officially planned the trip ahead of time, so the visit was a bit impromptu. But he'd already scared the hell out of his family once this week with a thwarted bomb threat. He had no intention of doing it twice by barging in unannounced when they were on a freakishly high security alert.

"Hello? Momma Billie? It's me," he called out, closing the door and entering the six-digit code to keep the alarm from going berserk. The keypads were specially outfitted to flash every time one of the doors opened since Hayley couldn't hear the chime. The one in the kitchen must have done its job, because a few seconds later, she came running down the hallway from the back of the house.

Luke! Oh my God, I'm so happy to see you. We've been so bored, and kind of scared, and—

His sister pulled up completely short, her tie-dyed Converse high tops squeaking to a stop at the sight of Quinn standing next to him on the floorboards. Hayley's shock lasted less than a second, though, before an ear-to-ear grin tore over her face.

Oh, shut up! she signed rapidly, her dark eyes sparking with excitement. *You brought a girl home! This is her, right? Your partner, Quinn? I knew she was pretty! Momma Billie is going to be so mad you didn't tell that detective to say anything when she called to tell us you were coming. I bet she would have started making something other than meatloaf if she'd known you were bringing a girl home. You know what, never mind. Oh my God, introduce me! Please?*

Luke lost the battle with his sigh. He hadn't brought a woman home since...well, okay, ever. He should have known Hayley would make a monster deal out of this.

"Okay, okay. Jeez, don't pull a hamstring." He spoke as he signed, not because Hayley needed him to, or even because she preferred to lip read. But he didn't want to exclude Quinn from the conversation, even if Hayley was probably about to make him regret it. "Quinn, this is my sister, Hayley. Hayley, this is my partner, Quinn."

Quinn smiled and slowly signed, speaking out loud as she went. "Hi, Hayley. It's so nice to meet you."

Hayley's brows traveled up. *She knows how to sign?*

"Yes, Quinn is learning to sign," he replied, trying to keep both his expression and his tone nonchalant. Not that he was having a truckload of luck in either department. "We treated a deaf patient a couple weeks ago, and ever since then, I've been teaching her a few basics."

Hayley took a step toward Quinn, facing her fully and

not even bothering to rein in her Cheshire-cat smile as she signed back, *It's nice to meet you, too. Like,* so *nice,* while Luke translated directly.

"I'm sorry," Quinn said, shifting her weight from one sandal to the other on the floorboards. "That's really all I know how to say so far. Unless you want to know that"—she paused, her brows furrowed with enough concentration to blow Luke's completely as she signed—"my favorite color is light blue and I really like cheeseburgers."

Hayley huffed out a soundless laugh, and okay, Luke had to laugh, too.

"What?" Quinn asked, starting to laugh herself. He started to answer, but Hayley shushed him in ASL, reaching out in a *may I?* gesture for Quinn's hands.

"This is the sign for light blue," Luke said, watching first as Hayley guided Quinn through it, then as Quinn repeated the sign on her own.

"Ohhh. Got it. Light...blue." She did it once more for good measure. "Wait. What did I say the first time?"

Unable to help himself, he grinned. "That your favorite color is rutabaga."

Quinn's smile was self-deprecating and utterly, flawlessly gorgeous as she looked at Hayley. "I'm sorry. I guess I'm not too great at ASL yet."

"That's okay," he translated as his sister shook her head. "I can lip read as long as I can see you."

Hayley turned her attention back to Luke, the sudden softer version of her smile catching him right in the solar plexus. *You really like her, don't you? And she likes you, too, because she tried really hard. I can tell she practiced.*

Making the executive decision to edit the conversation to preserve his pride, he relayed the part about Quinn having signed well, switching to ASL only as he said to Hayley, *Now*

*no more side conversations. Momma Billie won't have it, and you
know they're not polite.*

Okay, okay, she responded with a dutiful nod.

And yes, he snuck in before the clack of his grandmother's shoes on the hallway floor turned into her presence in the foyer, unable to keep the squeeze in his chest from translating to a smile as he signed, *I really like her.*

Hayley smiled. *I like her, too.*

Thankfully, both the inquisitive look on Quinn's face and the odd but so-damned-good feeling in Luke's rib cage fell prey to his grandmother's voice a second later. "Luke! Oh, thank God you're here. I've been so worried...*oh.*"

Although Momma Billie's halt at the end of the hallway was more graceful than Hayley's, Luke knew the woman well enough to recognize the depth of her surprise.

"It's okay. I'm safe," he said, wanting to address her concern. While both Sinclair and Detective Hale had sworn up, down, and sideways that they'd assured his grandmother of his safety while the search for Ice was ongoing, Luke had known she wouldn't believe it until she saw him with the eyes God had given her. "I'm really fine, Momma Billie."

"Well, let me see you, then." Not even the fact that he'd brought company could keep her from opening her arms and grabbing him into a fierce hug.

Luke's throat tightened, and he let her hold on to him for a few beats longer than usual before pulling back with a sheepish smile. "I didn't mean to barge in on you, but I ah. Wanted to make sure you're okay. I also want you to meet my partner, Quinn. Quinn Copeland, this is my grandmother, Wilhelmina Turner."

"I'm a tough old bird. Just fine. And you can't barge in on family," his grandmother tsked, but the smile tugging at the corners of her mouth gave her away. "Quinn, it's lovely to meet you. Welcome."

"The pleasure's mine, Mrs. Turner." Quinn reached out to shake Momma Billie's hand, and now the smile on his grandmother's mouth made a full showing.

"Oh no, we'll have none of that, now. I appreciate your manners, sweetheart, but Mrs. Turner was my mother-in-law. You can call me Billie, or Miss Billie if you'd rather."

"Miss Billie," Quinn agreed. "Thank you for your welcome. I know I'm here with Luke unexpectedly."

"It's no trouble at all. We've had quite a few unexpected circumstances over the last few days." Just like that, his grandmother's smile slipped away. "Are you two alright? I can't even imagine…"

The look on her face—the one that suggested that she not only *could* imagine, but had done so in Technicolor for the past twenty-four hours—sent unease rolling down Luke's spine. He needed to focus on the end game. Talking about the kidnapping and the bomb threat would only terrify her.

"We're okay," he said, making sure to look Momma Billie in the eye so she'd know he meant it. "The intelligence unit has a good plan. They're going to catch this guy really soon."

Did he really say he was going to hurt you? Or come hurt us? Hayley asked, and shit. Shit, shit, shit, Luke had no good answer to her question. At least not one that wouldn't frighten her out of her mind or be a bald-faced lie.

Quinn looked at him, her concern clear, and he relayed Hayley's question. He grasped for something—pretty much anything at this point would do—but then Quinn shocked the hell out of him by turning toward Hayley.

"Ice said a lot of terrible things. But you don't have to worry, because none of them are true. Your brother's tough, and even though some of the things the detectives in the intelligence unit told you are pretty scary, they really are doing everything they can to keep us all safe."

Oh. Hayley paused, clearly processing what Quinn had said. *Well, I guess that makes sense. And the detectives do seem really smart.*

Luke translated for Quinn, while Momma Billie placed a squeeze on Hayley's shoulder.

"Come now," she said, her stare soft yet serious in the warm, cozy light of the foyer. "No more talk of bad men and empty threats. The police are doing their job, and Luke and Quinn are here, safe and sound. That's what matters."

Okay. Hayley nodded, and Luke saw the glint forming in her eyes just a second too late. *So if we're changing the subject to happier things, does that mean I can tell Quinn about the time Luke put on a tiara and a feather boa to have tea with me when I was little?*

"Hayley," Momma Billie warned. But something that had been buried for far too long broke free in Luke's chest, and he shook his head with a slow smile.

"No, it's okay. Hayley's right. We should be focusing on happier things." He turned his attention to Quinn, whose curiosity was wildly obvious. "My adorable sister here"—Luke paused to let Hayley roll her eyes—"wants to know if she can tell you about the time she talked me into wearing a tiara and a feather boa so we could have high tea on her eighth birthday."

Quinn, who had zero poker face to begin with, barked out a laugh. "Oh, *please* tell me there are pictures. Because—"

"No pictures," Luke said, because as much as he loved his sister, he also wasn't insane. "It's a great story, though. If you want to hear it."

Wait. Are you seriously going to let me tell her? Hayley asked, her lips parted in surprise.

But Luke didn't hesitate. "Yep. I am going to let you tell her."

"Well." Momma Billie brushed her fingers over the front of her blouse, and there was no missing the emotion in her smile. "I suppose all of our best stories do get told in the kitchen."

Quinn peered down the hallway. "Oh, can I help with dinner?"

She gestured to the dish towel that took up permanent residence over Momma Billie's shoulder whenever the woman cooked, and oh Lord, he'd never live down the raft of stories that were about to come out of the woodwork now.

Funny, for the first time ever, that felt okay.

Momma Billie put her arm around Quinn, flashing her a conspiratorial smile. "Everyone helps in the kitchen, honey. That's how this family works."

Quinn shot a glance over her shoulder, her blond brows winging up as she looked at him. "You wore a tiara *and* you can cook?"

Ah, busted. But it wasn't as if he'd been willing to confess something as personal as learning how to cook at fourteen out of necessity before now.

"A little," Luke hedged, caving under the pressure of both his sister and his grandmother's I-call-foul frowns. "Okay, okay! Yes, I can cook."

He makes the best marinara sauce in the world, Hayley signed.

Upon hearing the translation, Quinn laughed. "You've been holding out on me."

Luke watched her make her way to the kitchen with his grandmother on one side and his sister on the other, the three of them conversing as easily as if they'd known each other for years, and his chest panged with a feeling that would have been dangerous if it wasn't so right.

"Yeah, well," he whispered to himself. "I'm not holding out anymore."

27

"Oh my God, I'm so full, I honestly think you'll need a wheelbarrow to get me back to my apartment."

Quinn rubbed a hand over her belly, making her way to the unmarked police car in front of Luke's grandmother's house even though each step took effort. Between the incredible dinner, the *very* incredible dessert (Quinn would never look at strawberry shortcake the same again, ever), and the side-splitting laughter she'd shared with his family over the last two and a half hours, she was certain she'd burst at any moment.

Even crazier? As full as her stomach was, it was nothing compared to her heart.

"Yeah, Momma Billie's cooking will do that to you," Luke said, leading the way over the dusky front walk.

"Nope. No way." Quinn laughed. "I saw you make that buttery, fluffy goodness you called mashed potatoes. That meal was a team effort."

"You're going to tell everyone at the fire house I can cook, aren't you?"

A few weeks ago, she would have worried that she couldn't read either Luke's guarded expression or the hard-to-discern tone of his question. But now she saw the playful glint hiding in his ice-blue stare, the slight yet definitely sexy twist of his full, firm mouth, and she didn't even think twice about saying, "Uh, yeah. If you think I'm going to pass up a shot at having those potatoes every time you draw kitchen duty, you're out of your mind."

"I knew I should've kept that close to the vest," Luke replied, and even though his smile marked the words as less than serious, Quinn's heart still squeezed.

He'd trusted her enough to let her in, past his armor and his defenses and all the things that scared him.

And now that she was there, she didn't ever want to let go.

"Well I'm glad you didn't, because I had an incredible time tonight," she said, threading her fingers through his. "Thanks for bringing me to meet your family. Your grandmother and sister are really great."

Luke's low laugh melted into the shadowy twilight. "I'm pretty sure they both feel the same way about you. In fact, I'm willing to bet that Hayley won't stop badgering me until I bring you back for another round of sign language lessons and crazy ambo stories."

While the four of them had spent a fantastic evening together, Hayley had shown a quick affection for Quinn that had been mutual. The kid was hilarious, not to mention wildly smart. Chatting with her via a combination of lip reading, white-board messages, and translation from Luke and Miss Billie had been all too easy, not to mention fun as hell. Although she'd never had a sibling of her own, Quinn had felt instantly at home with Hayley.

"I'd love to come back, and I promise to keep the ambo

stories as PG-13 as possible. I'm pretty sure your grand-mother wouldn't appreciate—"

Out of the corner of her eye, something moved in the shadows beside the house, sending an immediate, scissor-sharp fear through her bloodstream that froze both her and her words right there on the pavement.

I will make every single person you care about feel what you're feeling right now, and then I'll make you watch while I blow their fucking brains all over the floor...

No. Oh God. No, no. Ice couldn't possibly be there, watching. He couldn't—

"Quinn? What's the matter?" Luke's body was bowstring tight and directly in front of hers in an instant. But then a breeze ruffled the thick canopy of leaves overhead, the light from the curbside streetlamp shifting to reveal nothing more than an alcove housing a pair of trash bins in the side yard of the house beside Luke's grandmother's, and Quinn's muscles went lax with relief.

"Nothing." She gave up a soft, self-deprecating laugh. "I thought I saw something in the side yard there, but...I swear, being under surveillance all the time is sending my imagi-nation into overdrive."

"Are you sure?" He lasered a stare over the yard. "Maybe we should have the officers check it out, just to be on the safe side."

Quinn took one last look at the shadowy space between the two houses before shaking her head. She wouldn't let these creepy, paranoid thoughts snuff out the fun of her evening, and she *definitely* wouldn't let them unnecessarily frighten Luke's grandmother and sister.

"No. They've been out here, keeping an eye on the house this whole time. If someone was out here, they'd know. Really," she said, nodding toward the unmarked car a few dozen feet away. "It was nothing. I promise."

"Okay," Luke said after a long second, pulling her close to complete the trip to the car. "Then let's go home."

The officers made quick work of both the fifteen-minute trip from Miss Billie's house to Quinn's building and the sweep of her apartment, proper, before offering up a polite goodnight. She kicked off her sandals, the warmth and safety and pure goodness of the last few hours wrapping back around her as Luke pulled her close.

"Hey."

"Hey," Quinn whispered back. She knew it should seem odd or even awkward that they were standing there in her living room, hanging on to each other without talking. But as crazy as it sounded, she didn't need words. She was safe, strong. Here, in his arms, nothing could touch her.

Here, she felt cared for. Beautiful just as she was.

Loved.

Quinn pushed up to her toes, slanting her mouth against Luke's. Forcing herself to ignore the provocative urge to rush, she let her lips rest on his with only the barest hint of pressure. His mouth was warm, soft, yet steady at the same time, as unique as a fingerprint, and she memorized the feel of him before beginning to move.

Slowly, she cautioned that part of her that still wanted to hurry. Quinn brushed her fingertips over Luke's shoulders, the cotton of his T-shirt giving way to bare skin as her hands skimmed up to his neck. His muscles flexed at her touch, pulling and releasing in response to each of her movements, and she couldn't help but press closer against his body in search of more.

"Quinn." He pressed back in a motion that fit hers perfectly, his hands at her hips, holding her tight. There was no mistaking the ridge of his cock against her lower belly, and the proof of his obvious arousal sent a curl of uncut lust to Quinn's core.

But she didn't give in to it. Instead, she dropped her mouth to the slope where his neck met his shoulder. Hooking her fingers around the neckline of his shirt, she tugged the fabric aside, parting her lips over his collarbone so she could taste him.

Luke stiffened at the contact, the blunt edges of his fingertips curling harder against her jeans. His breath coasted over her shoulder in a heavy exhale that threatened to rock her steadiness. It wasn't that she couldn't be patient —God, she'd wait all night if it meant she could have Luke in her bed, his cock buried between her legs until they both forgot their names. It was how much he clearly wanted *her* that pushed at her composure.

Quinn didn't want to hold back. She wanted to give him her body. Her mind. Her heart.

She wanted to give him everything.

Parting her lips wider, she kissed the column of his neck, trailing upward to the hinge of his jaw. The friction of Luke's lightly stubbled skin sent little sparks of want through her blood, and she pressed up to her toes to angle closer.

"Do you know what I see when I look at you?" Quinn whispered, selfishly letting her mouth linger over his pulse point just to feel it hammer and jump.

"No." His answer slid down her shoulder on a warm exhale. Even though her mind and body sent up matching protests, something deeper made her let go of his shoulders and take a step back. Grabbing his hand, she led him to her bedroom, turning on the small lamp on her dresser before turning to look at him in the soft, golden light.

"You're fierce. Steadfast," she said, stepping in close and

brushing her fingers over his temples. Slowly, she coasted them down his face—God, how had she never seen the subtle play of emotions there?—before lowering her touch to Luke's chest.

Quinn's heart beat faster, in time with his. But holding back now wasn't an option, and what's more, she didn't want to.

She didn't just want him. She wanted him to *know*.

"But you're also kind and honest. And I love you. You don't have to say it back," she added quickly as his eyes went round with shock. "In fact, you don't have to say anything. But it's how I feel. When I look at you, that's what I see."

For a minute, Luke simply stared. But then the surprise on his face became intensity, and he pulled her close until only a few inches remained between their mouths.

"I do have to say it back, Quinn. Not out of obligation." He held her even tighter, their bodies fused from shoulders to chests to hips. "But because it's true, and you deserve to hear it. I love you, too."

He lowered his mouth to hers, and just like that, Quinn was lost. She opened to his kiss, letting him search and find and take before claiming the lead and doing the same to him. Luke gave it readily, their back and forth building with ease that was both familiar and incredibly erotic.

She slid her fingers beneath the hem of his T-shirt. A sudden urge tore through her, refusing to be denied, and she lifted the cotton just enough to take the edge off of it.

"I want to see you." Holding the fabric with one hand, Quinn ran the other over the hard, flat plane of Luke's abs. "I want to see all of you."

He answered with a nod. A shot of desire bloomed between her legs as he let her lift his T-shirt over his shoulders, growing stronger still when she reached for the button on his jeans. She forced herself not to rush, to feel the glide of his skin, hear the shush of her fingertips on the cotton and denim as she undressed him. Finally, Luke stood in front of her bed in nothing but his boxers, and oh, she'd never wanted anyone so much in her life. But the hunger was so much more than a sexual pull to have him strip her bare or slip his fingers into the wet, slippery heat that had built between her thighs or push his cock into her harder and harder until she flew apart at the seams.

Luke had given her the power to find what she needed. And now, she wanted to take care of him.

"Quinn."

The whisper was all permission, and she didn't hesitate to take it. She brushed her fingers over the curve of his biceps, marveling at the way his muscles tightened and flexed at her touch. Her hands traveled the expanse of his chest, her breath catching in time with his exhale as she skimmed the flat disk of one dark brown nipple. Luke watched her in the muted lamplight, and the intensity on his face amped her want even higher, making her heart pound and turning her nipples to hard peaks beneath her tank top.

"God, baby. Please," he hissed, his hips bucking into the hand she'd lowered to his waistband. One swift tug had his cock springing free, and Quinn wrapped her fingers around him for a long, purposeful stroke.

"Yes. Fuck, *yes*." Luke dropped his stare to her hand, watching as she pumped from root to tip. Swiping her thumb over the bead of moisture there, she let her touch linger over the head of his cock for just a second before returning to the slow up and down rhythm. Luke kept his stare in place, and Quinn couldn't help but do the same, the provocative sight of her fingers working his body making her clit throb.

A moan escaped from her chest. Still, she didn't slow her movements, testing out different speeds and pressure until Luke moaned right along with her. He thrust into her palm, his movements growing firmer and firmer, until finally, he pulled back from her with a sharp curse.

"No more waiting." Reaching down, Luke grabbed the edge of her tank top, guiding it over her head in one fluid yank. Her shorts were next, gone with an economical set of twists and tugs, and Quinn's pulse sailed through her veins. Her bra and panties lasted only a few seconds longer, the lace barely having hit the floor beside them before Luke guided her back over the bed.

"This is supposed to be for you," she whispered, parting her knees to accommodate his body as he leaned in to cover her mouth with a long, sweeping kiss.

"Don't you see? This is what I want." He paused just long enough to draw one finger over her sex, smiling wickedly when an involuntary sigh rolled from her throat. "I love you, Quinn. I want *you*."

Kissing a path over her breasts and belly, he slid his way lower, settling his shoulders beneath her thighs. Her clit ached with need and want and a thousand other things she couldn't name. But Luke seemed to need to touch her as much as she yearned for him to give it, and he angled forward to lick her in one long, firm stroke.

"Ahhh!" Quinn arched off the bed, her pussy clenching at the contact. His lips quirked in a smile that sent shivers over her hyper-sensitive skin, and oh God, oh God, she needed this man.

"You want to give me something?" he asked, repeating

the mind-blowing move in reverse. "You want this to be for me?"

"Yes," she moaned, her hands turning to fists over the sheets beside her.

Luke looked up at her. "Then let go and come for me, baby. I only want you."

The words broke her, shattering her control and making her reckless. Quinn lifted her hips against his mouth—or maybe he met her halfway, she really didn't know. Skipping all the pleasantries of soft touches and gentle movements, he circled her clit with a punishing slide of his tongue. Sparks danced across her field of vision, growing stronger with every pass, and when he pressed a finger deep inside, her breath escaped on a gasp.

Too much. Not enough. "Luke." She opened wider in a silent bid for more. *More.* "I need…"

"I know," he whispered, sliding another finger inside her pussy with ease. "I need it too."

He dropped his mouth back to her body, pleasuring her with long strokes of his tongue and fingers. Release built deep in Quinn's belly, growing and strengthening like a perfect, beautiful storm as it crashed into her in waves. Luke worked her through her orgasm, softening his movements only when her cries became heavy exhales and her body went loose. He shifted back to grab a condom from her bedside table drawer, and by the time he'd returned to the rumpled bed sheets where she lay, the climax that had just barreled through her had begun its first twinges of rebuilding.

"Come here," Quinn said. Luke didn't pause, pressing over her and balancing his weight on one forearm as he edged the head of his cock past her entrance. Her breath caught and held, unspooling on a sigh as he tested her body in slow thrusts until finally—oh God, yes, please, yes—he was seated fully inside of her.

"Jesus, Quinn. You feel…"

Rather than finish the sentence, he began to move, and all at once, she understood what he meant.

"Luke."

His eyes flashed over hers, ice blue and wild with an emotion she'd never seen on his face. But her body, her mind, her heart, they all said the same thing.

Mine.

"Come for me, baby," Quinn said, lifting and lowering her hips. "I only want you, too."

With a heavy exhale, he started to move, thrusting into her in steady strokes. The pressure bordered on pleasure/pain, filling her pussy so completely she was tempted to scream. Luke was exactly where she wanted him, though, and each glide of his cock made her greedy for the next. Pushing deeper, he levered his hips forward, the change in angle providing direct contact with her clit. The slide above combined with the pressure below to create a pleasure like nothing Quinn had ever felt, her inner muscles tightening harder with every thrust.

"Oh. *Oh.*" Reaching around his hips, she splayed her hands over the firm curve of his ass to hold their bodies completely flush. She dug her heels into the mattress, rocking her hips wildly against him as a second climax rushed up from deep inside of her, taking her by surprise. Luke pulled back—only an inch, but the friction of his thrust in return was enough—triggering another wave of release from low in her belly. His expression changed, then, his movements growing faster and more primal. But Quinn didn't scale back or shy away from the intensity. Instead, she opened her knees wider, letting Luke find what he needed over and over until, with one last thrust, he began to shake.

She whispered his name, softening her motions little by little as his body relaxed and his own movements slowed. Eventually, they found their way beneath the blankets, their bodies curving in tight like spoons, and in that moment, lying there in the safety of Luke's arms, Quinn felt like nothing—no bombs or bullets or bad guys—could ever touch them.

28

Ice stood in the shadows and thought of two dozen ways he'd like to murder those paramedics with nothing but a rusty spoon. That they'd somehow managed to contact the RPD and defuse the bomb Rusty had planted before he could detonate it was enough to sign their death warrants in permanent ink. But the blonde was *seriously* starting to piss him off. Ice had gone out of his way to hand-craft extra fear in her because she'd been the weaker link. She was a drone. Predictable.

That she'd grown ballsy enough to take pictures of him *and* turn them over to the cops, when she damn well knew the price? The second this deal with Sorenson was in the bag, Ice was going to torture that treacherous bitch in ways she couldn't imagine.

Not even with all that knowledge of human anatomy.

While the thought of making her pay for her sudden snap of bravery took the edge off his anger, he still had to focus on the bigger picture, which meant flying way under the radar for the next two days. Unlike his appearance outside of Three Brothers last week, Ice hadn't intended for anyone to see him at the fire house yesterday. He'd only gone to make sure the job got done, to hammer home the chaos that would have eliminated the threat from those paramedics and let him make good on his threat to kill them all in one tidy little blast. Instead, he was dealing with eight-by-ten printouts of his face being wallpapered to every store-front and telephone pole in the fucking city.

On second thought, he was going to kill that blonde twice, just for good measure.

"Patience," Ice murmured, his voice disappearing into the nighttime breeze. As much as he wanted to kill both her and the boyfriend tonight and be done with it, he needed to stick to his timeline now more than ever. The bomb not going off in time was unforeseen and unfortunate, but he was smart enough to adapt his business plan and still keep his ass covered. He hadn't led the Vipers for this long only to let two paramedics be the end of him.

He knew what he was doing. The gun deal was set. It would make him the biggest, most powerful gang leader in Remington.

And he'd earned every ounce of the respect that would come with it.

Ice's cell phone vibrated, pulling him from his thoughts. Although he'd had more than enough cover not to be seen or heard for the past four hours—patrol cops were so easily fooled, it was pathetic—he still triple-checked his surround-ings before sliding his phone from his back pocket to look at the screen.

Incoming Call: Brady Sorenson.

"Mr. Sorenson," he said, keeping his voice low and neutral even though he was on full alert. They might be business partners with a common goal, but the call was unexpected, and the last thing Ice needed right now was another fucking surprise.

"Mr. Howard." The edge in Sorenson's voice was enough to send a spear of unease through Ice's gut. "It seems you've been busy."

Ice selected his words with extreme care before answering. "Yes. I've been finalizing the last of the preparations for our meeting."

Orchestrating a deal this big, with buyers he could trust and who had enough cash to buy in, plus finding a location for the exchange that was neutral, private, and easily controlled had been just shy of impossible. Not that it had kept Ice from making it happen. "Speaking of which, I've got coordinates for your team," he added, knowing full well Sorenson would want to do advance recon on the site. After all, that's what Ice would do.

"What you've got is a big problem," Sorenson said. "My sources tell me you're experiencing a visibility issue, and that it isn't small."

"There's no issue."

Anger shoved the words out of Ice's mouth too fast, and the prickly silence that followed told him that Sorenson had heard the mistake, loud and goddamned clear.

"I can assure you my sources are extremely well-informed. If they tell me there's an issue, believe me, there is," he said, and a flare of irritation made Ice's heartbeat pulse louder through the quiet night.

"Of course," he bit out. He counted to three, imagining how he'd cut the blonde's Achilles tendons to make sure she couldn't run before he started to kill her. "I understand you want to protect your assets, Mr. Sorenson. What I meant was, there's no problem."

For fuck's sake, he'd been watching the cops look for

him for the past twenty-four hours. They knew a thing or two, but so did he. Namely, all of their patterns and schedules for shift changes. He knew who they watched, from where, and when, which meant he knew their weaknesses and how to exploit them. It was how his livelihood worked, for fuck's sake.

He was the best.

Sorenson's snort caught Ice right in the chest plate. "I'm not sure I agree. I made it very clear that security was my number one priority. Yet you obviously don't seem to recall that conversation, since your face is currently being broadcast over half the city. I told you this deal was yours to lose, Mr. Howard. Well, you just lost it."

This motherfucker had to be kidding. "You're backing out of our agreement?"

"I'm telling you your services are no longer required."

"I have buyers on the line," Ice argued, but Sorenson was unmoved.

"And I have buyers across three states. I'd been hoping we could do business, but I'm not interested in any unwanted attention, and your current situation makes you a liability."

Ice's molars came together with a clack, his words seething out from between them. "I can guarantee—"

"Nothing," Sorenson said, his tone wrapped in barbed wire. "You can guarantee nothing. Which is why we're done here. It's a shame you're not ready for the big leagues."

And then the line went dead.

It took every ounce of Ice's control to focus on the tiny bedroom window he'd been watching from a distance so he didn't scream out loud. He had not—had *not*—lost the deal he'd spent months preparing for and years deserving because of that stupid whore of a paramedic.

Except...he had.

His hands cranked into fists, hard enough that he'd likely feel it later, but right now he didn't care. Right now, he only wanted one thing.

Revenge.

And this time, *nothing* would stand in his way.

THE FIRST THING Luke had learned at the academy was that being a first responder didn't allow for waking up slowly, or for grogginess of any kind. But when someone was slamming their fist into the front door of the apartment where you were in protective custody and you were just one pair of basketball shorts away from naked, the cobwebs pretty much took a backseat to your adrenal gland anyway.

Luke was out of bed in an instant, his muscles coiled tight and his survival instinct roaring full speed ahead. "Lock yourself in the bathroom and call Isabella," he said to Quinn, who might be equally less-than-dressed in her tank top and panties, but she was also equally alert.

"Luke, wait." Her eyes were saucer-wide, her hair a riot of messy curls around her sleep-shocked face, but at least she had her cell phone to her ear. Whoever was at the door went for another round of wham-wham-wham, and nope. No way.

Not waiting.

With his heart locked in his throat, Luke grabbed the Louisville Slugger he'd parked by Quinn's bedside table last week. He got three steps from her front door before a familiar voice sounded off from the other side, and his bare feet slapped to a messy halt on the floorboards.

"Slater. Copeland. It's me and Moreno. Open up."

"Hollister?" What the fuck?

Luke checked the peep hole, relief funneling through him at the sight of the detectives on the threshold. Quinn lowered her cell phone and grabbed a long cardigan sweater from one of the hooks by the door, and Luke undid the chain and popped the dead bolt, opening the door with a quick tug.

"What's going on?" he asked, his seconds-old relief growing heavy and cold as both Hollister and Moreno moved into Quinn's apartment with their hands resting on their holstered weapons.

"Are you both secure?" Isabella asked, her dark brown stare moving over the living space in a meticulous three-sixty while her partner's did the same from the opposite direction.

"What? Yes," Quinn said. When neither detective moved so much as a trigger finger, she scrambled to add, "Oh my God, Omaha. Of course we're both secure. The officer who brought us home a few hours ago checked my apartment and we've been locked in ever since."

Hollister's shoulders let go of his neck, but only by a fraction. "I'll call it in," he said to Isabella, who answered with a tight nod.

"What the hell is going on?" Luke asked, his patience threatening to detonate.

Isabella exhaled, swapping a covert look with Hollister that peppered Luke's gut with holes. "We've had a...security breach."

"Here?" His adrenaline surged again like high tide. "Did Ice try to get into the building?"

"No," Isabella said, although between her tone and her expression, the word created more questions than anything else. Hollister moved into the kitchen, murmuring into his cell phone in hushed tones that Luke couldn't hear enough of to turn into answers, and Isabella split a glance between him and Quinn. "Why don't you both get dressed? Liam and I need to take you to the Thirty-Third anyway. Sinclair will update you when we get there."

Quinn paled. "Who's dead?"

The word sent fear skidding through Luke's rib cage, rendering him unable to breathe, let alone ask what the hell Quinn was talking about.

Isabella said, "Quinn, I really think—"

"No." She took a step forward on the floorboards. "I've heard enough family notifications to know one when I see it. The first names, the 'let's go down to the station so you can talk to my boss' line. So who is it, Isabella?" Her voice wavered. "Who's dead?"

"No one is dead," Isabella replied after a silence that felt like an ice age even though in reality, it had only lasted a beat or two. "But we do have a dangerous situation right now, and it could be life threatening."

"Please." Luke looked at her, unable to keep his composure on lockdown for another second. "Just tell us what the hell is going on."

The detective nodded, and although Luke had learned how to read people like the Sunday Post over the last ten years, he'd never seen an expression quite like the one Isabella wore as she turned to look at him.

"It seems Ice managed to disable the alarm system at your grandmother's house, and he snuck in to kidnap Hayley."

All the air vanished from the room. No. No, no, no, that couldn't be—"Ice has my sister?"

Quinn sucked in a breath. "What about Miss Billie?"

Sweet Jesus. Luke's world tilted in a way that suggested he'd never see right-side-up again, but Isabella shook her head, adamant.

"Your grandmother is completely safe. She's at the Thirty-Third, and we've got crime scene techs scouring her house for evidence as we speak."

Terror mingled with a thread of disbelief in his brain, muffling all of his thoughts. How could this have happened? For Chrissake, he'd trusted them. They'd had a *plan*. "I want to know everything you know," he said to Isabella, an odd chill forming in his belly. "Right now."

"Okay," she replied as Hollister returned from Quinn's kitchen. "Your grandmother and sister checked in as usual about an hour after you left. But then we got a frantic call from your grandmother about forty minutes ago. She'd gotten up for a glass of water and went to check on Hayley on her way back to bed."

Something twisted deep in Luke's chest. "Yeah, we do that a lot, just in case she needs anything. Or I guess I used to do it when I lived there."

Isabella nodded. "Hayley wasn't in her bed when your grandmother checked on her, but her cell phone and her shoes were both in her room. Your grandmother was smart and called us immediately. We had a unit standing by and we were able to act fast to get her to safety. At this point, everyone at Seventeen has been accounted for. It seems Hayley is the only person missing for now."

"For now?" Quinn asked, her lips parting on a puff of shock. "You think Ice is going to go after more of us?"

"We are going to do our very best to make sure that doesn't happen," Hollister said. "But for now, we have to err on the side of extreme caution. Everyone's down at the Thirty-Third."

"So, wait." Luke's brain played an epic game of catch up as he pieced together everything Isabella had said. Something didn't quite add up. "How do you know for sure that"— he forced his lips to form the words even though they felt like razor wire jammed between his teeth—"Ice has my sister?"

Isabella hesitated before removing her cell phone from the pocket of her jeans. "Because this was delivered to the intelligence unit's inbox about twenty minutes ago."

She pulled up a video before handing the phone over to Luke. His physiology betrayed him by making his hands shake, and even though a small part of him screamed not to tap the triangle on the otherwise black screen, he scraped in a breath and did it anyway.

"Well, well," came Ice's voice, followed by a barely visible shot of his menacing face a second later, and Luke would have given anything—*anything*—for the chance to crawl through the screen to choke the motherfucker. "By now I see you've figured out that I have a guest."

The camera swung to the side, and Luke's knees threatened a labor strike. "Oh, Hayley," Quinn whispered shakily as an image of his sister flashed over the screen, lasting only long enough to prove that she was both conscious and terrified before Ice returned in front of the camera.

"As you can see, she's not hurt. But that *is* going to change. See, those two paramedics knew what would come to them if they opened their mouths. I know that blonde thinks she got the best of me with those pictures. She thinks she's brave. Safe. But she's wrong."

Quinn stiffened beside him, her breath catching audibly as Ice continued. "So this one's for you, sweetheart. I don't care if it takes years, but I *will* find everyone you care about, and I'll kill them slowly while you watch, just like I said I would. You're going to pay for what you did to me," he said, his expression hardening in the dim light. "And I'm going to get back the respect I deserve. Stay tuned while I get ready. Starting at midnight, this one dies."

"Moreno," Luke managed, but it was all he could get past the fear sailing through his central nervous system. Ice had Hayley. His baby sister, who Luke had sworn he'd always take care of.

He was going to kill her, slowly and viciously, and Luke couldn't stop him.

"We're not going to let it happen, Slater. Capelli's already all over the video, and if anyone can trace it quickly, he can. The entire unit is at the precinct and on this case right now. We're *going* to find him before he can hurt her."

"I..." *should have been there*. God, his grandmother and sister shouldn't have been in that house alone, police patrol or not. He should never have left them, not even for a minute. "I'd like to be with my grandmother, please."

"Of course," Hollister said. "We can take you whenever you're ready, man."

Nodding, Luke heel-toed a path down the hallway to get a shirt and a pair of shoes. Stupid, really, that he could be doing something so ordinary as reaching for his Nikes when his sister was somewhere out there in the dark, terrified and taking her last breaths.

"Luke." Quinn crossed the threshold of her bedroom less than a step behind him, reaching for his hand. "This is going to be okay. The intelligence unit will figure this out, just like they did with the bomb."

His laugh in reply was all bitterness. "The intelligence unit had a plan to keep us safe, too, and it failed. That psychopath has Hayley, Quinn. Not me, not you, but my seventeen-year-old *sister*. He has her and he's going to kill her in less than two hours. So, no. Nothing about this is going to be okay."

"They'll get her back. I know you're upset—"

But just like that, Luke's last thread of composure disintegrated like hot ash. "I should have been there. I should have been in that house, protecting them from the danger that I brought to their door."

Quinn's eyes went wide, her fingers tightening over his. "You had no way of knowing Ice would do this."

"I had every way of knowing!" Luke snapped. "Christ, he fucking *told* us from the beginning he was going to go after the people we cared about, and what did I do? Instead of protecting Momma Billie and Hayley like I should have, I went and trusted other people." He pulled his hand from Quinn's, turning to snatch his T-shirt from the chair at her bedside and yank the thing over his head. "I trusted the intelligence unit, I trusted you—God, I lowered my guard and let you all in like a fucking idiot, when what I should have done was just keep to myself like I always do."

"You think letting me in was a mistake?" she whispered. For a split second, he registered the tears wobbling on her eyelashes, the hurt in the words he'd just said, the emotions hurtling around in his chest.

But emotions were what had gotten him into this mess. They'd let him rely on other people. They'd let him get distracted. They'd let him *care*.

If there was one thing Luke knew, it was how much caring would wreck you in the end. So he did what he should have done right from the start.

He stamped out the feelings in his chest until the only thing left there was a dull, hollow ache.

"If I hadn't been here with you instead of with my family where I belong, none of this would've happened. So, yeah. This thing between me and you—between me and *all* of you —was a mistake."

And then he turned and walked out of her bedroom.

29

Quinn sat on one of the hard plastic chairs in the intelligence office's meeting room and wished she could go numb. She'd only been in the small, rectangular space with her station-mates for twenty-two minutes, but each one had felt like a freaking century. Between the slow crawl of time, the lack of any further updates, and the cold terror that washed through her every time she thought of Hayley being anywhere near Ice, Quinn's nerves were thoroughly shot.

Add in the fact that her heart had been smashed into no less than a dozen jagged pieces, and yeah, numb was definitely at the top spot on her wish list right now.

"Hey. How are you holding up?" Shae asked, sliding into the standard-issue office chair beside her. After the initial relieved greetings Quinn had shared with everyone on engine and squad, she'd gone tight-lipped enough that they'd all given her some space to decompress.

Right. Ice had Hayley, and he was going to hurt her unspeakably all because of Quinn.

How the hell was she supposed to do anything other than scream?

"Fine," she said, and great. Guess the other F-word was back in her vocabulary. "I mean, you know. Considering."

"How about Slater? Have you heard anything?"

"No."

At least this wasn't a lie. She and Luke hadn't spoken a word to each other since they'd been in her bedroom. After they'd arrived here at the precinct, he'd chosen to stay with his grandmother in the sergeant's office, where there was a couch for her to lie down. Although Quinn had made sure her cell phone was fully charged and readily available in her back pocket and she'd seen Luke's in his hand when they'd been buzzed upstairs, he hadn't texted her with any sort of update, or any sort of anything.

This thing between me and you was a mistake...

Quinn cleared her throat, the rock-hard seatback of her chair digging into her shoulder blades as she straightened. "Yeah, I ah. I'm sure he wants to be with his grandmother. The poor woman is probably worried sick."

"I'll bet," Shae said, although her green eyes creased with enough intuition to tell Quinn that her friend's spider senses were definitely tingling. God, Quinn hated being a bad liar. "But the intelligence unit is full of pit bulls and piranhas. They're going to find Slater's sister."

"Yeah," Quinn said. *Unless they don't.* Ice was stone-cold diabolical, and it was already a few minutes after eleven. The intelligence unit might be good, but could they really dial up a miracle?

"Copeland."

Quinn jumped about a mile out of her skin before turning toward the source of the voice beside her. "Jeez! Gamble, you startled me." For a guy whose shoulders filled an entire doorframe jamb to jamb, he was unnaturally stealthy.

"Sorry," he said. "I just wanted to know if you need anything."

Gamble had never been a man of many words—or, okay, any more words than were blatantly necessary. But the concern in his stare was obvious enough to send a twinge through Quinn's chest.

"That's really sweet of you. But you don't have to take care of me."

One dark brow lifted. "Why not? You take care of all of us."

"Oh." The words sent a pang through her gut, reminding her how spectacularly she'd failed at keeping all of them safe, and damn it, the last thing she needed right now was to cry in front of everyone in this room.

"You know what, I think I'm going to walk the halls," she said, pushing her way out of her chair/torture device.

"Do you want some company?" Shae asked, but Quinn slapped together what she hoped was a convincing smile.

"No, thanks. I just want to clear my head." *And cry. A lot.*

Shae nodded. "Okay. Just let me know if you change your mind."

Quinn slipped past the door, making it about six steps down the empty hallway before allowing the tears in her eyes to fall. But she didn't want to attract attention from anyone who might pass by and see her bawling like a baby, so she forced her feet to keep moving, down to the end of the hall leading to the main room of the intelligence office.

"We've got a time-sensitive situation here, with an asset in grave danger. Give me something I can use."

Sinclair's sandpaper voice caught Quinn's attention, full-on. She knew she shouldn't eavesdrop—when they were talking about a case, it might even be illegal for all she knew. But still, this was Hayley they were talking about. She had to know what was happening.

"The phone used to shoot the video was a burner, so that's a dead end," Addison said, and Sinclair made a noise of displeasure.

"How did Ice get past the alarm?"

"Looks like he used a pretty simple signal jammer." That was Capelli. "They're illegal, but unfortunately not *that* hard to find. Even easier to use once you've had a tutorial. But they don't leave a trail, so that's another dead end."

Quinn's heart pounded in her ears. The intelligence unit had to have a plan. They *had* to.

"Tell me you have good news on the video," Sinclair said.

The rapid-fire clack of a keyboard accompanied Capelli's answer. "I'm getting closer, but the signal was bounced around more than an NFL game ball. It's going to take a little more time to locate the asset."

The *asset*? Wait, were they talking about Hayley?

"It's twenty-three twenty. We don't have any time," Sinclair pointed out. "What else?"

"I've got something," Garza said. "Word just came in from the gang unit. There's buzz all over the place that this deal between the Vipers and Sorenson is off. Apparently Sorenson backed out."

"Whoa," Addison murmured. "Too much heat on Ice?"

"Looks that way. But it makes sense. He blamed Copeland in the video, and she's the one who took the pictures. Now he's looking for revenge."

Quinn's chest constricted beneath her T-shirt, and she placed one hand against the wall for support. Oh God. Oh God oh God, this was all her fault.

"He did say he had to get ready," Isabella said. "Which means he wasn't when he sent the video."

"And *that* means he's acting on impulse," Garza continued. "Which makes him weak."

"Or a wild card," Maxwell said. "With an asset he sees as clearly expendable."

Again with the asset thing. What was wrong with them? Couldn't they see that Hayley was a bright, smart, funny kid, one who was terrified and in dire need?

"Ah! I've got him!" Capelli's voice sent Quinn's heart pinballing through her rib cage. "Sneaky fucker. The video signal came from an abandoned warehouse on the edge of North Point, over on Beaumont. The address matches the original kidnapping site where Damien snatched Copeland and Slater."

"Jesus, he really is getting brash," Garza muttered. "We need to extract that asset right now."

The sound of chairs scraping over linoleum told Quinn they meant business, but Sinclair stopped their movements with one word.

"Wait."

"Wait? Sarge, we're in a bit of a time crunch here, and there's an asset on the line," Hollister said.

"Exactly," the sergeant replied. "There is an asset on the line, and we can't barge in there like gangbusters without knowing what we're dealing with. Ice could have the place swarming with Vipers, or worse. Let's not forget this asshole planted a bomb at Seventeen. If we aren't smart about this, we're only creating a bigger risk, for the asset and for ourselves. We need site recon and a tactical plan, which means we need time."

"But you just said we don't have any," Addison pointed out.

"We're going to have to make some."

Quinn released a shaky exhale into the empty hallway. She knew whatever plan the intelligence unit came up with would work. They knew where Ice was, and they'd take him down. All they needed to make that happen was a little time. Time they didn't have.

Time she could give them.

What Ice wanted above all else was to make *her* pay. She'd been the one to go to the police in the first place after he'd told her not to. She'd been the one to take the pictures of him that had apparently cost him this big gun deal.

And she was the one who could take care of Hayley, who wasn't an "asset" or part of some tactical mission. She was a kid. A kid Quinn had put in danger.

Gamble was right. Quinn took care of the people who mattered to her. She could take care of this.

Even if it killed her.

$\sim$

LUKE PACED the floor in Sinclair's office for the six trillionth time in forty minutes. Momma Billie watched him from her spot on the couch, and Christ, what the hell was the intelligence unit doing right now that they couldn't come down here and tell them *something*?

Ice had his sister. He was going to kill her in less than twenty minutes.

And Luke would never, *ever* forgive himself.

"Is Quinn alright?"

His grandmother's question sounded off like a canon in the quiet room, stunning him into place.

"What?"

"Quinn," she repeated, her hands folded tightly in her

lap over her dark gray slacks. "She must be worried about you."

Luke dodged the topic, his old skills coming back like a bad habit. "There are way bigger things to be worried about right now."

"I know," Momma Billie said, her voice catching but her gaze remaining steel-strong. "But I can't think about those things and stay calm, so let me worry about you."

"I'm so sorry." The words flung themselves from Luke's mouth completely unbidden. But once they were out, he couldn't stop the rest. "I should have been there with you. I should have protected her. I—"

Momma Billie stood, planting herself directly in front of him on the floor tiles. "Luke Matthew, you stop that right now. You've done nothing but care for your sister and me since you were a boy. You did the right thing by telling the police what happened to you and Quinn, and by trusting them to take care of it. The only person at fault here is that monster."

"But—"

"No." Momma Billie lifted a finger in her trademark I-mean-it gesture. "You are a good grandson, a good brother, and a good man. I won't have you thinking otherwise. None of what happened here is your fault."

Luke exhaled, all shock. Could she be right? "I'm just really scared."

"I know, baby. I am, too. But the police are working hard. They'll get your sister back. Have faith."

Luke bit down on his tongue. He wanted to have faith, he really did. He wanted to believe there was a plan that would work, that Hayley would be fine, that Ice would go to jail where he fucking belonged.

He wanted Quinn. Even if she probably hated him right now.

Luke's cell phone buzzed from the pocket of his shorts, and shit, he'd forgotten he'd even had the damned thing with him. Sliding it free, he went to silence it, but the text message on the screen turned his blood into ice.

I'm in Omaha. Tell the intelligence unit there aren't any other gang members at the warehouse with Ice. And in case I don't get to say this later, I'm sorry. I love you.

"I'll be right back," Luke said. But his hand was already on the doorknob, his body already in motion, and he launched himself toward the main office.

"Stop!" he shouted, realizing only belatedly that every detective in the unit was covered in Kevlar and armed to the teeth.

"We've got a location on your sister and we're falling out," Hollister said, throwing his badge over his neck. "We can't stop."

"You have to," Luke tried again. "I have a message from Quinn, and it's for you. She says she's at the warehouse."

Everyone in the room stopped moving except for Sinclair. "Give it to me."

Luke read the message, handing over his phone a second later. A thousand questions raced through his gray matter, but they were nothing compared to the pure adrenaline pumping through his veins.

"Ping Copeland's phone. Right now."

Capelli didn't appear to waste so much as a single keystroke. Thank fuck. "Oh, shit. She's at the location."

"How the hell did she know where to go?" Hale asked, her blond brows sky-high. "Or that we needed that information?"

"It doesn't matter," Garza clipped out. "She's there, and frankly, she's buying us time."

"She gave up the code word, so her intel is legit," Isabella said. "Sarge, the clock is ticking. We need—"

"To go," Sinclair said. "Let's fall out, people. Right now."

"I'm going with you," Luke said, scrambling to catch up as the detectives followed Sinclair down the hallway.

Garza looked at him as if he'd lost his mind. "Too dangerous. Ice already has his hands on one asset, and he may well double that if he finds Quinn."

"An asset?" Was this guy seriously for real?

"It's what we call people who have been kidnapped," Isabella said, not unkindly, as she started to hustle down the stairs. "We do it to keep ourselves on the level and our heads in the game. We have to keep our emotions out of it so we can do our jobs. That's all."

Luke pressed forward to the bottom of the stairs, standing in Isabella and Garza's path even though he knew it would probably earn him a top-shelf ass chewing later. "I get that you have to keep your emotions out of this, but I *can't*. My sister and the woman I love are out there. So you can either throw me in jail or take me with you. Those are your choices right now."

"You're staying in the car," Isabella said, sending a spiral of relief through Luke's gut and a solid shot of are-you-kidding-me over Garza's face as they started to move again. "Trust me, Garza. Once you find someone who makes you this crazy, there won't be any arguing with you, either. Now come on. Let's go catch a bad guy."

30

In hindsight, borrowing-slash-stealing Shae's Jeep from the precinct parking lot had been easier than Quinn had anticipated. She'd have to thank her friend later. And tell her not to always hide her keys in the visor.

Provided that she lived through this, and that there would even *be* a later.

The intelligence unit has a plan. Get them the time to make it work.

Sliding her clammy palms over her denim-clad jeans, Quinn set her sights on the front of the warehouse. Ice's Escalade was the only vehicle on the block, which was as deserted as she remembered it. The one dingy streetlamp a handful of buildings away offered more shadows than light, which had been horror-movie freaky at first. But once her eyes had adjusted to her surroundings and she'd taken a careful trip around the perimeter of the warehouse, Quinn had realized that things were dark and quiet for a reason.

Ice was acting alone.

She slipped her cell phone into her palm, taking care to shield it well to hide the glare before checking the time.

23:57

"Okay. You can do this." By now, Luke had certainly given the intelligence unit the message she'd sent a few minutes ago. They'd be on their way, for her and for Hayley.

Now all she had to do was buy them the time to get here.

Moving cautiously so her boots wouldn't crunch on the gravel, Quinn walked up to the front of the warehouse. A small light bloomed from behind the grimy windows, and she took a slow peek inside. But between the crates and the filthy glass, seeing anything definite was impossible.

Right. Plan B.

Quinn gulped down a breath, putting one shaking hand on the doorknob. Miraculously—*yes*—it turned, and she edged her way inside to the soundtrack of her pounding heart.

"It's almost time."

Ice's voice curdled Quinn's blood, stopping her in her tracks. She couldn't see him—he had to be closer to the center of the cavernous room—and she crept forward even though her knees felt like they were loaded with Silly Putty.

"Ah, I forgot. You can't hear me, can you?" Ice said, and okay, this was good. Hayley had to be really close by. "It made it easy to take you, you know. You didn't even budge in your bed before I sedated you just enough to keep you from kicking. Sufentanil is a beautiful thing." He paused, the awful, menacing smile in his tone raising goose bumps on Quinn's arms. "And now here you are, wide awake."

With a deep inhale, she kept moving toward his voice. *Steady. Steady.*

"It's a shame you can't scream, though. That's always the best part, hearing the scream. Ah well. That stupid bitch will get the message when I gut you from stem to stern. Do you know how much blood is in the human body, sweetheart? Why don't you smile for the camera and then we'll find out?"

"Four point seven liters."

The sound of her own voice shocked the hell out of Quinn, but somehow, it didn't waver. Ice's chin whipped up from the spot where he stood in front of Hayley about ten feet away, and he swung toward her, gun raised.

"What the fuck are you doing here?" he spat, that cold, dead stare pinning her into place, and fear threatened to make her falter.

You can do this. You're strong enough to do this.

Quinn kept her focus right on Ice, even though her instincts howled for her to look at Hayley, to at least try to tell her with a look that everything would be okay. But Quinn couldn't risk turning his attention back to the girl, so she settled for a lift of one shoulder.

"I'm answering your question. Not that it matters, though. You're not going to prove that little science lesson today."

"But I am," Ice bit out, his nearly black eyes glittering with rage as he stalked closer to her. "I have to admit, I'm surprised you cranked up the balls to play hero. You always stink of so much fear. But it's just as well. Now that you're here, you can watch in person while I skin this one alive."

"You won't have time." Please, God, let them hurry. "The intelligence unit knows exactly where you are."

Ah, that got him. "They wouldn't have sent you in here," Ice said slowly. "You're bluffing to try and save the girl."

Quinn shook her head. *Just keep him talking.* "You're half-right. The intelligence unit wouldn't have sent me in here. In fact, I'm sure they'll be pissed that I came. But they know about everything, Ice. The kidnapping, the bomb at the fire house. The deal with Sorenson. They know where you are, and they're on their way here. I'd say you've got three, maybe five minutes to run."

His loud, ominous laughter drove straight into her bones. "Run? You think I would *run*?"

Quinn's belly dropped under the sheer force of her dread. "If you don't, they're going to catch you."

"The cost of revenge is steep sometimes," he said, a horrific smile bending his features. "But that deal was mine. I earned it. I've been running drugs in this city since I was in goddamn middle school. Made my first kill at sixteen, then washed up and had a sandwich. I'm not just good at what I do. I'm the best. I *own* this city. Then you come in here, taking pictures and talking to the cops after I told you not to, and all of a sudden, that deal is gone? No."

Ice moved closer, sending Quinn's pulse into overdrive, but she stood her ground on the dusty warehouse floor, listening as he continued. "See, people don't betray me. If they do, they end up like Cherise, or like that ignorant fuck, Dixon. I'm sure the prison guards will be finding his body any minute now. Christ, it was all too easy to have him shanked and left to bleed out. Easier yet to pin the whole thing on Damien. But they both fucked with me, and now they've paid the price. That's how respect is earned."

His stare glinted in the low light. "I don't tolerate disloyalty. You did something I told you not to do, and it cost me something I deserved. Now I'm going to take it out of you, piece by piece."

He lifted his gun, and Quinn's mouth went dry with fear, tears pouring down her face in a sudden stream. Oh God, she was out of time. Ice was going to shoot her—she could see it on his face. She looked at Hayley, her heart slamming and breaking all at once as she mouthed, *look away*.

But Hayley shook her head and made one sign,

mouthing the word that went with it. Then everything in the room stretched into slow motion as the girl opened her mouth and screamed.

Luke heard a scream, followed by the pop-pop-pop of gunfire, and screw waiting in the car. His feet stabbed into the gravel path in front of the warehouse, his breath shellacked to his lungs as he damn near tore the warehouse door off its hinges. A riot of voices rang out in sawed-off tones, followed by the heavy thunder of boots on concrete, and he tore through the maze of shipping crates leading to the center of the room.

"RPD!" came a shout, then a quick, "Clear!" after it, and Hale holstered the weapon she'd just pointed at him. "You're supposed to be in the car," she scolded, stepping back. Only then did he realize she'd put herself in front of someone else, and he damn near collapsed in relief.

"Hayley!"

He grabbed his sister, giving her a visual sweep from head to toe before restarting the process with his hands. "Are you hurt?" he asked, unsure whether she was shaking or if it was just his hands.

Hayley shook her head, grabbing his hands to still them. *I'm fine. I'm fine. Go get Quinn. Please. You have to go get Quinn.*

Hale stepped in to look at him. "I have her, Slater. I swear. There are ambos en route. But they're going to need you in there. Go."

Ambos? Why would they need more than one? And why would they need him right—

Oh, no. No, no.

"*Quinn!*" The word tore past his lips, announcing his

arrival as he sprinted through the rest of the maze, his feet crashing to a halt as he reached the last shipping container.

"Quinn? Quinn!" Luke said, his gaze whipping wildly around the dimly lit space. Then, all at once, he saw why he was needed.

Quinn sat in the middle of the concrete floor, covered in blood.

And it wasn't hers.

"What are you doing?" Luke asked, certain he wasn't seeing properly. Because no way, no *way* could she be treating the bullet wound of the man who had just tried to kill her.

"Chest compressions," she said, looking up at him with a fierce blue stare. "Now are you going to help me save this asshole so he can spend the rest of his life rotting in jail, or not?"

Quinn scrubbed the last of the blood off her hands and finally chanced a look at herself in the mirror. Her hair qualified as a category three hurricane, and the pale green scrubs the intake nurse had given her to change into did zilch for her fear-paled complexion. But she was here, at Remington Memorial Hospital, standing and breathing.

She was alive, and so was Hayley. That was all that mattered.

Tossing her blood-soaked clothes into the biohazard bin in the corner of the bathroom, she took one last breath before turning toward the door. The intelligence unit probably wanted to question her, not to mention yell at her for a while. She might as well get it over with.

But when she opened the door, the person waiting for her in the hallway wasn't from the intelligence unit at all.

"What are you doing here?" Quinn asked, her cheeks heating at the idiocy of her question. Of course Luke was here. He'd ridden over in the same ambulance that she had, and apparently scored himself a pair of matching scrubs. How come they looked so great on him?

Because he's gorgeous, dummy. Also, not yours.

"Actually, I was waiting for you. There's something I need to tell you."

"Oh. Is Hayley okay?" She'd looked fine when Addison had hustled her out of the warehouse, but everything had happened so fast. Plus, she'd been through a lot. She could be in shock, or—

"Hayley's fine," Luke said. "The paramedics from Twenty-Nine gave her the all-clear on the way here. She's resting in one of the curtain areas with my grandmother. But that's not what I wanted to tell you."

Quinn paused, her stomach twisting. "Is it Ice?"

"Ice went up to surgery." A chill moved over Luke's light blue stare. "The trauma surgeon said it's going to be a long night, but that you probably saved his life by initiating CPR when you did."

"Oh." God, talk about irony. But if she'd let him bleed out, she would have been living by his code, not her own. She saved people. That's what she was made for—it was who she was. Plus, saving Ice's life ensured he'd spend the rest of it locked up, with no power to hurt anyone, ever again.

And for him, that was worse than dying.

"Thank you for the updates," Quinn said, and Luke nodded.

"You're welcome. But that's also not what I wanted to tell you."

"Okay." Her brows lifted. "So what do you want to tell me, then?"

The emotion he'd clearly been keeping at bay slipped over his face, and wait. Wait, wait...

Luke stepped forward, cradling her face in his hands. "I want to tell you that I love you."

A soft gasp escaped from her chest. "But you said—"

"I know what I said. I was scared and stupid, but it doesn't change the fact that it hurt you. Not to mention it was wrong, and I didn't mean it. I'm so sorry, Quinn." He paused to let the words sink in. "You are the best thing that's ever happened to me. You saved my sister's life tonight, but before that, you saved mine, too. I love you."

"Oh." Her eyes filled with tears, but she didn't even try to hold them back. "Well I suppose that'll work since I love you, too."

"You forgive me for being a heartless ass?" Luke asked, thumbing the tears from her cheeks.

Quinn laughed. "You weren't an ass, and you could never be heartless. You were scared. And I know all too well what that's like, so yes. Of course I forgive you."

"I was scared," he admitted. "I thought I'd lose you both."

"Well there's more than one reason you didn't. I might have kept Ice from hurting Hayley, but she saved my life, too."

Luke pulled back in shock. "She did?"

"She did," Quinn confirmed with a nod. "Ice was going to shoot me, but Hayley saw Garza and Isabella closing in from the shadows. She knew they'd need a distraction to keep him from shooting me, so she told me to drop." Quinn made a fist, then opened it. "And then she screamed."

"That was Hayley?" Luke asked, clearly poleaxed.

"That was Hayley. Your sister is one tough kid."

"She is," he agreed, pulling her closer. "And you're pretty tough, too. I don't know what I'd do without you."

"Hmmm," Quinn said, stepping back in to put her arms around Luke, where they belonged. "Lucky for you, you're never going to have to find out."

EPILOGUE

"Seriously, Faurier. If you take the last of those home fries—"

"Gates, pass the coffee, would you? Otherwise McCullough's going to get Slater to tap a vein for her so she can mainline it."

"Y'all better stop jawin' and get to eating. Letting those pancakes get soggy is a sacrilege, now."

Oh, how good it felt to be home.

"You ready for your last run on ambo today?" Quinn asked, a bittersweet pang moving through her chest as she nudged Luke with an elbow. They'd both insisted on coming back to work with everyone else on A-shift, and after a big batch of grumbling from Bridges, he'd finally agreed. Quinn had had to promise to continue seeing Dallas on a weekly basis for a while, but that was cool. Dr. Phil was actually starting to grow on her, and their session really did help keep her on the level.

"I guess," Luke said, spearing a forkful of home fries from Quinn's plate and popping them into his mouth. "But I'll miss it, too."

She raised a brow, trying on her very best stern look. "Um, you're going to be *in* it if you take my home fries again."

"No, I'm not." Luke grinned, swiping another bite from her plate before leaning over to whisper in her ear. "Because if you take me out of commission, I won't be able to take off your panties and—"

"Quinn?" January poked her head into the common room, and oh God, saved by the bestie. "Captain Bridges would like to see you and Slater in his office, please."

"Jesus, you two. Shift isn't even an hour old yet," Kellan said from across the table. "What'd you do now?"

"I don't know," Quinn said. "We finished all the stuff for the case yesterday."

After a hard-nosed talking-to from both Sinclair and Bridges, a lengthy conversation with the D.A., a raid on several residences in North Point, Ice had woken from his seven-hour surgery to discover that he was being arrested on more felony counts than he could count on his fingers and toes.

He would spend the rest of his life in jail. And every day, he'd wake up and know that it was because Quinn had been brave enough to save him.

Luke stood, falling into step with her as she walked into the hallway. "Probably just some paperwork to get me back on engine. Parker will be back at next shift, right?"

"That's what the schedule says, but he's not supposed to be back in Remington until tonight." His brother's cabin was way out in the sticks, so she hadn't been entirely shocked not to hear from him. She doubted he even had cell service. "I'm sure he'll call me when he gets in. But other than paperwork, I have no clue what this could be about."

They made their way down the hall, then to the captain's office. After a quick knock, Quinn walked over the threshold...

And found herself staring face-to-face with Parker.

"Holy crap! When did you get back into town?" she asked, moving forward to give him a stunned hug.

"Hey, partner," he said, but funny, the word sounded just the tiniest bit odd as it traveled from her ears to her belly. "I came back a little early. Just got in a few hours ago. Hey, Slater. How's it going?"

"Good, man." They paused to shake hands. "It's good to see you."

"You, too." Parker swung back to look at her, a metric ton of concern winging through his dark brown eyes. "Seems you two have been through a lot while I was gone. Jesus, Copeland. A kidnapping? And a rescue at gunpoint? Are you sure you're okay?"

Quinn bit her lip. "Yeah. I wanted to tell you, but for a while, I couldn't, and then after that..."

"It's alright. I'm just glad you weren't hurt." Parker glanced at Bridges, and God, what was that look on his face? "Look, I know I've kind of been keeping my distance since I left town. I've had a lot of time to think since I got hurt, and I wanted you to hear this from me."

Quinn's pulse knocked at her throat. "Parker? What's going on?"

"I'm leaving Seventeen."

She blinked once. Twice. Then the words got all the way in. "You're not taking that job at Six, are you? Because there's no way—"

"No. God, no. I'm not going to another house," Parker said over a soft chuckle. "I'm going back to medical school. I talked to some people, who pulled a few strings to let me bypass the applications deadlines...and I landed a spot in Remington University's medical program. I'm starting in a few weeks."

Holy. *Shit*. "You're going to be a doctor?" Quinn asked, and he nodded.

"I did a lot of soul searching while I was gone, and I realized it's now or never. I've spent six years on ambo, and they've been some of my best. But this isn't where I belong. Just like sitting second chair on that rig isn't where *you* belong."

Bridges cleared his throat. "And that's where I come in. In order to make replacing Parker as painless as possible, I'd like to do it with you, Quinn. You have more than proven yourself. If you want the job as lead paramedic of A-shift, it's yours."

"I don't...I don't know what to say." She'd loved the routine of the last five years, the familiarity and comfort of her job. But Parker was right. She *was* ready.

"How about yes?" Parker asked. "I wouldn't feel right leaving here unless I knew my spot was in the very best hands."

Quinn's heart squeezed. "Okay. Yes, I'd love to accept the position."

"Excellent," Bridges said. "Slater, if you're amenable to one more shift on ambo after today, I'll do my best to find someone from the float pool to cover the rest of the time it takes us to find someone to ride with Quinn permanently."

"Respectfully, sir, I'd like to be considered for the position," Luke said.

"What?" Quinn's jaw dropped, but he just smiled.

"I want it. I want the job on ambo permanently."

"Whoa," Parker murmured, and even Captain Bridges took a second before answering.

"Well, good paramedics are in short supply, and your training is nearly complete. I think you'd be an excellent candidate for the position, and there's a new class of rookies coming out of the academy in a few weeks. I'd hate to replace you on engine, but I could make it happen." He put his elbows on his desk, his face growing stern as he continued with, "However, we do have another factor to discuss. I understand you two are involved."

As much as her cheeks wanted to burn at the topic of her sex life being brought up by her boss, she also wasn't about to cover anything up.

"Yes, sir," Quinn said, and Luke echoed her answer.

"There are no specific rules against two paramedics fraternizing. While it's not a situation I'd prefer, I also know you both to be professional and dedicated. If it's not an issue for either of you, it's not an issue for me."

Luke shook his head. "It's not an issue for me, sir."

"Me either," Quinn added.

"Excellent." Bridges pushed back from his desk and stood. "Now, if you'll excuse me and Parker, I'm going to take him to go let the rest of the house know about his plans. January will draw up all the paperwork for your new positions. Welcome to ambo, both of you."

Quinn turned to look at Luke as soon as the door closed. "Did that just...happen?"

"Pretty sure it did," he said, breaking into a huge smile that went all the way up to his eyes.

God, she loved him. "And you're sure? If you take this job, you'll be giving up engine for good."

"I know," Luke said, reaching for her hand. "But I am

your partner, and you"—he paused to squeeze her fingers
—"are my everything. I belong on ambo, taking care of
people. But more importantly, I belong with you."

"Okay," Quinn replied, squeezing back. "Then let's get to
work, partner."

EXCERPT FROM SKIN DEEP

Want more Station Seventeen? Check out this excerpt from SKIN DEEP...

Kellan Walker stood with an ax in one hand and a sledge-hammer in the other, thanking his lucky fucking stars he didn't have an office job. Not that pushing paper was a bad way to go, necessarily—honest work, and all that. But a nine to five fit him about as well as a suit and tie, and since he hadn't sported those particular torture devices since his father's funeral ten years ago, he was all too happy to stick to the helmet and turnout gear he wore every day for the Remington Fire Department.

Better that the fires were literal than figurative. At least *those* he could put out.

"Is that a sledgehammer in your pocket or are you just happy to see me?"

Kellan looked up from his spot in Station Seventeen's triple-wide engine bay, chuffing out a laugh at the familiar, feminine voice greeting him from the doorway. "I'm always happy to see you when I'm doing inventory, McCullough. Care to help out a brother in need?"

"You want me to pick up your slack again, Walker?" His fellow engine-mate Shae McCullough arched a honey-colored brow at him, and Christ, even in her sleep she probably had enough brass for a band. Cue up the number one reason Kellan liked her.

"I prefer to think of it more as lending your professional expertise. Sharing *is* caring," he reminded her, putting just enough of a cocky smile to the words to make her cave. Ball-breaker or not, Shae always had his back, just like he'd had hers since the minute he'd crossed the threshold at Seventeen two years ago. Being a firefighter was the closest thing he'd found to the seven years he'd spent in the Army. He and Shae were part of a team, along with everyone else on engine, squad, and even Parker and Quinn on the ambo. They didn't just carry their weight. They carried each other equally.

Still, Kellan knew better than to think McCullough would lower her brass knuckles all the way on his account.

"Caring, my ass. You owe me," she grumbled, although the slight lift of her lips negated any sting the words might otherwise hold.

"I can live with that."

Kellan let go of a laugh along with the words, his work boots scuffing over the smooth concrete of the engine bay floor as he returned both the ax and the sledge to their respective storage compartments in Engine Seventeen. But before he and Shae could pop open the next one down to do a head count on the Halligan bars, the piercing sound of the all-call echoed off the cinder block walls of the engine bay.

"*Engine Seventeen, Squad Six, Ambulance Twenty-Two,*

structure fire, ninety-three hundred block of Glendale Avenue, requesting immediate response."

Just like that, Kellan's pulse tripped into go mode in his veins. "Nothing like a crispy job right out of the chute," he said, double-checking that the storage compartments were all latched tight before quickly hanging the inventory clipboard in his grasp back on the nearby support post. Damn, they'd barely taken a chunk out of their morning shift-change duties. Not that it mattered in the grander scheme of things catching fire.

"You're not complaining, are you?" Shae shot a disbelieving glance over the shoulder of her navy blue uniform shirt as she pulled herself into the operator's seat, throwing on her headset and kicking the engine over into a low growl.

Kellan clambered into the back step behind her, moving all the way down to the spot diagonal from hers, directly behind the officer's seat. "Hell no," he said, because as crazy as it might seem to civilians, he'd rather be busy than bored. He hadn't become a firefighter to sit around the station. Give him the chance to run into a shit storm while all others were running out, and Kellan would take it every day of the week. Twice on Sundays.

He parked himself in the seat where he'd stowed his turnout gear barely fifteen minutes ago, inhaling to counter the physiological responses tempting his body to get jacked up. His heart might want to charge full speed ahead against his sternum and flatten his lungs to boot, but he'd learned how to show his adrenal gland who was boss long before day one at the Remington Fire Academy. Being a sniper for the Rangers tended to teach a guy how to keep his shit in check. After two tours in Afghanistan, the methods for managing his adrenaline were pretty much stitched into Kellan's DNA.

Deep breaths. Quick decisions. Precise movements. No dwelling on what was in front of you or what was already done.

Ever.

Kellan's lieutenant, Ian Gamble, slid his huge frame into the officer's seat in the front of the engine at the same time Station Seventeen's rookie, Luke Slater, scrambled into the back step to sit behind Shae. Gamble turned to pin the rookie with a you-got-lucky-you-weren't-last-in stare, hooking his headset over his ears and jutting his darkly-stubbled chin at Shae in a nonverbal "let's go."

Both Kellan and Slater grabbed the headsets hanging over their respective seats, because between the hundred and thirty decibel sirens and the rattle and whoosh of cabin noise inside the engine's boxy interior, they didn't have a prayer of hearing their lieutenant otherwise.

"Okay you guys, buckle down because this looks like the real deal," Gamble cut out into his mic, the scraped-up edges of his voice a perfect match for his gruff demeanor. He leaned forward to look at the screen built into the dashboard that connected them with Remington's emergency services system. "Dispatch is reporting flames showing at a residence on the north side of the district. Nearest cross street is Woodmoor," he said, mostly for Shae's benefit.

Of course, she probably didn't need the assist. Shae had operated Engine Seventeen since before Kellan had even set his baby toe in the firehouse for his first shift. She knew Remington's streets as well as she knew her own reflection.

Case in point. "That's up in North Point," she said. "The neighborhood's not pretty." While the fact didn't matter an ounce in terms of how hard they'd fight the blaze, it could have an impact on the scene.

"Mmm," Gamble acknowledged. "Well, if we haul ass"—

he paused to slide a glance at Shae, whose resulting grin Kellan could just make out in profile from his spot in the back step—"we'll be first on-scene, so gear up and be ready to look alive. Squad and ambo are on our six, and Captain Bridges is along for the ride."

"Copy that," Kellan said, tugging the headset from his ears. Continuing the smooth circuit of his inhale/exhale, he reached down for his bunker pants, pulling them over his uniform in one methodical move.

"Must be a hell of a fire if all hands are on deck, right?" Slater's dark eyes flashed wide and round from his spot next to Kellan in the step, giving away his jitters despite the guy's obvious attempt at a poker face.

Ah, rookies. Still, while some guys might be tempted to haze a newbie for being a little rattled on his first big fire call, giving the kid shit for turning out to be human after only three weeks on the job seemed a touch indecent.

"Not necessarily," Kellan said, trying to lead by example as he got the rest of his gear into place. "Bridges is a hands-on kind of captain, and squad goes on all the fire calls in the district no matter what." Those guys weren't elite for shits and giggles, that was for damn sure. "But it's not a drill, so keep your head on a swivel and stay on Gamble's hip. And Slater?" He didn't wait for the candidate to acknowledge him, because Christ, the kid looked two seconds away from stroking out. "Breathe in on a three count and out on a five. You're gonna need your legs under you all the way. You copy?"

Slater nodded, his stare turning focused, and what do you know, he actually took Kellan's advice. Good goddamn thing, too, because they were about T-minus two minutes from rolling up on the scene of this fire, and if the thick column of smoke Kellan had spotted through his window was anything to go by, something was burning pretty good.

Time to go to work.

Want to find out what happens, right now? Click here!
Skin Deep

MORE BY KIMBERLY KINCAID

Want hot heroes, exclusive freebies, and all the latest updates on new releases? Sign up for Kimberly Kincaid's newsletter, and check out these other sexy titles, available at your favorite retailers!

The Station Seventeen series:
    Deep Trouble (prequel)
    Skin Deep
    Deep Check
    Deep Burn

The Cross Creek series:
    Crossing Hearts
    Crossing the Line

The Line series:
    Love On the Line

Drawing the Line
Outside the Lines
Pushing the Line

The Pine Mountain Series:

The Sugar Cookie Sweetheart Swap, with Donna Kauffman and Kate Angell

Turn Up the Heat
Gimme Some Sugar
Stirring Up Trouble
Fire Me Up
Just One Taste
All Wrapped Up

The Rescue Squad series:

Reckless
Fearless

Stand-alones:

Something Borrowed
Play Me

And don't forget to come find Kimberly on Facebook, join her street team The Taste Testers, and follow her on Twitter, Pinterest, and Instagram!

Kimberly Kincaid writes contemporary romance that splits the difference between sexy and sweet and hot and edgy romantic suspense. When she's not sitting cross-legged in an ancient desk chair known as "The Pleather Bomber", she can be found practicing obscene amounts of yoga, whipping up anything from enchiladas to éclairs in her kitchen, or curled up with her nose in a book. Kimberly is a *USA Today* best-selling author and a 2016 and 2015 RWA RITA® finalist and 2014 Bookseller's Best nominee who lives (and writes!) by the mantra that food is love. Kimberly resides in Virginia with her wildly patient husband and their three daughters. Visit her any time at www.kimberlykincaid.com

Made in the USA
Monee, IL
25 January 2020